Julia Fitzgeral[illegible] AL SLAVE, SLA[illegible] SALAMAND[illegible] successful writers of roma[illegible]ction. She has two children and her interests include history, health and medicine (especially new discoveries), Persian cats, mythology and astrology. Miss Fitzgerald, who also writes under the pen names of Julia Watson and Julia Hamilton, lives in Chester.

Also by Julia Fitzgerald

ROYAL SLAVE
SLAVE LADY
SCARLET WOMAN
SALAMANDER
FALLEN WOMAN
LOVE SONG (as Julia Watson)

Julia Fitzgerald

Venus Rising

Futura
Macdonald & Co
London & Sydney

A Troubadour Book

First published in Great Britain in 1982
by Futura Publications, a division of
Macdonald & Co (Publishers) Ltd
London & Sydney
Reprinted 1984

ISBN 0 7107 3026 8

Photoset by Rowland Phototypesetting Ltd,
Bury St Edmunds, Suffolk
and printed in Great Britain by
Hazell Watson & Viney Limited,
Member of the BPCC Group,
Aylesbury, Bucks

Futura Publications
A Division of
Macdonald & Co (Publishers) Ltd
Maxwell House
74 Worship Street
London EC2A 2EN
A BPCC plc Company

Love, thou art absolute sole Lord of life and death.
Richard Crashaw, 1613–1649

Happiness is beneficial for the body but it is grief that develops the powers of the mind.
Marcel Proust

FOR DANIELLE DE WINTERS,
a storyteller after my own heart.

CONTENTS

PROLOGUE:

THE FEUD

'Then cherish pity, lest you drive an angel from your door.'

William Blake, 1757–1827

PROLOGUE

The rider on horseback had the carriage of a military man, a young, daredevil captain perhaps, who had seen extensive service in the King's army, had seen Old Nick face to face and sent him scuttling off, his tail between his knees.

Straight of back, proud, almost arrogant, his head high, bronze eyes barely noticing the verdant landscape, he rode like one obsessed – or possessed. There was anguish in the mouth, but it was rigidly controlled, and the hands on the reins were slender, tanned, yet strong. Birdsong did not reach the ears of this man, nor did the vibrant hue of hedgerow flowers and berries entice his eye. There was an urgency in his bearing, the tension of a panther preparing to spring, yet the sculpted lines of his mouth did not suggest a violent nature, and the eyes, although closed to his surroundings, were noble and intelligent.

Trees lined the road like great panniers outspread on a woman's skirts, their branches crinolines above him, adorned by birds and darting squirrels. There was the raucous, catch-me-if-you-can cry of crows wheeling high above, and the chenille-velvet coo of doves. Had there been silence, or a battle being fought, he would not have heeded that, either.

The house would appear soon. How well he knew its palladian lines, its beautiful, clean white stone so welcoming, so gracious. To come back under such circumstances was hellish, a finely drawn-out torture. There was the house. Cromer Manor. Its name rang like a honeyed bell in his mind. Haven; home; comfort; solace; joy. It had meant all of these things to him and more, much more. Once.

There had been a man who had always greeted him like a father, running down the steps of the Manor to fling his arms about him, to cry 'Welcome, welcome!' But no longer. Death was the one thing which could not be controlled. It visited when the whim took it, and it did not leave until it had taken what it wanted. Fabian had been sixty-one, but no one would have guessed that he was past fifty, for he had been a man of action, restless, brilliant, indefatigable.

Pulling in his horse, the man stared up at the façade of the house, wishing it could all have been different, but no one would have guessed what was going on in his mind. His handsome, boldly-sculpted face was as inscrutable as ever, the mouth and rich bronze eyes had assumed the mocking air which they displayed to all he met.

He had ridden like the devil to be here for the funeral and the reading of the will, but he was not even slightly weary. Strength and determination emanated from him in vibrant waves. He had the appearance of one who could change Fate if he so chose. He had never known what it was to be daunted. He had always taken what he wanted, in generous measure, coming back for more if it pleased him, especially where women were concerned.

The windows of the Manor were swathed in black. Servants stood to attention in the hall, their faces wretched. Their late lord had been dearly loved and deeply respected. His sudden, tragic death had shocked them all. They felt lost, without an anchor, which was only fitting for they had been the servants of Fabian, Lord

Cromer, the man whose *soubriquet* had been the Great Sea Lord.

Flinging off his dusty riding cape, the newcomer glanced round the vast echoing hall with its pink marble floor and stairway. There was no other hall like it in England, which was what Fabian had intended when he had ordered the old flooring and stairs to be ripped out and replaced with the rare, rose-pink marble. But with the master of this place no longer here it was like a mausoleum.

'Where is my uncle's bier?' the man asked the nearest lackey.

'In the library, my lord.'

As he stood on the threshold of the library, the man saw the bier in the centre of the floor. It was draped with embroidered silk in the Cromer colours, sea-blue and sea-green, unique shades to represent a unique empire built on the oceans of the world. On top of the bier, in a voluminous robe, lay his uncle's body. How peaceful he looked, how still and silent for the first time in his life. But it was not his life, was it? It was his death. The man felt grief explode in his chest. If only he could have been here at the end to bid Fabian goodbye, but the heart seizure had taken him so unexpectedly.

Stepping closer, the man came to a sudden halt, his eyes darkening. He was not alone. There kneeling beside the bier was a woman dressed in black. She was petite, her head was bowed, and veils shrouded her, but even so her voluptuous curves were discernible. Beneath the veils there was a luxuriant glossy mane of black hair, and a proud, straight back. The hands linked together in prayer were tiny, pallid as new ivory freshly carved, their nails minute and faintly pink, their fingers ringless. Small, shapely feet peeped out from the hem of her mourning gown, and were encased in black satin pumps. Behind the closed lids there were eyes of a rich Celtic blue but they were red and strained from crying, the flesh swollen.

At the sound of a footfall, she looked up, startled.

'*Kitty McDonagh*!' the man rasped, his voice thick with revulsion.

'My lord,' came the icy response, but there was trepidation in the veiled eyes. She could not stay here now. Getting to her feet, the woman lowered her head and slipped from the library. She wanted no harsh words spoken over the dead man's body. Let him rest in peace as he deserved. She hurried outside, seeking the tranquillity of the little Ionic temple in the gardens. There, sitting beneath its roof, where she had so often sat with Fabian, radiant with love for him, she strove to assemble her thoughts. It was virtually impossible. Sighing, she leaned back against the white stone seat. Until now, she had not given a thought to her future, for the truth was that she had expected Fabian to live many more years. She had not wanted him to die, *ever*.

She bent over her tightly-linked hands. 'Fabian, Fabian, come back!' she wept. '*How can I live without you*?' He had been everything to her, father, brother, lover. In his care, she had blossomed. He had taught her all she knew; he had shown her what it meant to be a lady of quality, and in return she had striven with all her heart and soul to make him happy.

The little temple was growing chilly. A thrush which had been carolling its heart out exuberantly was now dozing on its branch. In the far distance, a cow lowed. It was a perfect sylvan scene, lacking only her heart's desire to make it joyous. Nature's perfection would never be complete for Kitty without a soulmate to love devotedly. Rising to her feet, she stood gazing out into the misty distance. She had never been as alone as this. Suddenly she felt very old. All her loved ones were dead, her mother, father, brothers, sisters, Fabian. Only she herself remained on this earth. How could there be beauty, happiness, after so many had died? What should she do? Go back to the house? What else was left to her? Fabian had said that she must always consider it her home, for as long as she wished.

'Live exactly as you would if I were still alive,' he had told her. 'Everything I have given you is yours to keep, to do with as you wish.' So she had no fears on that score, none at all. If she could just be left in peace after the reading of the will, she would ask no more. She must have time to mourn, and she suspected that it would be a long time. Then, later, she would have to try and settle down to some sort of gaunt, loveless existence without Fabian.

As she went up the steps of Cromer Manor, she felt a fresh wave of grief. She had put so many considerations aside when she went to Fabian's bed, religion, beliefs, the distinction of right from wrong. But tonight she would stay by his bier and pray, if she had not forgotten how. Adjusting the veiling to hide her face, she stepped inside the Manor.

The man's dreams were strange and sensual that night. In them, he saw the Irish girl in a scarlet gown, a colour which he believed suited her nature exactly, and her heavy breasts were thrusting out from the shiny silk. Soft, white, round globes, gleaming like satin, they seemed to beckon to him to touch them, to kiss them. He wanted to resist her, but he could not, and his dream self slipped into her embrace, to be cradled against those magnificent breasts. He woke suddenly, angrily, to find himself fiercely roused, his loins aching.

Some hours before dawn, Kitty McDonagh fell asleep as she prayed, but, determined, she forced her eyes open and continued. Then, still sad, she kissed Fabian's hands tenderly, her tears cascading onto his fingers. How chilling and stony was his skin, so heavy and graceless in her clasp. There was nothing of him left now but mortal flesh. The spirit she had worshipped was gone. Shoulders sagging, she climbed the stairs to her chamber and fell into bed fully-clothed, to sleep as if she too were dead.

The atmosphere in the drawing room was sombre. George Thorley, Fabian's lawyer, was shuffling the papers which rested on his knee. When there was total silence, he cleared his throat and began to read out loud the last will and testament of Fabian, Lord Cromer.

'*I, Fabian Alexander Sutherland Cromer, being of sound mind and body, do hereby bequeath all my possessions, estates, manors, properties, trading posts and companies, fleets, ships, and the shipping empire known as the Cromer Trading Company, together with all my worldly goods, treasures, collections of jade, of black pearls, emeralds, lapis lazuli, and that collection known as the Treasures of the Tomb of Nanubia, Queen of Asia, all of these and everything else which is mine to bequeath, to my beloved nephew and sole heir, Carrick Hamilton Scott Cromer.*'

As the lawyer finished speaking, an extraordinary silence fell on the room. Kitty's face had set in lines of shock and disbelief – she was ashen, her mouth pinched.

The silence lengthened, seemed almost palpable. Finally, Kitty broke it, her voice faint.

'There is – is nothing else in the will, Master Thorley?'

'Nothing, my dear. I have read out every word.' The

lawyer leaned forward, his eyes limpid with sympathy. 'His lordship did not leave any letter with you to be opened in the event of his death?'

'No, Master Thorley.' Kitty's voice cracked, colour flooding her cheeks.

'Ah, then that is it, my dear. I am so sorry.'

'Thank you, Master Thorley.' Somehow, Kitty managed to get to her feet. Faltering only once, she went to the door and let herself out. As she went, she could feel the new Lord Cromer's bronze eyes boring into her back. She could imagine the look on his face.

Kitty stayed in her room for the remainder of that day. Her head was throbbing; she felt shaken to the heart. There was no place here for her now; Fabian had not loved her enough to leave her so much as a tiny cottage on the estate, and she knew that there would be no help from his heir. Had Fabian loved her at all? She fought back tears. No use appearing in front of his heir with a swollen, ugly face. She knew that she would have to face the man, find out what he planned, when she had to leave – if leave she must. She must gather her courage and do what must be done, much as she would loathe it. It amounted to little more than begging, and that she had never done in her life.

No, she could not beg. Never, never – certainly not to *him*. He would think her broken, wrecked. Well, she would not give him so much pleasure. She would go downstairs for dinner, and if he was there at the table, she would be as cool and distant with him as he was with her.

The dining room was empty, and she breathed a sigh of relief. He would not be there after all. Then she saw that there were two places laid, one for herself and one for him. She wanted to pick up his knife and fork and fling them out of the window. He appeared a few moments later, as if he had been waiting for her arrival. Nodding stiffly, he seated himself, while she straightened her back even more and raised her head. He was not going to see her crushed.

The meal was eaten in a chilling silence. Kitty consumed very little and only sipped at her wine. She was trying with all her might to imagine that the figure opposite her was that of Fabian. Tears began to gather inside her, but she fought them down angrily. She would not cry. She would *not*! As the last course was served, selected cheeses, red, white, Stilton, apples and port wine – which Kitty declined – she noticed that his eyes were staring at her across the table.

He was trying to stare her out. How *dared* he! He had been drinking freely throughout the courses, but he did not seem to be the worse for it, save for his eyes which glowed at her like living bronzed leaves from a ripe autumnal tree. She felt almost skewered upon them; it was a most unpleasant sensation.

'We must talk after this.' The sound of his voice shocked her.

'There is nothing to talk about,' she said in clipped tones.

'Ah, but there is,' he insisted.

'No, there is not!' She glared at him.

He did not reply. A few minutes later, she rose and made for the door but to her dismay found that he was there first, blocking her way.

'Let me pass!' she cried.

'I said we must talk.'

'There is no must about it, my lord. Let me pass!'

For a second or two, she thought that he was not going to acquiesce, then he stepped aside, his face mocking.

'You are an extremely desirable woman, Kitty McDonagh.'

Her mouth fell open. She could not believe what he was saying.

'You look somewhat surprised . . .'

'As well I ought. You are jesting with me, I think, my lord.'

'Jesting is not what I want to do with you, Kitty McDonagh.' His eyes were slumbrous with passion.

Her face flamed as she absorbed his meaning. 'How dare you, so soon after –' She could not continue. Could not say Fabian's name.

'You are, I think, in need of a roof over your head?' He leaned against the door, his long hard body insolent in its masculine splendour.

'And what is that to *you*, my lord?'

'I can provide you with one.'

'I think not!'

'You are the proudest bitch that I ever had the misfortune to tangle with . . .' he growled.

'No one is asking you to tangle with me! If you will just let me pass . . .'

She was feeling faint, her head swimming. The strain and shock of the past few days had been too much and now she was paying the price for it. If she could just get to her room before she collapsed . . .

When she came round to see the ceiling swirling above her head, she found, to her horror that she was in his arms, being carried into the withdrawing room. Heat swept through her body, making her cheeks flame.

'Put me down!' she gasped.

'That is what I intend to do when I find some suitable piece of furniture to put you on.'

He seemed to take an age looking round the room,

eyeing each chair, chaise longue and settle, and deciding against it. Meanwhile, she was pressed against his hard chest, unable to breathe without inhaling the powerful, clean, male scent of him. An expression crossed her face; it might have been distaste, or a realisation which stunned and alarmed her. Again, she ordered him to put her down.

At last he did, placing her not ungently on a chaise longue. Then he stood looking down at her with his legs slightly apart – a pose which would not have looked amiss on a Sultan surveying one of his odalisques.

'I am quite all right – if you would just leave me . . .'

'Leave you in this state? That would be most ungallant of me. Can I get you something? Do you want your maid?'

'No, I –' Her face burned, and she turned her head away, longing for him to go. He looked so threatening standing there. She had never been so near to him before and it was having an extraordinary effect on her.

'Look, I am not an ogre,' he said, 'I am sure that we can come to some amicable agreement. You are a very attractive woman.'

'Agreement, what do you mean?'

'As I said, you are very attractive. Very attractive indeed.' He sat down beside her on the chaise; she did not know which was more intolerable – his standing over her, virile and autocratic, or his sitting so intimately close with his hard thighs pressed against hers. She did not speak, but her expression showed her feelings.

'You look alarmed – surely there is nothing in what I have said to surprise you?'

She could not help but be conscious of his overpowering masculinity, his panther-like grace, the blazing dark-gold eyes which were like the eyes of some ancient Greek king carved from rich metal. They dazzled her. She leaned back against the cushions, her hand across her face.

Reaching out, he took her hand, pulled it down from her cheek and clasped it tightly in his.

A wave of disbelief swept over her. This could not be happening. *Must not happen* . . . Angry now, yet confused by her emotions, she attempted to pull her hand away, only to find it caged. And then her other hand was caged too.

'*Let me go*!' she cried, trying to wrench herself away from him.

'Why this firebrand behaviour? We know each other of old, do we not?'

She stared at him. She had never understood him, nor ever would, she was sure.

'You need a home,' he went on, 'and I can provide it for you. Ah, I see you bridle at that thought. Why? Is it not a sensible one? Would you not . . .'

'Stop, *stop*!' she cried, fighting to pull her hand free. His grip was stopping her blood flow, and her arms were becoming numb. In vain she tried to free herself. Even as she struggled she could not fail to comprehend the effect that this dazzling man was having upon her senses. He was emanating power and authority, it was as if his eyes were controlling her . . . But she must fight it with all her strength!

Then she was in his arms, crushed against his muscular chest, and he smelt of fresh linen, leather, male sexuality. The age-old response of a woman to a man was guiding her reactions. There was comfort too in his embrace, for she needed consolation desperately, and so she weakened, her body relaxing, and his mouth came down upon hers, like dew falling upon a rose, bringing it life, rebirth. Her eyelids closed and a frost of tears sprang behind them, for she wanted this to be Fabian, *needed* it to be him.

When he pulled away, she felt cold and bereft, unsure, but his next words were to change all that.

'I see we are in agreement at last. They say bad blood will out. Once a whore, always a whore.'

He stood up, thumbs in his belt, standing over her like a judge, his expression cold and arrogant.

She could not believe what she was hearing. Although there was a pounding in her ears, she leapt to her feet, bunching her fists and striking out wildly at him.

'You devil, you *cur*! How dare you, how *dare* you!'

He looked down at her, a lazy, taunting smile on his lips. 'I dare do anything, Kitty McDonagh. Anything at all. As you will learn soon enough.'

She stepped back, two spots of colour in her cheeks, outrage thudding in her heart.

'You are the most loathsome, despicable swine I have ever had the misfortune to tangle with!' she cried.

'So at least you can be honest in some things,' he mocked, reaching out for her again.

She stepped back hastily. 'I have never been anything other than honest, and well you know it!'

He laughed out loud. 'I am sure that in your profession it pays more to lie than to speak the truth to your clients.'

'I have never lied to anyone – and I am no whore. That is a terrible, terrible accusation to make!' The colour had fled from her cheeks and she looked desperately pale.

'You will not be the first harlot who has fancied herself to be an honest woman. Pretend with anyone you please, but not with me. I fancy that I shall pay you far more generously than the other men who have had you – those starving bogmen in Ireland can hardly have had much more than a stale crust to offer you.'

'How dare you speak of my countrymen like that! No one has ever paid me in that way, nor ever will! You can believe any vile lies you wish, but they will be lies all the same!' Kitty's face was scarlet now.

The bronze eyes were laughing at her. 'A whore who knows the difference between the truth and lies! Next it will be harlots wanting to take a man's place in the world.'

She had heard enough. Storming past him, she flung herself out of the room and ran up the stairs as fast as she could. As she went, she heard his low, mocking laughter behind her.

The man was an ogre, a monster! She wanted Fabian back with all her heart – she could not live if he were not in the world.

Part One:

THE LORD PROTECTOR

‘Prosperity is not without many fears and distastes; and adversity is not without comforts and hopes.’

Francis Bacon, 1561-1626

CHAPTER ONE

No one had told the flowers that there was a famine. They swamped the roadsides: milky white daisies, acid yellow and blood-red poppies, the tiny rosy leaves of the cranberry, cinque-foil, the dazzling flame of the bog asphodel. The hedgerows teemed with life, trilling birds, darting rabbits and, in the distance, a vixen loped, head hanging down with exhaustion, blood pouring from one leg where she had been temporarily trapped by a snare set by starving men who had hoped to catch something they could eat. Rabbit, hare or fox, they were no longer fussy.

Kitty McDonagh lay nestled in a mossy dip in the roadside, her eyes opening suddenly on the morning. For a few seconds she lay there staring up at the cornflower-blue sky, the birdsong obliterating every other sound, the scent of moss and shrubby undergrowth sweet in her nostrils. How could all this beauty continue in the midst of such despair and tragedy? Tears filled her eyes as she remembered. Back along the road there was a cottage where she had been born and grown up with her brothers and sisters, her mother and father. A cottage dazzling to the eye when the sun shone because it was was so immaculately painted with whitewash, so lovingly tended in every respect, the neat little garden weeded and tidied, the interwoven fence kept in perfect condition, and nearby the scrupulously tended vegetable plot.

Turning on her side, Kitty closed her eyes again, hugging herself with her arms. It had been a happy home. There were the usual family squabbles, it is true, but so much laughter, so much loving, hugs and kisses. What right had the good Lord to take all that happiness, all that loving away? No, she must not think like that, there must never be bitterness against God. Nora McDonagh, her mother, was always saying that what the good Lord had given, the good Lord could so easily take away, and thus had stoically faced the loss of two infant sons. Nora McDonagh had been a saint, but not a plaster saint, a loving, warm, caring saint with comforting arms and a cheering, sweet smile for her family.

'What good is it to lie in a ditch and weep?' Kitty asked herself. 'Have ye not weeped a thousand tears in the past few days? And where has crying ever got ye?'

Picking up her bundle she got to her feet, looking round her. There was not a soul to be seen. Once these fields had been carefully nurtured, packed with row after row of sunny yellow potato blossom. But there would be no potato crop this time, nor had there been last time, or the time before. There was a limit to what the people could endure. There had been crop failures before, and hunger on a comparatively tolerable scale, but nothing like the horror of the past two years, years during which Kitty had watched her family dying of starvation one by one, leaving her as sole survivor.

Terrible things had happened during the past two years, things which no human being should be asked to endure. Her daddy had died in her mammy's arms and then her mammy had died in hers, and after them Donal, Joseph, Patrick, Maura, Kathleen, and Corinne. Little sweethearts all of them and she, the eldest, trying to keep them alive in every way possible. She had gone hunting for forest creatures, weeping when her clumsy and inept attempts failed to catch her any. Over the months, however, she had had a little more success and she had learned how to spear fish with a long piece of bone, lying in wait until she became part of the scenery. Sometimes by the time she had caught the fish she would be so ravenous that she would want to tear at its raw and uncooked body with her teeth, but one day she had done so, biting into the tough scales with difficulty, chewing off a leathery piece, swallowing it and then vomiting it all up immediately. Sometimes the nauseating taste of that raw fish would return to her in her dreams. Now she could not even smell fish without feeling sick.

It had broken her heart to have to net the birds which she had always loved. All her life she had thrilled to their sweet songs, marvelling at their endurance, at the way they sat high up in branches on cold and wet days, singing as though their lungs would burst, singing as though the sun were always shining. The need to find some food for her starving brothers and sisters had driven her out with her net, which she had flung up into the trees. Sometimes she was lucky, sometimes not. It was always a traumatic experience to see the terrified birds fluttering and screeching in the net and to have to put them out of their misery with a blow to their heads. Her dreams were littered with bird corpses, too; for what she had done to those poor helpless creatures she would never forgive herself. Taking them back to the cottage in a bag, she would harden herself, quickly plucking out their feathers, cutting off their heads and legs and putting the little bodies to stew in the pot over the fire. Then she would add moss and grass, leaves, and anything else she thought might be edible. She had never told her sisters what they were eating, but some of the boys had known, for, on occasion, they too helped to catch the food. Kitty was the eldest by five years and she had been on the heavy side with puppy fat when the first potato failure had taken place, so she had more to lose. Her brothers and father had always been on the scrawny side, however much they had eaten in the past, so they had no reserves when the bad times came.

One day she had come in to find her mother retching, her mouth stained with berry juice. A few hours later the child Nora McDonagh was expecting had been aborted.

'I had to do it, Kitty,' her mother had whispered, her face white as bone, her eyes sunken. 'I know 'tis a crime and I'll go to hell for it, but 'tis a worse crime to bring a child into the world when I have seven already and they're starvin'. God forgive me for what I've done, for I'll never forgive myself.' Nora's voice had cracked, for she adored her babies.

After that she and Kitty's father had not slept together again and when the priest came by to ask about the christening he was told simply that Nora had lost the baby she was expecting. Anyway, who could have accused the loving, kind-hearted Nora McDonagh of any crime? It was unthinkable. And yet it was the truth. The famine had made it so, had changed devoted mothers into murderesses and zealous priests into feeble skeletons, strong family men into stumbling wrecks and the tender-hearted Irish into dead men, vagabonds and criminals.

All around Kitty stretched County Tipperary. Somewhere to her left was Lough Derg, which was haunted by some of her countrymen who had been put to death by Cromwell's soldiers years before. They had said Cromwell was the worst scourge of Ireland, the stony zealot who had decimated Drogheda and Wexford in the name of God and the Puritan religion.

The spring sunshine proclaimed that it was noon, so she sank down on a mossy patch beneath some trees, untied the knot which kept her bundle together and took out some herbs, which were all she had to eat. As she chewed on them she found herself longing for more solid food; for hot baked potatoes flung from one scorched palm to another and then broken in two so that their fluffy white middles were revealed, to be washed down with delicious buttermilk. What wouldn't she give for a dish of her mother's hare stew in its succulent juices, with a huge wedge of soda bread. The memory of past mealtimes floated before her eyes so vividly that she thought her family were really there before her, their eyes bright, their faces ruddy, as they had been before the repeated potato failures.

'Mammy,' she whispered, but the smiling woman she saw before her in a hazy dream did not look in her direction. Indeed none of the faces were looking in her direction or could be made to do so, however hard she exerted her will, and after a time she realised why. Their faces were turned in the direction of Heaven.

The herbs were filling her mouth with bitterness, the juice acrid in her throat. Looking round, she hoped to see hawthorn, whose blossom was not unpalatable, but there was none. She saw the deep blue flowers of the bugle, the five-petalled yellow pimpernel which was the colour of fresh butter, the stalwart ox-eye daisy standing straight and bold in the meadow grass, and purply-pink wild orchids. So much beauty, so much colour, yet none of it could stop the gnawing hunger she was feeling. Closing her lids tightly over eyes which were as blue as the gentians growing on the Burren, she plunged her head into her hands, her silky black hair falling forward over her face. Where was she going? She had no idea. After digging the last grave and fixing a crucifix of twigs over it she had snatched up her bundle and run from the haunted cottage as fast as her wasted legs would carry her. The cottage to her had become the coldest, clammiest crypt that ever any church had seen, the laughter which had once run round its walls having been snatched by death. She could not have slept another night in that place, but she had nowhere to go and no money to take her there. She had heard of towns and villages not touched by the famine, where people still lived and slept and ate exactly as they had always done, where potatoes flourished in the fields and pigs, cows and horses dotted the landscape. If she reached such a paradise what would they think of her, in her rags with her feet bare, the hair tangled round her hollow cheeks? Who knew what sort of welcome she would be given, for some people cursed beggars and that was surely what she was now: a beggar-girl.

But what good would fretting do? She had to go on, there was no turning back. Perhaps she would come upon a village soon and be given some food, bread thick with yellow butter, a mug of milk, strips of bacon, crisp and sweet. Oh, what she would give for any of those! Getting up she plodded on, then, coming to a stream which ran quite deep, an idea came into her head. Dropping her bundle, she stripped of the ragged dress which she had worn for over a year and which she had long ago outgrown. Then she put one foot after the other into the rushing water, shuddering at its iciness. Standing calf-deep in the stream, she splashed the crystal water over her stomach, breasts and thighs, not stopping until her hair was drenched, her feet rosy with the cold but alive with a blissful tingling. She knew she must present a scrawny picture but there was no one to see. How often had her mother said that cleanliness was next to godliness, how often had the priest said that an unclean body offends God's eye. She only wished that she had some lye soap to do the job properly. She thought of happy bathtimes in the cottage in days gone by, the little ones splashing and giggling in the frothing water, their laughter rapidly changing to squeals when soap stung their eyes. She could almost feel the pink and chubby little bodies in her arms again.

She rolled in the grass to dry herself, thinking of how the priest would have scolded to find her there naked in the open air. But he was dead too now, like all the others. She thought of a favourite saying of his, 'Always do the best that it is possible for you to do, for you cannot go back in time, you cannot put back the clock,' and she knew that no amount of sobbing and weeping could return her to those happy days and bring back her beloved family. She was on her own now and she must not rail against it, for it was all part of God's plan.

Dried, she put on her old brown dress of rough cloth, patched and threadbare though it was, and far too small for her. The herbs she had chewed had done little to assuage her hunger, the deep psychological longing for food and love and family, which were indivisible.

'You cannot put back the clock.' When would she think of that statement without the deep twisting grief inside her?

A bird circled high up in the air overhead looking for prey; a fieldmouse or vole, perhaps, would soon be filling its stomach. Nature had provided well for its animals but had little compassion for its people. Ireland, reliant on potatoes for centuries since the first experimental crops had been grown there, had depended absolutely on these as a staple diet. At that time, through ignorance, men had been known to die from eating raw potato, not knowing that it was essential that it be cooked; now men were dying because there was no potato to eat, raw, baked or boiled.

The McDonaghs had been more fortunate than most, for they had owned their house. Thousands of others in the best of times lived a hand to mouth existence, growing their most nutritious crops to pay the rent and not eating these themselves, even when death knocked at their doors in the form of potato curl. Ways of cooking and eating the miniature, necrotic potatoes had been devised by the starving. The disgustingly decayed black parts cut off, what little remained was cooked in the usual way then mashed with bran and salt. The resulting gluey and inedible mass, which tasted like poison, caused vomiting and prostration. Finally there was only the coarse, rough bran left, then that too had gone. Grass, herbs and nettles went into the pot, and weeds. Raw fish and bitter green food; Kitty would never forget them.

She was approaching a village now, a cluster of whitewashed cottages with pretty thatched roofs. To her delight the village looked well-tended, neat and tidy; the gardens were full of flowers and lushly verdant. A dog stood in the middle of the baked earth road, the colour of baked earth itself, its coat ragged but shining. When it saw her it barked convulsively and bared its teeth. Ignoring it, she knocked at the door of the first cottage. Oh, what a long wait standing there, while it seemed that her life was slowly ebbing away, her pulses throbbing, her mouth aching with the longing for food.

The door opening a crack or two, a woman's angry eyes looked out at her. Beneath the fierce gaze was a bulbous nose like a faded strawberry, the mouth a spiteful gash; the mobcap she wore was clean and neatly pressed, her gown of a pleasant, woven material.

Beg for food, this is your chance, the voice in Kitty's

head told her: beg or you will starve. But even so it took her all her willpower to force the words from her lips, to quell her pride and put herself at another's mercy.

'Please, mistress, I haven't eaten a proper meal in weeks. If ye have a crust or mug of milk –'

'A beggar! Joshua, there's a beggar at the door – a beggar-girl!' the woman screeched. A man appeared behind her, his face contorted into angry lines. Raising his fist, he advanced on Kitty, a stream of abuse gushing from his mouth. They were English, and what did the English know of the loving hospitality in the South? Nothing, that was plainly obvious.

Head held high, mustering all her dignity, the muscles in her legs shivering, Kitty walked on to the next cottage.

'No one'll help you there, either,' the man roared after her. 'We do not tolerate beggars here in Dungarry. This is a Protestant village and not for the likes o' Papists.'

How had he known she was a Catholic? Stung into a retort, Kitty called out, 'There is but one God and He is the same for all of us, and 'tis the same God who said feed my sheep and lambs.'

The man's face seemed to swell and turn to the colour of an angry bruise. He looked as if he wanted to box Kitty's ears, but his wife was now tugging at his sleeve and urging him to come back into the house. Plainly neither of them had envisaged a beggar who could talk back and quote the Bible at them. Husband and wife retreated into their little cottage, which was dim from the lack of every sort of light.

No one answered Kitty's knock at the next cottage or the next, for the altercation had been heard and decisions made. No one was going to offer alms to a pauper girl, ragged, unwashed and louse-ridden as she would surely be. Dungarry had laid up its stores and protected itself from the results of the potato curl, believing its survival was due entirely to a benevolent and loving Protestant God.

Steal food out of their gardens, for they deserve no better, urged the tempting demon in Kitty's mind. But she had been raised with a healthy flourishing conscience: stealing was wrong and punishable. Would God forgive her for becoming a thief to save her own life? She did not know the answer to that profound question. But if he intended her to die, then he would probably not forgive her for trying to thwart his plan.

Flocks of snowy hawthorn drooping over a fence made her mouth water. Pulling off handfuls of the blossom, she crammed it into her mouth. It was called bread and cheese by the poor but she had never known why, for it certainly did not taste like that to her. However, the starving do not pause to savour taste. Her cheeks crammed, she turned at the sound of a shout to see a man with a cudgel running down the road towards her, accompanied by the snarling dog. Turning on her heel, she ran, not stopping until the village was long out of sight behind her, and then she could not believe what she saw. A huge, roughly-shaped loaf of soda bread lying in the middle of the dusty track. It must have fallen off a cart. She fell on it, stuffing chunks into her mouth. It was stale and leathery, but that did not matter, nor did it matter that the taste of soda had increased as it was apt to do when the bread was not eaten fresh. Salty, hard and odd-tasting as it was, she devoured it all. Never in her life had she enjoyed food so much or known it taste so good. Nor, having eaten, did she forget to say a prayer of thanks. Tired after her feast, she curled up in a verdant hollow by the roadside and slept, needing all her strength to digest the food.

She woke to find the sun blazing in her face, the taste of

soda still acrid in her mouth, and three men staring down at her.

'Don't ye be after taking any trouble wi' her, yer lordship. Seth an' I will deal wi' her. The ragged urchin, how dare she lie down to sleep here on your land!' one of the men was saying.

Kitty had leapt to her feet, her head spinning. Who were the men, where was she? For a moment she was dazed and could not remember. The men stared at her unrelentingly, faces grim. Two were dressed in rough homespun doublets and baggy breeches, with coarse woollen hose and clumsy shoes with buckles. The third man had something strange on his head, the likes of which she had never seen before. It looked like hair and yet it was not, it was stiff and white, formed in artificial curls sweeping from the crown of his head down to his shoulders. Could it be a wig? She had heard her mother speak of the gentry who wore such things on their heads. The third man's clothes were beautiful, his jacket of a shiny material like sunshine on water, sparkling, a profusion of lace at his wrists and throat. He was the man addressed as 'your lordship' and the fact that he was the first titled man Kitty had ever met in her entire fifteen years caused her much more inner turmoil than the fierce expressions on the faces of his servants.

Making as if to run, she found her arm gripped by a beautifully-manicured, slender white hand. Looking down at the fingers curled round her arm, she was dazzled by the blaze of jewels, red, green and transparent as water they stared back up at her. Such beauty? Even terrified as she was their loveliness invaded her senses making an indelible impression on her mind. A sweet pungent smell issued from the man. It was not unpleasing, although she had never smelt scent on a man or woman before in her life. She stood there, half of her wanting to run, but the rest becoming calmer beneath the gaze of the bewigged gentleman. His eyes were a calm greenish-grey, steady and unwinking, his skin pale, the bones of his face fine and shapely, his mouth full. There was a deep dimple in his chin and his lashes were sandy, but not the ugly sandiness which gives an uncouth look.

'Stay, my child, there is nothing to be afraid of. Where have you come from, have you lost your way?'

It had been a long time since anyone had called her my child; not since the priest had died, in fact. It was good to hear those words on a man's lips again, solid and comforting, and something in her broke. She wanted to fling herself into the man's arms and sob on his chest like a child with her father. Unthinkable, of course. He was a wealthy stranger, a lord, English, maybe even a Protestant; the barriers of class, creed and sex seemed insurmountable to her. When she did not answer, he took her arm more gently urging her to come with him, telling his servants to follow behind. They walked some way, Kitty unable to find her voice; she was too overawed, too amazed by this turn of events. Now and again her companion passed a comment about the scenery or the weather and she nodded dumbly, wondering where they were going but not really caring. Could this be a dream? Perhaps she was still lying asleep at the roadside imagining it all.

After a time they came in sight of the most beautiful house Kitty had ever seen; beside it all the cottages she had ever known looked like hovels. She could not help but gasp out loud.

'Aha, I see you are impressed by my home. Its name is Cromer House and I am the Earl of Cromer. Come inside and I shall give you something to eat.' His lordship's green eyes twinkled.

Through the great front door they went and into a cool, wide hallway of marble and oak, gleaming, sumptuous, smelling of lavender and beeswax. The hall was like a miraculous vision to Kitty; she gazed round it, her mouth hanging open, then squeezed her eyes tightly shut before opening them again. Yes, the hall was still there and so was the man, a smile playing on his aristocratic mouth, a twinkle in his opal-green eyes. Suddenly she felt faint, overcome with all that had happened. She must have gone white, for Lord Cromer helped her towards a carved bench and called for his housekeeper. She was plump and motherly, dressed in Irish green with an enormous sparkling white apron from neck to toes, most of her hair, the colour of orange poppies, tucked into a mobcap. How different her reaction was from that of the villagers.

'Alanna, have the hounds been after tearing at your gown? 'Tis all full of holes along the hem, and how thin ye are! When did ye last have a good sound meal? Your lordship, where is the girl come from, how did ye find her?'

'Asleep in a ditch, Mrs McGuire.'

'Asleep in a ditch, Holy Mother of God preserve us! Have you no home to go to, alanna?'

Kitty shook her head. She felt very weak inside and shaky. She could not forget how she had been so rudely sent packing by the villagers who lived just over the rise. The distress of that had led to the discovery of the stale loaf of bread in the road, that discovery leading on to an even greater miracle: this richly-dressed lord who had all but scooped her up from the roadside, apparently not at all repulsed by her pauper clothes and bare feet. He was looking at her now, a gently questioning look in his eyes which she would have called critical, had she known that word. He was leaning with one arm resting on the beautifully-carved banister, one booted foot on the lower stair.

Suddenly the feeling of weakness got the better of her and she keeled over. When she came round she was being borne upstairs in Lord Cromer's arms, so close to him that she could see the silvery white hairs in his sandy brows, the v-shaped laughter lines at the corners of his opal-green eyes. He was much older than she had at first thought, but he had a hard and vigorous body and was barely out of breath at all as they reached the top of the stairs and turned left down the corridor. Her head felt strange, woolly, and even though she had eaten the soda bread some hours before it still lay like a rock in her stomach. She was sure that both of these sensations would have been paramount had she not been in the arms of this strong and beautiful man.

Turning in through a door, Lord Cromer carried her over to a vast fourposter bed, placing her gently down upon it. When Mrs McGuire bustled into the room he went over to the window, and stood staring out into the gardens beyond. The fine day was over; the rain was plummeting down like long glass pins, thundering against the bushes and trees outside, smacking against the earth and rebounding.

Inside the room was now gloomy as if seen through a watery haze. Turning back the covers, Mrs McGuire told Kitty to sit on the sheets and then helped her to strip off the ancient outworn dress, but she had pulled the bed-curtains together first so that they would not be overlooked.

'Mother o' God, there's very little dirt on ye, I'm thinking,' Mrs McGuire clucked. 'I was expectin' to have to scrape it off ye with a knife.'

'I washed in a stream,' Kitty said, her voice dull, emotionless, for she was still in something of a stupor.

'Even so, we'll get some soap onto your skin, for that old dress was none too clean.'

'I would like to wash myself, if you please,' Kitty said, her chin jutting out a little.

'An independent miss I see,' Mrs McGuire said, tilting her head to the left and shrugging her shoulder against it, in what Kitty would come to recognise as a characteristic gesture.

'I am fifteen now –'

'A great old age indeed, and I'm wondering if ye'll survive such advanced years. Here, take this bowl and this soap and wash yourself all over while I fetch ye a clean gown. Ye can go in the tub later when ye are stronger.'

'Thank you,' Kitty murmured.

Never had she known soap so smooth and silky, so sweetly scented; it smelt of all the most beautiful flowers in a garden. She would not have minded leaving it on her body instead of rinsing it off. The smell of it took away so many anguishes, so much pain that it was like a panacea for all ills. She was clean, had dried herself and was yawning deeply when Mrs McGuire returned with a soft lawn nightrobe. While the housekeeper was out of the room Kitty had not heard a sound from Lord Cromer, but she had wondered what he was doing. Was he still in the room, still staring out of the window to protect her modesty? He was much older than she, probably old enough to be her grandfather; perhaps to him she was nothing more than a child.

The robe was soft cream lawn, frilled with a fragile and rich cream spidery lace at the neck and cuffs. Suddenly her tiredness became too much for her. She lay down on the lavender-scented sheets, her head cushioned by the soft spotless pillow, and closed her eyes, sinking instantly into the deepest sleep.

She did not see Mrs McGuire gazing down upon her with the fond look of a mother who has raised fifteen children of her own and who loved to see a child cosily asleep. Nor did she see what happened after Mrs McGuire had tiptoed out, for it was then that Lord Cromer came across the room from the window to the fourposter bed to stand beside Kitty, looking down at her thoughtfully. Had she been awake and seen it she would have been none the wiser, for she could never have gauged the thoughts that were marching through Lord Cromer's head. He was not having very much success analysing them himself, as it happened.

CHAPTER TWO

It had been said of the young Lord Cromer that he had three mistresses: his shipping empire, the trading company he had inherited from his uncle, and gold. An alliance of the first two had given birth to a great quantity of the third. By the time he was forty Alexander Sutherland, Lord Cromer, was a legend in his own time with only one shadow to mar his phenomenal success, and that was the lack of a son. The arranged marriage of his youth had ended tragically when Deborah, his young bride of two years, had died of the smallpox. Conquering his grief with hard work, he had spent the next ten years expanding his empire, opening new trading centres in far-flung spots round the world, increasing his fleet and sending his captains into as yet unexplored regions of the earth in search of ivory and spices, hides, precious minerals, coffee, and jade. It was said that three-quarters of the coffee houses in the country were supplied by the Cromer Shipping Company.

To have one of his crews discover some new, rare and extraordinary commodity was his greatest delight, but it meant that there must be constant vigilance, constant rivalry and competition between his company and others who wished to replace him as the premier British merchant, or the Great Sea Lord as he was known by both friends and rivals. Consequently he had had little time for women. With nauseating regularity young heiresses were thrust in his direction, for he was not only possessed of wealth and high reputation but he was also a splendid figure of a man, six feet tall, with lean, broad shoulders and a physique finely honed from constant activity. He had the astute mind and burning ambition of those born in late December under the sign of Capricorn. Capricorn men and women are said to improve with age and, like the Saturn-born, he had gone grey early, but it was not a harsh dull grey; his hair was a silky silver hue which made his opal-green eyes all the brighter and more shrewd-looking.

As the years passed following Deborah's death, his retainers despaired of hearing their master laugh as he had done before he was widowed, or of seeing the bold and generous smile which used to light up his face, lacing his eyes with laughter lines. But then when he was fifty-two Lord Cromer married a second time. Eschewing the unschooled and brittle heiresses who were dangled before him by anxious mothers, he chose a mature woman of meagre property, aged twenty-seven, who was both handsome, discreet and intelligent. Her father was the impoverished Earl of Dauby, whose Irish properties were adjacent to those of Cromer. Lady Marianne Violet Dauby, freed for the first time in her life from her father's oppressive dominance, had looked on marriage to the handsome and cultured Lord Cromer as a miraculous release from what had become an intolerable situation.

Marianne, believing that her new husband adored her, and that marriage would give her completely free rein for her personality, had seemed at first to be more than contented with the balls and supper parties to which her husband took her, in order to introduce her to his business colleagues and associates and their families. However, very soon, having also led herself to believe that her opinion was of great importance to her husband, she began to offer it all too freely. When her unwanted advice was treated with an amused and dismissive tolerance, Lady Cromer became more strident still.

Lord Cromer remembered their bitter disagreements about a wife's role as he stood over the bed watching the peasant waif asleep. The waif's colouring was very much like Marianne's, which must have jolted his memory. He remembered how Marianne had become altogether more subdued during her first pregnancy, and how relieved he had been at first. But when she had become pallid and listless, going three and then four weeks beyond her time and sobbing because she could not feel the infant kicking inside her any more, it had turned into a tragedy. Neither mother nor child had been saved. Marianne had been buried with his still-born son wrapped in her cold, dead arms. Looking down on them before the lid was placed on her coffin, Cromer had wept for the first and last time in his life, needle-sharp tears, choking sobs which bruised his lungs.

Afterwards, he had returned to work, throwing himself into his business activities with an even greater fervour than before. A few weeks later he ordered everything of Marianne's to be removed from their home in London, their manor in the south and Cromer House in County Tipperary. He could not bear to set eyes on a single fragment of lace, on any of her dresses, or so much as one tiny silk bow or slipper. All of it had been cleared out, her memory totally erased. Once more, work was his obsession.

It was quite by accident that he found it possible to love a child other than one of his own siring. A few years before his second wife's death, his sister Emmelina had given birth to a son, Carrick. Although present at

Carrick's christening service, Fabian had taken little interest in the baby, at first disdaining his sister's invitations to the nursery. But as Fabian's visits to his sister's home were reasonably frequent it was only natural that one day he would encounter the boy in circumstances which would force him to notice the child. As it happened it was at the age of ten that Carrick saved Fabian's favourite dog from drowning.

Solomon was an old dog who liked to think himself a pup still. One day he had followed the younger dogs, many of whom were his sons, down to the lake. He splashed into the water joyously, remembering long-gone days when he was only two or three summers old, indefatigable, fearless and strong. Pedalling out after the younger dogs, he tried to copy their hearty barking, but the waters of the lake were colder than he had anticipated and the chill took his breath away. Very soon he was at the centre of the lake and the cold was turning his arthritic limbs to lead. Once, twice, he had plunged beneath the lake's surface, swallowing water, his eyes bulging with terror.

Glancing out of one of the windows of the house, Fabian had seen what was happening down at the lake but he knew that he would not be in time; the dog was going under for the third time, the ripples of the lake above his head growing smooth. Solomon had drowned. Tearing down the steps of the terrace and out across the lawns, Fabian ran with all the vigour of a twenty-year-old. But before he could get halfway across the lawns, believing that he was too late, he saw his nephew Carrick fling aside his jacket and boots and dive headlong into the lake. The boy was an excellent swimmer, soon reached the centre of the water, and there dived repeatedly until he found Solomon.

Meanwhile, Emmelina had also reached the lakeside and stood beside her brother, her hands first over her eyes and then her cheeks as she moaned, 'Oh, the reeds, the reeds, they are so thick in that spot. They will tie themselves round his ankles and pull him down and he will be drowned. Oh, I cannot look, I cannot look. Brother, save him, *save him*!'

But there was no need, for at that moment Carrick surfaced, hair wetly plastered to his head, Solomon clutched in his arms. Within minutes Solomon was being briskly rubbed down and massaged until his lungs voided the water he had swallowed. Fabian, who had enjoyed some of his most satisfying and rewarding hunting trips with Solomon bounding at his horse's side, looked at Carrick with new eyes. A nephew with mettle, and the boy only ten years old. To think that he had wasted ten years and barely exchanged more than a few words with the child. A boy after his own heart and, quite probably, the only boy in the world who would ever carry his blood, for the physicians had said it was unlikely his sister would have any more children.

Two weeks after the courageous rescue, Fabian made Carrick his legal heir. When he died his entire trading and shipping empire would go to the boy. It was strange what a deep contentment that deed had brought him, and shortly Carrick was his son in everything but name. He now went to his sister's house to see him, taking the boy gifts, curios and novelties from all over the world. A sinister-looking carving with a gargoyle's face from Haiti, carved ivory elephants from Africa, a scarlet, gold and emerald green silk dressing-gown from Tartary with embroidered silk slippers to match, embossed and enamelled plates and dishes from India, the face of a russet and gold tiger snarling from the centre of each. And jade statuettes of every hue. Many people believed that jade could only be green, but in fact there were different hues: semi-translucent milky white, dull dandelion yellow, different shades of red and brown, bluish-greens, and many more.

Motes of the past gathered in Fabian's head, floating through his thoughts one after the other. So many years of application, of dedication – and escape. He stared down at the sleeping Irish girl, feeling a sudden knot of compassion in his breast. Starving beggar-maids were ten-a-penny in Ireland, the precariousness of the national diet, totally dependent as it was upon the even more precarious British weather, saw to that. He had never ceased to be amazed at the amount of potatoes a sturdy Irish farmer or labourer could devour. Fourteen pounds of potatoes a day was what they would eat if they could get it; they liked oats, buttermilk, and leeks, too. The Irish had hearty appetites and insatiable thirsts, they relished their food more than most races. To send them famine was a doubly harsh punishment.

This child had rough red hands which were split and cracked at the knuckles, round the nails and in the clefts between the fingers; they looked tender and inflamed. How long had this poor creature been stumbling her way through Ireland's lush greenery, the verdant paradise which could so swiftly become purgatory for the poor? And where were her parents? Did they not care for her, did they not wonder where she was? He would have left no daughter of his to sleep in a ditch.

The truth was that he had been deeply disturbed to see the girl asleep in broad daylight, her ragged dress years too small for her body. Anywhere else in this stricken country he would not have been surprised, but here on his own lands which his family had nurtured and protected since 1602 when they had been given in gift from the Virgin Queen, Elizabeth Tudor, to one of Fabian's direct ancestors, Collingswell Cromer. Ten, twenty years ago, he would have walked past the girl sleeping in her earthy ditch, but much had happened recently; his sister Emmelina's death, which had been unexpected and painful and which had left him the guardian of his nephew, Carrick. The knowledge that he was no longer young, a knowledge which had scored itself into his mind when he had woken one morning the previous winter with stiffened fingers and aching joints. A brief attack, soon cured by herbal medicaments and careful attention to diet, but disturbing all the same, for hitherto he had never known a moment's indisposition in his life.

Lord Cromer reached out to touch the sheet covering the child. His gesture was almost absent-minded but to his amazement he found his hand resting on her hair, soft black silky hair, which he had expected would be bristly and coarse to the touch. Looking closer, he saw that she might well be older than the twelve or thirteen years which he had first thought her. She was small of course, because she was malnourished, but her features were not those of a snub-faced child, they were clearly sculpted like those of an adult or one on the verge of adulthood. Had he or the housekeeper asked her name? If they had he could not remember what she had answered. He found himself thinking of Solomon, bedraggled, wet and shuddering after his near-drowning in the lake; he had never been immune to the more desperate straits of those in need, which was exactly why he had always kept himself removed from them where possible. Except for this child, who had thrust herself into his life without asking his permission.

If flame had no heat and he could feel its flickering painlessly against his palm, he imagined that it would feel just as her hair felt now, a curl looping itself possessively around his forefinger almost as if it wanted to hold him and prevent his escape. The fanciful imaginings of an old man, he chided himself, drawing his hand away swiftly, tucking his thumb in his belt so that it would not stray again.

Turning on his heel, he strode out of the room. When the child had recovered her health he would take her to an orphanage in England and there she would be well cared for until she was old enough to set out in the world alone. Really he could not be expected to do any more than that.

CHAPTER THREE

The child filled out with remarkable rapidity, growing taller before Fabian's eyes. One day he saw a bony, skeletal wraith, the next a fifteen-year-old girl of dignity and comeliness. At first, Kitty had eaten like a starving hound, tearing at her food, dribbling broth down her chin, stuffing her mouth with Mrs McGuire's freshly baked bread and chunks of strong golden Tipperary cheese. Watching her, Fabian found himself experiencing the strangest sensation: after some time he was able to put a name to it. It was fondness he felt for the girl, the same fondness he had felt for Solomon as a pup; an all-embracing, tender, caring emotion which hit him in the throat and chest, melting his bones. She had spirit, the bog-waif, and very soon he was admiring her for it. And so it had started with the very best beginning of all: respect and tenderness, such as he would have felt for a young hound following him devotedly at his heels on long hunting treks. In many ways she was exactly like a puppy, wild, untamed, raw-speaking, and then, as her energies slowly began to return, she became ebullient and restless. But even as she filled out over the following weeks, the shadow remained in her face, the shadow of anguish, of loss and past suffering which no fifteen-year-old should have had to bear.

On finding that the skinny, bedraggled child was on the

verge of womanhood – Fabian realised that he faced a problem. Kitty was almost too old for an orphanage in London, yet too wild and unschooled to be sent to a Finishing Academy, and her education was abysmal. She spoke of a priest who had obviously meant a great deal to her, a man who had discussed theology with her as he would have done with one of his fellows, who had taught her much of what he knew of the past, the Bible, and of life itself. Kitty thought she could do well because she could scrawl her name and a fair amount of other words, but Fabian found her pride in this minute accomplishment the most shocking thing of all. Her calligraphy was blotched and unruly, surging across the parchment like a charging infant. When she had filled the page she would look up at Fabian, her eyes the colour of morning-blue skies, entreating him to praise her for her efforts.

Strange, unfamiliar emotions swirled inside him at such moments, emotions which he could accept when they were directed towards a beloved hound or his adored nephew, Carrick, but which when evoked by a tragic, raw-speaking Irish girl of some fifteen years made him prey to a tumult of doubts, uncertainties and – although he would never admit it – fears.

Life slipped into a simple routine. While Mrs McGuire filled Kitty with food, nourishing broth and drinks at every available opportunity, inventing new times for eating so that elevenses were joined by tenses, threeses, sixes, and so on, Lord Cromer attended to Kitty's first formal education. His business was not yet done in Ireland. The overseers he had sent out to make reports for him had not returned; letters he had dispatched to his major landlords had not been answered. In fact, things were as they always were in Southern Ireland, leisurely and relaxed. Long ago he had learned that one could not fight the lack of momentum in Irish life, one must adjust or perish. At any other time, however, he would have been fuming to return to Cromer Manor in Surrey, where he was surrounded by all the curios and artefacts which he treasured. But now his hours were filled with re-shaping and refining Kitty McDonagh in preparation for their return to England. He also began to see that although Kitty certainly needed refining, she did not need re-shaping, for her body rapidly filled out. She seemed to grow taller before his eyes, her breasts and hips swelling into a sweet curvaceousness, while her waist remained slender and sinuous, her stomach flat.

She had already grown out of the first rough-woven dress which Mrs McGuire had given her, but she had to be persuaded to part with it all the same, for she had never owned such a fine gown in all her life. The touches of white at collar and cuffs had brought a glow to her cheeks. Only when Mrs McGuire produced a larger and finer dress would Kitty finally relinquish the rough-woven gown. The new one was a cast-off like the other but handsome all the same, being of soft blue woollen material with lappets of blue linen at the cuffs and neck. Having bathed – a pastime which Kitty enjoyed with all the enthusiasm of a young child – she slipped on the new blue dress and brushed her glossy black curls until they shone. Then, barefoot, she ran down the stairs to the library where her lord protector was waiting.

He looked up as she came into the room, thinking how good it was to see the rose in her cheeks and the fullness of the face which had been hollow and haggard when she had first come into the house. Then his eyes had slipped down her body slowly, thoughtfully. She would be sixteen in a few weeks and she was beginning to look her age. Perhaps marriage would be a better solution for her, if he could succeed in smoothing the rough edges and present her to one of his stewards or gamekeepers back home. Tom Blart and Ned Evans were still unwed and they were good, honest men who would care for a pretty young wife. Pretty? Yes, she was pretty now that her health had returned. Such very blue eyes, the colour of cornflowers, and the wild raven-black hair clustering round her fresh cream skin.

Fabian felt a stab of regret, which he half-heartedly analysed as a wish that this radiant young girl might have been his own daughter. Then, as she sat down beside him, smiling broadly, he stopped the uncharacteristic analysis of his feelings towards another human being and started to question her about what he had taught her the previous day.

Her memory was excellent. She was a satisfying student: bright, avid for learning, she lapped up all he told her. Only her childish, scrawling handwriting displayed something other than competence, but he hoped that would improve in time. It was certainly not imperative that a gamekeeper's wife should know how to write, especially when her husband could do so tolerably well, but, with his customary dedication to whatever interested him, Fabian insisted that Kitty practise her letters until her arm ached. Philanthropy of this kind being new to him, perhaps he was over-harsh, but she seemed such a willing student and so eager to please that he took advantage of it.

Then one day, after writing and re-writing her name for something like three hours, Kitty suddenly hunched over the sheets of parchment spread all around her and broke into heartbreaking tears. It was a reaction to all she had gone through, a conglomeration of shock and grief and over-tiredness, but Fabian, who had had little experience of women in dire emotional need, found himself thrown into something like panic. He had loved his sister but she had been raised by nursemaids in the customary fashion, and when she had wept or been upset it had been her servants who had tended her. When had he last comforted a tearful woman towards whom he felt particularly protective? He could not remember. Had there, in fact, ever been such a moment?

Hesitating only momentarily before putting his arms round the sobbing girl, Fabian found a sweet consolation. Her response was immediate. She flung herself against his hard chest, her arms gripping round his neck as if she were terrified, while the tears gushed out of her eyes, making a huge soaking patch on his shirt.

'Oh, you are so g-good to me!' Kitty sobbed. 'If it were not for you I would be dead like my brothers and sisters, my mother and father. They all starved to death, you know. I tried to feed them, oh yes, truly I did. I did terrible things. Killing birds, poor defenceless little creatures, but there was just not enough food whatever I did, and they died, they all died, and it was my fault because I could not keep them alive. I killed them all – I killed them, truly I did. I am a murderess!' Kitty sobbed heartbreakingly, a surging heat engulfing her body.

Fabian listened in horror. It was the first time she had spoken of her past, but now it all came pouring out, her anguish, grief and suffering. In God's Name, what had the child been through? Smoothing back her hair, he kissed her forehead tenderly.

'Weep, weep, little one. Let all the tears come out,' he said. 'Let them all come out.'

'Death lived with us in our cottage,' Kitty went on. He was everywhere: he climbed into bed with us; he sat at our table; he hunted with us in the woods. Sometimes I would wake in the night, knowing that I heard his laughter, cold and chilling. We were his prey, his victims. He lived off our deaths; he inhaled our dying breaths to give himself strength. Oh my lord, how can I describe it to you? How can I make you see what it was like? As each one of my brothers and sisters died I wanted to die with them, but I had to go on for the others. I had nothing to live for, and yet everything. Every time one of them died a part of me died with them, so that soon I was nothing more than an empty shell. Oh Joseph, Joseph, my brother, my favourite brother! He died in my arms with my kisses on his mouth. I tried to kiss him back to life, I tried to give him my breath, my heart, but there was nothing I could do.' Kitty sagged against Lord Cromer's chest, exhausted at this revival of her worst memories. 'There will never be peace for me again in this life, not ever, not anywhere. When I go to sleep I see their faces, my mother and father, Patrick and Maura, Katherine, Corin and Donal, and Joseph – always Joseph. He and I were so close. We did everything together; we understood one another. I am so lonely now.'

Fabian, more moved than he had ever been in his entire life, gathered the young girl into his arms, her body a rage of heat against him. The fires of grief were burning brightly inside her but the tears were helping to quench them, and he told her so.

'Tears are the great healer, Kitty. Now that you can cry you will get better.'

'But the pain! The pain has never been so bad as at this moment,' Kitty protested, looking up, red-eyed, into Lord Cromer's face.

'Things always have to get worse before they get better, Kitty. You should know that.' Remembering something his sister had said, he added: 'Do not fear the storms, for afterwards comes peace.'

'Who said that, who said it?' Kitty asked, her voice insistent.

'An anchoress long ago, Mother Julian of Norwich. She shut herself away and communed with God and he sent her many messages by way of miracles and she wrote about them. My sister used to read her works. They were called the Revelations, I believe. The book will still be somewhere around the house, I imagine.'

'This house or your house in Surrey, Lord Cromer? Would this Mother Julian have been a Catholic, then?'

'Yes, indeed she was, for that was before the dissolution of the monasteries in Henry the Eighth's day.'

' "After the storms comes peace," ' Kitty quoted, absorbing the words which were like a balm. ' "After the storms comes peace." Was your sister a Catholic, then?'

'No, we are not a Catholic family. But she always used to say that there was only one God and it was stupid to try and divide that God into two different deities with different rules and laws.'

'But Protestants do not worship the Blessed Virgin.'

'They respect and revere her as the Mother of Christ.'

'That is not the same. I was always told that the Blessed Virgin could never refuse her faithful followers whatever they asked.'

'Then ask something of her now, Kitty, for it seems to me that you ask too little for yourself. Ask your Blessed Virgin to comfort you, to bring you peace and tranquillity, to heal the grief and the painful memories inside you.'

'I have not prayed since I was brought here. I think I have forgotten how to pray.'

Cromer, who had never been a religiously committed man, found himself acting as something of a father confessor. To say that he was astonished by this would have been an understatement. The child, who was not really a child at all, had wheedled her way into his heart. Now he ached to help her in more than material ways.

Stroking her silky night-dark hair, her little head supported by his hand, his other arm gently curved round her waist, he found that she was giving him as much comfort as he was giving her. She had revived emotions which he had long forgotten; she had created in him feelings which he had never known he could experience; she made him feel a whole, rounded person. The interaction was complicated. He had been a son, a husband, a brother, and a surrogate father to Carrick. Now, with this anguished, suffering girl, he could experience at one and the same time the entire multiplicity of roles which he had known in his lifetime. He found himself immeasurably humbled by this knowledge, and tenderness leapt into life in his breast, a tiny exquisite flower brought to life by Kitty's tears.

A few days before Kitty's sixteenth birthday they left Southern Ireland to return to Surrey. The journey at sea seemed interminable to Kitty: hour after long hour in the bleak and dewy air. Fortunately the sea was calm, but even so Kitty was filled with trepidation for this, her first sea voyage. She could not relax with a great expanse of water beneath her feet. She was homesick; she felt somehow that she was deserting her dead family, leaving them behind in their lonely, stony graves in Tipperary. The empty cottage would stand for all time, forlorn and lonely, with not so much as the echo of one peal of a child's laughter, with weeds and brambles tangling round its door and over the eaves. A house of weeds where once it had been a house of love.

Kitty stood at the rail of the ship, a forlorn figure in her heavy cloak. How cold and menacing was the air; nothing to be seen but miles and miles of flat lacklustre seas with a pale, pearly sky above and mist like a winding sheet round the sun. No trees, no flowers, no greenery, no birds this far out at sea. Nothing but the slicing arc of the horizon to capture the eye. Silently she vowed to herself that she would have to have a very good reason indeed before ever setting out to sea again.

Returning to her cabin, she sank onto her bunk, head in her hands, and whispered: 'Goodbye, mammy and daddy. Goodbye, Joseph and Donal, Patrick and Maura, Katherine and Corin. Goodbye. I'll never forget you. Rest happily, my family.'

Tears were slipping down her cheeks and through her fingers, when she heard the creak of the cabin door and Fabian stepped over the raised threshold. He was carrying a tray with a flask of wine and two goblets. On seeing her tears, he immediately poured the wine into one of the goblets and handed it to her.

'Here, drink this, Kitty. The sea can be a bleak experience when you're not used to it.'

'It's like a grave; the whole sea is like a great big grave,' Kitty said mournfully.

'Well, I wouldn't go so far as to say that.' Fabian quirked his brows, half-amused, half-pitying. 'Although it is true that many people have died out here in the Irish Channel.'

'Died! Died – I knew it, I *knew* it!' Kitty cried, her hands shaking so much that wine slopped over the edge of the goblet. 'I could feel all their spirits pleading for proper burial. Oh, 'tis horrible, horrible! I never want to set foot on a ship again ever, *ever*.'

'Then do not, my dearest; it is as simple as that.' Filling

her now half-empty goblet, Cromer told her to drink deeply. 'This is a special fortifying wine, Kitty. It will make you feel strong.'

Obeying, she drank too fast and started to choke. Patting her on the back, Fabian found that his arm had crept round her and she was leaning against him, looking up at him with her Celtic blue eyes filled with honesty, trust and hope.

'Kitty – Kitty, you are adorable,' Fabian heard himself say, and it was as if he were not himself any more, as if he were possessed by a far younger man, one with a romantic, loving and sensual heart and all the time in the world was standing still in preparation for what must surely come now. Stroking back the skeins of her hair, he gemmed her face with kisses, across her forehead, down one cheek and round the other cheek and then the tip of her nose and her eyelids. Gem after gem of kisses, until her face was covered with the jewels of his love and sparkling with the reflection of his feeling for her. The little face with its great blue eyes and pointed chin which he had so come to love. Then he knew what he was experiencing: a revelation of love which was just as profound as those experienced by Mother Julian of Norwich centuries before. For that was what it was: a profound and tender revelation. He loved Kitty. Send her to an orphanage? Never! She would stay with him, be his love, share his life, be his pretty little ingenue.

Her face was tilted up towards his, her mouth slightly parted. It was a full, soft mouth with a perfect Cupid's bow, and suddenly the world was rushing round and round in his head, demanding that he kiss the girl in his arms. Not the gentle, fatherly kisses of previous occasions, but the sensual, devouring and romantic kisses of love.

Her mouth quivered beneath his, a fledgling trying to raise its wings to be free and then ceasing to fight. Long, long moments passed while their lips imprinted themselves against one another, forming the ancient bond of love. Mouth to mouth, heart to heart, locked tightly together, while time raced and yet was still, and the world changed a million times and yet remained the same. Lightning and rain and thunder lashed about them and yet there was no storm. The sun's rays scored their bodies and yet the sun was shrouded by mist. Gulls screeched high above them, yet there was not a bird in sight. And the gulf between them of decades was now no gulf at all, for they were lovers.

Fabian's exploratory hands found Kitty's breasts. They were larger than he had imagined, full and rounded, and he groaned with the longing for a thousand years of loving between them when he knew there was so little time. Why could he not have met her when he was young?

Their kisses were fiercer now: a celebration. Fabian unlaced Kitty's bodice, freeing her milk-velvet breasts and covering them with kisses. Her neck was slender but strong and that, too, was soon burning from his lips. She was soft and relaxed in his arms, like a half-sleeping doll, yet weariness was the very last expression in her eyes. Wryly, he remembered the time when he had thought her eligible for one of his gamekeepers. Ludicrous, for he would never part with her. Give her to a crude and leather-handed peasant? Indeed he would not. She would wear silks and velvets and lie in his bed.

He groaned as age-old passions seared their way through his body. Gently he took Kitty's soft little hand and placed it between his thighs, where it rested like velvet against iron. He groaned again, for it had been a very long time since he had done this. Pressing his hand over hers, he squeezed her fingers tightly round him, moving her hand up and down, his breath rasping in his throat. She stared at him wonderingly, wanting to please, yet not sure exactly what was happening. Very soon it was over; the iron hardness had gone and her hand lay against a warm wetness. She was too innocent to know whether his reactions had meant pleasure or frustration, and she dared not ask.

'Kitty – Kitty, my sweet, that was beautiful, too beautiful. Next time it will be better for you, I promise; much better. It has been so long since I did this, I could not hold back, I am sorry.'

She put her arms round his neck. 'Have I pleased you, my lord?'

'Yes, yes. Infinitely,' he said.

She sighed as his arms came round her, powerful and enveloping. All she wanted in the whole world was to please him, her lord protector.

Somehow, after that, the journey seemed to fly. They reached land, where Lord Cromer's carriage awaited them to take them to Surrey, Kitty sleeping for most of the journey, her eyelids fluttering open now and again to see her lord protector's outline next to her and thus to know that all was right with the world. He loved her now and she had always loved him.

It was dark when they arrived at Cromer Manor. Fabian carried her up to his room where, after gently undressing her, he tucked her into his bed. A feeling of profound bliss enveloped her before she floated away into sleep.

Next morning they were served hot chocolate, bread and honey in bed by a sombre-faced footman resplendent in the Cromer colours of sea-green and sea-blue. The man was entirely discreet; he might well have been serving his master alone; he gave no sign of having seen a pretty, naked girl in the bed. When the footman had gone, Kitty came out from her cache beneath the covers, leaned back against the pillows and sipped at the delicious hot chocolate. She could feel her lord protector's opal-green eyes upon her admiringly, appreciatively, and she wondered if he would start to kiss her again. A thrill of excitement speared her body. His kisses to her were sweeter than hot chocolate or honey, and she wanted more and more and more of them. She was finding that she was only half alive outside his arms.

It was a simple transition for the great storehouse of love which she had nurtured for her family to be transferred to her lord protector. Before, all that love had been directed towards her parents and her brothers and sisters; now it was directed towards Lord Cromer. She felt no guilt or fear of him. She had cut herself off from the piety of her youth. For the moment everything was a dream, rosy and gauze-clouded; later, perhaps, would come the inner conflicts and the remorse; later, when she had done more than simply lie in Fabian's arms.

The chocolate drunk, the tray put aside, Cromer said: 'I will buy you a string of beautiful pearls for your birthday, the exact colour of your skin.'

'Pearls?' Kitty's eyes opened in wonderment.

'You shall have anything you want; anything, just ask.' Then, seeing her flushed cheeks, he realised that he was overwhelming her.

She had never asked for anything for herself; she was undemanding, almost diffident, urgent to please him and, as a consequence, he wanted to please her. For as long as he could remember, people had looked to him as a source of wealth and opportunity. Kitty did not. When he looked into her eyes he saw his true identity, he saw himself as she saw him: kindly, benevolent, generous-hearted. Someone who made him feel like that deserved the finest rewards possible and he would see that she got them.

She was staring at him now, with her eyes plainly adoring him. All his life he had collected beautiful curios: jade and jewels, statuettes, and now here, lying beside him in his bed, was a beautiful ivory figurine with sapphire eyes and carved ebony hair, all his very own. Warm, loving and lively as she was, he would never want to shut her away in a glass case to admire from a distance. This *objet d'art* was for his bed, not his display cabinet.

Reaching out, he touched the soft white globes which on a statuette would be chilly marble. Kitty's breasts were warm and swelling velvet with nipples the colour of tea-rose petals. Suddenly he wanted to lie with his head between her breasts, cushioned on their plump softness, and this he did, revelling in the rosy scent of her flesh.

Nothing could have been simpler or sweeter than what followed. Fabian in so many ways was young for his years, and Kitty, because of her experiences, so much older than her age. As she relaxed with Fabian's arms around her, revelling in the soothing balm of love, she gave no thought for his age. Because he had been all things to her she was ready to be all things to him. When the pupil is ready then the master will appear, Cromer was thinking almost wryly, unsure who was the pupil here and who was master. Kitty was made for love: in that she had a great advantage over him, although she would hotly deny that if it were put to her. They were together and that was all that mattered. Outside, there might be a world which would scorn, ridicule and revile them, but they would face it as one being.

His lips suddenly began to move over her breasts, exploratory yet soft as velvet. He planned to be gentle with her, slow and coaxing and tender; gradually he would lead her along the paths of rapture, taking care never to frighten her. He was prepared for her to show great maidenly modesty, Irish girls being famed for this, and he was prepared too, despite the feeling he had for her now, to forgo his longings until she was older if she became too upset by his advances. This sweet, trusting ingenue was too precious, too fragile a flower to be crushed and broken in his embrace.

Strange spangling sensations trickled over Kitty's flesh as Fabian kissed her breasts, her lips, then her breasts again. Her cheeks flushed a bright rosy pink, her breathing quickened. This is Fabian who saved me from death, she thought, as she responded to his cautious lovemaking. Fabian saved me from death and now he is my life, she thought, arching her hips to meet his, her arms sliding round his neck and clinging tightly. Thereafter she returned his kisses ardently, writhing against him, taking him entirely by surprise with her response. Sliding his hands over her soft and shapely little body, he found himself violently roused. When he found her dewy centre, pushing hard against its barrier, he was past the point of control. Within seconds it was all over, finished, nothing to remind Kitty of what had happened except the flaming sensation between her thighs being cooled by a sudden wetness.

'Forgive me, sweetheart, it will be better next time,' Fabian said.

But she did not seem angry or impatient with him, although he was feeling unutterably selfish. What was it that made him like this in her arms – his long abstinence beforehand? Could there be some guilt because until recently he had considered her almost as a daughter? Had he made the transition too violently from father to lover?

But he was not a man to be cast down by problems. He was quite sure that in time, the correct adjustment would be made. He had time and was determined to spend it upon Kitty. She was lovely, lying there against the pillows, her cheeks radiant, her eyes a magnificent blue, tendrils of silk-soft raven hair like circlets round her head. She was smiling a little, her lips gently curved. She did not look frustrated or angry or impatient; she was no self-centred strumpet, no demanding harlot, like others he had tarried with. Sweetness, virtue, shone from her eyes – and perhaps that was the reason for his present difficulties. He felt that somehow he was sullying a young innocent.

Lying in her arms, he resolved that he would always do the right thing by her. Oh, not marriage of course, for that was unthinkable: she was an Irish pauper girl, he was a peer of the realm. But he would secure a safe future for her, shower jewels and gifts and treasures upon her which, after his death, she could sell if she were in any financial difficulty. And, of course, he would leave her an annuity in his will. He was bursting with good intentions: the age difference was immense and she must be protected.

Should he leave the cementing of their sexual relationship a little while longer or should he persevere? Kitty's eyes were upon him. Sometimes he found their gaze inscrutable. What was she thinking? Had he taken this enormous step too soon? If only he could put a name to what he felt for her. Love? Was that too strong for the unique bond between them? It was unlike him to delve so deeply into a relationship, and he realised that what he felt for Kitty was indeed the beginnings of love. A spring bride for a winter lover, he thought. Then he pushed aside the regrets for what might have been so that he could enjoy what he had – what they had.

CHAPTER FOUR

Having had no experience of servants in a great household save for the kindly, easy-going and tolerant staff of Cromer House in Ireland, Kitty was unprepared for the formality of the household in Surrey. Here, rigid-backed servants in the Cromer colours of sea-green and sea-blue piped in ivory paraded hither and thither with all the regimentation of an army. Yet, over it all, was an atmosphere to which Kitty responded wholeheartedly, and that was one of happiness and contentment. It had been a bachelor household for some years, and although Kitty did not know it Lord Cromer's servants had despaired of his ever bringing a lady into the house. Knowing as they did that he was an ardent and cultured gentleman, it was only natural that he should require a lady of equal standing to share his life with him. The Irish girl was pretty and dimpled, her movements well on the way to being graceful and genteel. In her new gowns of pastel silks, embroidered with rosebuds and seed pearls, the silky panniers flowing like waterfalls at her hips, she was an enchanting picture. But overruling all that were her origins. Lowborn, it was said that she had been found by their master lying in a ditch, dressed in rags, half-starved and near death.

At first, there was some hostility towards her, because of this. There were murmurs of 'fortune-hunter' and 'schemer', but these were soon silenced when they saw how very happy their master was in her company. Transformed, in fact, from a lonely, strained and sometimes snappish man who drove himself too hard and who seemed to have lost the capacity for enjoying life, into a man who had rediscovered the art of laughter and leisure.

With hounds bounding at their heels, Lord Cromer and his pretty young companion were seen all over the Cromer estates, sometimes on foot, sometimes on horseback. Fabian was teaching Kitty to ride, and had carefully selected for her a tranquil and phlegmatic hunter called Dimsie. On Kitty's sixteenth birthday in June, she and Fabian had an al fresco lunch in the gardens, the sun blazing down on them benevolently, birds chirping and carolling in a never-ending birthday greeting. Chicken and apricot pie, succulent roast ham, egg and herb pasties, cheeses and strawberry sorbet were washed down with fragrant sparkling wine from Champagne in France and then, afterwards, while they were lying back replete, Fabian took something from the deep pocket of his lavender-embroidered silk coat. Kitty heard a faint clink and then something cold and serpentine was lying across her neck. Reaching up a hand, she felt the slippery satin of pearls white as summer clouds, their clasp fashioned out of one enormous sapphire studded with diamonds.

'Sometimes it is pearls for swine, if you will pardon the expression, Kitty, but this time it is pearls for a pearl.' Fabian grinned down at her. Then fastened the sapphire and diamond clasp at the back of her neck, bending his head to kiss her soft white skin, her curving swan-like throat.

The scene and the moment were too much for Kitty and dewy tears rolled down her cheeks, splashing onto

Fabian's hands. Taken aback, he cried out her name, sounding so reproachful that she turned round to fling herself into his arms.

'Forgive me, my lord,' she wept. 'Such kindness as this is too much for me – I do not deserve it. It – it overwhelms me. Last year I was starving, dressed in rags, and now you shower me with silks and jewels.'

'To make you happy, Kitty. Only to make you happy, not to make you weep, sweetheart.'

'Give me time to adjust, my lord. So much has happened to me in such a short space of time that I am confused, bewildered.' Kitty covered her face with her hands.

To make her lord protector happy was the greatest motivation in her life, her only reason for being, yet when she became upset, as at moments like these, she knew that she was causing him distress and not joy. To please him, she wanted to subjugate every unwelcome emotion in her body: grief, pain, distress, restlessness, and all the other reactions to the shocks and bereavements of her childhood. It could not be done of course, but she wanted to make herself the most perfect woman on earth, to be all that she was sure Fabian wanted her to be. Would he give her such priceless pearls if he did not have the highest expectations for her? And she would live up to them, she would!

'This is your birthday, not your funeral,' Fabian was saying, rather ironically. 'I intended to make you happy not plunge you into despair.'

'But I am happy, my lord, so very, very happy. I do not mean to upset you, it is just that the pearls are so heavenly and no one has ever given me such a beautiful gift before – and – and – I love you, oh I love you, my lord.'

Fabian, who could tolerate women's tears if he could

staunch them quickly, found himself whispering that he too loved her, that he would care for her always, that she would always be safe with him.

'Oh, I feel it, my lord; I feel safe with you. I know you will care for me forever and that nothing will ever come between us. I feel that so strongly. Please do not let us ever be parted for I could not bear it. How could I ever survive without you, my lord?'

'As ill as would I without you, I imagine,' Fabian replied, with an honesty that startled him.

He, the old roué, was declaring undying love to a slip of a girl who had captured his heart for evermore. Was it a case of there is no fool like an old fool? No, he would not spoil it by being cynical. She loved him, she was touchingly grateful, his little Irish enchantress who could sometimes be so fey that it unnerved him. She seemed to know when she was predicting the future, stating a truth hidden from ordinary eyes. He did love her; they were together forever; he was never going to leave her. For as long as he lived she would be mistress of all the manors and estates which he possessed, regardless of scandal or gossip.

Gradually Kitty was absorbed into the social life of Fabian's peers. Dressmakers were summoned from London to supply her with a wardrobe which would have done justice to a duchess. In rapid succession, she was to learn all about the latest fashions. Struggles ensued when Kitty's ambitious dressmaker, Madame Aristide, a voluble French-woman who could not have been more than four feet tall and who looked like a bowling hoop in her enormous panniers, declared that she wished Kitty to look like a ballerina. Kitty had no idea what a ballerina was, and she had to wait in mystification for Madame

Aristide to produce the gowns she had designed and made in the style of the great Parisian ballets of the day. Her short sojourn in England had taught Kitty that it was shocking for a lady to show her ankles and so, when Madame Aristide produced a dress which she declared was styled upon that of the ballet and which revealed no less than five inches of Kitty's silk-clad ankles, there was a scene which some would have said resembled a confrontation between the French milliner and her client. Worse confrontations were to follow when Madame Aristide produced befrilled and beribboned hats which reared high upon the head and were exuberantly decorated with baskets of fruit, windmills and even a three-masted frigate with its sails billowing. As it was, Kitty did not take to wearing wigs; she found them hot and uncomfortable, and she was shocked when Madame Aristide suggested that she shave her head so that her wig would fit more closely to her scalp and make her feel cooler.

'Shave off my hair!' she exclaimed, her voice rising. 'Go bald? But how would I face his lordship when I remove my wig? His lordship is very fond of my hair.'

Madame Aristide, who for twenty-five years had put fashion before men, sniffed, shrugged her shoulders and raised her eyes heavenwards.

'Mademoiselle either wants to look the fashionable or mademoiselle does not want to look the fashionable. The choice is up to mademoiselle. All the ladies of the *haute monde* wear the *coiffure artificiale*. For *le petit six* to *neuf livres,* mademoiselle can be *dans la plus belle mode* – as grand as any Queen.'

'But I am not a Queen,' said Kitty, struggling to understand what the Frenchwoman, with her cumbersome accent, was saying.

'Of course, I want to look attractive,' Kitty went on,

'and to do justice to his lordship. But this is not the Court and I am not the Queen, and these corsets into which you have just laced me are pinching me so much that I fear any moment I shall have to scream very loudly indeed.' Kitty wafted a hand in front of her face. 'Is it absolutely necessary that I wear such a heavy, tight corset even in the height of summer, Madame Aristide?'

'*Oui, oui. Enfin, c'est absolument necessaire. Autre chose serait une catastrophe totale*!'

Hands on hips, blue eyes flashing, Kitty faced Madame Aristide and this time she spoke to her in Gaelic, rattling out at full speed exactly what she thought of the woman who persisted in speaking French to her.

Taken aback, Madame Aristide's jaw dropped open. 'What is that you say, mademoiselle, eh, *eh*?' she questioned, drawing herself to her full four feet in height.

But Kitty was not to be halted in her tirade. Having envisaged herself spending the rest of her life gasping for breath inside a heavy and rigid corset, a veritable bird's nest on her head, and the panniers of her gown so wide that all the doorways of Cromer Manor had to be extended to allow her entry, she had decided that enough was enough. She would be what was called the great English eccentric. She would wear no wig, nor would she powder her hair; she would refuse to be imprisoned in a massive whalebone cage which flattened her bosom to the point of extinction. It was bad enough that she had had to become accustomed to tight satin shoes with heels which were three and a half inches high and with pointed toes which crushed her feet – feet which were accustomed to running barefoot on Irish peat and moss.

The sessions with Madame Aristide would have been intolerable for Kitty had she not been anxious to please her lord protector. For him, she wanted to be serene and ladylike, so that no one would ever guess she had walked barefoot like a gypsy. But she found the effort chastening, to say the least. She thought of the Irish beauties she had known in her childhood: girls with speedwell-blue eyes, milky white skin and rosy blossoming cheeks, sturdy girls accustomed to the open air. Many of them had worn shoes only on Sundays, few, if any, wearing corsets, and as for powdering their hair, well that was an undiscovered oddity. Fingers rather than combs tidied their hair and a clean, handwoven shawl would be put over the shoulders for going to church. Those rosy, glowing, healthy girls had always been Kitty's idea of true beauty and she could not say that her conception had changed. As yet she had not seen anyone in England whom she could call beautiful; deportment and composure seemed paramount here, certainly among those with whom her lord protector mingled. To enunciate clearly, to smile becomingly, to gesture with grace and delicacy; such things as these were essential for a lady of the upper classes or for a lady who wished to ape her betters.

Sometimes Kitty despaired of ever raising herself to the higher echelons. It all seemed too much to cope with at once: eradicating her Irish accent, teetering along in the toe-crushing shoes when she wanted to fling them across the room and run freely through the long grass, barefoot. As for the rib-deforming corsets which made her feel so giddy the first few times she wore them, well the less said about those the better. After years of taking no more than a few minutes to fling on her clothes, Kitty found that the pantomime of dressing in the morning took longer and longer.

During her *lêvée*, which was what Madame Aristide affectedly called it, she dearly wished to dress herself, but found herself fumbling amongst stomachers, stays, underskirts, bodices, chemises, stockings and garters, yet more petticoats, fans (and for these there was a whole language to be learned), ruffles, and the panniers, or false hips, which jutted out at either side of the waist like walls. She was ready to eschew forever all things aristocratic. However, the look of delight upon Fabian's face when she appeared in her modish attire was more than reward for the hours of frustration and struggle she had endured. Whether she wore a pretty polonaise gown in satin, with the overskirt looped up and secured with bows, the underskirt of striped taffeta, or an ornate and stately evening gown with a stiff bodice, bared shoulders and ruffled silk ruching, it was obvious that Fabian relished her newly sophisticated appearance.

Eventually, the problem of the weighty panniers was solved, for Madame Aristide produced an adaptation of these, a lighter, more manoeuvreable mode which she called, with only the slightest curl of her lip, a pocket pannier. With this there was no need for the enormous, swaying cage of metal or whalebone to support the skirts, for the overskirt was pulled through pocketholes and draped in graceful, bowlike loops on each hip. Soon after, Madame Aristide announced that lighter materials were now in vogue, and so even more weight was taken off Kitty's shoulders, but the dressmaker's invention was proffered with such ill grace that Kitty felt very much an offender.

'If mademoiselle so desperately requires a change in *la mode*,' Madame Aristide declared afterwards as she departed huffily, 'then, as mademoiselle is a Catholic, I suggest that she prays for it.' And with that the Frenchwoman flounced out.

Kitty felt few qualms for upsetting the dressmaker as she did. The woman had obviously made a great deal of money from dressing the aristocracy, and Kitty was sure that she was the only customer who did not meekly accept Madame Aristide's every word. It was not that she did not love all the beautiful rich materials, the satins and taffetas, the lace and ruffles, the silk stockings, bows, frills, brocades, feathers and flowers and, most especially, the sumptuous pearls which Fabian had given her. It was that she longed to have had one of these gowns or the string of pearls, a pair of the silver-heeled scarlet leather shoes, to sell to keep her family alive. The sale of her present wardrobe would have kept her parents, brothers and sisters in great comfort for the rest of their lives, and that knowledge brought her an avalanche of guilt. Who was she to have survived when they had died?

Some days she would adorn herself in the beautiful clothes, pirouetting before the cheval glass, as light-hearted and exhilarated as any sixteen-year-old girl. On others she suffered a tightly-knotted twist of guilt and grief deep inside her, making her want to tear at all the materials adorning her body, strip it all from her and leave it lying in shreds around her on the floor. Why should she have such finery when her family did not even have shrouds in the graves which she had dug for them?

One day she was standing before her glass, fingers hooked into the collar of her gown, tugging at it, her cheeks scarlet, tears beading her lashes. That was how Fabian found her as he strode into the room unexpectedly. Startled, she blinked back the tears, pretending that she was arranging the ruffles at her shoulders.

'What ails you, little one?' he asked, putting his hard white hands where a moment before her own had been.

'Nothing. This gown does not fit me. Madame Aristide, for all that she pretends, knows very little about what she calls "oot couture".'

'Do you not mean *haute*, little one? That means high fashion.'

'I know that. Madame Aristide tells me nothing else.'

'And so you are in high dudgeon about high fashion, is that it?' Fabian smiled, dropping a kiss on the back of her neck.

'Why does that woman come here and try to force me into these suits of armour? This corset is like chainmail, and these shoes make my feet feel crippled.'

'Perhaps Kitty McDonagh would like to return to wearing the gown she was in when I found her in a ditch?' Fabian said softly.

'I have outgrown that now,' Kitty retorted.

'You have outgrown a lot of things, Kitty, and it is time you faced up to it. Childish displays, for whatever reason, are certainly something which must be next on your list to be outgrown. I remember a saying of my sister's, it was something she often used to tell her son, my nephew. She used to say that one of the first things you must learn when you grow up is that tempers must be tempered.'

Twirling round, Kitty faced Fabian with sparkling eyes, two spots of peony colour in her cheeks. 'I do not have a temper, I have never had a temper! I have no trouble *whatsoever* in controlling my feelings.'

'It is true that sometimes anger is more healing than tears, but too much anger can show that there are too many tears behind it.'

Kitty stared at him uncomprehendingly. Sometimes his perceptive comments made shivers go down her spine. How was it that he knew what she was feeling: was she so transparent? There were no traces of tears on her lashes now and she was almost snapping at him, her back rigid, yet he knew that she had been about to burst into weeping when he entered the room.

'Kitty, I am not a religious man; I have never felt it necessary to go to church. But you grew up with a very religious background and since you came to live in my household you have not visited church. I feel that it would do you good to attend Mass, to have Masses said for the souls of your family, perhaps. Is that not something which Catholics do?'

'It is indeed. Masses for their souls – that is a marvellous idea. Why did I not think of it myself. Of course, Masses for their souls!' Kitty clasped her hands together at her breast, eyes shining.

'We will have it done immediately. There is a Catholic church a few miles from here, the Church of Blessed Mary the Virgin, I believe it is called. We will ask for Masses to be said for the souls of your loved ones to ensure that they rest in peace, to ensure that you too rest in peace, Kitty, my little one. And I think it would be a good idea if you attended as many of those Masses as you wish. One of my men will be only too pleased to drive you into the next village at the relevant time. Forget about all these fripperies.'

Fabian was considering her past. As a Southern Irish girl, she would have been raised to think of the preservation of her soul as being of vital importance. Souls must be nurtured and protected, nourished and purified: covering a tormented soul with bows and frills and taffeta would never heal the wounds underneath. He must do the right thing by her – had he now vowed to do just that whenever possible? She had done so much for him: giving him a meaning, a purpose in life; saved him from sinking into the lethargy of a spiritless old age. She was a divine companion, undemanding, bright of mind, eager to learn, lively, yet never so much so that she exhausted him. He could look back ruefully to the first weeks he had known her, when he had wished that she were his daughter. Now, such a wish was the farthest thing from his mind. His weeks with Kitty had been an enchantment, a beautiful rich indulgence, a serenity filled with laughter and warmth. He knew, of course, that the outer world must soon intrude, for visitors were imminent.

One, for example, was the captain of the *Keita*, one of his merchant ships which, in the past, had been accustomed to trading in the Alacanti isles. The island chieftain, Bunruratti, had always greeted the *Keita* and its crew with open arms, trading pearls, tortoiseshell, mother-of-pearl, coral, and exotic tropical fruit for whatever Captain Blaney had brought him. However, on the latest visit of the *Keita*, Captain Blaney had been greeted by a range of spears and Bunruratti and his men kitted out in warpaint. Retreating hastily, Captain Blaney had been forced to stoop to a little espionage to discover why Bunruratti was no longer amicable to trade with him. The reason had quickly become obvious. A rival trading company going by the name of Killingham and run by a man calling himself Ebenezer Killingham was entrenched upon the islands distributing cheap and glittery gew-gaws, a rot-gut liquor which had already made some of the natives seriously ill, and bottles of a brew which Killingham claimed would increase the virility and fecundity of the chief and his wives, but the price of which was ruinously high.

Having obtained a bottle of the brew, Captain Blaney had tasted it, his face wrinkling with disgust.

'That wretch Killingham is a confidence-trickster, a cheat, a liar and a rogue!' he had roared. 'This brew is nothing more than cheap alcohol laced with herbs and sugar. Increase their virility, indeed – all it will do is rot their teeth.'

However, Chief Bunruratti was adamant that he was not going to deal with the Cromer Trading Company ever again: he preferred Ebenezer Killingham, and that was that. Quite coincidentally, his oldest wife, who had failed to become pregnant for some years, had announced that she was expecting a child. Bunruratti naturally attributed this to Killingham's brew.

While Fabian waited in his library for Captain Blaney to arrive, his eyes rested appreciatively on Kitty's throat. She was sitting by the window, reading, and the soft orchid-yellow sunlight was falling across her shoulders in a gentle shaft, lighting up the lustrous pearls which he had given her for her sixteenth birthday, pearls which had come from the Alacanti islands, and whose beauty and perfection had helped to establish the Cromer Trading Company in its early years. Now it seemed that the Cromer monopoly was threatened, if not actually permanently overcome. It was a situation which could not be allowed to continue.

When he arrived Captain Blaney was full of apologies for the situation in the Alacanti islands but also full of disgust for Ebenezer Killingham. What he really wanted to do was to let loose a string of blue rhetoric, but having seen the pretty young lady sitting by the window, he felt obliged to search for words which would not send her into the vapours.

That problem was soon overcome, for Lord Cromer launched into the local dialect of the Alacanti islands which he had learned on his many visits there in past years. Blaney too, of course, was well versed in the dialect and so the two men conversed for a time in Alacantian. Having safely told the story of how Chief Bunruratti's eldest wife had insisted on walking round the island wearing only a gaily-coloured turban to ensure that everyone saw her swelling stomach, the two men returned to conversing in English.

Kitty had been watching the scene with great interest, whilst simultaneously appearing to devour the book on her lap. She saw how Captain Blaney's dark brown eyes bulged as he uttered certain words which sounded to her very much like expletives of the coarser kind, but as they were in a foreign language she could not of course understand. '*Guhurundi*' Captain Blaney had said, And '*barrawali*' – and then '*buluhurundi barrawali*', his face growing redder and beads of sweat popping out on his brow.

Leaning forward, eyes narrowed, Lord Cromer listened raptly to what Captain Blaney was saying, and then he slammed his fist into his palm, emitted a sound closely resembling a roar, and leapt to his feet to stalk round the library.

A servant entered, bearing a tray of wine and wafers, took one look at Lord Cromer's leonine visage, hastily put down the tray and fled. So they have seen him like this before, thought Kitty, who had never before seen her lord in anything but a gentle mood.

Having filled three goblets with the wine and distributed it, Fabian emptied his in one gulp, Kitty wishing that she knew more of what was going on, what was making him angry and how she could help. She felt sure that she could offer some sort of assistance if only she were allowed to do so. Once or twice she looked up, mouth opening, ready to speak, wanting to ask questions. But the men's faces were so fierce, so absorbed in their conversation, that she decided against it. The book on myths and legends of ancient Greece which she had begun with such enthusiasm had paled into insignificance. What did she care for the lives of long-dead heroes when her own hero was so obviously distressed? Her fingers curled round the book so tightly that her knuckles gleamed whitely. Almost forgetting to breathe, she strained her ears to hear what the two men were saying, for they had now gone into a huddle, voices low, heads close together. Finally, their conversation over, Captain Blaney rose to be shown to his room, for he was staying the night before returning to London.

When the man had gone, Kitty jumped up, and went to sit by Fabian. 'What was all that about, my lord? Please do tell me I am longing to know. Can I be of help in some way? Captain Blaney seemed very upset and so did you, lord. Why was he here? Do please tell me.'

Fabian's face froze; the green opal eyes which she adored became almost opaque in their coldness.

'Such matters are not for young ladies to trouble their heads over,' he said icily, drawing back from her. 'My business concerns are entirely private; I will brook no interference from ones who should know their place. That will be the last time you will ever stay with me when I am discussing business matters with anyone.' He rose, face rigid, ready to stride from the library.

Kitty's mouth had dropped open. Her legs had turned to water; she knew that if she had been standing up she would have collapsed. Her warm, loving lord protector had turned into a chilling stranger, a man with green stone eyes and an expression to match. She was shocked and chilled, as he had meant her to be; her hands were trembling, tears like pins behind her lids, and a wave of longing for her cosy family cottage in Tipperary engulfed her – and with it the longing for her mammy's arms round her.

Before she could gather her wits to speak, Fabian had gone, the library door crashing shut behind him, the ruffles on her dress lifting in the draught of air.

In no small way she had been told to mind her place, not

to meddle in her lord protector's concerns, and she felt stricken. But the message was clear: stay in your place or feel the brunt of my anger. Shakily she got to her feet, the weight of loneliness pressing down on her. At that moment it was an intolerable burden. She had done everything she could to please him: laced into tight corsets, crushed into tiny shoes, holding her back straight at all times, enduring hours with Madame Aristide, spending an hour every morning, sometimes two, dressing. All these things she had done for him, offering herself and them up to him as a sacrifice. Everything she had to offer was now under control, she felt: her waist, her feet, and her spine being only part of it, for her tongue, too, was now so tightly laced that it no longer uttered Irish words, but only coolly cultured English ones. Until this moment she had thought that her mind was to be allowed the freedom it desired, but now she knew that her mind, too, was to be leashed: all of her bound up and lashed down like some irksome rebellious cargo on one of his lordship's merchant vessels.

The moment of decimating weakness was rapidly thrust aside as fury born of deep hurt replaced it. Tightly lashed and bound was she? To be kept in her place like some low servant, was that it? Bending down, she tore off her tiny satin shoes one after the other and flung them across the library so that the brilliantly coloured Oriental vase standing on its thin-legged table swayed, teetered sideways and crashed to the ground before she could save it. The vase had been a favourite of her lord protector's sister, as he had told her on more than one occasion, and now it was smashed in smithereens, spikes and slivers and squares of the china littering the polished oak floorboards.

Staring aghast, Kitty went hot and then cold, wishing that the floorboards would open and engulf her so that she need never face the consequences of her bout of temper. If he had been angry before what would he be like now?

Hand to her mouth, she ran from the library in terror, down the corridors, through the hall, heaving at the great front door until she finally managed to open it, and then burst out into the fresh air, her bare feet stabbed by the gravel of the main drive. Sobbing, she fled heedlessly across lawns, through copses and over hillocks, as far as she could run with her breathing impeded by the restricting whalebone corsets she wore. Her feet were bare it was true, but then she had spent the first fifteen years of her life barefoot; her feet had softened, but the bones were strong and accustomed to hardship.

It had been late afternoon when she set out and it was dusk when she stopped running. She had no idea where she was; she did not care if she were lost, for she knew that everything was over if her lord protector flung her out because of what she had done. The woods and hills of Surrey were no more daunting than those of Southern Ireland where she had roamed as a child, nor were the pangs of hunger which had become commonplace to her at one time. Finding a mossy dell, she curled up in it, staring up through the shivering, undulating leaves of the oaks high above her. They were black against a silvered moonlit sky, sequinned with stars. She might have been in Tipperary – and now she longed to be there, but before the bad times. She ached, yearned, craved to be back with her family, sitting at the table with mammy and daddy and her brothers and sisters, with a plate of hot roast tatties on the table before them and a jug of buttermilk to be shared out.

She was drifting away into the past: sitting at that table, biting into the soft, hot and fluffy potato, when she heard the voice of the old priest.

'*You cannot put back the clock*. You cannot put back the clock. . . . Live for the moment, do not scour the past for memories, do not waste the short span of life in bitter recollections and grief for what is over and gone forever.'

'*You cannot put back the clock*,' Kitty whispered. And she knew then with a wrenching clarity that she had taken a great step towards maturity. She knew what the old priest would have said if he had been with her: 'We must all face the consequences of our actions, Kitty. Facing those consequences is what makes us into adults, and strong adults at that. Now listen here to me, if you run then you will spend all your life running and you will be a prisoner of your fears. For the man or woman who faces up to the consequences of their actions is free, learning one of the great lessons of life which, in the end, makes us strong and invincible.'

'Yes, Father,' she whispered, as if he were really there sitting beside her. Perhaps he was, for she felt his presence very powerfully.

She must have fallen asleep, for the next minute strong arms were scooping her up from the earth and she was being crushed against a broad, muscular chest. She knew that the eyes looking into hers would be opal-green, even though she could not see them for the night was now velvet black.

'Never, never do that again, Kitty,' Fabian admonished as he carried her over the uneven ground to where his horse waited. When he had seated himself in the saddle, placed Kitty in front of him and caged her in his arms, he said grimly:

'A lady should know better than to be picked out of a ditch twice by the same man.'

She was tired, frightened, guilty, and terribly fearful of his wrath, so she snapped back at him: 'Then you want me to find another man to do it next time? I am sure that there are many who would be more than willing.'

She felt him go rigid, and she berated herself for a fool and an ungrateful idiot, but she was cold, drained of emotion, and exhausted. Curving against his chest, she rested her head and soon she slept, the rest of the journey passing in silence.

When they reached Cromer Manor, Fabian left her with his servants while he vanished into his study. Later, as she lay alone in bed, shivering despite the warming-pan at her feet, she longed for him to be in the bed beside her, his flat stomach pressed against her back, his thighs curving against hers. If they woke in the night to move, he would kiss the back of her neck, scooping her hair into his hands to brush its silky tendrils against his mouth, lavishing it with kisses. 'Hello, my little love,' he would say admiringly, and she had adored every moment of it. Now she was paying the price for her rebellion. He was displeased with her – perhaps he had stopped caring for her and in the morning she would be sent to an orphanage.

Not to have Fabian's love, not to have his eyes twinkling at her, not to have his face lit by the benevolent yet boyish smile she treasured so much. She could not live without him: she did not want to. Oh, she could not lie here shivering in dread! Slipping out of the warm bed, she pulled on her robe and pushed her feet into feathered mules. In a few seconds she was running down the stairway towards the study where Fabian had entrenched himself. She could see a light peeping under the door, she could smell tobacco smoke. So, he was sitting in there thinking and smoking a rare pipe, something which he only did when he was greatly troubled.

'Fabian,' she whispered through the door, 'Fabian, I am sorry. Will you forgive me?' No reply. She tried again.

'Fabian, *please* let me in. *Please*, I am so sorry. I do not know what came over me. I shall never say anything so terrible again, nor will I ever lose my temper again, I promise you.' Still no reply.

She tried tapping at the door, then knocking harder with her knuckles. Then finally she banged on it with her open palms.

'Please, please, Fabian, let me in! Please forgive me, I will do anything, anything.'

Tears rolling down her cheeks, she waited for his response, for the sound of his footfall on the polished oak boards near the door, for the sound of his beloved voice. Nothing. Desperate, she rattled at the handle: the door was locked. A wave of impotence consumed her so that she fell weakly against the woodwork, pressing her forehead against the polished surface.

Once more she tried, calling his name and begging him to open the door, begging him to forgive her. But he did not reply, and finally, broken, she crept back up to her bed, sliding between the sheets and lying there, lonely and cold, hands clenched into tight fists.

She had been a fool, a stupid fool, but she would pay the price in the orphanage. She knew that now. Oh, if only he had put her in there in the first place so that she had not had time to grow fond of him, to learn to love him as she did. Everyone, everything, she had ever loved had been torn from her; now he too would go and she would be an orphan again, adrift in a world of lovelessness and poverty.

'God forgive me,' she wept. But even if He did would she ever forgive herself?

CHAPTER FIVE

Fabian's door remained closed, much to Kitty's misery, nor did he share her bed that night. At dawn she was woken by the cracking of hooves on cobbles, and on rushing to the window, saw Cromer galloping off into the distance, accompanied by a small retinue of servants.

There are times when the longing to reverse what has been done is unbearable. Standing at the window, fists clenched to her chin, Kitty understood what she had done: spoiled an idyll, marred a dream. And how she needed her dreams, *ached* to have them. And what had she done to her lord protector? Shown him that she was a spoilt and wilful child, ungrateful, hysterical. Men were contemptuous of spoilt hysterical women. Somewhere along the way she had learned that and decided that she would never be guilty on that score. But she was. She had Irish peasant blood, fit only for goosegirls and swineherds, not for serene, sweet-scented ladies who were in control at all times.

How could she make amends? More to the point, would she be allowed to? What if it were all over forever?

'Over forever,' she whispered, pressing her nails to her lips. An orphan again, with no home, no one to love . . .

Crossing the room, she sank down onto her bed and proceeded to pummel the pillows with all the force of pent-up frustration and disappointment. Having done so and angrily dashed away the two tears which her control had let slip, she sat brooding for another hour or so, then she rose with a solid determination. Fabian wanted her to be a lady and a lady she would be, even if – Blessed Mother forbid – it was too late.

She bathed carefully, using the rose and lavender-scented soap balls which she loved, shampooing her hair twice and rinsing it until it squeaked. Maddy, her temporary maid, brought jug after jug of cleansing water then combed out the wet black curls, after patting them dry with a towel. Afterwards Kitty rubbed rose-scented oils into her arms, legs, stomach and breasts, dabbing rose-water at the base of her throat, behind her ears, in the crooks of her arms and between her breasts.

Recently she had read a book from Fabian's collection which was entitled *The Sultan's Harem*, and she had been very taken with the lives and habits of the odalisques. They bathed continuously, rubbing rare oils and unguents into their bodies, shaving all the hair from under their arms and between their thighs and painting their hands and feet with henna. Although she had no intention of attempting some of these more exotic feats, she liked to think of herself as an odalisque and Fabian her sultan. Certainly she had been as pampered and protected as any concubine. Had been . . .

Brushing out her silky hair, she pushed the sad thoughts from her mind. Which gown would she wear for her Sultan's return? Rose-pink satin striped with sky-blue and trimmed with ivory bows, or the cerise taffeta frilled with apple-green velvet? To match the array of gowns she now possessed silk stockings of every hue, satin shoes with diamanté heels, bows, ribbons and clips for her hair, painted fans with pictures of Greek goddesses performing their miraculous feats. One fan, depicting Venus with

Mars stretched out sensuously on couches, always made Kitty think of herself and Fabian. Venus and Mars, the quintessential woman and man: one curving, feminine and sensual, the other hard-limbed, sun browned, worldly and valorous – yet devoted to his woman. But she must put these fancies aside. When Fabian returned she would be waiting, groomed to perfection, serene, smelling divine, superbly composed.

Maddy was not the most skilled of coiffeuses, but she managed Kitty's abundant hair tolerably well, the various finishing touches being done by Kitty herself. When it was all over, what Kitty had always secretly called 'the performance', and she was corsetted, laced, compressed and squeezed into the fashionable shape, her hair coiled and curled, bosom rising in ivory curves from the tight bodice of a gold and green brocade stomacher with a striped skirt in matching colours, she waited in the drawing-room.

Midday passed, but she could not eat. Afternoon came and went, then evening. Reluctantly, she sipped hot chocolate and nibbled a cherry cake, not wishing to spoil her appetite for the dinner she would eat with her lord on his return.

It was two o'clock in the morning when she finally gave in, falling asleep fully clothed on the library couch. Fabian had not come home, nor had he left a message for her with any of the servants. No one, it appeared, knew when he would return nor, it was intimated, was this unusual, for his lordship would frequently depart without saying what his plans were. After all, he was the master.

Breakfasting alone, Kitty had little appetite for food but a great craving for Fabian to be sitting opposite her. He always enjoyed breakfast tremendously, eating heartily: scrambled eggs, devilled kidneys, ham, smoked fish, toast, coffee, and fruit in season to follow. Kitty was happy with eggs and toast, but today she found food lacklustre and unappetising, the tea bland. How she had revelled in such meals at Cromer House in Tipperary, giving silent thanks for every mouthful. Now, without Fabian, food was the ashes of love.

For the next three days she bathed, groomed and dressed herself as before to await his homecoming, and each day she was disappointed afresh. On the fourth day she attempted to go about her normal everyday tasks, but with little heart. A week passed, then two, then three, during which time she became a very regular attender at the church in the nearby village. She and Maddy would drive out in the dogcart, suitably attired for church, and spend an hour or so at the service and prayers before going back to Cromer Manor.

Maddy was a stolid country girl who said little but was company of a sort. Red-nosed, she had rough red hands to match, but was attempting to soften these with goosefat now that she was elevated to the post of temporary lady's maid. Her small hazel eyes peered out stoically from rust-red lashes and a marvellously freckled face. Her hair was a paler rust-red, thick and tangled as barbed-wire, though she battled dutifully with it each morning. As a child, in despair, she had once hacked it all off with a kitchen knife, so she knew something of what her mistress was going through with all the corsetting, panniers and toe-crushing shoes.

At eighteen, Maddy had given up all hope of ever being anything more than a dogsbody at Cromer Manor. Not that she would complain, for she came from a family of seventeen children and to have any work at all was a blessing. Not only that, but she was able to send home a shilling or two to her mother now and again. Maddy's mother, pregnant for the eighteenth time, was still only forty and her health was precarious. Maddy's father had lost an arm in an accident while cutting down a tree, and Maddy often thought that he had tried to compensate for the loss of an arm by using too freely what protuberances were left to him.

Sitting scrubbed and tightly-laced next to her mistress in Dingley church, Maddy would muse on her past. Childhood had been hunger, squalling babies, the acrid smell of urine-soaked pallets on the floor, the strange guttural noises her father made as he lay on top of her mother each night. Strangely, despite it all, her mother seemed to respond with a buoyant jerkiness, head twisting from side to side, knees clutching her husband's waist, while an odd mewing sound came from her lips. Sometimes, secretly watching when they thought her asleep, Maddy would feel her heart begin to pound, a wetness seeping between her thighs, overcome with a longing to be crushed beneath a man in that same way, yet not truly understanding what it was all about. Her father's climaxes were noisey and sometimes when he had finished and slept, snoring loudly, Maddy would slide her fingers between her legs and rub the moist centre there until she writhed in her own orgasm. She still did this regularly, for after Jack there had been no man in her life.

As the service droned on, her mistress intent upon her worshipping, Maddy would think of Jack, the chief stableboy at Cromer Manor, who had taken her virginity when she was thirteen. He had been blond and blue-eyed, with a smile which lit up his whole face with a sweet kindness which she soon grew to treasure. Twenty-two years old, he had worked hard for his place and intended to keep it. Women had had little place in his life, but when he saw Maddy with the thicket of terracotta curls and the hardy, bright eyes he had been smitten. A few days later he had taken her up into the hayloft. There she had melted blissfully while he kissed her over and over, his hands pulling her breasts free of her bodice. Hot and red-cheeked, barely able to breathe in her excitement, Maddy had felt her hand being placed around something hard and projecting. It was very hot and steely yet velvet-skinned, and it pulsed against her palm. Squeezing her hand tightly round the hardness, Jack had shown her how to arouse him so that he gasped and writhed, bucked his hips and groaned as a stream of liquid gushed over her arm. Surprised, she watched it spreading while Jack stared at her, his eyes half-closed, face beaded with sweat.

'What is it?' she had whispered in wonderment.

''Tis called spending,' he had told her.

'Can I do it too?'

'Aye, women can an' all, but ye might be too young.'

'Not I,' she had blushed. 'There is – well, I've done something very like while on my own.'

'You hot little minx,' Jack had teased. 'Was it like this?' And he had pushed up her skirts, touching her at her centre until she could not suppress her moans of pleasure. When she had climaxed Jack was ready again, and he had laid siege to her maidenhead in true manly style, thrusting against her until he slid inside into the creaminess which was more than ready for him.

Maddy was a passionate girl, and once Jack had roused her she longed for him continually. When they were not together she dreamed of him thrusting deep and hard inside her, his breath rasping in her ear, his strong knees and elbows supporting him. How hot they would become, kissing one another's damp lips so fiercely that it would seem they were forged together, hot flesh welded. She had wanted all of him over and over, could never get enough. However many times he made love to her, however many times they kissed and hugged and caressed, she dreamed of the next time, could not wait for the next time. He had been everything to her; days merged into a sequence of passionate hours in Jack's arms. She had wanted nothing else, dreamed of nothing else. When she saw him about the estate he would give her that ready, sweet smile which twisted her heart. When he smiled like that the sun shone out of his face, striking deep into her. Jack had been her sunshine and they had been planning to marry.

She had blessed every day, filling a modest dower chest with hand-sewn linen and other small items for their cottage after the wedding. Her fourteenth birthday had passed and Jack had given her a pottery horse which she had treasured. She still had it, wrapped in lint and placed at the back of one of her drawers. Sometimes when she was alone she would take it out and look at it, run her fingers over its cool glacé surface and press her lips to it, remembering Jack. How many people are fortunate enough to adore one another, thrill together sexually and also to suit one another's temperaments? They had, and life had stretched before them, offering them every joy.

When the accident had happened Maddy had been inconsolable; she had wept for days. Why had Jack been given to her only to be snatched away? she had sobbed over and over. For he had been snatched away – kicked in the head by an ill-tempered stallion. They had carried him to his bed and when she had been told the news she had run to him.

'Jack, oh Jack,' she had whispered, panic like a ball in her throat, her cheeks scorching, then icy in turn. 'Can ye hear me, Jack? Can ye speak to me? Oh, tell me how ye feel,' she had pleaded.

But he could not speak. The blue eyes she had loved

stared up at her entreatingly, filled with love and longing and regret. There was a kind of apology in them too, and that stabbed at her most of all. He tried to smile: she could see the corners of his mouth beginning to dimple. He knew how she loved his smile, the smile which had always changed his face from that of a sad, lonely man to a light-hearted, sweet-natured boy.

As her tears splashed onto his dear face, a baptism of love, his blue eyes closed, the smile faded forever, and she was alone. Her mind had screamed but no sound escaped her lips. They had dragged her from his body and she had lain in a stupor for a week, wanting to keep her eyes closed because then she could see in her mind's eye Jack's smiling face, and if she could not see that then she did not want to live.

Months, then years had passed but she had never been the same Maddy again, a part of her would always be with Jack, wherever he was. And, though she would never say it to anyone, she lived only for the day when she could be with him again.

Because of their losses there was a great bond between herself and her mistress, and every likelihood that what had started out as a temporary post would become a permanent one for Maddy. They were air and earth together, but that was no disadvantage in such a relationship. She knew that her mistress was in torment at the moment, and as she heard the minister's voice droning out a verse from Timothy: 'having food and raiment let us be therewith content', Maddy's mouth twisted wryly, for that was all they both had at this moment: food and raiment.

'Have you ever been in love?' Kitty asked her maid a few days later.

'Aye, that I have, miss,' Maddy said, a nerve flickering in her left eyelid so that her rusty eyelashes fluttered.

'What became of him, for you have not wed?' Kitty put her head on one side.

'He died, miss. Before we could wed, that is. Oh, we were going to, but then he died.' Maddy's eyelid jumped convulsively and she hunched her shoulders as if holding them protectively over the emotions buried deep inside her.

'So we have both lost loved ones, Maddy.'

'Aye, miss.'

'Sometimes I think I am cursed, you know,' Kitty went on. 'I only have to love someone and they go away.'

'The master will be back, miss, don't ye fret over that.'

'He is punishing me, you know. I lost my temper; it was very stupid, I said things I regret bitterly.'

'We all do that from time to time, miss.'

'But what if you do not get a second chance? What if he was the only chance I shall ever have and I have thrown it away?'

'He'll be back, miss. He do love you deeply, we all knows that. It do show in his face.'

'Tell me about your man, Maddy.'

'He was called Jack, miss, and he loved me madly and I loved him the same. Got on like two flames in the same fireplace, we did. Nothing was ever the same after he died.'

'I know exactly how you feel, Maddy. I felt just the same when I lost my family. It seems to me that loving someone makes them a part of you and you a part of them, so that to survive happily you must be together, the parts fitting one another, so to speak. There are parts of me buried in Tipperary which I think I will never find again.'

'Me too with Jack, miss.' Mistress and maid looked at one another mournfully.

'Love hurts,' Kitty whispered.

'Even after everything I've been through, miss, 'tis a hurt I would not have wished to do without,' Maddy said frankly.

'I expect you're right,' Kitty said, but she did not sound convinced. Suddenly the whole burden of living and loving was too much for her, the punishment for her feelings was too great. She longed to be tougher, insensitive, hardy as others were, for she saw herself as a very frail flower indeed, bowed to the ground by the first dash of rain that came along. Even though she longed for release from her feelings she was becoming more and more entangled in them: there was no absolution now.

'It seems to me,' said Maddy stoically, 'that the best thing to do when ye lose someone ye love is to find someone else to replace them. Not that I've done that nor ever could, but seems to me all the same that it's the best thing.'

'I agree about that.' Kitty stood up, walked to the window and stared out on an expanse of silvery summer rain. 'Find a replacement – oh yes indeed, you are right, Maddy. Who would want to do otherwise? Who could remain sane if they did not? We all need someone to love. Would you have time for another suitor, Maddy?'

'Never, miss.' Maddy thrust back her shoulders, head erect. 'I could never be unfaithful to my Jack. We were made for one another.' The corners of her mouth drooped.

'A torn dress can be mended, a heel nailed back on a shoe. Hair can be washed, stockings darned, but no one can mend a broken heart. That seems so inane, does it not? Hearts lying broken all over the place, so many of them, and no one knows how to mend them.'

Four days later Fabian returned. He looked pale and there was a new tautness in his face, a tension in the way he held his shoulders. Inwardly trembling, Kitty stood in the hallway to greet him. With all her heart she wanted to throw her arms round him and sob against his chest, but she had no idea what his mood was, how he would react to such lack of control on her part. In his absence she had come to question every emotion deeply, whereas before she had been a creature of impetuous instinct.

Dismounting, Fabian stood for a few seconds looking around him, his face inscrutable. Then, turning, he walked towards Kitty. She could not tell what he was thinking as his eyes absorbed her in her ivory satin gown with its ruched overskirt prettily striped in icing pink. Suddenly her heart felt too big for her chest, as if it had grown and swelled and was finding itself too cumbersome to beat. Her head felt so light that she thought it would float away.

'Kitty, sweeting, have you missed me?' Fabian held out his arms.

It was her darling lord protector come back. The breath tearing in her throat, she flung herself into his arms and was safe again.

That night they had a glorious reunion. She did not know what Fabian had done or thought while he was away, but it was plain that now he was back he regretted his absence and planned to make it up to her. He had brought her a jade figurine of the goddess Venus Aphrodite with her doves, and a chubby, smiling, winged infant at her shoulder.

'Cupid,' Fabian smiled. 'He is the god of love, the son of Aphrodite.'

'And who was his father?'

'There is some doubt about that, sweeting. You may

take your choice from Mars, Jupiter or Mercury.'

'And why is he carrying a bow and arrow?'

'They are the arrows of love which he fires himself. Some of them are golden and create love in the heart where they land, but others are lead and produce the opposite effect.'

'And why does he have a blindfold over his eyes?'

'Have you not heard it said that love is blind?'

Kitty looked at her lover with the colour stealing into her cheeks. His tanned hand was warm against her shoulder – she had been so long out of his arms. But she knew that what he said was right: love was blind, for had she not given herself to him blindly with every intention of continuing in exactly the same way?

'Why did you stay away so long, Fabian?' she whispered.

'No questions, Kitty; I am back now and that is all that matters. Come, let us make up for lost time.'

'You will not leave me again, Fabian?' Kitty begged, as her lover lowered his body over hers.

'Never, never,' he said huskily. 'You will always have a place here – this will always be your home and you must consider it so, whatever happens.'

'Do not speak of anything happening,' Kitty's voice trembled. 'Oh, how I have missed you.'

'And I you. I have realised many things while I was away, Kitty. Anything which causes a barrier between a man and a woman is wrong. I am an old man and set in my ways –'

'Not old, *never* old, Fabian!'

'Definitely set in my ways, Kitty, and they are ways which have proved a support and a defence in the past, but now they are a wedge between us so they must go. But do not expect me to change overnight, habits die hard at my age.'

His kisses made her cheeks bloom and then her lips, and she closed her arms round his neck to hold him inside her, clinging to him as if he were her life, which indeed he was. His invasion of her body was sweet and promising but, as always, it was brief, although in her deep and innocent love for him, and knowing no better, she was content.

Shuddering against her, his body hot, hers still cool, he slept while she lay on her back imprisoned by his weight, thinking that it was a miracle to have him back and that she did not deserve it.

In the weeks and months that followed Kitty was always by Fabian's side: in the drawing-room, the library, or wherever he happened to meet his colleagues and employees. Sometimes she would read, sometimes she would embroider shirts or kerchiefs for Fabian, sometimes she would be writing letters on a small inlaid desk or the carved ivory writing box which Fabian had given her. But whatever she was doing she was always fully conscious of what was going on in the room, of the talk, gossip, reminiscences, business discussions, the raising, discussion and solving of problems associated with the Cromer Trading Company, and, sometimes, if Fabian's face were set in particularly amiable lines she would ask him a gentle question or two, bring him out and learn his thoughts on the matter. Occasionally she would offer a suggestion or two herself, delighted when Fabian looked at her with new eyes because she had proffered a solution which had eluded him.

There were no more ugly scenes. These days their relationship was much more harmonious; a deeper understanding had sprung between them, and as the months passed they settled into a gentle and amicable routine, Fabian endeavouring one way or another to spend the greater part of each day with Kitty. There were diversions, of course; fêtes and balls, a masque which everyone attended in fancy dress. Fabian attired as a dashing pirate captain with a patch over one eye set many hearts aflutter, but he had eyes only for Kitty who, in a charming pink and blue shepherdess's gown and carrying a woolly toy lamb under one arm, captivated many male attentions. But, as the evening progressed, it became obvious that they had eyes only for one another, much to the chagrin of those who would have wished to entice their attentions elsewhere. Many were the envious glances in their direction, not only from unattached would-be suitors but also from much-married ladies and gentlemen who saw their own long-lost courting days revived before their eyes.

That there was a vast difference between the ages of the couple concerned mattered little. They were handsome, in love, and, perhaps more relevant, Fabian, Lord Cromer, was one of the richest men in the country. What a poor man will be branded for, or lose an ear or be sent to the Colonies, a wealthy man, especially if he possesses a title, can do with equanimity.

It was soon after this masked ball that Kitty was to meet Fabian's nephew for the first time. Carrick had been absent on a long sea voyage and was only now returning. The night he was due to meet Kitty, Fabian looked white and strained. It was not the first time that he had done so, although there were long periods in between when he seemed perfectly normal, as indefatigable as ever. This time, however, he did not show signs of throwing off his malaise and so servants were despatched to postpone Carrick's arrival at Cromer Manor. Tenderly Kitty cared for her lord protector in the ensuing days, feeding him nourishing broths and coddled eggs, honeyed wine and dried fruits which were said to hearten the patient. She recoiled when Fabian's physician bled him on the grounds that this would remove the poisonous humours from his system. She watched dismayed as the tiny sharply-honed knife slit his inner arm until drops of crimson blood dripped into the bowl beneath. It was considered a sovereign remedy for all ills, but she found the whole ritual repugnant. However, her fears seemed unfounded for within two or three weeks, Fabian was his old self again, ebullient and impatient to be out of bed.

Beltower, the physician, seemed much against his patient returning to normal life and he warned against it, but Fabian thrust his objections aside.

'The truth is, Beltower, that you know you will get no fee while I am well and on my feet. That is it, is it not? A little avarice, eh?'

Beltower harrumphed. 'I am not short of patients, m'lord. Sickness is all too prevalent in these unhappy days.'

'Is it not true that physicians only feel confident when they have a patient in need of them? Where would you be if we all bristled with health, eh?' Fabian laughed, throwing his head back in a carefree boyish gesture, which softened Kitty's heart. He looked so well, he seemed to be thriving. Oh, how she loved him and how relieved she was to see him recovered.

Beltower, whose medical knowledge, but not his confidence, exceeded that of Lord Cromer, withdrew in a huff, at which Kitty ran into Fabian's arms to kiss him on each cheek, to tell him that she would care for him lovingly.

''Tis not care I need now, Kitty sweetheart. It is a normal life again, and the sooner the better,' he grinned at her suggestively. Resting her head on his shoulder, she slid her fingers into the thick waves of hair at his neck, feeling the warmth of his scalp beneath them. He was alive, her Fabian was alive and he would remain so. All was well now. She knew with a passionate fervour that nothing would ever part them.

Life slipped back into its gentle, rhythmic movement. There were pearly dawns in one another's arms, golden afternoons entwined together, dusky purple-blue evenings irradiated by candle glow. All bliss, all contentment, and their whole lives stretching out before them.

Kitty woke one morning feeling chilly. The banked up fire had died completely in the bedroom and she could hear the long peewit sound of what must be a water bird of some kind, its penetrating soulful cry splitting through the black night with merciless efficiency. Shuddering, she cuddled against Fabian for warmth, her hand falling lightly across his chest. He felt cold too, so she reached down to pull up the coverlet which had slipped off them.

Suddenly the room was silent and unearthly and she knew why, the knowledge inching along her flesh like creeping, sharp-tipped fingers. There was only one heart beating in the room and that her own, but suddenly it was beating loudly enough for two: juddering, pounding, swinging painfully from left to right in her chest so that she thought it would escape from her bones.

She began to scream, 'No, oh *no*! Not this! Not again, not *this*!' Over and over again she screamed it, and by the time Maddy arrived she was too insensible to know that her maid's arms were strongly holding her, the gentle, earthy voice soothing in her ear.

CHAPTER SIX

She was dead too, she knew it. Strange, compelling thoughts filled her head – she wanted to follow Fabian, to be with him. She was sure that somewhere, not too far away, he was waiting, longing for her as she was longing for him. She dreamed of him, when she was awake and when she was asleep, and when she closed her eyes his image was so bright behind her lids that she thought he was still there with her in the room. Sometimes she wept until she felt that she would break in two, and at other times she lived as if in a dream, thinking that none of it was true, that he was still alive in another room in the house, or out riding, or on his way back from a journey to London. When she was in the salon she would think that he was in the library, and when she was in the library she would think that he was in the stables. She was alternately bemused, stupefied and stricken. But although she did not know it at the time, and perhaps never would, this multiplicity of disorganised emotions was her barrier through the gruelling times ahead.

When the new Lord Cromer arrived, tall, bright and handsome, a third of Fabian's age, redolent with health and vigour, straight-backed, broad-shouldered, slim-hipped, with his thick glossy bronze hair and the cynical, glittering bronze eyes like harsh topaz jewels, uncut and polished, jagged in his aquiline face, Kitty felt as if some strange, primitive, all-powerful god had been sculpted from fire, brook and heath. His violent energy transmitted itself to her like a threat. She felt endangered, weak, wholly at his mercy. He was so young and strong and virile – why could he not have given some of that power to his uncle to prolong his life? The thought cracked inside her like the splitting of fragile bones so that she felt she would crumble and fall.

Carrick hated her, loathed her: she could see that at first sight. When he told her that he blamed her for Fabian's death, she clasped her palms over her ears to shut out this terrible accusation. She could not bear to stay in the same house as him. Running out, she sought the peace of the gardens. But there was no more peace out there than in the house: perhaps there would never be peace for her again – perhaps all that was over and done with? A sweet interlude, she thought, all that she was to be allowed of happiness in life: one brief, sweet interlude. Her heart was full of grief but her arms were empty. She would never hold Fabian again, never see his opal-green eyes afire with love for her. He had died in silence without complaint, suffering no pain, for which she thanked God, but if only she could have kissed him goodbye before he went.

She plunged her face into her hands.

Then came the reading of the will and the most insulting offer of a bargain Kitty had ever received.

The next morning Kitty breakfasted alone in her room, unable to eat more than a mouthful of egg. Food: how could she ever want food again when her heart was dead? Pushing the tray aside, she ran her hands over the pillow and sheets by her side, trying to conjure up the warmth that would have been left had Fabian arisen only moments before. If she closed her eyes she could visualise him lying there, but when she raised her lids the emptiness of the room was a harsh, bright light which struck against her senses. Flinging herself onto the empty side of the bed, she began to sob.

Later, wearing a robe trimmed with swansdown, she sat at her dressing-table staring into the carved gilt mirror. Her face was bloodless, her eyes dull, their colour seeming faded. She did not want to dress, for even the simplest routine seemed a mockery now. To dress up would be to celebrate an event which she was mourning deeply. She had sent Maddy away, telling her that she wanted to be alone.

Then, to her astonishment, her door suddenly crashed open, admitting the new Lord Cromer. Leaping to her feet, hands clenched, she faced him, heart pounding.

'My friends will be arriving in due course to pay their respects. I want you out of here by then. You can take all your jewels and furs and any other gifts that my late uncle gave you, just so long as you never show your face here again. Do not ever try to make any claim on me or my uncle's estate for any reason.'

Furious and full of hurt pride, smarting beneath the dislike and disdain in his burning bronze eyes, and recalling only too well what had taken place between them the previous night, Kitty stood her ground.

'I shall not be taking anything with me,' she said, her voice low and controlled. 'What I loved and needed most in this house is now gone forever. No jewels or furs can ever replace that. I shall manage very well on my own, have no doubt of it.'

She moved to turn her back on him, but now he was close to her, his strong brown hands gripping her wrists.

'You took many gifts from my uncle, now here is a parting gift from me,' he said, crushing her mouth beneath his.

She struggled fiercely but he was a powerful man who had spent his life in athletic pursuits, travelling, adventuring, riding and fencing, superintending his estates; he had never lost a duel. She was unable to fight him off. His nearness, the male scent of his body, was an aphrodisiac which rifled her senses, tearing emotion from her though she had believed it all quenched.

His lips freeing hers for a moment, she hissed, 'This is not seemly! How can you behave like this when your uncle is newly dead? Had you no love for him, no respect?'

'What do you know of love or respect, a stargazer like you?'

Hearing the most derogatory name for a hedge-whore, a girl whose home was the streets, whose roof was the stars, Kitty blushed furiously, opening her mouth to cry protest. But his mouth was fiercely clamping hers again. Then his hand was grasping the front of her peignoir and tearing it from her neck to her knees, freeing her heavy, creamy breasts, revealing the silky black tangle of pubic hair. He had her in such a steely grip that she could not move her arms or evade his questing fingers, which sought out the contours of her body with a ruthless vigour. He was driving his hardness against her thigh, thrusting against her, as his hand encircled her breasts, teasing her nipples into hardness.

'I could have you here and now, on this floor, on the bed, wherever I chose,' he said, his eyes glittering like gold pieces.

'I dare you!' she lashed back. 'I would expect nothing better of you, *sir*.' Contempt thickened her voice.

She tried to draw back but there was no way she could release herself from his imprisoning embrace. She was frail and insubstantial, tiny, delicate bones encased in shapely velvet flesh, beside his great height and steely muscles. The contest was unequal even before it had begun; she knew that, but it did not seem that he was aware of it.

Once again his bronze head descended, a nimbus of rich deep gold, to trap her mouth, his tongue thrusting between her teeth so that her head was forced back painfully. But she was not aware of the pain. A thousand pins could well have been sticking into her but she would not have felt it while she was in the bondage of his arms. Dizzy, she went slack, her lids closing, while stars erupted and exploded behind her lids. She could feel the sensations blossoming from his kiss, sensations which filtered and darted through her body in the most extraordinary fashion. Her will, her spirit, her separateness, were all vanquished when he held her and, struggle as she might, she could not control her reactions, even though she knew what he would make of them: how contemptuous he would be, how he would put her response down to the ways of a worldly-wise, much-practised stargazer – a hedge-whore who lived and slept in ditches and there coupled with men, not caring who looked on.

Hours, days, nights, seemed to pass as he kissed her, her life seeming to speed by and yet not move. She thought he was going to force her back on the bed for his rigid hardness was painfully bruising her thigh and he was breathing heavily, moving his hips against hers. Then suddenly his arms fell away and he stepped back, staring at her through slitted eyes and, before she could speak, he had turned on his heel and was gone.

She felt like a branch which has been broken from its tree in a storm and left to lie shattered on the ground. She could not gather her wits, nor stay the trembling in her body. When Maddy rushed in, her face all concern, Kitty flung herself into her maid's arms, sobbing on her shoulder.

'He is a devil, Maddy,' she wailed repeatedly. 'He *is* the devil! Oh, why could he not have been the one who died.'

Next morning, wan and yawning, Kitty rose to continue gathering together the few possessions she had decided she would take with her. She would not be taking the clothes, jewels and furs which Fabian had given her, for she did not even know where she would be sleeping, let alone where she could put so many belongings. But that was not the real reason she was leaving them behind: the real reason was her pride. Let Carrick think what he might, she would leave here as she had come: a pauper. Her destiny was no longer in this house but out in the world and that would be where she would seek it. And why should she be afraid? Had she not in her short life experienced every vicissitude? Was she not well experienced and ably prepared for whatever might come, whether it be work, a stroke of good fortune, penury, or starvation?

Maddy's face was tight and closed. She had begged to be allowed to go with her mistress but Kitty, refusing, had remained adamant.

'Stay here where you will always have work and a roof over your head,' she had said, and nothing that Maddy said could change her mistress's mind.

'Miss, I'll go without pay, I'll sell my clothes to come with you, to keep us. I'll –'

'Maddy, you have hardly any clothes to sell, and as for going without your pay, well, why should two of us starve when only one of us need do so?' Kitty gave a strained smile.

Separation from the second person she had ever loved was affecting Maddy badly. Her heart seemed to have shrunk and she could barely breathe. Her mistress was so strong-willed and brave, but how would she survive out in the world alone? Oh, if only the master had not died! If he were still here everything would be exactly as it had been, everyone would be happy and content. There were some who radiated joy and there were others who radiated badness, and she knew very well what the new lord displayed. He was a barbarian. He had no heart: he treated the horses in his stables better than he was treating her lovely mistress. With all her heart she wanted things to be as they had been only a few days ago, but she knew that it was a forlorn hope.

Chin trembling, she said, 'Miss, I'll go with you anywhere. I would rather starve with you than stay here.'

Kitty's face softened. She put out a hand and grasped Maddy's shoulder. 'You're dear and loyal to me, Maddy, and I shall never forget it, but you must stay here and carry on your life as before. You will soon forget me, believe me.'

Tears welled in Maddy's light brown eyes. 'Never, miss,' she choked, '*never*!'

'I have managed alone before, Maddy. I am not afraid.'

'You shouldn't have to be alone, miss. He – the late master – he always wanted ye to live here, to be happy, to go on with your life just as ye did when he was alive. We all know that, all the servants know that, miss.'

'Well, it can't be helped, Maddy. It won't be the first reversal in my life and probably not the last.'

'It isn't fair, miss, it just isn't fair.' Maddy's face crumpled.

'I learned very long ago that nothing is fair, Maddy. I've had roses for the past few years while Lord Cromer was alive, now it's time for some thorns.'

'Can't you *make* him let you stay, miss? Can't you force him? Surely he knew how his uncle felt about you.'

'I think he does, Maddy. That's probably why he feels like he does towards me. I think he looked on his lordship as a father, you know, and he saw me as something of a usurper. You know what they say about wicked stepmothers, and I wasn't even married to Lord Cromer.' Her mouth twisted.

'You should ha' been, miss! He should ha' married ye by rights.'

'That's as may be, Maddy, but it's all in the past now and I must make my way alone again. It won't hurt me; I've done it before, I can do it again. No, it's no good going on with this conversation, Maddy. Come, help me collect my bits and pieces together. I'll wrap them in this shawl, for that can be easily carried.'

'You're going now, miss, now, at this very moment?' Maddy looked aghast.

'Is that not what we have been discussing, Maddy?' Tension made Kitty sound terse. Despite herself she shivered. A fear had come into her head: no doubt the new Lord Cromer was hoping that some man would pick her up as soon as possible, take her away and occupy her fully so that he would never have to see her again or be troubled by her existence at any future date. In all the times she had spent with Fabian he had never once made her feel cheap or immoral or a whore, while his nephew had made her feel all three. Yet the most astonishing reaction he had forged in her was a deep, galvanic response, which had ruptured her heart, she suspected, irreparably. She had experienced nothing like it before; it was so strange, so disturbing, that she did not dare to try to name it.

What was she to do? Shriek and scream, rampage round the room, smashing all the delicate china and figurines, ripping at the priceless bedhangings with her nails, aim scent bottles and cream pots at the windows? Run out barefoot into the wild to lie huddled in a hollow until Fabian came to rescue her and carry her back home on his horse? Her mouth twisted. *Oh God, oh God, if only he could*!

Her thoughts were interrupted at that moment by the sound of carriage wheels scrunching on the gravel of the drive. A horse whinnied, then came the sound of voices. She felt little curiosity but Maddy rushed to the window, leaning out to see who was there.

'Why, 'tis Lord Huntley. He cannot have heard about his lordship's death or he would not be here, and dressed in such finery, too – mulberry velvet with silver lace. Do look out, miss. He has brought some friends with him, too; a fine rabble they are, dicing and gambling and drinking all the night long if I know them.'

'I am not interested,' Kitty said.

'Lord Huntley is a kind man. He will give ye a lift if ye ask him.'

'And ride off in a stranger's carriage with his lordship's nephew smirking out of the window to watch us go while he thinks, "I was right about her, she is anybody's?" ' Getting up, Kitty stormed across the room, glaring out of the window, arms akimbo, cheeks pink as peonies. The last thing on her mind was curiosity about Lord Huntley; rather, she was thinking about picking up one of the large imposing vases in the room and dropping it out of the window on his head. Why should he, a complete stranger to her, be allowed to visit here when she had been ordered to get out?

At that moment one of Lord Huntley's companions

glanced up and saw Kitty and her maid at the window.

'Look, Huntley, two pretty maids – well, one pretty maid and one hearty lass. You can have the hearty lass and I will have the brunette.'

At this moment Kitty's fury reached eruption point.

'How dare you, how *dare* you!' she cried.

'A dare? She has dared you, Huntley. Now you will have to respond. What do you wager, pretty maid? I vow it cannot be your maidenhead, for that you will surely have lost long ago.'

'And would a man like yourself be able to recognise one if he saw one?' Kitty riposted.

'A pretty lass with mettle,' Huntley grinned. 'She'll not take your taunts lying down, Scott.'

'Then perhaps she'll have me standing up.' Scott leered up at the window.

Who knows what bawdiness might have followed had not Carrick joined his friends on the forecourt.

Kitty saw him looking up, eyes and mouth set in grim lines.

'Who is the maid?' she heard the man called Scott ask Carrick.

'She is of no account,' Carrick shrugged.

'What? A comely lass like that of no account? If you think that, Carrick, then you must be getting old.' Scott slapped Carrick on the back, a gesture which he plainly disliked intensely. 'Let the lass come down and drink with us, it can do no harm. Or are you keeping her for yourself, is that it?'

'No, that is not it,' Carrick growled. 'If you want her company call her down yourself. No doubt she'll be more than willing to come.'

'What is her name, Carrick?'

'Find out for yourself.' Turning on his heel, Carrick

stalked back into the house.

Huntley and Scott looked up at Kitty, who had been listening angrily to this exchange.

'Come down and dine with us, pretty lass. His lordship has given you permission.'

'Permission indeed!' cried Kitty, slamming the window shut and drawing the curtains across it in one tempestuous gesture. 'What do they think I am? What has he let them think I am?' She turned to Maddy. 'He wants to blacken my honour, destroy my reputation! Why, why? What have I ever done to hurt him?'

'He was his uncle's favourite until you came along, miss.'

'So he was jealous? What a childish emotion that is. If he had truly loved his uncle he would have been overjoyed to see him happy with me, not jealous. Surely he has enough women of his own?'

'Many, miss. He has a great reputation for being a ladykiller.'

'So I am not the first woman he has tried to destroy?' Kitty attempted a feeble jest. 'Well, he shall not get the better of me. I will not have it. I will do *exactly* as I want. If his friends want me to join them I shall do so, and I shall defy him if he wants to tell me to get out in front of them. He can do it, and much good may it do him.'

Later, in a gown of pewter-grey watered silk which had been one of Fabian's favourites, she entered the solar where Carrick and his friends were ensconced. Carrick was sprawled back in a velvet armchair, one knee over the arm. His face alight, he was making an expansive gesture with his hands as he told his cronies some tale or other. However, on seeing Kitty step into the room, his hands clenched and his expression became steely.

Bracing herself, Kitty walked across the polished dark

oak floor to stand half-facing the men. She appeared so nonchalant and totally at ease that her insouciance could have been taken for arrogance.

Huntley spoke first, glancing uneasily at Carrick as he did so. 'We are mortified to learn of the late Lord Cromer's death, mistress. Had we known we would never have arrived like this unannounced, and believe me our departure is imminent. You – you were a friend of the late Lord Cromer's?' He looked again at Carrick, who had offered no clue as to the identity of the beautiful young girl who stood before them now, gowned in sombre but elegant grey silk.

Conscious of the contemptuous expression on Carrick's face, Kitty said, 'It has been a tragic time for us all. Lord Cromer – that is the late Lord Cromer – was loved by us all dearly. The world will not be the same without him.'

She knew that the strangers could see that she meant what she said, but she was aware of Carrick's frank scepticism. She had expected no more and yet even in front of these men, even in such difficult circumstances, she could not help but remember how Carrick had kissed her. His name was burned into her heart, just as she had burned the names of her mother and father, brothers and sisters, on the rough wooden crosses which she had placed over their makeshift graves. But she would fight it, oh how she would fight it, with every fibre and sinew in her body.

One of the men, realising that he had forgotten his manners, rose to offer her his chair, which she accepted in one graceful, fluid movement. She knew that the strangers' eyes were upon her admiringly, acquisitively, and that Carrick was enraged by that. Maddy had said that Lord Huntley was a kind man, that he would give her a lift in his carriage. Well, why not? She had nothing to lose and a journey to gain. A journey, yes, but where to? Did it matter? Did anything matter now that she was homeless and an outcast once again? Fabian had rescued her from a ditch and now his nephew was ditching her, so she must force down her anguish, her trepidation about the future, and try to put herself first for a change. But it would be bitterly hard. Be nice to Huntley, said the survivor in her, let him see that you like him, for he does appear to be an affable young man. You might as well ride away from here in his carriage as on foot.

After exchanging a few sentences of stilted conversation, conscious all the while of Carrick glowering, his mouth a trap, Kitty knew that she must find out when Lord Huntely planned to leave.

By way of reply he repeated that he had planned only to make a short, surprise visit. 'Under the circumstances we shall, of course, leave as soon as possible.'

'You must stay the night, Huntley,' Carrick said grudgingly. 'Tonight there is capon pie and syllabub.'

At that Huntley brightened considerably. 'Well, in that case, Carrick my good friend, we shall indeed be delighted to stay overnight.'

As always, dinner was cooked superbly, the complementing wines carefully chosen by Carrick, but Kitty was to wish that she had not insisted on joining the men. She felt a continent away from the sparkling, witty-tongued girl she would have been had Fabian been sitting with them. Now and again she was asked a question by one of the men, a question which put her in a quandary. It was obvious that they were curious about her, wanting to know more, and as Carrick would offer no enlightenment, the burden was upon her. No, she would not be staying long at Cromer Manor, she told Huntely, and no, she did not have relatives in the area whom she would be visiting.

'Have you been to Hampstead?' Huntley wanted to

know. 'That is where I live with my sister, Amalia. Our house is situated at the edge of the Heath in a most diverting situation.'

'No, I have not been to Hampstead, my lord, but I have heard that it is the acme of the modish world. There is a spa there, is there not?'

'Indeed there is, a place regularly attended by all the leaders of fashion. But they do not come so much for the waters as for the attractive setting and for the healthy air and tranquillity after the dirt and bustle of London.'

'And how far is Hampstead from London?' By making polite conversation Kitty hoped to divert attention from herself.

'Hampstead is north west, past Chalk Farm and up Haverstock Hill and then Red Lion Hill; all beautiful open countryside. I believe that something like three hundred and fifty six acres of farmland comprise the entire estate. Sir Thomas Spencer Wilson is one of the main landowners; then there is Henry Samuel Eyre and John Powell.'

'I would imagine that so beautiful and healthy a place is much sought after. Will it not one day become as crowded as the city itself?'

'That is not possible, Mistress McDonagh, for most of the land is farming land and, as such, brings in more money to its owners when it is let for that purpose than for building. Then, there are family trusts and so on which prevent new houses being erected. Hampstead Hill itself, which is too hilly for farming, is the centre of activity. I assure you that you would take to the place instantly were you only to see it.'

'You tempt me, my lord,' Kitty said thoughtfully. Why not Hampstead? She might as well go there as anywhere. What she would do when she got there – or anywhere for that matter – was something else again. But even after her great loss and Carrick's brutal kisses and even more brutal insults, she was not faint-hearted. She would fight on, she would take what was offered and with all the enthusiasm she could muster she would put it to good use.

Suddenly Carrick spoke. 'Yes, why not Hampstead, Mistress McDonagh,' he sneered, lounging back in his chair, a goblet of brandy in his hand. 'There's a poorhouse at the top of Holly Hill, so I believe, and as one poorhouse is much the same as another you might as well be there as here.'

A stunned silence fell on the assembled company while Kitty flushed bright pink, refusing to meet Carrick's eyes.

But having begun, Carrick was determined to continue. Leaning forward, he said, eyes narrowed, 'Of course, if such a mean room should meet with your dissatisfaction then I am sure that a more luxurious abode will soon become available to one as practised as yourself, Mistress McDonagh. Why waste your time sitting in a poorhouse where crusts are given for nothing, when you might have the deep satisfaction of giving your body in return?'

A wave of nausea gripped Kitty as she went hot and then cold at his words. To assassinate her character like this, in front of his friends, and so misguidedly too. How could he, oh how could he? Grief welled up in her. Unsteadily she rose to her feet, swallowing with difficulty, for her throat felt charred. Not daring to trust her voice, she nodded slightly at Huntley and his friends, then walked from the room as regally as she could manage, head high, back straight.

In her room, the door locked behind her, she sank to her bed and sobbed. She felt alone and adrift without an anchor, without loving arms to hold her, so vulnerable and very much a victim.

She must have slept, for her dreams were disordered and she woke with a jolt. Night curtained the windows. She felt restless and uneasy, and desperately thirsty after crying for so long. Pulling on a cashmere shawl, she unlocked the door and slipped out into the corridor. The house was silent. Everyone must be in bed, she thought, as she slipped down the stairs. Her shoulders drooped as she approached the library door, for her darling Fabian was no longer in there poring over his books. What she would give to fling open the door and step inside into his arms. Pausing for a moment, she savoured the sweetness of her memories. It was then that she heard the voices.

'What is between you and Mistress McDonagh?' She heard Lord Huntley ask.

'Between us? Why, what in God's name could ever be between us?' growled Carrick.

'She is a pretty wench, attractive and spirited, with a lively mind. I meant no harm. Why should you not –'

'Do you not recognise an adventuress when you see one? She was a common whore, a strumpet, and my late uncle, God rest his soul, found her in a ditch in Southern Ireland. The rest of her family were all dead of the famine, but she had survived the only way she knew how, by selling her body.'

'Her family are all dead?' Huntley's voice was soft with compassion. 'The poor child.'

'Not poor for long, not after she met my uncle. He was usually so shrewd, but about her he seemed to have little common sense.'

'If she made him happy –'

'*Happy*?' Carrick snorted. 'Yes, for a price maybe she did bring him some spurious contentment.'

'You say she was a whore. I do not mean to doubt your explanation, Carrick my good friend, but are you quite positive about that? She looks so beautiful, so wholesome and healthy; she has such composure, such dignity. One can hardly imagine her rolling in a ditch with some loathsome, filthy, Irish peasant between her thighs.'

'I heard it from my uncle's own lips. She was a hedge-whore, the lowest of women.'

'But surely, only because she was driven to such desperate straits by the tragedy of her situation, the loss of her family?'

'Would your sister Amalia sell her body to survive?' Carrick cut in harshly.

Huntley coughed, taken aback. 'You do not expect me to answer that, Carrick, surely?'

'You do not want to answer it because you know that she would never do such a thing. Any decent, respectable and honourable young lady would rather die than sell her body.'

'But how can one say what one would do in such an abnormal situation?'

'If you do not believe me, Huntley, go up to her room now and I vow that she will be yours in exchange for any trinket you might have about your person.'

'Oh, surely not – I do not think – well, I could hardly –'

'Feel free,' Carrick sneered. 'You came here for some entertainment, so why not take some? Get her on her back and see if I am right or wrong.'

'You sound as if you have – well, that is, have you –?'

'I told you that she means nothing to me. In truth, she has monopolised too much of our conversation, Huntley. Tell me how my fiancée looked when you saw her at Lord Finchley's ball?'

'Rapturously beautiful as ever, Carrick. How could Lady Dulcie ever look otherwise? Even if she were ugly as an old hag, with a fortune that size men would call her a

Helen of Troy. But before we change the subject, would you mind very much if I took Mistress McDonagh back to Hampstead with me? My sister is in residence, as you know, and she will act as chaperone, so you need have no fear that I have any ulterior motive.'

'Take the scheming little hussy, you are welcome to her!' Carrick retorted. 'And the sooner the better. I can hardly bring my bride here when there is a resident whore.'

Outside in the dark hallway, Kitty wrapped her arms round her waist, trying to soothe the sickening pain which had formed there. Carrick was a fiend, a beast. He had a fiancée, a beautiful young lady of vast fortune, Huntley had said, and yet he had tried to make her his mistress. No wonder he wanted to get rid of her as soon as possible! He wanted her out of the way before Lady Dulcie arrived. Kitty was having trouble breathing, she felt as if an iron hand were gripping her throat. Leaning against the linen-fold panelling of the hallway, she attempted to gain some sort of control over the jumbled, anguished and confused emotions thronging in her head.

Too shocked and subdued to weep, she somehow found her way back up to her bedroom, where she lay on the coverlet staring at the ceiling with blank eyes. Chubby, painted Cupids rioted up there, the love messengers of Venus Aphrodite. But for her there would be no such message ever again; love had gone from her life and as yet, in her bemused and stupefied state, she did not know what was left or, indeed, if there was anything left at all. To shut her eyes and die seemed a totally appropriate and apt solution. But when she finally did close her eyes it was to sink into a stupefied slumber which did nothing to alleviate her dejection and misery.

CHAPTER SEVEN

Next morning Kitty set off for Hampstead with Lord Huntley and his companions. She looked pale, as well she might, after parting from stolid, loyal Maddy who had begged to come with her, and leaving the home where she had been so loved for the last few years.

Carrick had lounged in the hall to watch her go. He had looked splendid, rivetingly handsome in a midnight-blue velvet jacket with oyster brocade breeches. But his bronze eyes were uncompromising, his jaw rigid. Head high, she had asked him to please let her pass, at which he had let his eyes linger arrogantly on her breasts. Then he had pulled her towards him as if she were a toy to be picked up and put down when it suited him. Next minute his iron-hard body was crushed against hers so fiercely she could feel that he was strongly roused; through all the layers of petticoats and underskirts she could feel him like iron, thrusting into her stomach. Then, as his velvet lips came down to imprison hers she felt her insides melt into a sparkling dew. She was malleable as fondant in his arms. It was her one great weakness but she was determined to fight it.

While his bronze head was lowered over hers and she was manacled by his arms, being left in no doubt that he desired her, she struggled to find the strength to resist him. No effort had ever been so hard. In her vivid imagination it was midnight, lustrous stars twinkling overhead, although in fact it was a grey, misty morning. Every time he touched her they seemed to be bathed in moonlight, the powerful, mystical, silvery rays somehow bonding them together like celestial twins. There was yearning and romance, love and passion, building inside her as the kiss endured. She could not move, he was crushing her so tightly, but her secret was that she did not want to. She wanted to be there, to be secure in his love for evermore.

Even while she succumbed to his passion she knew that she was in the land of fools, that this love was to be taken from her as surely as the love of her parents, her brothers and sisters and Fabian himself. Nonetheless, there was courage and resoluteness in her resignation, for her relationship with Fabian had allowed her to let down much of her guard. He had nurtured her as if she were a tender flower and, like a tender flower given the loving care that it needs, she had blossomed. Her flowering was complete as she stood in the doorway of Cromer Manor in Carrick's arms. She could not help it even though she knew that he entertained nothing but contempt for her, even though she knew that he would have bedded her without thought for her needs or emotions or feelings, and despite the fact that in a few moments' time she would be stepping through this door because he had ordered her out of his home.

She was awash with tumultuous bliss when he took his lips from hers. Slowly, as if in a dream, she opened her lids to gaze up at him and saw that his eyes were black with what she took to be lust – and something else: a little sequin of astonishment? To feel anger at her loss was an emotion with which she was deeply familiar, and it was anger which rose now as she tugged herself free of his arms, stepping back to glare at him.

'How dare you take advantage of my weakness!' she stormed. 'You think that you have only to pull me into your arms and I shall be your willing mistress. To use your physical strength in such a way is utterly, *totally* contemptible! I have never hated anyone in my life as much as I hate you, Carrick Cromer – *never*!' The last word came out in a hiss as, swinging up her arm with all the force she could summon, she crashed her palm against his cheek. Then, lifting up her skirts with her hands, she ran down the steps and out onto the drive, her face ashen except for two blotches of scarlet on her cheeks as Huntley helped her into the carriage.

She did not look back – what was there to look back at? She did not see Carrick standing in the doorway, a bemused and vulnerable expression on his face, the scarlet imprint of her hand clearly showing like a livid scar beneath his eye. It would have done no good if she had seen, for his guard would have been clamped down again instantly. It was an excellent guard, and one which had stood him in superb stead for over two decades. No woman had ever inched her way behind it, not even Lady Dulcie Madingly, the woman to whom he was betrothed.

As the carriage bowled and twisted its way through Surrey and up towards London, Kitty found herself with little to say. For their part, Huntley and his companions were jocular and attentive. As to her eventual destination, no enquiries were raised, but it seemd, by all accounts, that Kitty was to be taken to meet the Lady Amalia, Huntley's sister.

'You will like Ammie,' Huntley said, 'she's a comet in frills and satin. Such verve, such buoyancy –'

'A girl after your own heart, in fact,' Scott put in, his

pale, rawboned face alight as he gazed admiringly at Kitty.

'I have had small experience with ladies of society,' Kitty began, but Huntley put up his hand.

'Please, Mistress McDonagh, there is no need to explain. I have been familiarised with your circumstances.'

'By the new Lord Cromer?' Kitty's body tensed.

'The very same.'

'And what did he tell you about me?' her heart fluttered, much to her annoyance.

'I imagine all that there is to know –'

'*All*?' Kitty was finding the coach distinctly warm. She would have preferred to be alone with Huntley while such a discussion as this was going on. Scott was hanging on their every word, and there was a lasciviousness lurking behind the admiration in his slightly protuberant eyes. She went on, steeling herself, 'I cannot imagine that his lordship knows very much, if anything, about me – we have met only very briefly and that under the most tragic circumstances.'

'That is true, mistress.'

'Is his lordship renowned for his perceptiveness?' Kitty asked acidly, her spine straighter than ever.

'You seem to assume that his lordship has been unflattering.' Huntley smiled.

'Knowing his lordship –'

'You would not put it past him?' Huntley interjected, grinning. 'And do you not believe that I am capable of making up my own mind? For myself I find you enchanting: have you any notion how rare it is to find beauty, grace and wit in one such diminutive package?'

Kitty was saved acute embarrassment by the sudden lurching of the coach, which now jolted into a ditch, throwing its occupants askew. Kitty had to brace herself against Scott's bony chest. He enjoyed it; she did not. His breath was malodorous, more than half of his teeth being badly decayed. Cheeks flushed, Kitty struggled to right herself, found Huntley's hands on her shoulders and leaned back into his arms momentarily before regaining her balance.

'Pass her to me next!' grinned Edward, Earl Riveden, who, having silently weighed Kitty up from every angle, now decided to show his interest.

'I am not a ball,' Kitty snapped, smoothing her cape and sleeves and, with that, sobriety reigned once more.

Hampstead was rural, quaint and picturesque; pretty, well-loved houses, cottages and farms cameod by emerald fields. Huntley's coach slowed as the road became steeper, past the White House occupied by the doughty Admiral Barton who had sailed on the *Temeraine* with Admiral Keppel, then been a castaway on the Barbary Coast and enslaved by the Moors until ransomed by the British Government.

'Enslaved by the Moors!' cried Kitty, recalling all that she had heard of that ferocious race and their barbarous treatment of women.

'He had to retire from the sea because of his health, but he has made his house into a ship,' Huntley told her. 'He has had railing erected round the roof of the White House so that it looks like the deck of a sailing vessel.'

'And he has two cannons in the grounds which are fired whenever we enjoy a victory at sea,' Scott said. 'He must be getting on now, Huntley. Seventy?'

'He must be about that, not that one would know it.' Huntley turned to Kitty. 'We have a goodly assortment of gentlemen eccentrics roundabout and ladies, too, but we are not inhospitable – more like a happy, closeknit family who will always welcome worthy new members.'

'Save for Atalina, Lady Dunbody. She lives in that rose-pink house over there. She is apt to take aim with her blunderbuss should a man be so foolhardy as to step into her gardens.'

'And what treatment do women get?' Kitty wanted to know.

'You will have to ask Amalia that. I've never been within shooting distance of the old trout.'

The hill was becoming increasingly steeper, and it was now that Kitty experienced a new fear. She was steeling herself for the meeting with the Lady Amalia. It was true that she had heard nothing but good of Huntley's sister, yet how would even the most generous and kind-hearted sister take to the introduction of a strange young lady into her home? Might there not at the very least be a coolness, perhaps even open hostility? She was prepared to chat briefly and politely to Amalia, perhaps take tea if she were invited, and then bid Amalia a polite goodbye and step out alone into the world.

This time there would be a small difference, however. This time she would be wearing shoes and her gown was of dove-grey taffeta trimmed with ivory lace, her cape fine, soft black wool edged with marten. The new Lord Cromer knew little of her possessions, her jewellery, furs, gowns and so on; she could have taken anything she wanted. She could have brought all her jewellery with her, but she had not, not even the pearls which Fabian had given her on her sixteenth birthday. She would take nothing which would further lower herself in Carrick Cromer's estimation – not that she could be lower, she imagined. For some reason known only to him he had her labelled and condemned, almost it seemed, before he had set eyes on her. Why she did not know. But that was all in the past now, like so many other painful things. It was unlikely that their paths would cross again. Poor Maddy. Was it not said that those who were left behind merited the greatest compassion?

Amalia was tall, slim and virtually flat-chested. She had a springing walk, wore no ornaments or jewellery, and would have been plain had it not been for her sparkling peridot-green eyes and arched, mink-coloured brows and lashes. Disdaining artifice, she wore no rouge on cheeks or lips, but she smelled very pleasantly of fresh lavender. Her gown was simple, without excessive panniers, the material being sepia-brown embossed brocade.

Unfortunatley, her first words to Kitty were: 'You are passing through Hampstead?' and as Huntley was still organising the removal of companions and luggage from the coach, he was not there to contradict. For answer, Kitty smiled and nodded. 'I was not expecting my brother back so soon. Usually when he and Carrick get together they are inseparable for weeks on end.'

'That would probably have been so this time, my lady, had not Lord Cromer died unexpectedly.' Kitty felt the blood draining from her head. It was exactly as if life were flowing away from her. She struggled to explain, before unconsciousness silenced her tongue. 'He – Lord Cromer, that is – he – I loved him.'

'I know,' said Amalia mysteriously, hastily stepping forward to support Kitty and lead her to a seat.

Amalia was stronger than she looked, and she had no trouble taking Kitty's weight.

'I – I'm sorry,' Kitty said as darkness receded a little.

'You young ladies are all the same,' Amalia said, but not with asperity. 'Always so ready to fall in love. It is not called falling for nothing, you know. Think what happens when you fall: at the least, you get a nasty bruise, at the worst you break something vital, perhaps quite seriously. And what is more serious than a broken heart? The heart is the seat of the emotions as everyone knows.'

Head spinning, Kitty rushed to defend Fabian. 'He loved me too, my lady, he did! We would still have been together had he not died. He was never, ever unkind to me, but always treated me with the utmost kindness and generosity of heart.'

'For which he received nothing in return, I suppose?' Amalia said drily, tut-tutting. 'No, do not try to speak. You are not well, I can see it, for the colour has quite vanished from your cheeks. Sit there and rest, and when you are feeling stronger come and lie on the chaise longue in the drawing room and have tea. Oh, you headstrong girls,' she added. 'You enter the lists of love with such naiveté, such foolhardiness. Then, when you are unseated, and lie bruised and broken in the dust, you bewail your fate.'

'Oh, but it was not like that at all, *not* with Fabian,' Kitty said, a little of her self-possession returning.

'Naturally you do not wish to speak ill of him now that he is dead.'

'Nor did I while he was alive, my lady. I am still not over his death, you see. It happened so suddenly and since then my life has been turned upside down. I had so much when he was alive.'

'Did he not leave you provided for? He always struck me as a man who would be prepared for every eventuality – a realist.'

Kitty shrugged, pressing the back of one hand to her cheek. 'He always told me that he had, that I would be provided for after his death, but I naturally did not want to hear him talking about such a painful possibility. It is true that he did promise me an annuity and a roof over my head for as long as I should need it.'

'Carrick is Lord Cromer now, is he not?' Kitty nodded.

'Do you think that he has destroyed the will in your favour? If Fabian left a separate letter perhaps Carrick knew where it was and burned it.'

'Oh, I am sure he would not do that!' Kitty gasped.

'You say that Fabian told you he had provided for you, yet you are homeless. I have guessed aright – you *are* homeless?'

Kitty nodded dumbly.

'When I get my hands on that Carrick I shall throttle him!' Amalia made a squeezing gesture with her hands.

Kitty's eyes widened in alarm. 'Oh no, you must not do that, my lady. You must say nothing, nothing at all. I have nothing to say to him and he has no more to say to me, I am sure. He will be married soon –'

'To Dulcie Madingly; yes, that is true. One of the most beautiful women in the country and an heiress to boot. They have been betrothed since childhood, did you know? It was Fabian's greatest wish that they marry, for Lord Madingly was his dearest friend until his death some ten years ago.'

So it was an arranged marriage, thought Kitty. Well, that did not make its impact any the less. Arranged or not, the Lady Dulcie was lawfully betrothed to Carrick and would, in the very near future, be his bride, and mistress of Cromer Manor.

'What is the Lady Dulcie like?' Kitty asked, eager to know, yet dreading what she would hear.

'She has buttercup-yellow hair, naturally curly, pansy-brown eyes, and a tip-tilted nose which would be the envy of any woman. She is petite, fragile, with a full bosom and a handspan waist. Her singing voice is as beautiful as a lark's; she is skilled at embroidery; dances like a nymph; and possesses one of the most impressive jewel collections in existence. She inherited the Biltingham Pearl, reputed to have been worn by Catherine de Medici, the Madingly diamonds and, of course, her betrothal ring is the famous Habsburg emerald which has been in the Cromer family for some two hundred years. Originally it was given to the Empress Isabella by her husband, Charles the Fifth.'

Kitty said nothing. What could one say on being told such a stunning list of virtues? No wonder Carrick had treated her with such contempt for she was indeed a pauper beside the illustrious and immensely wealthy Lady Dulcie. How well she knew the aristocracy's penchant for arranged marriages which would bring families, houses, and fortunes together. So crushed was she by Lady Amalia's litany of Dulcie Madingly's virtues that she did not hear the note of irony in Amalia's voice, nor discern the dislike in her eyes. All she knew was that Dulcie was a paragon and a wealthy paragon at that, and that she, Kitty, owned nothing but the clothes she stood up in.

'It may interest you to know, Mistress McDonagh, that you have been the subject of extensive and conflicting rumour hereabouts.'

'*Here*, in London?'

'Where else? I can think of only one other place which thrives on rumour in the same way and that is Dublin, a city which will not be unknown to you.'

'I know of it,' said Kitty.

'Did you not pass through it on your way home?'

'I seem to remember being asleep for much of the journey.'

'I am always dreadfully seasick in the Irish Channel.'

'No, I do not think I was that, but it is all so long ago now,' Kitty sighed.

'Time flies, does it not? They say it is a particular conjunction of the planets. What natal sign are you?'

'I was born in June.'

'So you are a Gemini, the Twins, a contradiction, with a lively, alert mind and two sides to your personality. Cerebral but all too willing to give your heart when you meet your soulmate, and from that moment you become one with him.'

Her soulmate. It should have been Fabian, but astonishingly the man who came instantly to mind at that phrase was Carrick. How could *he* be her twin? Ah, but if only he were, a little voice erupted in her mind.

'Look, you must stay here,' Amalia said suddenly, leaning forward, eyes alight. 'Men – they're all the same – users, heartless, with their brains here –' Amalia gestured to her lower stomach. 'Best to armour oneself against them at all times, prepare as if for war. Expect war and strengthen yourself in readiness. We shall be Amazons together in the battle against manhood.' Amalia flung back her head, carried away by the spirit of her words. 'Do you know about the Amazons?'

Kitty shook her head.

'They were a mythical race of powerful women who founded their own city, Themiscyra. They had a queen, Hippolyta; and all female infants had their right breasts cut off to facilitate the use of the bow. One of the Labours of Hercules was to take Hippolyta's girdle from her . . . All male children were destroyed at birth . . .' Amalia's eyes twinkled. 'I have often thought that certain males of my acquaintance merited such a fate.'

'Then I would *never* find my soulmate . . .' Kitty said, a little of the sparkle returning to her eyes. She was finding Amalia both extremely likable, lively and sympathetic, even if her butterfly mind took some keeping up with.

'That is true, but you would be saved a lifetime's misery in your search for him, would you not?'

'Then do you believe I shall ever find him?'

'That is up to the Moirae.'

'Who is the Moirae?'

'Who *are* they, you mean. Clotho, Lachesis and Atropos, the three Fates. One spins the web of life, one assigns man to his fate and Atropos is the fate that cannot be evaded. All gods and men must submit to them; they are the divinities which govern the lives of mortals.'

Absorbing this colourful but heretical statement, Kitty stayed silent. Fates in female form, three of them, just like the Holy Trinity, governing the human destiny. Three seemed to her to be a sacred number, for it regularly occurred with divine reference. God, the Son, the Holy Ghost. Mother, Father, Son. Love, hate, indifference.

'You have nothing to say?' Amalia said finally, cocking her head on one side. 'But no, of course not. I am, as ever, being callous. What you must have been through of late, my dear – forgive me. I will call for refreshments and you must lie on the chaise longue and take tea with me.'

When they had retired to the apricot, ivory and sky-blue salon and were sipping a very pleasantly flavoured tea, and eating cinnamon and almond buns, her hostess repeated her invitation to Kitty.

'Feel free to stay with us. I am in dire need of a diversion. Truth to tell, Huntley House is a morgue since our parents died two years ago. They drowned. The ship they were in sank off the Cornish coast in a storm as they were returning from a trip to the Continent. Then –' Amalia swallowed, putting aside her fragile, gilded porcelain tea dish, ' – then my beloved cat died. He – he was so beautiful, so loving. He ate out of my hand, he followed at my heels like a doting hound, he slept on my bed.' Tears gemmed Amalia's lashes. 'He died suddenly, without pain, I am relieved to say, and I was nursing him at the time. I had always known that he would die in my arms.

He – his breathing became shallow, faint, then he took a deep shuddering breath, then another, and then a third, with little faint breaths in between. Then it was over – over,' Amalia said as if to herself. 'Can you imagine what it is like to have a loved one die in your arms?'

'I think so,' Kitty said, swallowing back tears herself. 'Yes, I think so.'

'Until it has happened you just cannot imagine. His name was Zeus, I had named him after the king of the gods. I thought it only fitting. It has happened only recently and my brother was away at the time, not that he would have been as upset as I, for he is devoted to his hounds, and anyway Zeus took little notice of anyone but me.'

Kitty said nothing, not one word about her family dying of starvation one after another in her arms and the way she had buried them with her own hands. To have declared this now would be almost insulting, somehow an inference that her hostess, for all her distress, could not possibly know the true meaning of grief.

Amalia's butterfly brain was back on the subject of Kitty staying with her. 'Did you not bring a maid with you?'

'I felt it best to leave my maid at Cromer Manor. Not knowing what my destination would be.' Kitty put down her porcelain tea dish. 'I feel that I must clarify the situation, my lady. It would be true to say that I am homeless, it would also be true to say that I am penniless. I left all but a few bits and pieces behind me at Cromer Manor. So, you see, I possess only this gown I am now wearing and my cloak and the contents of the shawl I brought with me. I can make no financial contribution to the household, nor repay your kindness to me. Perhaps now I have explained my circumstances fully you will withdraw your invitation. If so I shall quite understand.'

'You have courage and pride.' Amalia looked pleased rather than shocked at Kitty's words. 'And I am most taken with the cut of your gown. Tell me, who is your dressmaker?'

'Madame Aristide.'

'And did she design your gown herself?'

'She made the gown but, in fact, it was from a design which I sketched myself.'

'So you design dresses, how exciting! I find the whole kerfuffle of being fitted for gowns wearisome beyond belief.'

'So do I,' admitted Kitty. 'That is why I started designing some of my own clothes myself, because I found it relieved some of the tedium. It is exciting to see a sketch transferred from paper into cloth.'

'Would you design a dress for me?'

'But of course.'

'I do not like frills and bows and suchlike, but I do like the line of a dress to be perfect.'

'There Madame Aristide would agree with you,' Kitty smiled.

'So, you see, you *can* do something for me after all,' Amalia said.

Kitty was given a very pleasant room in ice-blue and tea-rose pink. The bed was a Tudor half-tester; Amalia told her guest that Queen Elizabeth the First had once slept in it when she was a young girl. Kitty was tucked up in that bed which now, thankfully, had a more comfortable mattress than the original. The time was approaching midnight. All was silent in Huntley House save for the incidental creaking and groaning of old woodwork as it settles at night. They had spent a pleasant evening together, she and Amalia, with Lord Huntley joining them after dinner for tea and sweetmeats. Amalia was addicted to tea, drinking it to the exclusion of all else. Now it was time to sleep, but rest was eluding Kitty. She felt unsettled despite Amalia's kindness. Then, as she lay awake in the darkness, she heard a series of creaks along the corridor which sounded as if someone were approaching her door. And then the creaks stopped outside her room and the handle of her door was turned round slowly. She had not thought to lock it – why should she when Carrick was miles away in Surrey?

'Who is that? Is it you, my lady?' she called out.

'It is I, do not be afraid,' Huntley's voice came back, at which she shrank against the pillows.

'My lord, what are you doing here in my room?'

'What else but visiting you, pretty lass.'

'Lord Huntley, you have me *much* mistaken! I am not what you think, nor what you would make me!' Kitty riposted.

Ignoring her words, Huntley approached her bed. He was holding a candelabrum, and by its unsteady light she could see his face, its planes seeming to undulate weirdly as if melting wax were running down them. By daylight he was reasonably attractive, although not handsome, but by this strange eerie light he looked forbidding, capable of every debauchery.

'You must know why my sister asked you to stay with us.' Placing the candelabrum on the bedside cabinet, Huntley sat down beside Kitty, who shrank back, pulling the coverlet up to her chin.

'Amalia asked me to stay because –'

'*Because* she knew that I would be happy to have such a

fair companion to warm me at night. That is it, Kitty, did you not guess?'

A wave of nausea swept over Kitty. But all the same, despite his words, she could not believe that the direct and lively Amalia could have concocted such a plot.

'I cannot believe you, my lord,' Kitty said, eyes flashing.

'Then do not believe me, my dear. All the same, I speak the truth. Surely in your heart of hearts you must know that. Why do you think I brought you all this way in my carriage?' Huntley moved towards Kitty so suddenly that his fur-trimmed robe fell open and she saw that he was naked beneath it. His body was broad, somewhat paunchy – although none would have guessed it with his clothes on – and it was covered in coarse dark hair. To her horror, Kitty saw that he was already in a state of arousal.

'My lord,' she cried, 'whatever you may have planned, whatever your sister may have planned – and, indeed, I cannot accept what you say about her as the truth – I do not seem to have been consulted on the matter *at all*! I have no intention of becoming your bed companion, as you put it. Now, if you would *please* leave my room.'

By way of reply, Huntley lunged at her but she moved sharply to one side, the kiss he had intended for her lips glancing off her shoulder. Leaping from the bed, Kitty's eyes shot round the room. A weapon, she needed a weapon. At first she thought there was only the candelabrum, but that was round the other side of the bed nearer Huntley and so out of her reach. Then she saw a vase with a heavy base and a long, fluted neck in the hearth, which looked as if were made from some bronze metal. Ideal, she thought, and within seconds her hands were curving round the fluted neck.

'If you come one step nearer to me, my lord, I shall hit

you with this,' she warned.

Huntley threw back his head and roared with laughter. 'A little thing like you, hit me with that? Why, you cannot be more than five feet tall, if that.' Huntley was standing up now, facing her, his robe swinging open. He did not seem in the least embarrassed by the fact that he was displaying himself openly.

'You are even more radiant when you are angered,' Huntley grinned, stepping towards her, his arms outthrust.

'Take one step nearer and I shall hit you with this, I promise you!' Kitty cried.

'Kitty my dear, do not think that I mean to use you and then discard you like the Cromers have done. I am not unkind, I shall be good to you. You shall become my mistress; I will find a little house for you, perhaps a little cottage in the Vale of Health, where the air is sweet and clean. You will live and there and I shall visit you. You will have everything you want. I shall pay you generously –'

'*Pay me*!' Kitty screamed. 'Pay me – how *dare* you speak about me as if I were a common whore! I am nothing of the sort and I never have been. If you come any closer I shall scream as loudly as I can and your sister will hear me, and then she can tell me to my face whether or not what you have said is true.'

Huntley's gleeful expression dimmed at that, his smile fading, and with it his ardour.

'Please do not scream, Kitty, I will not come any closer. You are so beautiful. Carrick said that you were –'

'What did he say about me?' Kitty almost snarled.

'That you – that you were –'

'A whore. He said I was a whore, did he not?'

Chastened, Huntley nodded.

'Well, he was wrong! I am no whore. I loved Fabian and he loved me, that is all there is to it, *all*!'

It was too much. Dropping the bronze vase with a loud clang, Kitty burst into tears: piercing sobs which made Huntley's face blush bright red.

'Now look here, Kitty – er – Mistress McDonagh – I – I'm sorry, forgive me. I didn't mean to upset you.'

'Get out, get out, you cur!' Kitty screamed through her tears.

'Yes, I – I'm going. Please – please stop screaming,' Huntley begged, clutching his robe around him and backing out of the room. He had fallen over a footstool, landing with a loud thud on his back, his feet sticking into the air, when Amalia rushed into the room.

'Holy Zeus, what is going on here, brother?'

'Am – Ammie,' Huntley gulped, struggling to get to his feet. Unfortunately, he trod on the hem of his robe and crashed to the floor a second time.

'Have you quite finished the acrobatics?' Amalia rasped. 'If so, please remove yourself from our guest's bedchamber.'

After Huntley had stumbled out, abashed and red-faced, Amalia put her arms round Kitty to lead her to the bed.

'Poor Kitty, I am so sorry this had to happen. My brother – well, let us call him a red-blooded male for want of a more cogent description. Can you forgive us?' Amalia stroked Kitty's forehead, smoothing back the tangled ebony curls.

'Your brother, he said you and he had – had arranged this together.'

'He said *what*? Wait until I get my hands on him, I shall box his ears, the skunk!'

'I thought it could not be true.'

'Never in one thousand years! Men will say anything to get between the sheets with a pretty girl. But it is all over now, my dear.'

'Yes. I must apologise too, my lady, for your brother must go without the reward he expected for bringing me here.'

'He needs a reward?' Amalia sounded scandalised. 'Indeed no. A slapped face yes, for misjudging you, and I shall be the happy person to slap his cheek – in fact, both cheeks. If he wants a whore he had only to step out into the street.'

Amalia helped Kitty to bed, tucking her in as if there were a generation between them instead of a handful of years. Then, a servant brought cinnamon milk and they sipped their drinks together, talking until drowsiness overcame Kitty and Amalia tiptoed away to her own room.

CHAPTER EIGHT

Huntley was absent from breakfast next morning.

'He has gone to see our old nursemaid,' Amalia explained. 'She lives in Camberwell – in a farm cottage – with her son and his family. Maggie Durrin will sort him out; he always flees to her when matters do not go right for him.'

'Did you – hit him?' Kitty hardly dared ask.

'I chastised him as firmly as he has ever been chastised, let us put it like that,' Amalia grinned, lavishing butter upon her toast. 'Now, on to brighter matters. You have a talent for design and I have a wardrobe full of boring, lacklustre dresses. If you will sketch me a ballgown – one suitable for a festive occasion – and a daydress or two to be going on with?'

'But of course.'

Later, having produced some half dozen designs, Kitty showed them to Amalia.

'I love that one, and that. Do you think this is really *me*?' A little frivolous, mayhap, with such a low décolletage and no fichu?'

'I think it would suit you, my lady. You are slender and tall; a heavier build could not stand it – but, of course, there is no reason why you should not have a detachable fichu. First try the gown without one and see what you think. You might well change your mind after seeing yourself in it. Had you thought of wearing apple-green to complement the colour of your eyes?'

'Green? If the truth be known I have always detested the colour of my eyes. Why could they not have been a mysterious amethyst or a rich dark brown instead of this silly pallid green?'

'But they are not pallid at all, they are a beautiful peridot-green, and you should enhance their colour with a choice of dress shade which sets them off to the greatest advantage.' Kitty could not help but smile then, for she was remembering her baptism of fire with Madame Aristide. How unwilling she had been to learn the essentials of fashion, but in the end she had absorbed them all and now was able to pass them on to Amalia.

'I have a maid who is all thumbs. Usually I end up dressing my hair myself. I do not suppose that you are skilled in that direction also?'

'I should be more than happy to show you what I can do,' Kitty said.

It was the start of a warm and amicable relationship, with Kitty designing a new wardrobe for Amalia, dressing her hair every morning, and generally playing the part of lady's maid when the occasion arose, although Amalia made it clear that Kitty must not consider herself as a servant.

'I want us to be good friends, Kitty. My brother is away so often, and I am lonely here; I miss my parents, I miss my cat. At times this house has seemed like a vast, echoing morgue without them, but it is different now that you are here. I enjoy your company very much, Kitty.'

'You are very kind, my lady,' Kitty blushed.

'We have a perfectly equal relationship, Kitty, with gratitude on both sides, I think. But when we are in public I do not want anyone to consider you my servant in any way, for indeed you are not, my dear. Friendships – and I believe in friendships with all my heart – can only be truly satisfying between equals.

'We seem to have got on extremely well from the first moment we met, my lady.'

'You really must stop calling me that, Kitty! Call me Amalia, for heaven's sake. Pomp and circumstance has always awed me. We Aquarians believe in equality, you know, as well as true friendships.'

'In that book on the stars you gave me to read it said that Aquarians and Geminians get on very well together because they are both part of the air trinity.'

'That is true, my dear. We are both airy types with butterfly brains. Aquarians, if anything, are wilder and more original than those who are June-born: we are the wild dreamers of the Zodiac. Of course, with all Zodiac signs there are two sides. There is the warm, caring Aquarian – and I like to think I am one of those – then there is the cool, detached Aquarian, usually of the male variety! But then isn't the male always worse than the female?' Amalia grinned. 'Now, Carrick Cromer, there is an example of the cool, detached Aquarian for you: self-seeking, arrogant and sardonic. To soften all that melodrama and quixotic temperament he would need a warm, romatic Venusian ascendant – and a passionate Scorpio moon would help greatly.'

'Let us not speak of him, please,' Kitty said suddenly, giving way to the surge of feelings inside her.

'He really hurt you, did he not, my dear?' Amalia sympathised. 'Those Aquarian men at their worst can be barbarians.'

The ball at the Honourable Wedgley Branton's home in the Vale of Health was to change Kitty's life. She had designed a gown in greengage velvet which Amalia was to wear with an overskirt of greengage and rose-pink taffeta with rosebud trim. At first, during the fittings, Amalia had declared that such an ultra-feminine gown was not for her, but Kitty had insisted and in the end Amalia had seen that she was right. Kitty had also designed her own gown for the ball, in a rich cerulean-blue silk taffeta with a white fur trim, and for once she was wearing panniers, albeit small ones. Every time that Amalia had chosen a bolt of cloth for herself she had insisted on Kitty selecting one too, so Kitty was no longer short of clothes.

The house where the ball was being held was about one hundred years old, elegant and beautifully tended. Lights blazed from the mullioned windows, which were flung open to the night, and airy, romantic dance music flowed out to greet Amalia and Kitty as they alighted from their carriage.

'They bankrupt themselves every year with this ball,' Amalia whispered as they approached the house. 'They jest about living on bread and water for the rest of the year.'

'Then why do they do it?'

'Status – prestige, my dear, what else?'

Footmen with ramrod-straight backs, white powdered wigs and emerald-green livery piped with gold, opened the doors for them and took their cloaks, then they were announced at the entrance to the ballroom.

'The Lady Amalia Huntley and Mistress Catherine McDonagh,' boomed the major-domo as all heads swivelled to stare at the newcomers.

'Do not worry about the stares, Kitty; the time to worry is when they do not look at you,' Amalia hissed.

Within moments, unattached gentlemen of Amalia's acquaintance were hurrying forward with invitations to dance, and before Amalia was whirled away she said in Kitty's ear: 'It must be the gown, Kitty,' at which Kitty grinned broadly before she, too, was swept onto the dance floor by a young gentleman with the looks of a Turkish prince.

The dance was a riotous one, leaving no breath for conversation, and when it was over both were in need of a drink. The young man lead Kitty to the refreshments table where he poured her a glass of punch.

'You are staying with Lady Amalia?' the young man asked.

'Yes.'

'She is a relative?'

'A friend – a very dear friend,' Kitty smiled. 'I did not catch your name when Lady Amalia introduced us.'

'Argoed, Frederick Argoed. You may have read some of my poetry. I write as Caliban.'

'I am afraid that I have not, but I shall amend that soon, of course,' Kitty smiled.

'I would not wish you to do that if you are not by nature a literary person,' Frederick Argoed frowned.

'I am sure I shall enjoy reading it.' She could not help but notice how the black eyes of the poet were burning into her, his silky black hair, unpowdered and worn loose, framing his somewhat pale but strongly-boned face like a ruff.

'Might I have your permission to dedicate a verse to you, Mistress McDonagh?'

'To me?' Kitty was taken aback, a reaction which rapidly gave way to deep pleasure. 'Why, of course you may, what a charming suggestion. I am honoured.'

The poet, taking her hand, pressed a burning kiss on

her upturned palm, his midnight-dark eyes gazing up at her through long black lashes.

'I shall call my poem Aphrodite Reborn,' Frederick Argoed breathed.

'Do you intend to monopolise the lady all evening?' a voice cut in, Kitty turning to see a tall young man with twinkling eyes and a bush of unruly blond hair. He was attired in an immaculate military uniform which she could not identify, knowing very little about such things.

The effect on Frederick Argoed was immediate. He scowled, his dramatic and romantic features unable to conceal fury at the interruption.

Kitty, who was not in the mood to be monopolised, beamed up at the military gentleman, who half-bowed and then led her out onto the dance floor.

'I feel that Master Argoed is not too pleased,' Kitty twinkled.

'Then that is too bad. Besides, as you may have guessed, it is not his pleasure which concerns me. Shall we introduce ourselves?'

'Indeed. I am Catherine McDonagh.'

'And I am Captain Benjamin Hawkley. Has Argoed promised you a poem?'

Kitty nodded.

'He would. No pretty girl is safe from his pen.'

'They say that the pen is mightier than the sword,' Kitty teased.

'So they do, but no battle was ever won with a quill.'

'Do you speak of war between countries or of the lists of love?'

'It is far more interesting when men and women battle with one another,' Captain Hawkley could not conceal an almost leering smile.

'You find human conflict amusing, then?' Kitty cocked

her head on one side.

''Tis better to be amused than sunk into melancholy,' the Captain answered.

'Must the choice be so extreme – is there no happy medium?'

'Then you do not find a jovial temperament attractive in a man?'

'But of course, although there are other things to be considered too.' Kitty could not decide whether Captain Hawkley's verbal tourney was planned to entice or repulse her, but as she intended to remain serenely aloof, it did not matter. She was not going to be cajoled into a physical relationship with a man at this precarious juncture. She was still grieving for Fabian, still saying prayers for him daily. Frequently, she would think of things to tell him, and then remember that she could never communicate with him again.

Captain Hawkley's grip was increasingly persistent and his palms were moist, which Kitty loathed. The heat in the room was becoming suffocating, but she could not suggest that they step outside into the gardens for a breath of fresh air. Across the room she saw Frederick Argoed dancing with Amalia. Amalia was considerably taller than Argoed, but the poet carried himself elegantly so it did not seem to matter. It was true that he had distinctive bone structure, strongly curving cheeks, a handsome yet not too sharp Roman nose, and this, allied with the glossy, wild black hair and burning black eyes, gave him a fiercely romantic aura. Kitty knew that she would rather be with the poet than with Hawkley, for a man of sensitivity – and she was sure that Argoed was that – was an all-too-rare and pleasant discovery.

Hearing Captain Hawkley coughing impatiently, she realised that he had been speaking. At that point, the music ended and she suggested that they have a seat.

'I will fetch you a glass of orange juice,' Hawkley said, before disappearing into the mêlée.

Kitty glanced round. She was totally surrounded by ageing fashionable ladies who were enlivening their evening by indulging in spicy gossip. Who was having an affair with whom, adultery, an elopement, a lady running off with her groom, a child born at full term when its father had been back from sea only six months. It was the usual smattering of scandal beloved by such people. And then Kitty heard the name of Cromer. Gracefully fanning herself and with eyes half-closed as if resting, her ear muscles became rigid.

'Yes, Lord Cromer – the *new* Lord Cromer, that is, handsome, arrogant young devil so we all thought him. But he has volunteered to pay for the infant's upkeep and its education when it reaches the relevant age.'

So Carrick has a bastard, Kitty thought, heart sinking. Well, what else could she have expected of him? A man of fiery passions, virile, ardent: he would naturally have offshoots of such ungovernable carnal desires. So he was paying for the child's upkeep and education, but he was not prepared to marry the mother, she thought, her lip curling. The two ladies deep in conversation continued.

'So that is the last time you will ever hear me call Lord Cromer arrogant, Lady Stella. There was no need for him to intervene, no need whatsoever, but the poor girl was distraught, threatening to kill herself because this dastard had run off and left her with child. Lord Cromer hardly knows of her. She is the distant cousin of an acquaintance of his and yet he has taken on the responsibility of her child, even though its father is a rapscallion and a knave.'

'But 'tis not the first time he has done this, Lady Marsha,' Lady Stella put in. 'There are twins being educated in Bath, two lovely fair-haired young girls, the children of a childhood friend of his. The friend – Archibald Trevellion – was killed in an unfortunate hunting accident. He left his widow and daughters penniless – they had to sell their home to pay his debts and then, on hearing what had happened, Cromer stepped in, gave the lady an annuity and has financed the daughters' education for some five years now. Lovely girls they are, eleven years old this very month, if I remember aright, but their mother, poor creature, has wretched health. She bore them late in life and never fully recovered her vigour.'

For a moment Kitty could not get her breath. She turned round, staring, rudely she knew, at the two dowagers. They would have been nondescript but for their flashy jewels, feather and flower head-dresses and garishly-rouged cheeks. But they knew more about the man who was responsible for her present plight than she. Blood thudded in her cheeks. Carrick, who had so insultingly suggested that she become his mistress, a philanthropist? Paying for orphans to be educated when they were not even of his blood? How many men would do that? Only one that she knew of, and he was dead. Could it be – could it possibly be that something of Fabian lived on in his nephew? That Carrick was not made entirely of ice and stone? She would need time to digest this knowledge, and this was definitely not the place to do it.

When Captain Hawkley returned she failed to notice him until he bent right over her, coughing raspingly to attract her attention.

'A reverie, Mistress McDonagh?'

'Forgive me. The heat . . .' Kitty forced a smile with lips as unresponsive as board. Taking the proffered fruit juice from the Captain, she sipped it, tasting nothing. Carrick, brutal, arrogant, self-seeking, insensitive Carrick – caring for fatherless children and a stranger's unborn bastard! It was like a thunderbolt and she was totally unprepared for its effect. She spent the rest of the evening in a haze, reacting mechanically, smiling, nodding, and recalling little of it all by the time she got into bed.

There, she gazed into the dark, seeing and hearing nothing. *Carrick.* His name pounded in her head. *Carrick. Carrick.* The last few hours had wrought an astonishing change in her opinion of him. How easy it had been to think that she hated him when she thought him a callous opportunist. Not so easy now when she knew there was another side to him – a side so like her adored Fabian. How could she continue to loathe a man who was doing for penniless children just what Fabian had done for her?

Hating Carrick was part of her existence, however, and the assimilation of today's information would take more than a day or two – and what would be at the end of it for her? A woman of perception, she believed that she might already suspect the answer, or at least a part of it. At the moment, turmoil reigned unrelentingly, and she felt drained by it.

If her animosity towards Carrick did fade, what would there be in its place? She closed her eyes, waiting for her turbulent thoughts to settle. What if she found that she could feel a new warmth towards him, even love? A shudder coursed through her body. Where would such a change of feeling get her? She knew the answer to that. Exactly where she had been before. Nowhere.

CHAPTER NINE

The next morning, Hetty, the maid, brought three calling cards in to Amalia and Kitty as they sat in the drawing room.

'You have made an impression,' Amalia beamed, as Kitty passed her first one card then another. 'Captain Hawkley, and Vernon de Torren – well, one can discount *him*, foreigners are so unreliable. Hawkley, now, he is a man of gentle birth with a large annuity from his late great-aunt, the Countess of Hazelly.'

'Birth is one thing but inclination is another,' Kitty retorted to Amalia's amusement.

'Do you mean Hawkley did not behave like a gentleman last night?'

'I distinctly felt that there was a hirsute barbarian lurking behind that immaculate uniform,' Kitty complained.

Amalia leaned forward, lips pursed. 'But is that not true of all healthy young men, my dear? You have led a very sheltered life, it seems to me – oh, do not look so embarrassed – all these rumours bruited about regarding your colourful reputation, well, they simply are not true, are they, my dear?'

'Did you believe them for one minute, that is, after having met me, I mean?' Kitty's voice was steady.

'No, but one had imagined perhaps two or three lovers

– such a pretty girl as yourself, such charisma . . .'

'One lover, Amalia.'

'Only one?'

'Only one.'

'Shall I let you into a secret? I am still virgo intacta,' Amalia gave a cheeky grin. 'Do you find that disturbing in one my age?'

'It would be disturbing if it were not of your choice, Amalia.'

'True, but it is. When the right man appears he can have all of me, heart, head and hymen. I vowed that when I was fourteen years of age. Now, let me see – from whom is the third card? Why, Frederick Argoed. Well, that does surprise me.' Amalia opened her mouth as if to say more, then closed it, then opened it again. 'I shall have to warn you, Kitty my dear, do not count on Argoed. He is – that is, he had, er, well a . . .' Amalia put her hand to her mouth. 'Oh dear, I am not explaining myself very well, am I?'

Kitty could not imagine what was coming so she smiled faintly.

'You see, sometimes artists, creative artists that is, are inclined to – well, they have strange proclivities, abnormal ones that is, with regard to sex . . .'

'You mean that Frederick Argoed is debauched?'

'In a way, but it is rather more than that. You see, Frederick Argoed had an affaire with a man.' Amalia's eyes glowed. 'A most unsavoury type,' she went on. 'A writer, but a writer of tawdry, cheap novelettes full of lust and gore and such distasteful subjects. They used to walk on the heath, arm in arm just like lovers, one black-haired, one golden-haired with blue blue eyes exactly like a girl's.'

'I see.' Kitty was struggling to absorb this extraordinary

information. Two men having an affaire together: how did it happen, what did they do together? For the life of her she could not imagine.

'The boy – Perry Patterson was his name – died of smallpox. Argoed was *distrait* – he took years to recover. Now he writes love poetry for pretty girls who take his fancy, if, that is, there is any fancy left for them to take, which I doubt.'

Further discussion was halted as the outer doors of Huntley House crashed shut.

'My brother is home,' Amalia cried happily, as Lord Huntley strode into the room, kissed his sister, then greeted Kitty with a breezy bow. Since the eventful night when he had burst into her bedroom neither had referred to that incident. It was best forgotten, and Lord Huntley had never tried such tactics again. Indeed, he was rarely at home, for the Huntleys too had a flourishing business closely affiliated with merchant trading, which was how Huntley and Lord Cromer had met.

'Dear young goddesses,' Huntley grinned. 'Diana and, yes, Venus –' he grinned at Kitty, 'I am in need of feminine benevolence. Advice, that is. Samples of material have arrived from Genoa – I need choices to be made. Would the fair young Venus care to divulge her preferences?'

'What is to be the destiny of the selected cloth?' Kitty asked, with great interest.

'Gowns for ladies of the haute monde, perhaps even for the King's Court, if the goods are what is wanted.'

'Since when have we been clothiers?' Amalia asked.

'Since the day I saw the samples and recalled your praise of Kitty's talents for design, Amalia. Besides, leather, brandy and spices can be numbingly boring. I saw peacock-blue silk from Genoa and visualised you in it,

Kitty, and a deep pink brocade for you, Amalia, instead of those sepia shades you seem to covet. Diana in pink and Venus in blue – why not?'

'You seem very pleased with yourself, brother. Is that the sole reason for this impromptu visit?' Amalia asked, eyes shrewd.

'Well, there is another little matter, just a very little, *petite*, tiny, infinitesimal matter,' Huntley grinned wickedly.

'You need some money.'

'Sister, you should be a sorceress! How did you guess?' Huntley dropped a kiss on Amalia's forehead.

'Experience,' Amalia sighed. 'How much?'

'Quite a lot, in fact. To pay for the Genoa order and a few other bills. Creditors are apt to become wolves when their bills are not paid. There seems to have been a lull in the sales of leather . . .'

'And spices?'

'The same.'

'Surely not brandy, too?'

'Well no, but . . .'

'But what?'

'Something has to pay for the losses. Thank the Lord, brandy is perennially popular.'

'But people cannot have given up spices in their food, surely, and are people now going barefoot?' Amalia asked acidly.

'*Ours*, sister – *our* spices and leather have been eschewed.'

'When papa left you in charge of the business he did *not* know what he was doing!'

'Sister, I cannot help trends – they are beyond my control – that is why I wish to branch out with a new line.'

'And have you put some serious thought into what this

new line should be? Or was it simply that you saw some pretty materials which took your eye? Have you any idea of the present condition of the fashionable world, the trends of the moment, the most popular fabrics and so on, or what colours are modish now?' Pausing, Amalia frowned. 'Tell me, brother, what is the most fashionable colour of the season?'

'This present season?'

'Yes, this present season, brother.'

Huntley's eyes slid thoughtfully over Kitty's gown and then Amalia's, at which Amalia said, 'You will get no help from looking at us, brother, for neither of us are wearing the particular shade in question.'

'Blue?' hazarded Huntley, but Amalia shook her head. 'Green?' he said next, Amalia shaking her head again. 'Why, of course, bright yellow – I saw Lady Mallington in bright yellow only the other day.'

Amalia shook her head again, while Kitty suppressed a smile. 'I'm afraid you are wrong all three times, brother. What shall we do with him, Kitty?'

By now, all of Huntley's foolhardy ebullience had evaporated. Stalking over to the sideboard, he prodded a bowl of fruit, then helped himself to a hefty measure of brandy, and stood staring out of the window, affecting an insouciance which he obviously did not feel. Then, turning to the two women, he said:

'I did ask for your assistance, ladies. I did remember what you had said about Kitty being a talented designer. Kitty, will you help me?'

'But of course, Lord Huntley, at least I will do my very best.'

'Will you come with me to our warehouse and inspect the material samples?'

'Yes, of course. I would be only too pleased to help.'

'And am I not invited, too?' Amalia put in almost pettishly.

'You too, dear sister. Why, how can I fail with Diana and Venus to aid me?' Huntley grinned, his spirits restored.

Amalia gasped when she saw the condition of their warehouse on the Thames.

'The place is falling down,' she cried. 'Ashley, you have been neglecting it! Why have those loose boards not been nailed back into place, and see, there is rain seeping in through the roof onto that pile of hides over there. No wonder our leather does not sell if it is all spotted with mould and mildew.'

'I am sure that is a new leak, sister.' Huntley went over to inspect the damage. 'Not too bad,' he pronounced.

'Everything is bad which interferes with our sales, brother. Surely it would not bankrupt us to repair this warehouse which houses all our precious merchandise?'

'I told you – finances are in a very precarious state at the moment.'

'You cannot spare a few pennies to have these boards nailed back into place and the roof patched up?' Amalia cried, swinging her arm upwards to point at the damage.

'Oh, I will do the repairs myself on the morrow.'

'Yourself? But . . .'

'Please, sister, you have my word on that. Now, do come and look at these samples.

Kitty followed Amalia and Huntley towards the back of the warehouse. There was indeed a smell of mildew in the air which would hardly be conducive to healthy storage of leather and spices, or for material either. As it turned out, the samples of cloth were superb. Genoese velvet in blood-red, brilliant emerald, russet, crushed strawberry, blackcurrant, and rich cream. Gauzy silks threaded in silver and gold, yet so transparent that when they were held aloft the shimmering strands seemed to hang unsupported in the air. Silky rustling taffetas, candy-striped in every hue imaginable. Black cloth of gold, rose cloth of gold, cloth of silver, on and on for bolt after beautiful bolt.

'These are magnificent,' Kitty said, imagining the different materials made up into sumptuous gowns. She saw the emerald cloth of gold on a Court gown with panniers like sails, the rose samite worn by a young girl at her first ball.

'Well, ladies, which do I choose? It's up to you,' Huntley urged.

'Is there a limit on our choice?' Kitty asked, knowing that she would like to choose virtually all the bolts of cloth if she were given a free hand.

'I thought a dozen to two dozen, at the very most. Remember, we are experimenting, branching out into a field where there are many competitors.'

'Then we must be even more careful about our selection. Might I be allowed to take home snippets of some of the materials so that I can think about them and sketch some designs? Then, when I have done that, I will give you my final choice. It will only take a day or two.'

'Thank you both.'

'I will make my choice, but where it differs from Kitty's then you must override it, for she is the talented one,' Amalia said.

The next two days were hectic as Kitty sketched and then painted in her designs. After having done so, she decided against three of the selected materials but remembered three which could replace them. Having finished her sketches, she showed them to Huntley and Amalia, who were full of praise.

'Now all we need is a skilled courturière to make them up in various sizes,' Kitty said.

'Have the dresses ready made?' Amalia gasped, astonished at this revolutionary idea.

'Yes, why not? You have said yourself how you loathe dress fittings, standing for hours while a seamstress pins and tucks and stitches.'

'But what if the dresses do not fit the ladies who require them?'

'Look at this design.' Kitty pointed to her sketch pad. 'Can you see these folds here?' Amalia nodded. 'Well, these are adjustable gowns. With a mere stitch or two they can be taken in or let out.'

'You are a genius, Kitty,' Huntley said, looking closer at the designs. 'Ready made gowns, who would have thought of it.'

'I had the idea some time ago when I was being subjected to non-stop dress fittings by Madam Aristide – remember, I told you about her, Amalia? I really used to fume, having to stand there for all those long hours while she altered gowns and took fittings and so on.'

'Think how convenient this will be,' said Amalia to her brother. 'Ladies who require a gown will no longer have to wait days, even weeks, for it to be prepared. They can come along to us and buy it ready made.'

'We can have the same style, or similar styles, made up in different materials,' Kitty went on, 'and if a particular style should prove very popular then we can have it made in all the most popular sizes.'

'We shall need a showroom, a base from which we can sell these ready made dresses.' Huntley frowned. 'Might we not also need young ladies to wear them – to display them, that is, when purchasers come to buy?'

'What a brilliant idea.' Amalia clapped her hands. 'But we can hardly display the gowns in the squalid surroundings of that old warehouse, brother. We shall need somewhere altogether more comfortable and luxurious if we want to attract the right clientele.' Amalia giggled. 'Clientele – how professional that sounds. Oh, I have such a strong feeling that this venture is going to prove a success!'

'I feel that way, too,' said Kitty, but she felt anxiety too, for it seemed to her that the whole venture rested on her shoulders.

What if her adjustable gowns proved a dismal failure? What if ladies of the haute monde refused to purchase ready made clothes? But she was not one to sit around contemplating disaster. She would design more dresses, they would have them made up by reputable seamstresses, then they would find a comfortable showroom and hold a gown show, a gala gown show, with free refreshments thrown in. Eyes sparkling, she put this idea to Amalia and Huntley, who looked at one another with glowing faces.

'We cannot fail,' Huntley said. 'There has never been anything like this before. We shall attract dozens of people – make history! Come, let us celebrate with wine.'

Preparations were soon under way, and if they had imagined that the next few weeks would be uneventful then they were proved wrong. Seamstresses had to be found, and this was by no means easy. Many were fully occupied for months ahead, and more than one or two went into the vapours at the mere mention of ready made gowns. 'Anathema!' one cried, reaching for her smelling salts, then having Amalia and Kitty shown to the door at high speed. Another declared that if her major client, the Duchess of Broome, discovered that she was embroiled in such a controversial and shocking scheme, then she would withdraw her custom instantly. Finally, having found a handful of dressmakers whose minds were open to innovation, negotiations began for the work to be carried out. This entailed Kitty spending long hours in the dressmaking establishments, three of them in all, discussing her designs, her ideas and how she wanted the gowns to be made. It was necessary for her to be present at each stage, for there was much confusion over the adjustable sizes. Patiently, she explained to all involved just what she had in mind, then she explained it again – and again – until everyone involved had absorbed her requirements.

The sewing women who worked in the establishments were hardy girls who began stitching at dawn and broke off for a few brief minutes once a day, to snatch a tasteless meal. Summer and winter, they pursued this routine, receiving a pittance in exchange and sometimes forfeiting their sight. More than a few were blind by the age of twenty five, for they had been sewing, virtually non-stop, since childhood, and most of that time by the light of a feeble, flickering candle. Their stitches had to be invisible, which further strained their eyesight.

On discovering this state of affairs, Kitty had been appalled. Girls going blind sewing gowns for rich socialites, and being paid a few meagre pence per week! No, she would not have that, even if it would ensure that all the gowns which she needed were ready by the required date. Conditions were improved, by her own order – Amalia's too. Better lighting, nourishing food, longer rest periods, shorter hours, and pay when off sick were just a few of the reforms introduced by the two women.

Madame Violette, proprietress of the largest establishment involved, and who had, hitherto, allowed Amalia and Kitty a free hand had blanched at these revolutionary improvements. Wailing, she had clasped her hands to her ears and swooped up and down her work room, issuing a sound which resembled that of a bird in a dire state of distress.

'My girls – zay will be spoiled – ruined – pampered to such weakness that they demand more and more until I, Madame Violette, am the screaming stock of London! No one will visit me, no one will consult me evair again! Aiee, I am regretting what I am doing!'

Gently, Kitty and Amalia had explained their plans – and they had also repeated the fact that, if the gala show was the success they hoped it would be, then Madame Violette would become more famous than she could possibly imagine.

'We shall finance the girls' needs during the coming weeks, Madame,' Amalia said, directing the full power of her charm towards the Frenchwoman. 'We shall pay all their bills – and so you will not be out of pocket at all. We promise you that.'

'But what of afterwards, when you 'ave gone? My girls will demand I give zem all this money, these long rest hours, the pay when sick . . .'

'Madame, afterwards you and your girls are likely to have so much work that you will be able to take on double your present work force, and of course make more than double the money you are now making. We shall need an eternal supply of ready-to-wear gowns – and you will be one of our chief suppliers – I thought we had made that quite clear? We have many leaders of fashion coming to the show – Countesses, Duchesses, Lady Rose Amesbury, and, it is hoped, at least one of the King's daughters . . .'

'Aiee!' wailed the Frenchwoman, but this time she exclaimed with delight, her cheeks suddenly pink. 'The King's daughter – the Lady Amesbury, that *belle femme*, who makes everything she wears look so marveilleuse!

Oh, oh, this is true – you 'ave not the jestings wiz me?'

'It is true, Madame – quite true. I am sure that you will never regret your involvement with us,' Amalia smiled.

'Oh, oh, the Lady Amesbury! The King's daughter, oh, oh!'

Clutching at her ears, and totally mollified, Madame Violette said not one further word of protestation.

Kitty forgot what sleep was like. A trestle bed was brought into Madame Violette's establishment so that she could snatch an hour or two's peace whenever possible. The sewing women had taken to her very warmly indeed, but, as with all such happy situations, it entailed responsibility. Sometimes, it seemed to Kitty, the whole world would judder to a halt if she did not stay wide awake and fully alert the clock round.

Every afternoon, there were rehearsals for the show, and at two of the clock each day, a chattering bevy of attractive young girls besieged Madame Violette's door. Selected carefully for their good looks and air of refinement, these girls were new to modelling gowns but not new to the eye of the public, for some were actresses or singers, and three were dancers in the classical mode who displayed sinuous grace, deportment and composure.

Training them was a different matter, however, and not without its frustrations and moments of anguish. Amalia and Kitty were always together for these afternoon sessions, for it needed two people to sort out the rivalries, disputes and wrangles which arose amongst the girls. Knowing that they were to be viewed by the aristocracy, and that it was quite possible that gentlemen would be present, each girl wanted to wear the most splendid gown and appear before the others on the dias. When Kitty explained that she and she alone would decide who wore the dresses and who came on first, she was treated to a display of charm, cajolery and flattery like nothing she had ever experienced before. She managed to survive it – with difficulty – comparing herself to a circus tightrope walker, and the girls to wild beasts snapping below, ready to devour her if she failed to provide the titbits they demanded. A sense of humour was paramount in those arduous and stressful weeks, when at times it looked as if nothing would go right, and as if the entire show would have to be postponed indefinitely.

All too soon, the day of the show approached, and with it Kitty's presentiment that it would be an abject and total disaster. However hard she tried, she could not throw off this feeling; her back was aching from weeks of sleeping in the uncomfortable trestle bed with its hard mattress, and from bending over materials and sketching boards and lifting and carrying boxes containing all the paraphernalia which was to adorn the hall where they would hold the show.

Every movement seemed to require double the usual effort, and her head was pounding when the news came, only hours before the opening, that the young girl who was to model the wedding gown – the highlight of the show – had slipped on the steps of her home and sprained her ankle.

On hearing this, Amalia folded her arms and looked at Kitty. 'You will have to do it – you are the same build as Becky, and the same height, so no last minute alterations will be needed.'

'I? But I have had no practice,' Kitty exclaimed, conscious of her pale face and throbbing head.

'You have a natural grace, my dear, which Becky never had for all her rehearsing.'

Kitty glanced at the sumptuous wedding dress on its hanger. Froth after froth of ivory lace, seeded generously with glossy white pearls, and the aureole headdress of white swan feathers from which was suspended the most fragile, shining silk veil trimmed with seed pearls. It was a heavenly creation and she adored it. Besides which, nothing of its like had ever been seen before; the veiling in particular being innovatory. While designing it, she had dreamed of wearing that gown herself as she married Fabian, and she had brushed away a secret tear or two as she thought of what could never be.

Bracing herself, she said, 'Of course, if there is no alternative than I shall wear the wedding gown.'

'Good girl.' Amalia patted her on the shoulder.

While the refreshments were being taken round by liveried footmen from the Huntley household, in the cramped dressing room Kitty and Amalia worked frantically to ensure that all went smoothly, straightening the models' hair, making sure that the gowns went on stage in the right order, finding lost shoes, matching jewellery, and so on. Then it was time for Kitty to don the wedding dress and step gracefully out into the centre of the hall for all eyes to rest upon her. She had not realised how disconcerting such a mass of people could be. She knew that more than two hundred were expected, and all of those carefully selected, but it seemed that they had each brought at least two friends. The hall was crammed, faces were staring unrelentingly in her direction, and there was not so much as a sniffle to be heard as she walked serenely down the centre of the hall, turning a little to the left, a little to the right, slowly circling at the bottom of the room then drifting back, a faint smile on her face, her eyes tranquil.

And then she saw Lord Cromer and her heart seemed to burst into a thousand fragments in her breast, each one piercing into her flesh. As beautiful, as arrogant as ever she remembered him, his glossy bronze hair thick and luxuriant, shining like polished gold, his powerful, glowing, bronze eyes boring into hers. She could not breathe, she could not swallow. She had a vague recollection of a beautiful young woman entwined round Cromer's arm, her head resting on his shoulder: a young woman with a mass of buttercup-yellow curls and tip-tilted nose, with a full, curvaceous bosom above a tiny waist.

Somehow Kitty finished her promenade of the room and vanished into the dark recesses of the corridor leading through to the dressing-room. There she paused, heart hammering, struggling for breath. Carrick, with his betrothed – the woman he was going to marry – watching her. She knew what he would be thinking, of course: he would be thinking that it was a farce for a whore to be wearing a white wedding gown, when white was the symbol of virginity. Anguish constricted her heart; she felt sick and dizzy. On tissue paper legs she managed to get back to the dressing-room, where she sank into a chair while Amalia fussed over her.

'How do you feel, my dear? Was it such an ordeal, then? Oh, you have no idea, the orders that are flooding in already! We shall have to duplicate so many of these gowns. We have explained to people that they will not be the only one to wear a certain design, but only one or two have turned up their noses at the idea of duplication. And, in fact, we can vary them – a bow here, a frill there, and so on. You look very white, was it so terrible?' Amalia chafed her hands. 'Everyone is applauding your skill as a designer. I vow that you will find yourself with other work to do besides ours, my dear.'

At that moment one of the pages ran in with a folded piece of parchment which he handed to Amalia. Opening it, Amalia read what was written there and then grinned broadly.

'Well, the wedding dress is sold, Kitty. Is that not marvellous? To such a beauty that she will surely be a superb advertisement for your skills as a designer. Oh, the orders will come flooding in!'

'Who has bought it, Amalia?' Kitty had very strong feelings about her wedding dress. While designing it she had felt closer to it than to any of her other creations. She knew that it was because she had visualised herself wearing that very dress while standing beside Fabian at the altar, but of course she could not speak of that to anyone.

'Who has bought it?' Amalia said, almost absently, putting a hand to her aching back. 'Why, Lady Dulcie, of course – you know, Lady Dulcie Madingley, Lord Cromer's fiancée. One cannot deny that she will look radiant in it – Kitty, *Kitty*! Oh dear, oh dear, how stupid of me to prattle on so. She has fainted. Ashley, Ashley, come quickly and help me with Kitty!'

After her faint, Kitty spent exactly one day in bed, then, despite Amalia's protests, she rose, dressed, and began to sketch a new series of designs. Determined not to submit to the desolation chilling her heart, seeing in her mind's eye the frozen image of Lord Cromer sitting entwined with his betrothed, Kitty sketched at furious speed; gown after gown appeared, along with headdresses, caps, slippers, gloves and fans. She would not weaken – she would not become a poor, feeble, weeping creature. No, no, not for any man, not even *him*.

She worked all through the morning, afternoon and early evening, refusing to break off for refreshments or meals although Amalia did her best to cajole. The floor around her was ankle-deep in sketches by the time she had finished, and as soon as she put down her pen she realised that her head was splitting, the back of her neck stiff and aching. She lay on her bed sipping the mulled wine with spices and honey which Hetty had brought her, but it tasted of ashes, as did everything which she ate or drank when thinking of Carrick.

She dozed, on and off, her dreams were wild and disordered. She was in bed with a man, his hard brown body naked against hers, a scintillating frisson coursing between them. Like magnets they clung, knotted together by love, and it was a symbolic knot, a mystical marriage, which, like the Gordion knot, no man could untie. Passions teemed through her body and mind in a smouldering, sensual halo which enveloped them both. She still felt submerged in that sensual halo as she awoke, its warm glow bathing her. To wake from that passionate dream to find herself alone in bed with an anaemic dawn pearling her bedchamber was intolerable, yet she knew that she must tolerate it, must learn how to cope with it. If she ran from it she would never be free: to stand and face it was the only solution.

Under her pillow was a little book which Amalia had given her. It contained a reading for every day of the year. Taking it out and opening the pages, she read the proverb for that morning: *Grapes must be destroyed before wine can be made*. She thought she knew what it meant: a reference to the struggles of the soul's journey, the rebirth and regeneration which must take place, the rise of the phoenix from its own ashes. Was she prepared to endure such torment? Did it mean that she must be destroyed, totally transmuted, before the end product, the 'wine', could be produced? Had she the courage to leave herself so boldly in God's hands or, as Amalia would have it, in the hands of the Moirae?

Closing the book, she slipped it back under her pillow, but not before she had remembered one of the daily sayings of the previous week: *The Lord is my shepherd; I shall not want.*

'There has never been anything like it, Kitty. The Duchess of Collingley, one of the richest women in the country, and her cousin, the Lady Araminta, who is renowned for being so difficult to please – they are all queuing up to buy our ready-made gowns.' Amalia clapped her hands together, pivotting round on one foot. 'And so many others too, you would not believe it – ladies who could afford to have a whole army of sewing women working week after week on their gowns, and yet they have come to us and ordered entire selections.'

'Now our only problem is to find an army of sewing women to make up the gowns,' Kitty smiled wryly, her thoughts still upon the sketch which she was completing. It was for a ball gown for one of their shortest customers, a lady as petite and fragile as a porcelain doll but who had an obsession about looking taller than she was.

'I wish you would leave that sketching and enjoy yourself more. You have hardly stopped work for days now.'

'With orders rolling in how can I do otherwise?'

'And what will happen if you become ill, my dear? Come, I will send for some hot chocolate and we will sit in the solar for a few moments and rest.'

'I do not think –' but Kitty's words were interrupted by the scrunch of carriage wheels on the drive and the piercing whinny of a horse.

'Now who can that be? We are not expecting any visitors.' Amalia went out into the hall, returning in a few moments, eyes wide. 'Kitty, guess who has come to call upon us – Dulcie Madingley.'

'She has called unannounced? Why is she here?' Kitty

gasped. To call unannounced was unthinkable.

'We shall soon find out. Will you come with me to greet her?'

'I would rather not.'

'She adored your wedding gown, my dear. Her enthusiasm has brought us many customers.'

Kitty averted her eyes. 'If you need me call me,' she said.

Shrugging, Amalia went out, closing the door quietly behind her, but she was back within a few minutes.

'She has come to see you, Kitty, you specifically.'

'Me?' Kitty's heart sank. 'Why should she want to see me?'

'Really, Kitty, sometimes I think your brains are addled. You designed her wedding gown, did you not? Well, she wants you to design her trousseau, too.'

On hearing that Kitty experienced a surge of almost crippling anger. How much more of this humiliation must she take?

'Oh, I can see that something has made you angry, Kitty.' Amalia touched her cheek. 'Is it the fact that she will be Lady Cromer very soon? Dear girl, you must put aside old resentments, old hostilities, for they will harm you more than they will ever harm the Cromers.'

Now was not the time to tell Amalia that she, Kitty, no longer hated Carrick Cromer – far from it. Their wealthy and fashionable client was waiting for her services and the fortunes of the Huntleys depended upon her. Their financial straits had been precarious for some time – far longer, in fact, than Lord Huntley had cared to admit at the start. But once he had opened the books to Kitty and his sister the full enormity of their position had become clear. There had been recriminations on Amalia's part, of course, but she was the first to admit that her lack of interest in business matters had helped contribute to this dilemma.

'Why is it,' she had said to Kitty, 'that a man can be the greatest fool and knave, yet everyone expects him to be able to handle business matters? Not that I am saying my brother is either of those things, of course, but it is the expectation that men will shine at business while women know nothing of such things that has allowed our affairs to get into such a disgraceful state. From this moment on, whoever can offer the most cogent advice on the situations we encounter shall have the final word, whatever their sex.'

Having collected herself, Kitty followed Amalia to the door, out into the hall, and through into the solar where Lady Dulcie Madingley awaited them. She was wearing a primrose-yellow wig, the exact shade of her natural hair; her eyes were wide and bright, but her mouth unsmiling. Her gown was fuschia silk embroidered with garlands of ivory roses, and she carried a fashionable gold-topped cane.

Having given Lady Dulcie a cursory glance, Kitty's eyes became riveted upon the third finger of her left hand. It bore the enormous Habsburg emerald which Amalia had mentioned earlier. This emerald, reputed to be the most flawless stone in existence, had been given to the Empress Isabella by her devoted husband, Charles the Fifth, the Great, and it was said, and strongly believed, that only true lovers might possess and wear the ring. Any lady wearing the ring who did not truly love her betrothed would be cursed, and to back up the superstition there was a string of stories about faithless fiancées who had dared to flaunt the ring then met unsavoury ends. One had tried to sell the ring so that she could elope with her squire; she had been decapitated by brigands, her secret lover mortally slain. Another who had lied to her fiancée about her purity had been publicly repudiated, then drowned herself.

'Lord Cromer and I are going to Paris for our honeymoon,' Lady Dulcie drawled. 'We shall be meeting my lord's distant cousins, the Duke and Duchess of Denver-Collis. The Duchess is a leader of fashion which, as you will appreciate, is quite an extraordinary accomplishment for an English lady in France.' Lady Dulcie leaned forward, her generous ivory breasts bulging from her excruciatingly tight bodice. On one stunning breast was a star-shaped patch centred with a dazzling diamond, on the other, a crescent moon spangled with scarlet and emerald sequins in the shape of a D. Privately, Kitty thought the patch was tasteless and overdone: the impact of the breasts themselves was more than enough without decorating them like yule boughs. Still, men were renowned for responding to such feminine ploys. Having no doubts about her own femininity, Kitty did not feel the need to resort to blatant sexual trimmings.

'Quite extraordinary, Lady Dulcie,' Kitty nodded agreement, flat-voiced.

'Naturally, I want to excel myself –'

'Excel *yourself*, my lady?' Kitty interrupted, eyes wide with apparent innocence.

'Well no, not myself, you stu – that is, I wish to excel the Parisiennes, who are, as we know, the foremost leaders of the haute courture.' Having decided that Kitty was a simpleton, Lady Dulcie enunciated each word loudly and clearly when addressing her. 'I want an entire trousseau of the most fabulous gowns ever created – and, of course, chemises de nuit.' She fluttered her eyelashes with something like a crude suggestiveness – or was it false modesty? Kitty could not decide. 'My future husband is a man of the most ardent, shall we say, appetites? I wish to be alluring and provocative in my night attire – I wish to drive him to a frenzy!' Lady Dulcie tittered, her breasts wobbling. From where Kitty stood it looked as if they were elbowing one another to get out of the breath-defying bodice.

Cheeks now scarlet, Kitty nodded again. 'I know exactly what you mean, my lady,' she said.

'*Your ladyship*! *Your ladyship* is the correct mode of address for a servant!' Lady Dulcie snapped at Kitty, who wanted to snap back at her before storming out of the room. But noticing Amalia with her knuckles pressed into her mouth, Kitty fought for control.

'How long will it take for the trousseau to be prepared? My lord is eager to wed me.'

'We must measure your ladyship, of course, and I have sketches – if your ladyship would like to view the designs we have available to your ladyship? If your ladyship would follow me . . .' Kitty led the way to the studio, whose walls were lined with her ink and wash sketches.

Five hours later, when Lady Dulcie had finally gone, Kitty collapsed from exhaustion, feeling that she had sold her body and soul – but not for anything would she let Amalia know how degraded she had been. Amalia was elated, clapping her hands together and saying that their fortune was made.

Yes, thought Kitty, fortunes are made as hearts are broken. But if Amalia, whom she loved dearly, could keep Huntley House and the family business, what did one shattered heart matter? No one had been more shocked than she when, some weeks before, it had become obvious that Amalia's home would have to be sold to pay her brother's business debts, unless money could be found from some other source. Wryly, Kitty recalled how she had looked on Amalia as her saviour when, in fact, the situation was the reverse.

Drained of energy, eyes closed, Kitty leaned back on the chaise longue. In the darkness behind her lids she could see Lady Dulcie, half naked, in one of the flimsy nightrobes that Kitty was to design for her, while Carrick kissed her throat, then tore open the transparent lace to bury his face in the sumptuous, cushiony breasts.

Torment, she was in torment!

'Kitty, are you ill?' Amalia's face loomed over her.

'No – just weary,' Kitty sighed.

'I will order some brandy wine with cream to restore you. You shouldn't work so hard. I do appreciate it, my dear.'

Later, back at her drawing board – for only in work could she find a semblance of peace – Kitty began to design Lady Dulcie's trousseau. The colours were to be ice-blue, syllabub-cream, bird feather-gold and gilly-flower-pink, colours which she had suggested to complement Lady Dulcie's colouring. She would begin with the travelling outfit, designing the nightwear last of all. She only wished that she could sketch that with her eyes shut.

CHAPTER TEN

As the months passed and Kitty's success multiplied, the Huntley trading business found its feet again, its debts were paid off and its profits were wisely invested. Gradually, Kitty grew restive. The trousseau for Lady Dulcie Madingley had been completed long ago and despatched to her ladyship, who had let everyone know that she was entranced with it. There had been the balls, the masques and parties to which Amalia had dragged Kitty, even when she was at the lowest ebb and had no wish to show her face outside the door.

The Lady Amalia Huntley, who had been renowned for her uninspired and sombre mode of dress, was now praised for her dress sense, and she had acquired suitors, too – Lord Frederick Clivedon de Moss and the Honourable Chevening Sawley-Beamish. Only that morning a basket had arrived for Amalia, and, on opening its lid, she had found an adorable kitten, a present from Lord Frederick. On closer examination, the kitten was found to be wearing a diamond-studded collar. Not rough stones but beautifully cut diamonds of a fair size, which quite took Amalia aback.

'I had no idea Lord Frederick was so serious,' she said, allowing the kitten to romp on her knee. 'What shall we call the little mite? Is he not the sweetest kitten? I think I shall call him Apollo, for he has brought so much sunshine into my life.' She looked up at Kitty. 'No, I must be fair – it is Lord Frederick who has done that.'

Kitty smiled. There was a new softness in Amalia's face. She was no longer so strident against men; she smiled more frequently and altogether seemed to enjoy being a woman. Kitty hoped that Lord Frederick would soon ask for Amalia's hand in marriage. Her dear friend deserved the happiness which such an alliance would bring her, for Lord Frederick was a warm-hearted man with insight, humour and generosity who had not for one moment been misled by Amalia's verbal diatribes against the male sex. On many occasions he had declared quite loudly, certainly always loud enough for Amalia to hear, that he preferred a woman of education and wit, one who could speak up for herself, who could quote from literature and who had more on her mind that the colour of embroidery silks and the latest perfume from Paris. But Lord Frederick's pièce de resistance was undoubtedly the kitten.

Kitty remembered one of the sayings from her little book of quotations: *A man who provides one with something to love will himself be loved.* She rejoiced for her friend's good fortune, even though she knew that it would leave her very much alone, for Amalia would be going to live at Moss House in Wiltshire. She could remain with a skeleton staff in Huntley House, Amalia had told her, but then there would be the problem of Huntley's presence when he was at home. Kitty knew that what she needed was a home of her own, but how she could arrange this she did not know. She knew that she would miss Amalia greatly, but she would be pestered even more ardently by Frederick Argoed and Captain Hawkley, who had continued to pursue her wherever and whenever possible during the months of her residence in Hampstead.

Argoed's poem had been written, dedicated to her, and duly delivered by special messenger. She could not say that she had been impressed by it. He had taken one or two outrageous liberties with the rhyming of words. Kitty thought that it should not be called *Aphrodite Reborn* but *Death of a Dream*. She had put the scroll of parchment at the back of one of her drawers and promptly forgotten about it.

Then she heard that Captain Hawkley was being posted abroad, and she felt that her time in Hampstead was coming to a close. It had served its purpose, elevating her from the blackest despair, rescuing the Huntleys from financial disaster and, in a roundabout way, finding a husband for Amalia. There was a studio crammed with designs which the Huntleys could use for many years to come and she would never hesitate to provide more designs on demand. Now there was nothing to do but to look forward to the Saturnalia Masque at the house of the Duke and Duchess of Cheshire. It was one of those events which Kitty viewed partly with anticipation, partly with hesitation. She knew nothing about the Cheshires, but Amalia wanted to win the custom of the Duchess. Because of this, Kitty had designed trend-setting extravaganzas for them both to wear. Amalia was to attend as Hera, Queen of the Gods, with a steepled gold headdress studded with gigantic mock sapphires and draped with shining silver veiling. Her gown was silver cloth of tissue, gleaming, floating, it looked an opaline blue-pink in certain lights. She was carrying a tall gold sceptre in her hand, while embroidered on her bodice, beaded and gemmed with sapphires and emeralds, was a peacock, Hera's symbol.

Kitty had deliberated long and hard over which identity she should adopt for the evening's festivities.

'Why not go as Diana, the goddess of hunting and young maidens?' Amalia suggested.

'I had hoped to find a goddess perhaps not quite so well known. What do you think of my going as Nemesis?'

'The goddess who metes out happiness and misery? I'm not sure about that. One can just imagine Nemesis deciding that one has too much happiness and snatching it away.'

'That is why I rather like the idea of dressing up as her,' Kitty half smiled. 'She has dealt me quite a few bad blows in my lifetime and I thought it would be pleasant to put myself in her place for once and imagine that I have her powers.'

'A pleasant fantasy, but I think that her robe would be too plain to do you justice – if you will pardon the pun.'

Eventually Kitty decided to go as Cassandra, daughter of Priam and Hecuba. As a King's daughter she could dress as richly as she wished, and should anyone ask her why she had chosen to be Cassandra she would reply mysteriously, thinking of her treatment at Carrick's hands: no one had believed a word that Cassandra said either.

The Cassandra outfit would be simple yet striking, for Kitty wanted to stand out in the bevy of overdressed masquers. Some six months earlier, she had come across a very rare material which neither she nor Amalia had ever before seen. It was a delicate silk lace, the whole gown when it was finished weighing little more than a few ounces. The colour was pale shell pink and under the gown Kitty put an underskirt and bodice of ivory cloth of gold, which gleamed through the lace like moonlight. Like Amalia, she would be wearing her hair in the Grecian fashion, looped up and with pendant curls.

When Amalia saw her dressed in the finished outfit she clapped her hands together with glee.

'What you need now is a scrying glass.'

'What is that?'

'Oh, all prophetesses and seers have a scrying glass – the famous Nostradamus had one. He looked in his mirror and prophesied the future for Queen Catherine de Medici.'

'Carrying a mirror around all evening would be somewhat inconvenient,' Kitty said.

'Then have a hand-mirror on a chain round your wrist. I have one which will match your outfit perfectly; it is silver set with very pale amethysts, almost pink.'

And so a silversmith attached a silver chain to the mirror and Kitty was to wear it round her wrist.

The arrival of their carriage was imminent, and Amalia was putting the finishing touches to her hair while Kitty slipped on her white fur cloak. Early on she had found that she had a passion for white fur, and she liked to add it to her own gowns and cloaks wherever possible. But white fur simply would not go with Cassandra's outfit, so she was wearing a sumptuous floor length cloak of it instead, lined with crimson velvet.

Once ready, the two women got into the coach and settled themselves, Amalia looking bright-eyed and excited, Kitty somewhat calmer.

'Oh Kitty, if the Duchess should become one of our clients! Lady Dulcie Madingley told me how much the Duchess admired her trousseau.'

'She is wearing her trousseau already?' asked Kitty, astonished. 'But she is not yet married to Lord Cromer.'

'I just heard the tale at third hand, I do not know whether she was actually wearing any of the clothes when the Duchess complimented her on them. Perhaps she visited Lady Dulcie and was shown them in her bedchamber, who knows?' Amalia shrugged. 'The Duchess is so beautiful, so young and slender, she is the ideal foil for your designs, Kitty. Every overweight, blowsy Dowager will imagine that she, too, can look like the Duchess of Cheshire if she wears your designs. That is what we are aiming for, is it not?'

'Such a situation would be delightful,' Kitty agreed, knowing that this aim seemed increasingly to be an empty and meaningless one. To work non-stop, hour after hour, to blot out her feelings for Carrick, to obliterate the thought of his marrying Lady Dulcie and their passionate honeymoon in Paris, yes, that had originally been her intention. Indeed she might well have succeeded in eradicating her longing, had Amalia's unexpected, yet joyous, attachment to Lord Frederick not disrupted their existence and shown Kitty that nothing had changed. No matter how long she worked, how hard she tried to blot out thoughts of Carrick, she knew now that she loved him. Time after time she marvelled over the effect he had had upon her: one violent embrace, one melting kiss, and she had handed her heart and soul into his keeping.

Amalia had warned her that the Duke and Duchess of Cheshire's annual masked ball was the high spot of the London season and that everyone who was anyone would be there, which meant, of course, that Lord Cromer and Lady Dulcie Madingley would probably attend. So Kitty was well prepared for what was to come that evening. She would see him. She would, of course, control her emotions superbly, as on so many occasions before. Holding her head high, she would stare straight ahead as if she had not seen him, she would keep her back straight and she would be more graceful and composed and lady-like than she had ever been in her whole life before. She would give

Fabian good reason to be proud of her this night. Carrick would never know – must never know – that she loved him, ached for him, dreamed of him night after night. She must think of the business, and nothing else but that. True, with Lord Frederick's marriage to Amalia, the Huntley fortunes would no longer need boosting, for he was reputed to be immensely wealthy. However, Kitty had her own future to think of now, and she was determined never to be an impotent pauper again. Whatever happened she would be independent, self-sufficient, her own mistress from now on.

She had not forgotten Maddy either. She hoped that one day her maid could join her, but first she would need sufficient funds of her own and possibily her own little house. She would dearly love to live in the Vale of Health amongst the artists, poets and writers in their picturesque homes, but she knew that she could not run a successful designing business from a tiny cottage, so her new home, when she finally chose it, would have to be reasonably imposing, a place to which no fashionable lady would disdain to come.

Pretty little Plum Cottage, which was painted that very colour, had captured her heart but had insufficient room for a studio and the storage of sample gowns and designs. Amalia had said that she might stay on as long as she wished at Huntley House but her brother, too, was now anticipating marriage and, of course, he would wish to reside there with his bride when that day came. How time changed everything. *You cannot put back the clock.* She remembered those words as if they had come from another age. But she was no longer the ingenue against whom every cut and thrust stabbed like steel. She was tougher now, altogether hardier. She had learned that she had a flair for business dealings and that she could handle even the most difficult of clients. The flow of her creative powers, once it had begun, was virtually ceaseless. When she was designing it was as if she were taken over by the demon of art. She knew that she was fortunate; there was an artist in the Vale of Health who was going through a very bad period at the moment and who spent much of his time striding up and down on the Heath, striving for inspiration. She had never had to do that. Indeed, sometimes the flow of inspiration, the sheer pressure of it, was so great that she longed for release.

Their carriage was arriving at the Cheshire mansion and Amalia and Kitty were being announced by the pompous, booming voice of the Cheshires' major-domo, whose acid yellow and flame-coloured livery was totally eclipsed tonight by the hectic colours of the guests' costumes.

The Duchess of Cheshire was weaving in and out of the assembled company, her face alight. This was her metier – she was one of society's leading hostesses, willing to spend a fortune every year to ensure that she remained so. Her costume was her own idea of what the real Britannia had worn, as she was at pains to tell everyone '*Not* the lady on the coins, who was King Charles's mistress, but the real life Britannia who lived so many centuries ago!' No one had the heart to tell her that there had never been such a person, that she was the figment of patriotic imagination. Nor did anyone during the evening comment upon her ensemble, which shrieked of colour, bad taste and indifferent design. However, nothing could detract from the porcelain beauty of her face, the incomparable beige-gold eyes which glowed like uncut topaz. She wore a steeple-like helmet of indeterminate origin, which kept sliding over one eye, and eventually, with a tinkling laugh, she threw it to one side. It landed in a dish of fruit jelly, splattering one of the valets with wobbling red splotches.

Imperturbably the man retrieved the helmet, cast it under the table out of sight, and resumed his former stiff-backed pose.

Candelabra blazed from one end of the great hall to the other. Up in the minstrels' gallery, built in Tudor times, an orchestra played lilting music. Kitty had become accustomed to these occasions where everyone seemed to speak at once, but of course there was one difference this time: this was a masked ball, and, until midnight, unmasking time, everyone was in disguise, save for the host and hostess.

Amalia had warned her about masked balls, where people who had known one another all their lives professed not to know each other merely because their eyes were covered by a flimsy mask. Astonishing things had come about as a result of these evenings, Amalia had told her, such as husbands paying court to women whom they did not recognise as the wives they believed themselves bored with. At unmasking time they had found that they were wildly in love with their own mates yet again. Others had found that a life-time's enemy had, in the space of a few hours, become a lover. The excitement of these occasions could be profound, Amalia had cautioned, and it was better to keep a level head at all times unless one was prepared to live with shame and regret.

But while she had been listening to Amalia, Kitty's mind had been on the possibility of seeing Carrick again in more relaxed social circumstances. Being masked, she would be able to observe him at a distance, for she knew that she would recognise him anywhere, even with his face concealed. Who could not recognise him? That blazing bronze hair – for he rarely wore a wig – his stance, height and straight back, the broad shoulders and slender, lean waist, could not be hidden.

She looked around for him now but could see him nowhere. Amalia had introduced various young men to her, all of whom were clamouring to lead her out onto the dance floor. She could not say that any of them in particular captivated her, but Frederick Argoed was the one now lightly clasping her hand as they circumvented the floor to a trilling piece of music.

'Where do you hide yourself away?' he was asking. 'I hardly ever see you. Is it true that you shut yourself behind closed doors and do nothing but work at your designs?'

'Do you have an objection to ladies being artists?' Kitty raised a brow.

'Not I. But is it not unusual for the fairer sex to work at a drawing board when they can be working at an embroidery frame or raising young children?'

'Would you have me chained so young?' Kitty smiled lightly.

'You call bearing children being chained?'

'And is it not? What freedom does a woman have after she has produced an infant? Is she not then expected to continue producing a child each year until her childbearing years are over?'

'There speaks a lady who has never been in love.' Argoed's passionate dark eyes bored into hers. 'Is it not well known that a lady in love thinks of nothing else but producing children of that union?'

'After the marriage ceremony, of course,' Kitty teased.

'But of course. I meant nothing immoral. Dare I ask it, Mistress McDonagh – have you, that is, are you in love with any particular gentleman at this moment?'

Kitty laughed. It seemed that wherever she met Argoed he was able to take up their conversation as if they saw one another regularly. Remembering all that Amalia had said about him, she did not intend to take his attentions seriously.

Enjoying the music, watching Argoed's face and thinking of ways to lightly tease him, Kitty did not notice Lord Cromer standing at the edge of the hall, watching her with piercing eagle eyes. His face was grim, closed and saturnine, his shoulders rigid. Various people had tried but failed to engage him in conversation. Now they had drifted away, so that he stood alone, sipping brandy from a crystal goblet. Lady Dulcie was late – he had called for her in his carriage but she had sent a message via her maidservant that she would be delayed and would follow later. She was arriving now, dressed as a water sprite, trailing seaweed and a dressmaker's version of exotic underwater plants, the whole outfit shimmering with diamonds, emeralds, seed pearls and sapphires. Soon she and Lord Cromer were whirling round the dance floor, smiling into each other's eyes, giving everyone the impression that they were devotedly happy.

As a flying piece of seaweed slapped against Kitty's back, she half turned to see what it was. Colour flooded her cheeks as she recognised Carrick, still unwigged, but dressed in the garb of what must surely be Apollo the sun god, for a blazing, golden sun gleamed on his broad chest.

With her Grecian veil partially obscuring her face and her mask over her eyes, Kitty believed that there was little chance of Carrick recognising her. Silkily, Lady Dulcie apologised for her errant seaweed and the handsome coupled undulated away. But not without leaving Kitty's heart hammering against her ribs, sounding so loud in her ears that it almost drowned out the noise of the music. Gripping her hand even more possessively, Argoed led her away. He seemed not to notice how pale she was, but her sudden unwillingness to communicate disturbed him.

'Have I offended you, Mistress McDonagh? Please do tell me. You are suddenly so silent that I feel I have said something unintentionally distressing.'

Kitty smiled cooly. 'Master Argoed, surely the whole point of a masked ball is that one does not recognise one's partner? And yet you must have called me by name several times. I fear that my disguise is a poor one.'

Argoed blushed a fiery red. 'You have culled me, Mistress McDonagh – er – that is, I mean, Mystery Lady.'

At any other time Kitty would have laughed aloud, but as it was she was watching Carrick and Lady Dulcie – whose petite fragility could not be concealed – and as she watched them she saw Carrick bend low to drop a light kiss upon Lady Dulcie's forehead. Lovers even in public, she thought, feeling empty and hollow inside. Midnight was approaching, when masks would be removed and exclamations of recognition, some genuine, some feigned, would be heard. Suddenly she did not want to be with Aroged. She wanted to be alone, somewhere secluded, without the black, passionate eyes scouring her soul. Excusing herself, she slipped away before Argoed could restrain her. She was unaware of his lustful black gaze following her from behind his mask.

Every corridor, every room she entered seeking solitude, seemed to be packed with a babbling throng, but eventually she found a peaceful library where a fire blazed and the faint odour of tobacco hung in the air, reminding her, heart-stoppingly, of Fabian. A book lay open on the carved oak desk, just as if someone had left it there only a moment ago. Sinking into the comfortable armchair by the fire, she relaxed, holding her toes out to the blaze, remembering how years ago she had done just the same in front of a peat fire in the cottage in Tipperary.

She must have been lightly dozing for she did not hear

the door to the library opening, but she did hear the footfalls sounding on the oak boards by her chair. She looked up in alarm. Carrick stood there. She made as if to jump up in alarm, but he put out a hand.

'Do not let me disturb you. I merely wish to have a few words with you. I knew you would land on your feet – or should I say on your back? But I have to hand it to you – what a scheme to put it about that you are a wealthy princess without a throne. What a splendid way of attracting rich clients! It takes a stroke of genius to concoct such a tale, and I must say that I did not think you had that quality.' Taking her hand, to her astonishment, he kissed the centre of its palm lingeringly, causing sparkles of desire to snake their way through her body. 'Just make sure that you do not tell your lies to any of my friends,' he drawled. Then his hard, probing fingers had slipped inside her gown, caressing her breast, teasing the nipple erect. 'If only you could teach your skills to others,' he said, almost wistfully, making her wonder what he could possibly mean. Her cheeks were burning, but she had not the strength to push him away. Her mind was in turmoil.

As always when he was anywhere near her, she felt helpless. And now, helplessly, she submitted to him, allowing his fingers to roam over her breasts, cradling, caressing. His hair was almost flame-red against the blazing fire and he looked as if he were indeed Apollo, pulsing with sunlight. She wanted that moment to continue for eternity; she wanted them to be frozen in time. It was blazingly real and yet a mirage; a strange sense of unreality penetrated her bones. Perhaps she was dreaming it all? Was he really there with her?

'What is your costume?' he wanted to know.

'I am Cassandra.' The words were a sigh.

'What a strange choice. No one believed her pronouncements, did they, and yet you have the whole of London believing that you are a Russian princess fleeing from some scoundrel in your homeland!'

As Kitty did not know what he was talking about, she did not reply to that, but she did say: 'You have never believed a word that I have said.'

'I know the truth when I hear it.'

'I have never spoken anything but the truth to you.'

'What are you feeling now?'

'Longing, passion, desire,' she whispered, as if mesmerised.

'I too.' Taking her hand, he placed it between his thighs. 'See what you do to me, Kitty McDonagh. Surely you guessed long ago what effect you have on me? I am a passionate man . . .'

She drew her hand away as if it had been scalded, remembering the brutally cavalier treatment she had endured from him before, and yet wanting to forget it. 'Touch me there again,' he said, his voice husky. 'See what you do to me, Kitty. Do not feel that I am forcing you; do it of your own free will.'

There was a roaring in her ears, a tumult of heat in her cheeks, as, unable to help herslef, she reached out and did as he requested. He was like iron, erect and ready. She heard his intake of breath as her fingers slipped inside his breeches to stroke his maleness. She could feel the crisp bronze hairs against her palm and suddenly she wanted to kiss him there. Again she drew back, startled at such a thought, savouring it in her mind but unsure, all the same.

Gently he drew her out of the chair, seating himself there in her place, and then he unlaced his breeches, gently pulling Kitty towards him, helping her onto his knee. At first she was a little unsure of what he wanted her to do and then she realised, and kneeled over him, circling him with her hand before poising herself above him and then gently lowering herself. He felt like fire against her, pushing at the entrance to her centre, and then he grasped her round the waist with his hands, thrusting himself up as hard as he pulled her down. It was unbelievable, exquisite bliss for her, like nothing she had ever known before, like being impaled, but a blissful torture. But she was shocked, too, – and not a little bemused. Were it not for the fierceness of her reaction, she would have thought it a dream.

They were in total harmony, eyes locked, bodies locked. At one, blissfully, erotically, at one. No experience, no desire, had ever been as sumptuously ecstatic as this. He moved rhythmically, pressingly, coercing her into an unavoidable response. Tingling shivers of mounting desire coruscated along her skin, a silvery tinselled fizzing which was simultaneously sweet and velvety.

His heart was thudding. She could feel the echoing beat inside her and she hung over him, weak with passion, while a tumult of sensations seared through her. Now she knew that she had been longing – yearning – to be in Carrick's arms – that she had never hated him, after all. That a much more powerful and enduring emotion was involved.

'Kitty,' he whispered her name, his bronze eyes slumbrous with love – or at least that was what she took it for. What he was giving her, what she was receiving and giving back was so very different from what she had known with Fabian that she knew it must be love. With Fabian it had been sweet, tender and affectionate but, she now knew, too gentle, too muted, to involve her deepest feelings – indeed, until she had met Carrick she had not known they existed. With Fabian she had been girl, with Carrick she was a woman.

She wanted to cry out: '*Do you love me? Tell me that you love me!*' for she needed those words from him as desperately as she needed food and drink. Carrick was her sustenance, her soul's nourishment. She now knew without doubt that they were meant for one another: a man and a woman forged for the same destiny.

His thrusts were becoming deeper and more penetrating now. She leaned forward, cradling her head against his chest, felt his lips brush the crown of her head once, twice, with the sweetest tenderness, while he was carving out his own place inside her.

'Do you love me?' she whispered, but there was no reply. She had hoped for some response. Surely he could not be so warm and loving, without that most important emotion being involved?

He began to move more urgently, the breath rasping in his throat, while Kitty almost sobbed with longing for the culmination of their lovemaking. It all seemed so right with him. She knew now that they were born to be together. He knew it too, that was why he had followed her into the library. He had come to tell her that he loved her, that it had all been a terrible mistake with Lady Dulcie, and that he would marry her, Kitty.

'Tell me, *tell me*!' she urged while he scythed in and out of her body, hot, steely and throbbing.

As his breath came quicker and quicker she urged him again, 'Tell me, tell me!' but he said nothing. She thought he chuckled deep in his throat, but she could not be sure. Looking up at him she saw the reflection of the scarlet flames in his eyes, so that the bronze became an unearthly crimson glow, like fiery gold. His mouth was curved in an enigmatic smile. He had never looked more handsome and desirable to her than he did at that moment. But still he remained silent.

Deeper and faster went his thrusts, and she knew that it would soon be over. Already it had seemed to last an incredible time. How could she ever have thought that Fabian was an accomplished lover? Here, in Carrick's arms, the world had ground to a halt; they seemed to have been making love for days.

'*Now*!' she heard him rasp, and then he soared into her with a blissful, splitting anguish and she felt the explosion deep within. As he emptied himself inside her, he kissed her mouth, so that she throbbed from head to toes, a sliver of delicious pulsating sensation.

For a few moments they lay still, then he said: 'Do not forget what I told you, Kitty. Tell whatever lies you like to strangers but not to my friends. Keep off my territory unless you present yourself there in a bona fide fashion, for I shall brook no skulduggery from you.'

She could not believe her ears. Was she hearing aright? Pulling herself away from his chest, she glared at him.

'Skulduggery!' she cried. 'How dare you! How *dare* you make love to me and then speak to me in such an insulting fashion! I have not lied to anyone nor do I intend to.'

'Have it your own way, Kitty,' he drawled. 'But heed my warning all the same or you will rue the day.'

'I could never rue something I have not done,' Kitty retaliated, pulling away from him angrily, climbing off his knee and straightening her disordered skirts.

'Do what you please unless it displeases me.' He gave a small yawn as if he were bored with the whole situation. She found this insolent gesture so insufferable that she wanted to slap his face. And yet, even more, she wanted him to pull her back into his arms, kiss her and tell her that he loved her. Ah yes, that would be the sweetest joy on earth. But it was obvious that he had no intention of doing anything of the sort, for he got to his feet in one graceful movement, adjusted his breeches and strolled to the door with his usual, panther-like grace. Stunned, she watched him go, indignation warring with heartbreak, as she realised how he had tricked her. He had taken advantage of her passionate need for him, waiting until her defences were low, then using and discarding her as he would a tattered kerchief.

'My lord,' she whispered, and at the door he turned, the bold bronze eyes inscrutable, mouth gently curving.

'Oh, I forgot,' he gave an almost apologetic smile, the sweet charm of which smote her right through the heart. Reaching into the pocket of his masque costume, he drew out a handful of gold coins. Holding out his hand, palm uppermost, showing the gleam of gold, he said, 'Your payment, Mistress McDonagh.'

Fury and tears biting inside her, she spat, 'What, no crust? Surely, my lord, you have a crust somewhere about you on your person? Remember what you told me about Irish whores willing to sell their bodies for bread? Do not tell me that you came unprepared! A loaf of bread, is there not a loaf of bread in the Duchess of Cheshire's kitchens where you may procure a crust?' Her cheeks were flaming, her body trembling. As the door closed behind him, she flung herself into the armchair where Carrick had made such passionate love to her and there she sobbed out her grief. Cassandra, whose word no man believed.

CHAPTER ELEVEN

The next morning Amalia could hardly contain her excitement.

'It is incredible what they are saying about you, Kitty,' she cried. 'Lord Frederick told me that the whole of London is convinced you are a foreign princess, an exile who has fled Catherine the Great's Court in Russia because of a scandalous love affair!'

Kitty blinked, too stunned to answer at first, while the memory of Carrick's words fluttered through her mind. She had slept badly the previous night, and when she had opened her proverbs book she had read: *To those who give all, all shall be given*. She had flung the book across the room.

'Did you not hear what I said, Kitty?' Amalia's voice sounded like a distant bell ringing far away.

'I heard. What do you think of this nonsense?'

'Nonsense? Why, I think it is delightful – great fun. What a lark, a tremendous lark! 'Tis amazing what fabrications people will invent when they cannot uncover the truth.'

'So I am an immoral Russian, a princess?' Kitty managed a feeble smile.

'Does that not intrigue you'"

'Perhaps it would if the truth were not more fantastic.'

'Kitty, you have never told me everything about yourself . . .'

'Do you believe the rumours, then?'

'No, no, of course not. I think I would have detected some proof of your being Russian and royal if it were so.' Amalia's eyes twinkled.

'I have no wish to speak of my past. The pain is put behind me now – as much it can ever be.'

'I am sorry to intrude, forgive me. It is just that, well, I thought it would be marvellous publicity for your – our – work if this rumour were allowed to flourish.'

'You want me to lie?'

'No, no, of course not.' Amalia's cheeks reddened.

'I will deny these rumours – they are not true, simply not true.' Kitty was remembering how Carrick had accused her of spreading lies for personal gain – the humiliation of such accusations was debasing. 'I am Irish, not Russian. A princess? That is laughable,' she said bitterly.

Amalia sighed. 'Perhaps you are right. It was wicked of me to think that I could persuade you otherwise.'

'Not wicked.' Kitty touched her friend's arm. 'I would like to do what you ask if you think it would really help the Company but . . .'

'You would not have to lie as such, Kitty, just do not deny the rumours. Smile mysteriously – do not confirm or deny.' Amalia poured more hot chocolate for them both. 'Kitty – you know I am to marry Lord Frederick soon. He is not agreeable to my continuing in what he calls common trade. He wants me to be mistress of Moss Manor, with my mind fully upon him and the sons I shall bear for him. That is what I want, too.'

Kitty nodded, saying nothing. She was thinking of the independent-spirited Amalia who had invited her to stay at Huntley House. Then, Amalia had bridled at the mere notion of any man engaging her affections or ruling her heart. How different things were now.

'I understand.'

'So you must think of yourself now, Kitty, my dear. Already your reputation is excellent. Your designs have captivated the country; next week you will meet the King and Queen. Once the Queen wears your gowns the rest of the Court will follow; all their relatives and children will follow, too. A great future lies before you, Kitty, and even the merest hint of your having royal blood will open so many doors. Amalia leaned forward, her eyes soft. 'I want them to open for you, Kitty. You have suffered so many losses, so many griefs, yet you have always put others first. Do not think that I am not aware of it, for I am. You even forgave my brother for his dreadful, insulting behaviour the night of your arrival in our house.'

Kitty blushed. She had not done any of it for rewards, verbal or otherwise. Amalia went on.

'Others would have grasped greedily at whatever fell in their path, but not you. It is time you benefited now, Kitty, you personally.'

'Amalia – you did not start these rumours, did you?'

'I?' Amalia looked shocked. 'Certainly not! I told you, Lord Frederick passed the information on to me – he was as startled as I.' Amalia turned away to reach for a piece of almond cake, her eyes glinting mischievously.

'Why on earth would such a rumour be spread about, let alone believed?'

'Who knows, my dear? Boredom, excruciating boredom? The rich and titled are prone to it, you know. They adore a jest – some spicy gossip or scandal to alleviate their tedium. And while not a word is said publicly about certain appalling things going on amongst the highest of all, there is no end of conjecture about the rest.'

Kitty had never been able to discern the least value in gossip, let alone entertainment, and this whole affair still seemed nonsensical to her. She supposed that she could not stop the rumours if people were determined to believe them.

Later that same day, while examining some new merchandise which had arrived at the Huntley warehouse, Kitty found two things which were to have a startling effect on her future. One was a fan – not hand-painted, as was the custom; the other, an old and dusty book, exquisitely illustrated by hand and showing the complete jewellery collection of Queen Farenefi, child bride of the Pharoah Nkha.

First she examined the fan. It was set on sticks of blond tortoiseshell, picked out in gilt, and the leaves were so neatly decorated in yellow, blue, green and ivory that Kitty did think at first that it was painted. But on closer inspection she found that no paint was involved and that the picture – a cornucopia of fruit and flowers – appeared to be flush with the delicate vellum leaves. Thoughtfully she closed the fan, slipping it in to her pocket.

The book was ancient, shabby and cobweb-strewn, but when opened, the beautifully illustrated paintings of collars, necklets and head-dresses stood out like jewels. Strange, animal-headed gods carved from gold and turquoise, mystical symbols – eyes, beetles – stuck with gems, all of which had belonged to the twelve-year-old bride of Pharoah Nkha, who had been famous for his worship of the heavenly star, Sa-lu-is. The handwriting in thc book was faded and spidery but authoritative. There was a date, which might have been 1699 or 1600, she could not tell which. The jewellery, so the writer claimed, had disappeared en route from Egypt to its new owner, the Comte de Joffrac of Paris.

Already a dozen designs were teeming in Kitty's head for fans painted – or printed– with the animal-headed gods and the many faceted representation of the venerated star, Sa-lu-is. For replicas of Queen Faranefi's jewellery using more modern gems and precious metals, for materials coloured in the bright, lucid turquoise of the Egyptian gemstones, the like of which Kitty had never seen before. She thought of the coming audience with Queen Charlotte. If only she could have had material in this colour to show her. She could try mixing her paints – perhaps china blue and lemon yellow together would create a similar hue. The book, too, went in the capacious pocket of her cloak and then, getting in the Huntley's carriage, she ordered the coachman home to Hampstead.

The sky was a fragile, pellucid gauze, petalled with milky clouds. The sun beamed, yet its heat was not too intense. The road swarmed with phaetons and dog-carts carrying people to and from the spa. Ruddy, bulging faces peered out from under over-curled wigs topped with lace and plumes: ladies who wished to indulge in the pleasures of the flesh, grow blowsy and bloated, then rush to take the waters when apoplexy was imminent. Men who were on an ever turning treadmill, with brandy, port and rich repasts at one end and blood-letting, starving and spa-soaking at the other. Kitty never ceased to be thankful that her weight remained constant and that her appetite – despite her early experiences – was not excessive.

Her thoughts returning to the Egyptian jewellery, she recalled what she knew of Queen Charlotte's colouring.

'The wedding is to be brought forward,' Amalia blushed, dimpling at Kitty. 'The truth is – and I am telling only you, of course, Kitty – the truth is, I'm with child.'

Kitty leaped to her feet, hugging Amalia. 'That is marvellous news, Amalia! Oh, I am so pleased for you!

Does Lord Frederick know yet?'

'Oh yes, he was the first to know – after the physician, of course. Is it not exciting, Kitty – my own child, my very own! My lord is overwhelmed.'

Kitty thought of the half-finished sketches for Amalia's wedding gown, which was to be of quilted pearl satin embroidered with Lord Frederick's family emblem, the iris.

'I had better finish the design of your wedding gown tonight.'

'You will be my maid of honour, Kitty?' Amalia took her hands.

'I have said yes, I will not change my mind.' Kitty smiled.

Knowing that the wedding guests would include Lord Cromer and his fiancée had caused Kitty to say at first that she would prefer not to be so publicly in view. She would be happy, she said, to attend amid the throng of guests, but not in the forefront. However, after Amalia had been visibly upset at her refusal, she had relented. What would be a few more hours of unease after what she had endured in the past? For her dearest Amalia she would do it. But after, when the ceremony was over and Amalia and her new husband had set off on their honeymoon to the Italian lakes, Kitty planned to shut herself away in Huntley House and produce an entire new season's designs of gowns, fans, caps and jewels based on the Egyptian designs. It would take her mind of what she would never have: a honeymoon with a man whom she adored.

There were gasps of awed delight as Amalia drifted down the aisle of St Margaret's Church, Westminster, in the snowy, bountiful wedding gown Kitty had created for her.

The panniers were like unfurled wings ruched with priceless antique lace, the quilted satin stiff and regal as a Spanish Infanta's Court gown.

Behind her, moving slowly, came Kitty in a simple satin gown of softest eau-de-nil frilled discreetly with creamy lace, and carrying in her hands a tiny bouquet of rosebuds caught with a dark green velvet bow. She kept her gaze straight ahead, not wanting to meet Carrick's eye or that of his fiancée, but she knew that her cheeks were burning as Amalia, reaching the altar, handed Kitty her bouquet of roses, stephanotis and orange blossom.

The ceremony was very moving, and tears welled in Kitty's eyes. When the bride and groom looked at one another and then, again, at the end when they kissed, their eyes were overflowing with love and tenderness for one another. That is how it should be, thought Kitty, knowing that it would never be like that for her. Never.

After Amalia had left in her travelling gown of deep cornflower blue, Kitty went back to Huntley House. As soon as she walked in through its front door she felt bereft. She knew that she was foolish to feel this way, for Amalia and her husband would only be away for six weeks. It was not a final separation. And yet she did feel bereft. As she climbed into bed she noticed something on her bedside table. It was a package neatly tied with blue ribbon and her name was written on it in Amalia's large, generous scrawl.

Inside was a letter and some papers covered in minute print, the phraseology of which was obscure and verbose. Peering closely, Kitty managed to decipher some of the sentences, her mouth dropping open. She found that she was the owner of a small trading company very much on the lines of that belonging to the Huntleys – a company which needed only a name, which she was to provide, and which could be run along lines of her own choosing. All the details were there, all the legal technicalities, every aspect carefully thought out and neatly arranged by Amalia and her brother. Kitty laughed out loud, but there was a sharpness to her laughter. That day Amalia had gained a husband and she, Kitty, had gained a trading company. She knew which she would rather have.

The first set of replicas of Queen Faranefi's jewellery arrived at Huntley House the following week. Kitty could not wait to put them on. Skilfully made by Amalia's jeweller, Humphrey Lecoq, they were breathtakingly beautiful. Standing before her cheval glass, Kitty stared at herself open-mouthed. The crescent-shaped mock gold collar was studded with turquoises, lapis lazuli, and brilliant enamel lozenges in amethyst and scarlet. It seemed to alter Kitty's whole being as she took in her reflection. Quickly she fitted the matching chandelier earrings which seemed to shimmer with a strange celestial light, almost like an ethereal half halo across her throat from ear to ear. The rings on her fingers, the wide matching bracelets on her arms, she imagined herself as Faranefi, the Pharoah's child-bride, wondering, not for the first time, what Nkha and his wife had been like. How would it feel to be a queen at twelve years old? How different from her own pauper childhood.

Fingering the collar, she felt the raised star shape which centred each piece of jewellery. This was the venerated star, Sa-lu-is, which in the illuminated book glittered like diamonds. Lecoq had made the stars from cut glass, but they did not look as they should. They seemed lifeless, somehow. Kitty felt she knew how they should be: bright, dazzling, effervescing with light. Regretfully, she replaced the jewels in their leather, musk-scented case. Without them she felt denuded, spiritless. She hoped that her clients would be as eager to possess similar replicas or different versions of the same.

The letter arrived the next day. Dirty, finger-marked and tattered, it was brought by an urchin with bare feet and cropped head. Having given the boy some coins and sent him to the kitchens to eat his fill, Kitty opened the letter. It was dated two weeks earlier and was headed St Mary of Bethlehem Hospital. Who on earth could be writing to her from the lunatic asylum? She soon found out. Slowy she read:

I WRITE THIS LETTER FOR MADDY BROOKS WHO IS RESTRAINED HERE, COMMITTED FOR LUNACY, BY THE BEADLE OF THE PARISH OF OXLEY. SHE BEGS THAT YOU HEED HER REQUEST AND VISIT WITH HER.

Kitty went white. Maddy – her Maddy – committed to the dreaded Bedlam, the hospital for the irretrievably insane – a place from which few, if any, were ever released. How had it happened? Why had Maddy left Cromer Manor? She would go to her at once, of course. Calling for the carriage, she put on her cloak.

After her mistress had gone, Maddy had missed her desperately – as desperately as she had missed Jack all those years before. She had tried to settle down, flinging herself into work, but to little avail. Headaches began to plague her. Cook called them 'megrims' and dosed her with a concoction of peppermint, rosemary, betony and marjoram. Still the head pains continued, sometimes three attacks per week. And then the dreams started. Jack came to her, but he was a weeping, hollow-eyed skeleton.

She woke screaming as she heard the splash of his tears on his fleshless bones.

The other servants began to complain that Maddy was not keeping herself clean and neat, in that order.

'The new mistress when she arrives won't be wantin' a slattern for a maid.' Cook wagged her finger. 'Yer'll 'ave ter clean yerself up, gel.'

Maddy had stared at her, glassy-eyed. Cook's sleeping draught of opium and Indian hemp, sipped on and off throughout the night, was the only way she could find a semblance of rest, but it left her dazed and stupefied during the day. Hands trembling, Maddy tried to nod that she understood, but her neck felt like cottonwool and her head wobbled.

'Get those greasy clothes off, m'gel, and into the tub wi' ye,' Cook had instructed, Maddy obeying meekly.

Within a week things were as bad again. Maddy was unable to concentrate. Forgetful, she threw a priceless lace cloth onto the fire, then folded a polishing rag in tissue to store it away, only half comprehending the mayhem which broke out as a result.

When Cook told her that she was going to stop giving her the sleeping draught, Maddy became hysterical. First she begged on her knees that Cook would not withhold the brew which brought her the only peace she knew. Then, when Cook remained adamant, Maddy went red in the face and her heart seemed to swell, threatening to burst out of her ribs. Feeling as if she were choking, she could not restrain the sudden anger which pulsed through her body. Picking up one of Cook's mixing bowls, she dashed it across the room.

'You will give it me, you will, you will!' Maddy screamed.

Cook, white-faced, reached for the handbell which she

kept on the ledge and began to ring it violently. Soon the kitchen was filled with valets and grooms, maids and gardeners.

Once more Maddy screamed: 'You will give it to me, you will!' and then she sank to her knees, tears streaming down her face, her elbows pressed together, her hands clenched and tightly thrust against her mouth.

No one could prise her arms apart. She had to be half-dragged, half-carried out of the kitchen and up to her room in the attics, where she lay as if in a stupor, hearing voices like those of ghosts around her.

'Some sort of seizure. Is it apoplexy?'

'No, it cannot be, she is too young. Besides, she don't seem to be in any pain.'

'What are we going to do? If his lordship were 'ere . . .'

'But he is not, so we shall 'ave to find a solution for ourselves. Doctor Murchison is in the next village delivering triplets. If she is still like this on the morrow we shall 'ave to summon him.'

'She's not been right since the young mistress left. 'Tis a tragedy.'

'Save your sympathy for those that can serve ye, Doris.'

'Yes, I suppose you're right.'

The voices drifted away, as did Maddy into sleep. The doctor never did arrive, and by the time she had fought her way back to health she had decided that she must leave Cromer Manor. She knew that her mistress had gone to somewhere called Hampstead; she thought it was near London. She was going to search for her, because she knew that she could never be happy again if she did not find her.

She set out with less than Kitty had done. Wearing her Sunday best dress and her patched, threadbare cloak, she left. Fortunately she had recently acquired a good, stout pair of shoes, so she had no fears for her feet on the journey. It was quite the usual thing for country folk to walk for miles and Maddy had done it regularly until coming to the Manor to work. However, she had forgotten that she was weaker now after her illness, nor had she expected her cache of life-savings to disappear so quickly. With her last few coins she bought a large loaf of coarse bread, some apples, a wedge of cheese and a mug of fresh goat's milk. All might have been well, for she was not all that far from London even on foot, and despite her pallor and the loss of a few pounds in weight while she was ill, she was still an attractive girl in a sturdy, peasant way. Her russet curls were like a beacon wherever she went.

She caught the eye of a sea captain who, having been back in the country only two weeks, was busily ploughing his way through as many females as he could find. He had come to Heckley for the market, for its beer was renowned. Two weeks on land had only partially compensated for his six months at sea. As a rule he was a peaceable man who preferred his women to be willing, but he had a bellyful of Heckley ale, and when he saw Maddy finish her drink, replace the mug on the market stall, pick up her packages and start to wend her way out of the throng of buyers and sellers, he followed her.

Maddy was out of earshot of the market when she heard the twig crack behind her. She glanced round immediately, her back going cold. The sea captain was a big man, strong and sexually roused but, to be fair, he did try to tempt her into responding willingly to him. Any other girl might have done but not Maddy, with her lifetime's vow to be true to Jack.

''Tis none of your business!' she shouted at the sea captain's questions, but he coiled a powerful arm round her waist, dragging her to him, digging his erection into her stomach. At that Maddy bunched her fists, beating violently against the man's chest, but she might as well have been trying to break iron. He laughed, throwing back his head, his big yellow teeth like dirty amber against the tangle of his wiry black beard. He smelled of beer and tobacco.

The man caught her wrists, manacling them with his steely hands, while Maddy continued to fight and scream, kicking out, trying to get her knee into his groin. But she was like a puppet doll being manipulated by its master.

'There's a nice pad of moss over there, lassie. Come on now, why fight, it's going to happen anyway. I've been a long time at sea; a man's needs are urgent after a long voyage. I'll pay ye.'

'How dare you, how dare you! Get off me, get off me, let go!' Maddy screamed in reply.

Laughing, the man dragged her to the pad of moss and flung her down so hard that the breath was jarred from her body. Then, while he pinned her to the ground with one great sea boot, he undid his breeches, fondled himself for a few moments, grinning, while she stared up at him in terror, her face crimson and beaded with sweat. Seconds later he had crashed down on top of her, taking her breath away. With one burly arm across her throat, half-choking her, he dragged her skirts up and tugged at her pubic hairs before plunging his fingers inside her, scraping her with his nails until he drew blood.

Maddy wanted to scream but the forearm across her throat was taking her to the edge of blackness. Desperately she prayed for someone to come along the track and come to her aid, but no one did.

'You can't fool me,' the sea captain said. 'I know you're enjoying this. There's no girl on earth who doesn't enjoy a good swiving. Ye all pretend to be prim misses but when it comes down to it ye're all the same. Whores, all of ye.'

The next minute the man was bludgeoning his way between her legs, bruising his way through without thought for her feelings, convinced that once inside her she would begin to enjoy rutting with him. Breathing stertorously, his foul beard and tobacco-laden breath billowing into her face, the man pounded inside her savagely, tearing at the tender lining of her womanhood.

'Told ye – ye'd – enjoy – it – didn' I,' he panted, his face blotched, a scarlet rash flooding his chest.

One word slipped from Maddy's lips before she became unconscious: 'Jack.'

The man jettisoned his seed inside her then rolled away on his back, grunting. Not looking at her, he recovered his breath, fastened up his breeches, then stuck his hand in his pocket to draw out a coin, which he dropped at her side on the moss.

'Hey,' he said, prodding her with his boot. But she did not move. He began to feel uneasy then – not that he thought he had killed her, but if someone came along and saw her lying there as if she were dead he would have a lot of explaining to do. Within minutes he was out of sight, far down the track, taking a cut through a copse so that the trees would shield him from passers by.

Rain woke Maddy. Bemused, she stared up at the darkening skies as memory returned. Then her face crumpled and she wept. She had betrayed Jack. What had her life come to? Not so long ago she had been so proud, so clean and hard-working, loving her mistress and serving her well. Now she was little more than a hedge-whore, a girl who slept in the open and gave her favours to any man. She saw a coin gleaming on the moss but she would not pick it up, much as she needed it. No, she would never take payment for letting a man use her body. It had been against her will, she had loathed every minute of it. Now all she wanted to do was try to forget it.

Getting up, she swayed with dizziness. Having walked on a few paces she remembered her package of food and went back to find it. It had landed in a bush so she retrieved it. She had never felt less hungry but she knew that later on she would be glad of the bread and fruit. She was sure that she could not be far from Hampstead now. Oh, how she longed for the sight of her mistress's face. In the whole world there had been only two people she had loved: Jack and Mistress McDonagh. To have lost one of them was intolerable; to lose two of them was a tragedy.

Tramping on along the track, she kept her mistress's face in her mind. She knew that Mistress McDonagh would greet her kindly when she found her. That she had no idea where her mistress was seemed not to have occurred to Maddy for, although she seemed physically fit, there were parts of her brain which had been permanently affected by the drugs she had taken. But her optimism had not been affected, and it was that which carried her forward.

Some hours after she had finished her package of food, when she was faint from hunger, she begged work from a farmer's wife. For one week she fed the hens, scrubbed out the dairy, helped with the butter-making, turning the enormous, creaking churn until her arms screamed with the agony of it. She gathered fruit, chopping herbs and making preserves and medicinal concoctions for the household, helping in the kitchens when the labourers came in at mealtimes clamouring to be fed.

On the seventh day she woke with a scalding pain between her legs and found that the passage of water was unbearably painful. Examining herself, she found something which resembled a small abscess with a pitted centre, but when she pressed it she felt no pain.

She remembered a girl in her village who had contracted what was called the burning. She had gone to the city, become a whore and then returned to the village to die of the loathsome disease which was the result of her sinning.

Maddy felt strange and lightheaded, petrified and yet at the same time satisfied, for if she were being punished for her sins she need no longer feel guily for betraying Jack, even though it had been through no fault of her own. God had taken the matter into his own hands and He was punishing her. There was a bitter but necessary justification in that.

She could not stay at the farmhouse, of course. She felt weak and sick and was no longer able to rise at six am and work until late at night. Besides, she feared that she was contagious, that she might spread her disease to the farmer's children. One night she crept out with her few paltry possessions. In the weeks that followed she worked in the taproom of a seedy inn where the landlord plagued her with his attentions until finally she left. Then she gathered herbs and wild flowers for an old simple woman now crippled by the rheum, who also lived in the same village. At last her symptoms went and she wondered if she had been mistaken. She felt almost her old self again. There was no sign of any sores, and the burning pain on passing water had gone. So she began to work in a dairy again, spending the next few weeks in the homely reassuring tasks of scalding churns and vats, churning butter and patting it into its moulds, then printing it with the farmer's own emblem, an acorn.

Her illness had set her back but she still intended to get to Hampstead one day. However, that desire was to become more and more of a dream with each passing month, for she now felt unclean, unworthy. Would her mistress want a maid who had sordidly contracted a loathsome disease? What if she passed the contagion on to her mistress? What if it somehow lingered even though she believed herself to be cured now? So ran her thoughts, for she was pitifully ignorant on such matters.

Finally, longing overcame her fears and she set out again, tramping along the roads until she reached the perimeters of London where, for the first time in her life, she smelled the malodours of the polluted Thames, the wide open sewer of the city, and the stench of ordure piled in the streets. Dead animals left to rot where they had fallen. Bundles of rags on street corners which, on closer approach, proved to be human beings. Drunken women with their breasts exposed and half-starved babies on their hips or drooping from their arms. Ravening dogs in search of hands and ankles to crunch. Brightly painted carriages bowling through the filth and stench, their wheels not always missing the beggar children crouched by the roadside. A man and woman rutting openly in a doorway, the man with his breeches down and buttocks exposed. Little flower-sellers whose bodies were for sale also. Blowsy whores, breasts out-thrust, nipples rouged, who were anybody's for a penny; sneak thieves, child pickpockets, beggars and a myriad more debauchees, malingerers, vargrants and criminals.

The effect on Maddy was stupefying. Trying to gather her disjointed wits, she asked one or two people the way to Hampstead, but no one seemed to have heard of that place. Moved to pity by a skeletal beggar woman wearing only a thin, ragged shift, she gave her her own shawl and then watched, horrified, as the woman was bludgeoned around the head, the shawl snatched from her by an attacker who vanished in seconds with his booty. Maddy tried to help the woman, but her body was stiff and her eyes glazed with shock. She was dead. Stunned, Maddy gaped at the blood on her palm where she had touched the woman's head, hoping to help support her. She had caused the woman's death: she felt horribly guilty.

For all the filth, poverty and misery there was a ribald, hearty, devil-may-care atmosphere in the London streets. Whatever their sufferings, the people seemed determined and able to live with them. Finally she found someone who did know where Hampstead was, and directed her on the right road. Then she knew that she would soon be with her mistress again. She felt light, happy. Dusk was falling as she tramped across the fields. There was a liquid, silver crescent moon in the sky and now and again she heard the lowing of cattle, the bark of a fox, the rustle of rabbits and other small creatures in the undergrowth. All this pastoral beauty so close to the open sewer of London.

She was taking a short cut through a little copse when the men sprung out on her – five of them, all desperate, starving for money and sex. When each one had raped her, the others standing around watching, eager, sexually excited to the point of no return, they bludgeoned Maddy on the head and left her for dead.

When she came round, hours later, soaked, battered and bloody, she had lost her sanity.

CHAPTER TWELVE

The first thing Kitty saw inside Bedlam was a bevy of plumed, bewigged, laughing men and women dressed in the very latest fashions, two of the gowns being of her own design, though she did not recognise the wearers. When she realised what the men and women were doing she felt sick. On the other side of a ricketty barricade cowered a gaggle of lunatics who were being poked and prodded with sticks specially provided for this purpose.

'Stick that one with the boss eye,' one of the dandies nudged his companion. 'Look, he knows we're talking about him – he's slobbering with excitement. Like to be the centre of attention, do you?' The dandy shrieked with laughter.

The lunatic curled back his wet, shiny lips in a grimace which was meant to convey laughter. Then, seeing that he had everyone's full attention, he screamed a string of what he imagined to be the foulest epithets he could concoct. Over and over he repeated the words, until he collapsed in a heap on the floor, white foam bubbling from his mouth.

'Cardew, stick that woman next,' said the dandy, 'the one with the black hair. Where has she got her hand? Oh, she is a filthy one and no mistake.'

Kitty, watching, aghast, fought back waves of nausea. Not only for the terrible, pitiable and neglected condition of the lunatics, but for the manner in which they were being treated as entertainment. Poor, helpless, mad creatures.

'You are despicable, revolting,' she cried to the dandy and his companions. 'You ought to be ashamed, all of you. Yes, yes, ashamed! Those poor creatures have done you no harm. Have you nothing better to do with your time than to plague them?'

The dandy looked momentarily taken aback, his cheeks paling beneath their carmine rouge and black crescent patches. Then he said with a sneer: 'It seems that one of the lunatics has escaped.'

Furious, Kitty cried: 'Who is madder – the one whom God makes mad or the one who deliberately maddens others?'

'Is that a riddle, mistress?' The dandy, scented hand on hip, surveyed Kitty haughtily. 'I do so love a good riddle.'

'Then thank the Lord you still have the wits to appreciate them!' Kitty rejoindered. 'For those poor lost men and women do not.'

'Ye take too much upon yourself, mistress,' the dandy began, face glowering. But Kitty had gone, for she had not come to this wretched and horrifying place to cross swords with such as he.

Maddy was somewhere in this infamous building and that remained her only purpose for being here. It was unthinkable, of course, to consider Maddy here; there had been some misunderstanding. What had probably happened was that Maddy had been mistaken for a vagrant while on her way to find her mistress, and as some parishes took a very dim view of people who did not have a permanent address they shut them away. As soon as she found Maddy she would get her out of here and take her back to Huntley House.

Hearing a heart-wrenching scream in the distance,

Kitty shrank inside herself. What need was there of a Hell when this place existed? There was a sour, foetid smell in the air which turned her stomach. Only the thought of being out of here soon with Maddy kept her going along the corridor to where the overseer was to meet her.

She found him lounging on a shabby wooden bench. She was not sure whether he was a physician or a nurse or simply an attendant without qualifications. From two feet away she could smell that he was doused in scent of the cheapest variety, an artificial and pungent violet odour. But she could forgive him his liberality with perfume, for if she had to work in this place she imagined that she would want to drown its sour smell, too.

Leaping to his feet, the man bowed low. His nose had been broken at some time and had been reset crookedly, so that the left nostril was on the same side as the right. But he seemed amiable enough, although his eyes did keep straying to the purse at her waist in obvious expectation of a large tip. He requested that she follow him and they went along more corridors where the doors became heavier and more solid. Now and again she heard a moan, a cry or a scream, and she longed to be free of the ominous atmosphere.

'The woman is in here.' The overseer stopped outside a great studded door. Still amiable, he smiled broadly as he reached for the heavy iron keys at his waist, found the required one and fitted it into the lock. As the door swung open Kitty stepped forward, her face alight, ready to greet Maddy.

The first thing that assailed her nostrils was a choking, animal smell. In the gloom of the cell, which had only a tiny window high up, and that barred, Kitty saw a small hunched body lying on a narrow wooden bed.

'Maddy!' she gasped. Then, turning to the overseer, she

said. 'This cannot be right, this cannot be the woman I have come to see.'

The man opened his mouth to reply but, as he did so, a small croaking voice from the bed said: 'Mistress, Mistress McDonagh, is that you? Do not – do not come too close.'

Kitty was across the room in a flash, squatting down beside the bed and its pallid, shivering occupant.

'Maddy, what has happened to you? Is it really you? How did you get inside this terrible place?'

Slowly, painfully, Maddy told her some of the things which had happened to her since she left Cromer Manor. Shocked, Kitty said that she would have Maddy out of Bedlam within the hour.

'I wish you could, mistress,' Maddy raised her face from the conglomeration of rags and tattered matress on which she lay, so that Kitty could see her face more clearly. Maddy's mouth was a circle of livid, purulent sores.

'Do not ask me what I have, mistress,' Maddy went on. 'Do not question me. I have something foul and loathsome which no respectable woman should have. God forgive me.'

'With proper nursing you will get well,' Kitty insisted. 'I shall take you home and get a good physician for you.' Turning to the overseer she said angrily: 'Get this poor woman something refreshing to drink, some orange juice.'

'Ye'll be payin', mistress?' said the man.

'But of course,' replied Kitty, her voice heavy with contempt.

'Ye'll not mind being locked in here with the mad woman while I fetch the juice?'

'No, I shall not,' Kitty said.

When the man had gone she took Maddy's hands in her

own, although her maid flinched, drawing back her fingers and saying once, then again, that she was contagious, that her mistress must not touch her or she would be infected too.

'No, of course I shall not,' Kitty half-smiled, although she felt far from benign. 'I shall take you home and you can have a lovely hot bath, clean clothes and proper treatment, and you will soon be well again.'

'What I have is incurable, mistress. The men who raped me – I got it from them, that was how I got it. There, I've told you now.' Tears welled in Maddy's eyes.

'There is a cure, I am sure that there is a cure,' Kitty insisted.

'No, no cure, mistress.'

'I shall take you home all the same, Maddy. It is unthinkable that you remain in this place.'

'But I am not alone, mistress. Jack is with me.'

'Jack?' For a moment Kitty could not think what Maddy meant.

'Yes, Jack. You remember him – he was to marry me but he died – a horse kicked him in the head. Broke my heart, it did. I thought he was dead, but he is not, you know. He is here in this room with me; he is standing behind you now and grinning at me.'

Gooseflesh crept along Kitty's shoulders and down her back. Maddy must have a fever and be suffering from delusions.

At that moment the key grated in the lock, making Kitty jump with fright, and then the overseer was in the room and handing her a jug of watery fruit juice. Holding the lip of the jug to Maddy's mouth, she helped her drink.

'You can see how weak I am,' Maddy said between gulps. 'I have not the strength to walk out of here. But I could not go now anyway. Jack is here, you see. I knew that I would find him again one day, I knew that we would be together again. Is it not strange that I came all this way to find you, mistress, and instead I found Jack? I did not know what I really wanted, you see, but God knew and so I have it now. My Jack. He will never leave me again, we shall always be together. He stays here in this room with me – he never goes away now.'

Kitty listened with sinking heart, realising that Maddy had no fever, for her brow was cool, her eyes normal in their brightness. Did she really think that Jack was with her, her tortured mind producing for her the one being whom she believed could provide her with comfort and protection?

'I am going to get you out of here, Maddy.' Tears blurred Kitty's vision. 'I shall not be long, I am going to speak to the person in charge of this hospital. You should not be in here.'

At the door Kitty blew a kiss.

'Don't go without saying goodbye to Jack,' Maddy instructed, almost arrogantly.

Swallowing, a shiver tingling across her body, Kitty said: 'Goodbye, Jack,' before following the overseer out into the corridor and waiting while he locked the door.

Silently she followed the man to the superintendent's office, where she spoke to the woman who was in charge that afternoon.

'There has been some mistake,' she began. 'The young woman whom you have taken into the hospital – her name is Maddy Brookes. I want to take her out of here immediately, this afternoon. I shall be caring for her myself at home.'

The assistant superintendent, a square-faced woman with hair the colour of undyed wool and of a similar cushiony texture, stared blankly at Kitty.

'Take her out? I am afraid that will not be possible.'

'She is my maid – was my maid. I want to care for her now that she is so sick.' Kitty's mouth felt wooden, her hands were trembling.

'As I said, that will not be possible. The girl has been certified insane. We do not have sane people in our establishment. This is St Mary of Bethlehem Hospital for the Insane. Surely you realise that? The insane,' the woman said again, as if she revelled in the use of that word.

'But she is not insane!' Kitty cried, 'she is just very sick. She has been through a terrible experience trying to find me.'

'Then you have no one but yourself to blame for her condition.' The superintendent glanced at her hands. They were rough and red, with bitten nails.

'That is beside the point and for my own conscience,' Kitty said. 'What we are discussing now is the fate of that maidservant. As I said, I wish to take her home and care for her myself.'

'There is no way that a lunatic can be removed from here, not even by the next of kin, never mind an employer.' The superintendent rose, shoulders squared. 'Even were it in my power to free this patient I would not do it. She has been certified insane, by the medical authorities. You do know what disease she has contracted?'

Kitty nodded. 'I have guessed.'

'You do know the course this disease runs? Even if she were not insane now she soon would be. The end is terrible, the victim bestial, violent and with nauseating physical symptoms. Sufferers have been known to commit murder in the final stages of this disease.' The woman was blinking a great deal and after every half dozen or so rapid movements of her eyelids she looked away.

'I am sure that with tender care, careful nursing and the right food . . .'

'There is no cure, mistress. We have kindly allowed you to see this woman, against our better judgement I might add, for the contagion is virulent.'

'I insisted on seeing her,' Kitty said quietly, although her heart was hammering loudly in her breast.

'That is true, you did insist, but normally we would not allow anyone such intimate contact.'

'Yet there is a crowd of onlookers baiting some of your patients in the forecourt. They actually seem to be prodding them with sticks and jeering at them. Do you not fear contagion there?'

'None of those wretches has a contagious disease, mistress.' The eyelids continued to blink convulsively.

'Is it regular practice to allow the public to come here and taunt the lunatics?'

'I do not see that it is any concern of yours, mistress. How we run this hospital . . .'

'Hospital you call it? What kind of medical care are these poor people receiving? I have seen none so far! Exposed to taunts and jeers, locked away in filthy cells.'

'Money is short.'

'Cleanliness costs nothing.'

'This is no concern of yours, mistress. You cannot take your maidservant away for she has been certified insane and that is an end to it.'

Having left the room in furious anger, Kitty immediately marched back to fling a purse of sovereigns on the woman's desk.

'Here, you say you are short of money, well, this will pay for Maddy Brooks to be given every comfort – a soft bed, clean linen, fresh fruit and meat – and I will send

Lord Huntley's physician to her tomorrow.'

'That will not be possible, mistress, but the luxuries shall be attended to. Our physicians here are excellent and Brookes is receiving their full attention.'

Kitty's face whitened, her eyes brilliant as sapphires. '*Mistress* Brookes is most certainly *not* receiving their full attention! However, these sovereigns will alter that, of course, will they not?'

With that Kitty left.

A few hours later, accompanied by Lord Huntley, Kitty came out of the residence of the Huntley's physician. She was downcast and Huntley had his arm around her to comfort her.

'I will not rest, I will get her out of that monstrous place!'

'Of course, Kitty,' Huntley said, not sounding convinced.

'You do not think I can, do you? Oh, she was so loyal to me – so devoted – why did this have to happen to her? I was going to send for her . . .'

'People get sick all the time, Kitty. And as for her setting out alone on the roads, well, she should have known better.'

'The poor travel like that all the time. What other means do they have of getting from one place to another?'

'You know more about that than I do. All the same, cutpurses and footpads abound on the highway.'

'She had nothing with her to steal except her womanliness,' Kitty's voice was low. It was all of eighteen months since she had vowed never to be at a man's mercy again, but for Maddy it was too late. No, it must not be too late!

'Huntley, I am going to the Queen. If Doctor Scott will not help us then I will go to the highest in the land.'

'The Queen? She is extremely sensitive on the subject of

madness, Kitty. With the King's mental condition being what it is . . .'

Richard Warren, the King's physician, had, in confidence, told the Duchess of Devonshire's mother that the King was mad and she had communicated this to Lord Frederick, who had told Amalia. The general public had been told a variety of stories about the King's illness: that he had dropsy and gout, a fever, melancholia. At one time his life had been despaired of, and, indeed, the previous November it had been believed that the King had died. Finally, to quash this belief, Doctor Warren had written a declaration stating that His Majesty had passed a quiet night but without any abatement in his complaints. After the declaration in the Morning Chronicle the rumours had evaporated.

'Surely it will make the Queen more sympathetic to my plea, not less, Huntley?' Kitty said. 'She will have some idea of what I am going through, will she not?'

'Your heart is in the right place, Kitty.' Huntley squeezed her arm.

'Not at the moment, Huntley – at the moment it is in Bedlam.'

Queen Charlotte Sophia of Mecklenburgh-Strelitz was a plain, serious-faced woman with a wide, humourless mouth and a long slender body with narrow shoulders. Whatever the Queen lacked in sparkling vivacity and light-heartedness, she more than compensated for by being a loving, devoted and faithful wife to the King and the mother of a very large family, all of whom were adored. Had Queen Charlotte been presented to King Henry the Eighth as his prospective bride it would have been a disaster as great as that of his marriage to Anne of

Cleves. In fact, she suited King George admirably, for he too was a plain-living, simple man, who, totally faithful, divided his time between his Queen, his children and his books.

Making a deep obeisance before the Queen, Kitty proceeded to tell Her Majesty of her dilemma. While speaking she noticed how the Queen had changed. She seemed altogether smaller and more bowed; she was very pale and her eyes dull. When Kitty had come to the Court to show her designs to Her Majesty, the Queen had been altogether brighter and more responsive – and so pleased with the sketches that she had ordered gowns for herself and all her daughters for their next public appearance.

Kitty had been carefully instructed about Court etiquette. She remained standing while telling the Queen about Maddy.

'Faithful servants are decidedly too few,' the Queen said when she had finished. Her Majesty, who spoke firmly and with a chunky German accent, seemed preoccupied.

'I could not agree with you more, Your Majesty,' Kitty said, lifting her shoulders a little and opening one hand, palm uppermost.

'Doctor Warren will know what to do . . .' the Queen's voice tailed off as if other thoughts were invading her mind, which indeed they were – thoughts of her beloved husband being forced to sleep apart from her for five months because of his perplexing illness; of the bevy of treatments which had been applied to the King without success: a diet of asses' milk, the waters at Cheltenham, rhubarb pills, a strong physic of castor oil and senna, laudanum, bark*, James's Powder . . . the linen

*Quinine

swaddling used to restrain His Majesty when he became turbulent. To see such a great monarch as her darling husband being constantly dosed, restrained and confined in such an unkingly manner upset Queen Charlotte almost as much as it upset King George.

When Doctor Warren joined them he did not look as if he had been racking his brains for days to think of fresh treatments which would cure the King. Nor did he look like a medical man. Wealthy, highly successful and sought after now that he was treating the King, Warren had society as well as the King eating out of his palm. Yet the fact was that Richard Warren loved golden guineas more than he did his patients, and it was said of him by the more cynical that when he inspected his own tongue in the mirror, he would automatically remove a guinea piece from his right pocket into his left.

Kitty did not like the look of him. She thought that his expression was venal, that, as she told him of Maddy, he was paying far more attention to the cut of her clothes, the richness of the fabric, the few pieces of jewellery that she wore. As to his professional response she could not complain. His questions were competent, thorough and, certainly on the face of it, sincere. When he had finished cross-examining her, Kitty told him that she regretted she could tell him no more about her maid's state of health.

'It sounds like a mild case – easy to treat. When you have removed the young woman from the Bethlehem Hospital I shall be pleased to treat her myself.'

'A mild case?' Kitty's face lit up. 'Then you think she can be cured?'

'But of course.' Having polished his immaculately manicured nails upon the lapel of his exquisitely-cut jacket, Doctor Warren admired their sheen.

Kitty felt weak with relief. 'Oh, I am so glad, Doctor

Warren! Will you help me get her out of the Bethlehem Hospital, for that seems to be the first hurdle?'

'But of course. It will be no trouble – no trouble at all. Indeed, I am surprised that she is in there at all, having no money.'

'It is true that she had no money when she was found, Doctor Warren, but I have left money to pay for her care.'

'Good.' Having noticed a speck of pus on his jacket sleeve, the Doctor grimaced. He must change his attire immediately, then he would get this maidservant creature out of the lunatic asylum and experiment upon her with some of his new cures. He was desperately short of victims on whom to experiment and one could hardly admit that the King of England was one's major guinea-pig. The brilliant-eyed, spirited young woman standing before him, despite her tasteless concern for her servant, was as ignorant as anyone about medical matters. With this serving-maid, as with the King, he would have a totally free hand: be God. Doctor God. He smirked to himself. Doctor God . . . With the power of life and death in his hands. That it was mostly death was beside the point. It was the power, the glory and the gold – not necessarily in that order – which interested him.

Coughers filled his coffers. The infirmities of the old brought him gold. To have confidence, that was all one needed: the confidence to gull one's patients and their families. One day he would hit on the right cure for King George and he would be hailed as a physician who could work miracles. But there was a limit to what he could try on the King at any one time, and, being a society doctor, he rarely saw the more mundane levels of insanity. For all he knew this creature – this Maddy Brookes – might provide the very key that he needed.

Part Two

THE MERCHANT OF VENICE

Love sought is good, but giv'n unsought is better.
Shakespeare. Twelfth Night.

CHAPTER THIRTEEN

The Venice Trading Company. Kitty smiled to herself. That was the name she had chosen for her business venture and she was delighted with it. The Venetians had long been famous for their great trading empire and theirs was a city of art and dreams and marvels, with exquisite designs, and a history, much like herself, in fact. So it seemed appropriate that her first trip as owner-manger of her own company should be to Venice itself.

She had tracked down the man who was pioneering the art of printing fans instead of painting them so that they could be mass-produced and, more exciting still, she had learned of the Count Tomaso Vincenti Barraccani, the man who now owned the jewels of Queen Faranefi. A strange, eccentric recluse who had in his day been something of a lecher and womaniser, the Count Barraccani now lived in a villa on one of the Venetian canals. He had not set foot out of doors for ten years so it was reputed, and it was unclear how he had acquired the Egyptian Queen's jewellery. Theft seemed improbable, for he was a wealthy and respected man, and had been the favoured friend of monarchs in his younger days. Nonetheless, the fact remained that the jewels had disappeared on their way to a Frenchman something like a century before.

Kitty was avidly curious to meet the Count and to see the jewels while she was in Venice commissioning the fanmaker, and treasure-hunting for materials, leather, lace and velvets.

She was very nearly packed, her passage was booked and she intended to stay in Italy for as long as was practicable. All was under control in London, her designs were being made up as usual, there was a date three months hence for another gala fashion show, and Amalia was keeping an eye on matters until she returned, for Amalia and her Lord Frederick were now back from their highly successful honeymoon in Italy.

Amalia had been full of sympathy over the tragedy of Maddy. That Doctor Warren had been too late to save her maidservant would give Kitty cause for guilt for the rest of her life. Maddy had died within hours of Kitty visiting her at the Bethlehem Hospital. Her last words had been a whisper, 'Jack, I'm coming, Jack . . .' and then she died, apparently quite peacefully. Kitty had been extraordinarily upset by the news and guessed that it was because the girl's tragic death had revived memories of her dead family.

After a few quiet, thoughtful days of prayer and meditation, Kitty stirred herself into action, naming her business the Venice Trading Company and mentally preparing herself for the new venture. She could barely wait to see the jewels of Queen Faranefi and the richly magnificent splendours of Venice.

Amalia learned of the whereabouts of the Pharoah's gems while on honeymoon. It seemed to be no secret in Italy. Amalia had sent word by despatch to Kitty, who had written to Count Barraccini at once. His reply had been rapid and extremely warm. Yes, by all means she must come and visit him and see the jewels while she was in Venice: any date would be convenient if she would give him a little advance warning. Friends of Amalia and Lord

Frederick lived within easy distance of Venice, and they too would be pleased to meet Kitty while she was there, so it seemed that the scene was set for a very pleasurable trip.

'If the Count is not as friendly as he seems, go straight to Gwendolyn,' Amalia said. 'She will be expecting you whenever you arrive. While it seems that Count Barraccini is getting on in years, and rarely seen in public these days, it is true that he was a great libertine in his youth. One does not want to land in a dangerous situation, and be at his mercy, does one?'

Kitty had laughed. 'If he is still a lecher at seventy, then I shall of course make straight for Gwendolyn, but I do not think that I have anything to worry about on that score. His letters are so sincere, so open.'

'Even so, take no risks, my dear. Remember what happened to Maddy when she ventured out into the world, and be sure that it does not happen to you.'

'I shall take care, never fear, Amalia. Truly I feel in the mood for an adventure to take my mind off things. I shall return all in one piece, I can assure you.'

Now her passage was booked on the *Adriatic Pearl* and all she had to do was to say goodbye to her friends in Hampstead.

CHAPTER FOURTEEN

At the tap on her cabin door, Kitty opened it to see a ruddy-faced boy standing there.

'Captain's compliments, Mistress McDonagh. If you would care to join him at his table this evening at eight of the clock?'

'Thank you, please tell the Captain that I will be pleased to accept his invitation.'

Kitty turned back to her hand luggage. The invitation posed a problem, for she had not dressed for a social occasion. She was wearing a travelling gown in the colour which she had named Egyptian blue and which was a direct copy of the colour of lapis lazuli, with a perky little hat in blue and white striped silk with peacock-green feathers dipping at the brim. Mellyn, the Welsh girl she had hired to accompany her during the journey, would be of little use for she was, at this very moment, lying groaning in her bunk in the next cabin, the victim of a decimating bout of seasickness.

Sitting on her bunk while she considered what she would wear that evening, Kitty's thoughts returned to that other sea voyage which she had taken with Fabian six years before. What a child she had been then, how ignorant and unaware, an innocent, infantile creature having no notion of what the future would bring. Yes, what a child – a victim of adversity. But she was no longer a victim. Today she was an adult, a woman of the world, something of a pioneer, one could even say a fashion-setter. She had striven to give herself everything that she wanted – that was, everything that was in her power to obtain. Of the other, the one thing that she could not have, well, she must put that aside, think of it as a business loss, which indeed it was.

A business loss! How much she had adjusted to her new rôle in life. Was she getting cynical? She truly hoped not.

'Fabian,' she spoke his name aloud and it hung on her lips like a wraith, a ghost from the past. Lifting her fingers, she brushed it from her mouth with a stoical resoluteness. *You cannot put back the clock*. No, nor put the clock forward until you were ready, and she was ready now.

At five minutes to eight she was dressed and ready in a gown of oyster taffeta embroidered with sea-green and sea-blue irises, the Cromer colours which she still liked to wear in memory of Fabian. She wore a necklace of green peridots, with matching earrings and bracelets, matching velvet ribbons and black osprey feathers in her hair.

Mellyn had tried to get up to help her dress and to coil up her hair, but after a few faltering steps she had gone so deathly white that she was forced to retire to her cabin. Having seen to her maid's needs, Kitty had set about getting herself ready. It was no hardship, not after a lifetime of such activity. If it had been she would long ago have found someone to replace Maddy. But perhaps the truth was that she would find it hard ever to replace her. She had chosen Mellyn because her lilting accent and dark, Welsh looks could never remind her of Maddy's beacon-red hair and sturdy, Home Counties accent.

A tap on the door announced the Captain's messenger boy.

'If ye'll follow me, mistress,' the boy said, which she

did, stretching out her arms to balance herself against the oak-panelled walls of the passageway. Knowing how narrow corridors were on board ship, she had purposely worn a skirt with reasonably small panniers.

Fortunately the sea was calm and the ship did not lurch as she followed the boy through the intricate network of corridors with the creak and groan of the *Adriatic Pearl* in her ears, the smell of tar, hemp and scouring soap in her nostrils.

From inside the Captain's dining-room came the hubbub of conversation, the scent of food and wine mingling with beeswax. Kitty knew very little about the Captain but she hoped to ask him some questions about Venice and the trading routes. She smiled at the cabin boy as he held open the door for her and she stepped over the threshold. She had to move carefully as she did so, lifting her skirts, for the threshold was raised quite a few inches.

'My God, not *you*! were the first words she heard.

'*You*!' she cried, as she saw who had spoken.

Carrick dwarfed the little dining room, standing before her like a primeval god, thick bronze hair burnished by the lamplight, his eyes incredulous on seeing her. He was wearing buff-coloured breeches, gleaming black top boots and spotless linen, with a dark jade green jacket embroidered tastefully in bronze silks. Had he been wearing sacking rags, he would have looked equally magnificent, handsome and heart-stopping.

Kitty swallowed, unable to find her voice. Somehow, she managed a taut smile, while colour raged in her cheeks. How was she going to eat in front of him? How could she sit down at the same table with him? She wanted to curse at him, to hit him, kick him, but most of all she wanted to fly into his arms and be kissed a thousand times over.

The Captain beamed happily. 'So you two know each other, do you? How fortunate, then I do not have to introduce you,' and with that he ordered the dinner to be served.

Kitty sat as far away as she could from Lord Cromer, but that was not far enough in this small room. There were five other guests, most of whom looked like merchants. Not wishing to make a scene and determined that she would not run off like a coward, Kitty smiled as the Captain introduced her to them. Throughout, she worked very hard at averting her eyes from Lord Cromer, which was not easy, for she was overpoweringly conscious of his nearness. He made the merchants, with their plump ruddy faces and plain clothes, look like homely little gnomes. What on earth was he doing on this ship? Where could he be going?

And then, as she sipped her wine and tasted the somewhat tough beef which was over salted, over spiced and yet virtually tasteless, a thought struck her. Carrick Cromer travelled widely, it was his business after all, the work that he had inherited from his uncle. When she had chosen a ship that would take her to her destination she had been most careful not to select one which she recognised and which had belonged to Fabian's fleet. She had been quite sure that the *Adriatic Pearl* was not one of the Cromer fleet, but of course, as they were expanding, the company might have acquired this ship. Anyway, it was too late now, whatever the reason. She would fix her mind on how loathsome he was, how contemptuous, callous, avaricious, self-seeking, lecherous and faithless. Not necessarily in that order. She never wanted to see him again let alone have to sit at the same table with him. His arrogance was insupportable, his prejuidce ungovernable. She thought all these things and more, with all the strength that she could muster, in her firm determination to erect an impenetrable barrier between them.

The wine was mundane and lacked sparkle; the food she would not have given to a dog – not that it seemed to be displeasing the merchants or the Captain, for they were all munching, crunching and chomping while quaffing great draughts of the wine and asking for their glasses to be refilled. It would have been a convivial scene had Carrick Cromer not been there. It would have made it much easier too if one or two of the merchants had brought along their wives. As it was, she was the only woman present.

The pungent scent from the oil lamps in the enclosed space was particularly nauseating. Perhaps it was this which made the merchant on her left, a cloth trader, start to choke, and turn an interesting shade of vermilion. Cromer rose instantly, strode round the table, and slapped the man hard on the back.

'Thank ye, thank ye, m'lord,' the man spluttered, gasping for breath. 'Stupid o' me, swallowed that hunk o' meat unchewed.'

Having spoken, and apparently partially recovered, the man suddenly made a guttural noise and slumped over the table.

'A seizure of the heart!' cried the Captain, instructing his cabinboy to fetch the ship's doctor as quickly as possible. The doctor would have been dining with them had a sailor not broken his leg only an hour or so earlier.

When the merchant had been carried out on a canvas stretcher made from a sail, Kitty turned to the Captain. Even though the man was beginning to recover from what, after all, had been only a slight seizure, she no longer felt like socialising and she told the Captain this, thanking him for his invitation and his hospitality.

As soon as she had finished speaking, Lord Cromer took her arm. 'I will escort you back to your cabin, Mistress McDonagh,' he said, quirking one dark bronze brow.

'Thank you, my lord, but I do not need escorting,' Kitty retorted haughtily, snatching her elbow away, and with that she made a rapid but dignified exit from the dining-room and along the narrow passageway which reeked of tar.

It grew darker as the light of the Captain's room faded behind her. She should have asked for the cabinboy, who would have guided her with a lighted lamp in his hand, but he was helping the physician. She would find her way, of course – she had an excellent head for direction. They had turned left here – or was it right? All the oak-panelled walls, the doors, looked alike. Pressing on, she came to another turning. By now it was very dark and the creaking and groaning of the ship's timbers was eerie and disconcerting. Was a storm brewing up, for the floorboards seemed to be tilting sharply? She wished that she were tucked up in her bunk, hard as it was.

Despairing of ever finding her way back, and as the ship tilted sharply, she clung to a lamp-fitting projecting from one of the walls. She imagined that somewhere up on deck the wind must be howling like a crazed beast, yet down here all she could hear was the noise of rending and straining oak. The ship suddenly tilted so violently in the opposite direction that her grip on the lamp-fitting was loosened and she was flung across the corridor in a most ungainly fashion, cracking her elbow and wincing with the pain.

And then what little light remained was blocked out by the massive bulk of a man's body. With all the noise that the ship was making she had not even heard him approach.

'That offer of an escort is still open,' an amused voice said, and as the ship rolled again she found herself pinioned by despotic arms which would not let her go.

'An offer, you said?' she glared up at him. 'This is hardly an offer – this is more like being chain ganged!'

'Some men who are chain ganged find that life at sea is the perfect setting for them.' Carrick Cromer's eyes twinkled but she could not see them in the dimness.

'And many find that they loathe it and cannot wait to get away!'

At her words, he dropped his arms so suddenly that she had to clutch at his jacket sleeves to stop herself falling.

'I thought you said that you would not take up my offer?' He smiled laconically.

'Indeed I am not!' Kitty cried, snatching back her hands and, with arms outstretched on either side, attempting to make her way back down the corridor.

He let her struggle on for some yards before calling out, 'By the way – you are going in the wrong direction. That is the way to the sailors' quarters. But I am sure that they would be pleased to see you – they are lamentably short of female company on board ship. Have a good time – you should make a handsome profit. They tell me that one can get accustomed to anything on board ship, even making love in a hammock.'

'You swine! You insulting, despicable swine!' Kitty cried, her cheeks scarlet.

'Such mild insults, Mistress McDonagh. Surely a lady of your reputation can concoct something a little more colourful than that? I have been called worse things in my time by dairymaids.'

'I can quite imagine it!' Kitty raged. 'There can be few women who have not had cause to curse you at one time or other.'

'Is my reputation as great as that?' Carrick grinned, hands on hips, feet apart, in true swashbuckling pirate style, while Kitty was struggling not to crash to the ground. He was grinning broadly while tears of anger were forming behind her lids.

'It is late, we cannot stand here all night exchanging repartee in this childish fashion.' Kitty flung up her head.

'Childish fashion – ah, now that is phrase with which you are well acquainted, Mistress McDonagh. I believe that you are attempting to make a livelihood from it.'

'You are the most gross, insulting man I have ever had the misfortune to encounter,' Kitty said through gritted teeth. 'My designs are not childish fashion, as you insinuate – they have been very well received and are highly successful.'

As he did not reply she began to walk along the corridor towards him, averting her eyes and struggling to regain her dignity. As she came nearer he folded his arms one across the other, surveying her as if he were a mighty Emperor selecting a new odalisque for his harem. But he did not attempt to move.

'If you will let me pass!'

'Now, how can I prevent it?'

'By standing in my way as you are doing.'

'As in so many things your judgement is erroneous,' he replied, before moving aside to let her pass.

As she walked along she could hear his boot heels thudding behind her and she was consumed by a powerful desire to shout back at him: 'Go away, *go away*!' but she restrained herself.

About to turn left, she heard him command: 'Right!' and her inner confiict made her cheeks burn more brightly. Was the right way as he had directed or was he deliberately leading her astray? She knew that she no more wanted to be instructed by him in the right way than she did in the wrong.

'You do not believe me.' Nonchalantly he leaned against the wall, looking like a giant in the enclosed space, and apparently quite unaffected by the roll of the ship.

'Give me one good reason why I should ever believe one word you say,' she retorted, glad that her enveloping skirts concealed from him the ungainly manner in which she was having to keep her legs wide apart to retain her footing.

'How different things were when we last met . . .' He sounded almost as if he were musing.

'Oh, *that*.' Furious at being reminded, she turned down the corridor, to feel his hand clamping her arm.

'I said not that way. It seems to me, Mistress McDonagh, that you have spent the whole of your life going along the wrong paths.'

'That is untrue, of course, totally untrue. But if it weren't, do you have the information which would put me in the right direction? Are you setting yourself up as some sort of teacher, an authority on wayward women?' She tugged at his fingers, trying to release their vice-like grip, but she was only too well aware of his strength and knew that her feeble efforts were as ineffectual as butterflies' wings beating to get out of a glass container. Finally, in exasperation, she cried: 'You have no right to try to stop me!'

'Then let me take you back to your cabin.'

'And then you will leave me in peace?'

'What else?'

'What else, indeed,' she stormed, allowing him to take her arm and lead her in the opposite direction.

He seemed to know everything about the *Adriatic Pearl*, all its corridors and decks, gangways and ladders, and very soon they were standing outside her cabin door. Reaching out her hand, she opened it, stepping over the high threshold into her room as rapidly as she could. She did not trust him: she wanted to have the door safely shut and locked behind her as soon as possible. She did not even stop to call goodnight or thank you.

Even so, she did not have time to think or to react to the deft, beautifully-controlled muscular power of him as he wrenched the door from her hand, stepping in behind her and closing it so that they were caged in the little room: the virile, omnipotent nephew of the Great Sea Lord and the fiery Irish peasant girl.

It was like history repeating itself, and she might have remembered it as such if there had been anything in Carrick to remind her of Fabian. But there was not. Fabian had been her father, her lord protector all rolled into one, and Carrick was her lifetime's love, her destiny, her karmic lover. For a moment there was terror in her eyes as she backed away from him, clutching at the harsh wood of her bunk while the floor slanted sideways.

As his mouth came down on hers she closed her lids, and her mind seemed to fill with a shimmering light. As if from a great distance, she saw a star coruscating in a black void, its spangled iridescence compelling her to bow to it. She was manacled by Carrick's arms, and yet the star was calling her and she was moving towards it inexorably. Yet her movement was not taking her away from Carrick. Far from it. For he too, in a strange, inexplicable way, seemed to be part of the star, as was she.

Her narrow bunk had seemed hard and lumpy when she had sat down on it alone, but now that Carrick was gently placing her there it might have been swansdown. And there was no longer any storm, only the electrical impulses darting backwards and forwards between their bodies . . .

His kisses were erotic and scintillating; she seemed to have been ravenous for them for years. She was the dish and goblet, he was the meat and wine, and he was filling her, filling her, with love. She had been clay which he could model and fashion into shape as he desired, and desire her he did, that was obvious.

'How did you engineer this little jaunt – have you been following my movements?'

For a moment anger broke through her bliss. 'It seems that every time we meet you accuse me of something underhand. What a woman of many parts you would have me – a harlot, an adventuress, a liar and a confidence trickster – and now a spy following your every movement. Perhaps I might have time for such activities if there were a hundred hours in each day and I did not have a living to earn. My designs,' she added firmly.

'Oh yes, the childish fashions,' he grinned, jewelling her forehead with kisses and then her nose, her cheeks, her chin, and finally her mouth, which received a ruby kiss, full-blooded and passionate, rich with feeling and emotion.

'If they are childish fasions then that makes the women who wear them children,' she retorted, dragging her mouth from his, but with a great effort.

'Most of them are, empty-headed, superficial children who will never grow up, pampered and spoiled from the moment they are born until the day they die.'

'Have you forgotten that one of them is your betrothed?'

'No.'

'Surely you are not planning to marry a child?'

'No.'

'So at least one of my customers is a mature lady who appreciates original designs?'

He did not reply. So there was loyalty of a kind somewhere inside him, even if he did not hesitate to betray his fiancée whenever the occasion arose. Having thought that, she wondered how many other women he was bedding or had bedded in the past, but the moment her mind formulated that question it received its reply: none now but you, and she knew, without hesitation, that this reply was the correct one.

Time sped by but neither was aware of it – they had thoughts only for one another. A molten silence seemed to have fallen over them so that neither spoke and yet all feeling, all emotion and thought was transmitted just the same. Gently, Carrick removed her clothes, which was something of a relief, for it had not been comfortable bunched into a bunk while wearing cumbersome panniers. The lacing of her bodice undone, he slid it over her shoulders and breasts, now covered only with a fine toile de Paris under-bodice edged with lace. She wore no stays, which seemed to amaze Carrick.

'This is your true shape,' he said wonderingly. 'That neat little waist is all your own.'

'It is indeed,' Kitty smiled, coiling her arms around his neck. 'I hope eventually so to influence fashion that women will abandon their corsets and wear more loose classical styles – like the one I wore at the Duchess of Cheshire's masque.'

'All women aren't as shapely as you, Kitty.'

'Is shape so important?'

'To a man it is. A woman has to go in and out in the right places. I thought that was understood.'

'It is – but men, dandies that is, they wear corsets, too . . .'

'Why are we talking of such mundane things? What I really wanted to tell you was . . .' he paused, looking as if his thoughts had caught him unawares. 'What I wanted to tell you was,' he paused again, looking faintly astonished and then, in silence, stood up, but only so that he could help her to her feet while she unlaced her skirts and panniers until she stood there, touchingly diminutive, in her toile de Paris shift, and white silk stockings caught at the knee with garland-embroidered garters. Next he took the pins out of her hair so that it tumbled onto her shoulders, dark and luxuriant like silky fur. In seconds he was undressed too and they were lying pressed close together in the bunk.

Passion was pulsing in her veins as he pushed down her shift, kissing her heavy, naked breasts, lapping her nipples with his tongue until they hardened like pearls. He was hard too, pulsing with ardour. Encircling him with her hand was like holding that source of immense power generated by the universe. All meaning, all purpose, reason, need and intention, was coursing between them as if they were the archetypal lovers, the creation, and, at the same time, the opus.

Later she would understand things about love which she had never realised before, but for the moment she was borne along by the radiation of sexual joy, the knowledge that she was in the arms of a man who was her love god, her entire body thrilling to his touch. It seemed entirely right that she should be there with him, beneath him, pliant, expectant, for she had learned long ago that the only time she was truly alive, truly knowing the purpose for her existence was when she was in his arms. It seemed a miracle that they should have found one another, that their desires and passions were in unity, the very rhythm of their love-making like a beautifully long rehearsed and graceful dance. It was as if they had been making love from the beginnings of time.

All time, all love, seemed to converge, the past falling away, the future beckoning, as he slid deeply inside her. She clung to him, Venus with her Mars, and there was no longer famine, starvation, nor death in the world, no anguish, suffering or pain, sickness or loneliness, but only the ageless meaning of their mystical union. Man and woman, the two halves of God, coming together again as if they had never been apart.

They both seemed surprised by their reactions. What had begun for Carrick as a routine seduction, at which he was highly competent and much experienced, was turning out to be the most moving and emotional experience of his life. He had fooled himself that what he wanted from this woman was a few moments of lustful satisfaction. She was beautiful, she had a superb body, and he had learned from previous occasions that she had a passion to equal his own. Surely that was the reason why he had wanted to make love to her now instead of leaving her at her cabin door? Of course it was – he would have been a fool not to take advantage of this marvellous opportunity: sex on a platter – what could be more tempting or more convenient?

Neither of them noticed the hard pallet or the narrowness of the bunk with its sharp, wooden edges. They might have been on a sandy, golden beach, lapped by the royal-blue and peacock-green Aegean Sea, with silver-sided fishes fleeting through the waters and a brilliant sun blazing down upon them, or in a magical oasis in the desert, with fantastical creatures lurking in the depths of the pool nearby and curving palms above them illuminated by a blade-sharp sickle moon. The call of weird, mythical beasts was in their ears, the dip and soar of marvellous wings, the scent of exotic and gargantuan blooms which, like their love, could not have sprung from anything so mundane as earth.

Imagination, senses, passions, longings, were all at their highest for both of them as Carrick surged in and out of her body, touching her as deeply as it was possible to do, then sliding out only to strike at her again, at her very depths, making her shudder and cling to him all the more, calling his name, but somehow managing to bar her lips to those three words which she most longed to say, for it was not her place to say them first. It was only right and proper for the man to say 'I love you' before the woman did. And she was sure now that he would say it soon, for she knew that his response to her had amazed him: she could see it in his eyes. He had sought her out for a carefree tumble but Eros was already winging his way between them, firing his arrows for all that he was worth. However, his targets were not going to submit so easily. Lord Cromer, when he married, wanted an aristocratic wife, one who would provide him with highborn sons. Pretty peasant girls and gypsies were an excellent choice for a brief sexual interlude but not for bearing one's legitimate heirs. He could never forget Fabian's distress and deep unhappiness at failing to sire a son to inherit his title, estates and the Cromer Trading Company. Carrick had no wish to be in that position himself, and yet the moment was right for love, for kissing and caressing and staring deeply into one another's eyes.

Kitty could feel her heart pounding so vibrantly that it was almost deafening in her ears.

'Whose heart is beating so loudly?' she whispered.

'Ours,' he replied softly.

It might have been dawn or dusk, they did not care. But for one another at this moment there was a bounty of care, acute, meaningful and passionate. The feud was as forgotten as if it had never been: whatever its origins they were now totally obscured. Man and woman, united by love, were what mattered to the exclusion of all else.

Powerful, erotic sensations were sparkling through Kitty's body, their vehemence beyond anything she had experienced before, even with Carrick– a feeling that she was about to split into a thousand, tiny, glittering fragments, each one pulsing with a life of its own yet remaining a part of her even though separate. A vision, not seen but felt deep within her heart and soul, a spiritual vision. Yet it was physical too, that was all too obvious as she melted to make his passage easier, delirious with joy that he should want her, return to her. The universe, life itself, was irrelevant while she was in his arms.

He seemed possessed of an infinite strength and sexualtiy. He did not seem to tire, nor grow short of breath; he was indefatigable, fired with the energy of the gods. Perhaps that was because he had found his goddess at last. Even when the gentle ripplings began deep inside her, gripping him, he did not lose control but hugged her tighter, whispering impassioned words in her ear, so that her orgasm when it came was greeted generously. Then, when she was silent, warm and rosy, barely able to move a muscle, he began to scythe deeply inside her again so that she felt a new excitement: a revelation, a second orgasm following on the first and another after it, so that she could no longer think or reason but only feel.

He grinned, leaning on one elbow and looking down at her, admiration in his eyes.

'It is good to know that I am appreciated.'

'Then you can tell?' she grinned back, adoring the way

that his luxuriant bronze hair fell across his forehead and round his face while he was leaning over her, the teasing but sensual sparkle in his eyes, the broad, encompassing strength of his shoulders, and she knew that she had longed for him all her life, wanted such a man as this, a lover, protector, husband, brother and father, all rolled into one. At heart she was still a staunchly monogamous Catholic girl, raised to believe in one love, one marriage and, as far as she was concerned, he was her one love, her one desire.

Tightly enclosing her in his arms again, he kissed her mouth, and then she felt him shudder, driving himself deep into her, and groaning in ecstasy as he poured out his love.

Resting silently afterwards, they realised that the storm had died down, the seas being calm again. Neither knew what time it was, nor did they wish to know. Sleep came swiftly and they had never needed it more.

The cabinboy brought Kitty's breakfast as usual, and she took it from him at the door without letting him in.

'Isn't it a little late to protect your reputation?' Carrick drawled from the bunk. He was propped on one elbow, grinning at her lazily.

Conscious of her state of undress, her cheeks reddened. Putting down the tray, she reached for a peignoir and pulled it round herself.

'You will have to make do with sharing my breakfast.'

'If I am invited.'

'But of course you are.'

They sat on the bunk, sipping hot chocolate and eating fresh white bread with delicious topaz-coloured honey. It was stimulating and yet a little embarrassing to have to share the same cup which, in view of what they had been doing only hours before, seemed strange. Kitty was beginning to feel downcast because she knew that this blissful interlude was now at an end. In a very short time the ship would be docking and they would be going ashore, going their own separate ways as on every other occasion.

Curving his forefinger under her chin, Carrick smiled at her teasingly. 'I have to award you full marks for finding out that I would be on the *Adriatic Pearl*. I kept this trip a total secret – no one knew in London.'

'I can assure you that I had no idea you would be on this ship . . .' Kitty began heatedly.

'So you sailed unaware that I would be your fellow passenger? You cannot expect me to believe that, my little Irish vixen.'

Bridling at that last phrase, Kitty slammed down her cup. 'You will have to believe it, for it is the truth.'

'Why should you be going to Venice of all places?'

'Why, to buy materials, of course. What better place?' she sounded surprised.

'That is a possibility, I admit.'

'It is always wiser to admit the truth. I would, if I were you.'

'Are you trying to accuse me of some sort of duplicity?'

'If I am then it is no more than you have done to me on more than one occasion.' She turned her face away, drawing her peignoir more closely around her. There was a heaviness in her heart; the morning had turned sour, their relationship was as contumacious as ever. They seemed fated to make love and then part in bad humour.

'It is a very long voyage just to find new materials.'

'So? I have next season's gowns to design, fans, jewels and so on.'

'Ah yes, those jewels.' He could not keep the glitter from his eyes. 'How did you find out about them?'

'To which ones do you refer?'

'The Pharoah jewels, of course.' He moved a little closer, his eyes narrowed. She saw that he could barely wait for her reply.

'I do not see that it is any concern of yours.'

'Oh, but it is, my dear.'

'How can that be?'

'Perhaps this name will mean something to you.' He repeated the name of the Frenchman who had waited in vain to receive the Pharoah jewels which he had bought in a previous century.

'Yes, I know that name. The jewels went astray on their way to him, did they not?'

'That is so. He was an ancestor on my father's side. I am his only living descendant; so you see, if those jewels are found, they belong to me, for I am their rightful owner by law.'

Standing up, Kitty went over to the tiny dark-wood dresser, where she proceeded to brush her hair vigorously, her thoughts racing. This was the last turn of events she had expected. If he had known of her adaptation of the original jewel design why had he not come forward sooner to ask her where she had got it. Why had he waited until now? Could he know the true reason for her journey to Venice? In the mirror she saw him watching her, his eyes hooded so that she could not see their expression. Of course, it might be some trick . . . they were old enemies, old rivals. How much more of a rival he would consider her when he knew that she had started her own trading company.

'Well?' Carrick's voice was stony.

Turning, she smiled winningly at him. 'Well what?'

'Where did you get the information about the Pharoah jewels?'

'Oh, in some old book I found.'

'The book told you where to find the jewels, you mean?'

'Oh no!' She frowned. 'Good Heavens, no. All that the book contained was a little information about the original owners and sketches of the jewels themselves.'

'You say an old book, how old?'

'It was not easy to read the date, but sometime during the last century.'

'How do I know you are not lying?'

Kitty stood up, her cheeks scarlet. 'This has gone quite far enough! How dare you interrogate me like this – accusing me of underhand tricks and lying? It would be bad enough if you had not so recently shared my bed, but in view of what we have just been doing together it is totally despicable and indefensible of you.'

'All I want to know is where those jewels are.'

'Is that why you followed me to my cabin? Is that why you slept with me? You were just using my body so that you could lull me into a false sense of security and then question me about the jewels. Yes, that is it, is it not?' Picking up her heavy silver hairbrush, she advanced towards him. 'You have not changed. You are still the most callous, self-seeking, ruthless and utterly avaricious man that I have ever had the misfortune to tangle with. You will get out now, and you will not come back. Do not attempt to approach me again, no, not for any reason. You are loathsome and revolting, a snake, a . . . a . . .'

'A bastard?' he suggested, snatching up his clothes.

'Yes, yes, a bastard!' she screamed, throwing her hairbrush after him with all her might, but he was out before the brush reached its destination and it thudded against the panels of the door.

Picking it up, Kitty surveyed the damage, running her fingers into the dent in the silver. It was a beautiful old brush and she loved it; it reminded her of one which Fabian had given her and which she had been forced to leave behind at Cromer Manor. Sinking down on the bunk, she clutched it tightly in her hands, trying to force back her tears. She failed, of course, as she always did where Carrick was concerned, for he seemed to have control of her emotions. When he insulted her she had to rage back; when he took her in his arms she melted into fire; when he left her she wept bitter tears. How could any human being have such power over another one? It was wrong, all wrong.

What was she going to do when she reached the Italian nobleman's villa? If what Carrick had said was true, then the Italian was in possession of stolen goods which had a rightful owner. Her anticipation had evaporated. There was little if anything to look forward to but a bleak passage through life which had no meaning, no warmth, no love.

Before preparing to disembark, she went over to her hand luggage and took out the facsimile of Queen Faranefi's necklace. Holding it up round her neck, she looked in the mirror, waiting for the delicious feeling of entrancement which always came when she wore it. But nothing happened; she felt as drained, as depressed, as ever, and the necklet looked what it was, a pale copy. Sa-lu-is, the star, was nothing more than colourless glass, vapid and lacklustre – which was exactly how she felt at this moment.

CHAPTER FIFTEEN

The Count's villa was snowy stucco with curving tympani and fairytale turrets. It stood in the centre of a confusing network of canals, its reflection shimmering in the waters. For centuries the Venetians had struggled against an ocean of mud and headstrong rivers to drain the land, dig canals and free fields of their water-logged existence. Now, all traffic went by water, water which was stagnant and because it received the city's waste products, often evil-smelling. However, by the Villa Aphrodite the air was sweet.

As soon as Kitty stepped into the ivory marble hallway of the Villa Aphrodite she felt her spirits lift. Cool and airy, it smelt of lilies, and the magnificent domed ceiling was painted with pastel-coloured frescoes of the gods and goddesses frolicking with Cupid. Portraits of aristocratic lords and ladies hung on the walls and a bevy of beautiful, dignified dogs lay by the hearth although there was no fire in the grate. Walking across to look more closely at the dogs, Kitty saw that there was an exquisite dove-grey cat lying between them – it had long soft fur and dark orange eyes. As she bent down to stroke it with a smile on her lips, it made a little mew as if to greet her.

'How beautiful you are,' she said in admiration. 'Would you mind if I picked you up?' When the cat mewed again, apparently in agreement, she gently lifted him into her arms and stood nursing him, her chin against his soft furry head.

That was how she was standing when the Count came into the hall.

'So you and Adam Kadmon have found one another. You are honoured, signorina, for Adam does not take to everyone.'

Kitty smiled. 'He is the most elegant and beautiful cat I have ever seen.'

'He is a very rare species from a strange and mysterious country many thousands of miles away. Have my servants brought in your bags, signorina?'

'They have, Count.'

'That is good, then come with me into the conservatory and we will have a little talk, *si*?'

As her maid followed the Count's servants upstairs to unpack her belongings, Kitty followed the Count out through the hall and along winding but sunny corridors towards a verdant terrazza, lavish with greenery and exotic, multi-coloured blooms whose pungent scent filled the air.

As they sat sipping a light Italian wine, they examined one another cautiously. The Count was not at all what Kitty had expected. She had heard that he was a great collector, a brilliant historian and philosopher, and an astrologer, too. She had pictured someone dark and sleek with brooding eyes and a saturnine expression. However, the Count was on the plump side, jolly and smiling, with a wild, shoulder-length thatch of liquorice-coloured hair and eyes to match. He had a mole on his right cheek, a deep crease across his forehead, very crooked, small, yellow teeth, and a deep dimple in his chin. Over the ubiquitous jacket and breeches, which were of fine Genoese velvet embroidered with silk, he wore a hip-length cloak in the Tudor style, its lining sparkling with symbols, stars and crescent moons. On his right forefinger he wore an enormous moonstone set in silver, and a matching moonstone dangled from his left ear. Staring at the stones, Kitty had the strangest sensation that there was movement inside them, that, if she stared hard enough, close enough, she would see strange pictures therein.

'Your friend and her husband enjoyed their stay in Italy?'

'Very much so, Count. They cannot wait to return again as soon as the opportunity arises.'

'That is excellent, my dear. Italy – especially Venice – was made for lovers.'

'I did not expect to see so much water.'

At that the Count smiled mischievously. 'The whole of Venice is really a great magical lagoon, with all the buildings floating on it. I will take you on a gondola one day; it is always better to explore the city that way – and, besides, there is an ancient legend that the first time a stranger visits the city and looks into the waters they will see the face of their future husband or wife. I am right in thinking that you are not yet married, my dear?'

'No, I am not.'

Adam Kadmon had found his way out onto the terrazza and was rubbing himself against Kitty's ankles, purring resonantly. Reaching down, she scooped him up into her arms, kissing his velvety head. He lay back as if enraptured and unable to believe his good fortune.

'Adam is an expert judge of character,' the Count twinkled. 'Normally he will not have anything to do with those of the fairer sex, but I see that he is already your slave.'

'And I am his,' Kitty laughed.

'Am I right in thinking that you were born under Gemini the Twins?' the Count said suddenly, leaning forward in his chair.

'Yes, you are right. Amalia – the lady who was recently on holiday in Italy – is also very interested in the stars.'

'Ah, not only the stars, my dear, but also the planets. It is the planets which are most important, for their movement through the galaxy makes us what we are. Did your friend Amalia ever speak of your rising sign?'

'My rising sign? No, I do not think she did – what is that?'

'The position of the sun on the eastern horizon at the moment of your birth, that moment when you take your first breath and are independent from your mother for the first time. I do not suppose that you know exactly when you were born – few people do unless something out of the ordinary occurs to fix it in the memory.

'As it happens I do, Count.' Kitty wrinkled her brow. 'My mother often spoke of the moment I was born. You see, the priest used to visit us regularly at the same time every week, nine in the morning sharp, and I arrived just a few moments before he did. My mother was very pleased, she told me, and she called me her gift for God.'

'Did she now,' the Count looked thoughtful, almost mysterious. 'A gift for God – she never followed that up, she never wanted you to go into a convent?'

'Oh no – you see,' Kitty paused, stroking Adam Kadmon as her thoughts ranged back over the years. 'You see, all my family died in one of the famines in Southern Ireland – it was caused by the potato curl. I was only a child when they died.'

'The sole survivor of your family.' The Count leaned forward again, his fingers smoothing over the moonstone in his ring.

'Yes, the sole survivor.'

'A girl of great courage.'

'No more than the hundreds of others who were left in the same plight.'

'And modest, too.' The Count seemed to be staring deeply into the moonstone, his sculpted black brows drawn together.

'If you will give me your birthdate I will draw up your natal chart and tell you your rising sign.'

'What will I learn from it?'

'It is a powerful part of one's chart; it governs the individual personality, the looks too. Then there is the moon sign, the mid-heaven or zenith, the descendant, the nadir and all the major planets, and the aspects between all these – there are so many intricacies, so many inter-related facts, to be studied.'

'You will tell me what it all means when you have finished, won't you?'

'But of course, Signorina, of course.'

'I would not like to be left in the dark . . .' Kitty's eyes twinkled.

'You will never be that, my dear.'

'If only that were true. Sometimes I feel that there is nothing but darkness in life, a deep, sad darkness . . .' Kitty stopped, astonished at herself for speaking like this to a stranger, and a foreigner at that – a man whom she had only just met.

'Go on,' the Count urged. 'Go on, feel free to speak.'

'That is all of it, really. I suppose that I am over the worst of losing all my family like that, but even the slightest loss brings it all back. Not long ago I lost a faithful maid and I blame myself for her death. If I had sent for her sooner, let her know that I still cared about her, she would still be alive now.'

'One cannot interfere in the destiny of others. It was her destiny to behave as she did, to die when she did.'

'But I could have stopped it, I know I could. I was too wrapped up in my own interests, my own needs.'

'If you know that then you have learned your lesson. Life is not meant to be a series of junkets and galas with merriment at every stage. Those who deserve pity are the ones who do not suffer, who have no losses, who are never so distressed or bereaved that they turn inwards and ponder upon the meaning of life. Out of all anguish comes a new hope, a new beginning; thus it has been from the origins of time. Feel sorry for those who are never plunged into the depths, because they can never reach the heights. In one day you will know more about living and loving, the meaning of life and the universe, than the majority of people will feel in their entire lifetimes.'

'But why is it like that, Count? Why do some drift through life with hardly a care and others have enough sufferings for two or three people?'

The Count gave a little bubbling laugh. 'Do you want an answer immediately or am I allowed to ponder on that for a few hours, my dear?'

Kitty looked up, thinking that he was serious, saw that he was laughing and joined in. At that moment a strangely bubbling purr escaped Adam Kadmon's furry mouth, just as if he were laughing too.

Count Barraccini did not seem in a hurry to show the Pharoah jewels to Kitty. After they had taken refreshments on the terrazza, Kitty was taken up to her room by the Count's housekeeper, a plump, dark lady with a black moustache, who spoke no English.

Kitty had been expecting one bedroom, but in fact she was given a suite of rooms of ornate and ethereal beauty.

Stucco walls of the most pleasing pastel colours, rich pineapple yellow, china blue and ivory made the sitting-room a delight to be in. On one wall there was a fresco of ladies in Medici-style clothes playing lutes with a back-gammon game laid out on the table between them. At the heels of one of them sat a little dog with a monkey-like face and doleful eyes.

One end of the room was a vast carved plaster fireplace reaching almost to the ceiling, with a statue of Venus on one side and a statue of Apollo on the other. Garlands of plaster flowers rioted between them across the mantel. Looking closer, Kitty saw that there was a design of hearts interwoven with the flowers and that inside each heart were the initials F and N. The initials were convoluted, curving round one another as if with fond intimacy. Perhaps this had been a lovers' room – a honeymoon suite at some time or another? Or perhaps those were the initials of the man who had built this house for the woman he had loved. There was something about the ambience of this room and the adjoining ones which appealed to Kitty tremendously. In a way it was a continuation of the atmosphere in the city itself, the magical city on an enchanted lagoon, as the Count had called it.

She stepped out onto the balcony to look at the view. Rows of stucco houses, cream and buff, beige and ivory, stared back at her. Some were newly painted, others shabby and peeling. Behind them the sky was dark turquoise blue with a froth of creamy clouds, and between her and the houses was the serpentine canal with its bare stone sides on which a press of people were rushing about their business, some laden with baskets of fruit and vegetables, others with bolts of cloth under their arms, others with parcels, boxes, bags and sticks.

On her arrival, Kitty had found the heat a great novelty.

Travelling across land after leaving the ship, she had enjoyed the countryside, the sunshine, the verdant fruits and flowers and colours which had made the journey a delight. Travelling with a group of merchants and their wives had ensured that she and Mellyn had been in secure and congenial company – not that either had been able to understand the others' language, but smiles and gesticulations had sufficed.

The water of the canal was changing from a dark oily blue to a muddy grey as a gondola wended its way past, its frontal carved rowlock proudly pointing the way like two inverted crescent moons side by side. A family was sitting in the boat, laughing and throwing wide their arms with typical Italian gusto, the father thrusting out his chest and plucking at his black bushy beard as if in imitation of an amusing acquaintance of theirs. She had thought that hungry longing for her family was over, but there was something about the jolly little group down below which destroyed her enjoyment of the day. Lost loved ones, so many lost . . .

Mellyn was clattering about in the bedchamber, laying out her gown for the evening. Kitty and the Count were dining with the Count's sister that night. The Contessa Estella Fennolloni was a widow and lived in seclusion in her own section of the villa, rarely taking part in public life.

'Estella always wanted to be a nun,' the Count had explained, 'but our father insisted upon her early marriage to Count Fennolloni. Unfortunately the Count died two years ago and my sister came here to live with me. It is an arrangement which suits us both admirably.'

Estella should have been a nun. Perhaps she, Kitty, should have gone into a convent, too – would that not have been an admirable solution for her? Lesser griefs than hers had driven women into a nunnery, and at times the thought of the peace and seclusion of such a place was greatly tempting.

'Mistress McDonagh.' She heard Mellyn's voice.

'Yes, Mellyn, what is it?'

'I cannot open this cupboard here on the wall. I want to put away your phials and cosmetic jars.'

Kitty walked into the bedchamber to look at the unusual hexagonal cupboard which was on the wall there. There were strange symbols on it, five of them, which she could not understand at all. She had never seen a cupboard with six points like a star, and she ran her fingers over the gleaming, polished wood which looked like walnut. Then she turned the key in the lock and tried to pull open the door, but it would not move.

'I expect the Count keeps some of his own private possessions in here and it has some sort of double lock. Anyway, my jars and so on can go on that carved cabinet over there. Do not unpack too much, Mellyn; we do not know how long we are staying.' Outwardly she was cautious, although in her heart she knew that she would be quite happy to stay in this villa for some time. Whatever else about her life had been unfortunate, her ability to feel at home in new surroundings had always stood her in good stead. She had loved Cromer House and Cromer Manor, Huntley House too; yet it was in the Barraccini villa that she felt most at home of all. While part of her said that everything here was new and strange, another part was saying that she had seen it all before somewhere, a long, long time ago. This villa was totally without danger for her, totally without fear.

The Count's sister, Estella, was dressed like a lady of elderly and sophisticated proclivities, but she had a youthful, unlined face and her hands were smooth, pale and unwrinkled. It was true that, although beautifully cut and of the most sumptuous apple-green and silver Genoese brocade, her gown was of a design much in fashion some fifty or so years before, yet the material appeared bright and new. If the dress were indeed fifty years old then surely it would have looked faded or shabby – and, besides, would it still have fitted Estella's figure after all these years? If she had worn this very gown in her youth that would make her at least seventy years old, yet she did not look it, nor did she carry herself like a woman of such advanced years. Her eyes were bright and sparkling, but of the palest china blue Kitty had ever seen, so pale that at certain angles they seemed to be transparent as glass, almost like the moonstones which the Count wore continually.

Dinner was served in a lofty room painted with frescoes of the stages of the Crucifixion. As Kitty looked round at the frescoes, thinking that they made somewhat strange adornment for a dining-room, the Count whispered in her ear:

'They are also the stages in life which one must go through before reaching heaven. As so many people think of little but filling their empty stomachs I thought it apt to make this room into a dining chamber. Even the courses of a meal can be compared to the stages of one's life. Usually, at the end of a large meal, one feels too full to contemplate one's spiritual condition but, this way, a little learning and contemplation can be done whilst eating.' The Count's eyes twinkled.

The table was of pale, glowing, golden spruce, polished like glass and laid with glittering crystal, silver and a centrepiece of blood-red flowers which looked quite real from a distance but, on closer inspection, proved to have been created from velvet and satin.

When Kitty sat down at her place she found a tiny scrap of paper by the side of her plate, and on opening it she read: *Be sure that you find me in Time*.

Looking up, she stared at the Count and then at his sister but both of them seemed to be absorbed with spreading their napkins on their knees and inspecting their knives and forks. Folding up the piece of paper, Kitty put it in her pocket.

The meal was beautifully cooked, tasty and fragrant. A citron sauce made the capon piquant and appetising, and the wines which accompanied each course were sanguine and sparkling without being heady. Little was said during the meal, but Kitty noticed that the Count often glanced up to look at the frescoes. After dinner the Count led his sister and Kitty into the salon adjoining the dining chamber.

A servant brought in a variety of drinks; soft, sweet wines from the south, fruit sherbets, so beloved by the Sultan of Turkey and his people, fresh herbal teas which smelled of new-mown hay. Spoilt for choice, Kitty finally decided upon the orange sherbet – it was very sweet and highly scented. Estella sipped hers noisily with obvious relish, then poured second helpings for them both. The Count had wine from the south, with its rich aromatic flavour redolent of muscatel grapes.

Outside, the moon was silver satin in an indigo sky, a billion stars pullulating around it, while the waters of the criss-crossed canals lapped secretively in the pewter shadows of the overhanging houses. A dog howled, desperate for solace, and a bevy of tomcats yodelled outside the nearby Villa di Fiorinelli, whose occupier owned a cat which was both beautiful, available and female.

'You would like to see the Pharoah jewels now?'

The Count's question took Kitty by surprise.

'Oh yes, yes, I would love to.'

'I will bring them in here.'

While the two women waited, Estella took a pack of cards out of the reticule hanging from her wrist. Thoughtfully she placed them one after the other on the table in front of her. Sitting opposite, Kitty could only see the pictures on the cards upside down, but even so she saw that they represented men and women. One looked like a queen, another a king, one was a woman in classical robes, another a gaunt black figure sitting astride a horse.

By now Kitty was accustomed to Estella's silences, so she leaned back, alternately looking at the cards then glancing round the room. Suddenly Estella spoke. 'So many deaths,' she said, her voice wistful. 'How have you borne it? Another would have died, too.'

Kitty swallowed. 'I – I – how did you know about that?'

'From the cards. Have you not seen the Tarot cards before? They never lie: they tell of your past, your present and your future.'

'The past has been bad enough, I do not think I could face knowing what the future holds, Contessa.'

The Contessa seemed not to hear. 'The Tower – ah, that means a change of some sort, a disruption.'

'That sounds like the past.'

'Sometimes our past is our future – sometimes those very things that we have wept over become the cause of our joy.'

'I cannot see that.'

'You try to be logical, practical. That is all to the good, but one must not deny the feminine force. There is a worldly man here, one whom you have called your enemy. He has caused you much sorrow and heartbreak, is that not so?'

Cheeks flushed, Kitty nodded.

'The Emperor card always means a worldly man – in

this case a strong man, a man of power and vigour, who is accustomed to getting his own way in all things. You are one of the things he wanted, am I right?'

Kitty nodded again, her cheeks burning.

'There is a card here to represent you. Now, if you had come up as the High Priestess I would have told you that this man was not for you, no, not under any circumstances. But see, here you are as the Empress who can never be complete without her Emperor.'

'That can never be,' Kitty sounded almost scornful. 'He is not the man for me, he is betrothed to another woman; he despises me, he has used me in the most despicable way.'

'You sound outraged, hurt, betrayed.'

'I am, I am.' Kitty stood up, filled with a restless energy. 'He has brought me nothing but unhappiness.'

'You think you are unhappy now, but the happiest people are those who can look back and think it was not better then.' The Countess was putting more Tarot cards on the table. 'Ah, and what do we have here – two more men, I see. Two more men deeply involved in your life, both of whom will want to marry you.'

'I cannot think who they are, nor do I wish to know. I have no time for anything but my work.'

'Work will not keep you warm in bed.' Estella's lagoon-pale eyes shimmered with a ghostly warmth.

'Nor does this man you refer to as my Emperor,' Kitty retorted. 'He will never be mine – no, no, never! I do not want him.'

'As you wish, so be it.' Estella seemed to lose interest in the cards, leaning back in her comfortable violet velvet armchair.

'If there is any truth in this nonsense of the cards I shall overrule it,' Kitty went on indignantly. 'No cards are going to dictate to me who I shall share my life with!'

'Not dictate, never dictate,' Estella looked shocked. 'They foretell the inevitable.'

'I do not believe that mere pieces of board can see into the future. How can that be?'

'I do not know how my mind works, yet it works very well indeed,' Estella said. 'The sun shines, the moon glows, even though I do not know how this happens. We breathe the air and without it we die, yet I do not know why this is. There are so many mysteries in life. If you knew the answer would it convince you?'

Kitty was about to reply when the Count entered, bearing a large box covered in imperial purple velvet.

'Here are the famous jewels,' he smiled.

Kitty's heart began to beat wildly. Placing the velvet box on the carved Italian marble table between them, the Count opened its lid and Kitty saw for the first time the magnificent jewels which had decorated the slender twelve-year-old body of Queen Faranefi. In the facsimiles which her jeweller had made for her and her clients, the centrepiece was of cold and empty glass, but the centrepiece of these, the original jewels, was a massive blazing diamond, so bright, so many-faceted, that Kitty was stunned into silence. Reaching out a hand, she ran her fingers over the diamonds, one for each piece of jewellery, the necklet, the earrings, the headpiece which fitted like a diadem across the brow, the armbands, the rings.

'These are nearly as old as time itself,' she whispered, finally able to find her voice. 'Thousands of years old and yet they still look so new, so bright. Do you know anything of the Pharoah and his wife? I have looked in books, questioned historians in London, but no one seems to know anything except their names.'

'Queen Faranefi was married to a much older man; she was eleven, he was in his sixties. They were cousins and before he died he wanted to leave her with child.' The Count sat down, warming to his story. 'Unfortunately he died and the Queen was still not in that happy condition. The Pharoah's heir was his nephew, Nkha, a vigorous young man in his middle twenties or thereabouts, who was a worshipper of the heavenly star Sa-lu-is.

As the late Pharoah had been a worshipper of the god Ra the new Pharoah's inauguration caused a total upheaval in the major religion of the land and there was much unrest, especially as Faranefi could not settle to the new religion and let her feelings be known. She was twelve by now, yet a vitally important person – the last link between the old Pharoah and the old religion and the new Pharoah and the new religion. She did not love the new Pharoah, nor did she wish to marry him, and a schism was developing. There were two factions, one for the young Queen and one for the new Pharoah, and war and insurrection were imminent.

Then the new Pharoah had the idea of trying to convert the Queen to his religion. With this in mind, he had this beautiful set of jewels made for her, representing the heavenly star Sa-lu-is, and he presented them to her. It is said that she refused them outright in the most arrogant manner, but then the new Pharoah urged her to try them on which, most reluctantly, she did.'

'And what happened then?' Kitty asked, but she felt that she already knew the answer.

'Why, the moment the diadem, the collar and the bracelets were placed round the Queen's body she was converted to the new religion and from that moment war and insurrection were avoided and two factions were united under the joint rule of Queen Faranefi and Pharoah Nkha.'

'Do you know if they were happy together? Did the

young Queen ever learn to love her new husband?'

'I do not think I would be overestimating their happiness if I said their union proved to be a blissful one, during which the Queen bore five children, the future Pharoah and his brothers and sisters.'

'Well, at least one Empress found her Emperor,' Kitty attempted a jest which sounded feeble the moment she had voiced it.

'Would you like to try on the jewels?' the Count said, at which Kitty's face lit up.

With Estella's help she donned the diadem, the collar and the rest of the gems, and then Estella led her over to the tall mirror on the wall at the end of the room. Staring into it, she saw herself wearing the Pharoah's jewels and then, as she stared harder, the great blazing diamonds seemed to swell and throb and grow, blazing with light so that she could see nothing but them, like living, blazing stars, her face and arms and shoulders fading away.

'The stars have won many people to their side over the centuries.' Estella's lagoon-pale eyes shimmered.

'Talking of the stars, I have worked out your chart, Signorina McDonagh, and on the morrow I will tell you more about it.'

Reluctantly Kitty turned from the mirror, away from the brilliant, dominating light of the jewellery. She felt strange and almost bemused, as if she were not herself and unsure of her surroundings.

'I am very lucky to have such kind people caring for me,' she smiled. 'When I came to this beautiful villa I had no idea how many riches I would find here and what good fortune.'

'This house is your fortune, Signorina,' the Countess said, and for a moment her wintry eyes glowed almost as brightly as the diamonds on the Pharoah jewels.

CHAPTER SIXTEEN

That night Kitty dreamt that she was at a wedding. It was a Royal wedding and she knew that it concerned her deeply, but she could not see the face of the bride, nor the groom. All she knew was that she was deliriously happy. The ceremony coming to an end, the bride turned towards the groom, who lifted back her veil, and then Kitty knew that the bride was indeed herself. Next, the groom reached out for something and, as if the wedding ceremony were also a coronation, he placed a necklet and diadem upon Kitty and she knew by their dazzling magnificence that they were the Pharoah jewels. The Emperor was crowning his Empress.

She woke feeling blissful, this emotion swiftly being followed by indignation. All this nonsense about the Emperor and that arrogant libertine, Cromer. She would have none of it – he was not for her, nor would he ever be, she would make sure of that.

Breakfast was brought to her on a tray in her room and afterwards she joined the Count on the terrazza, where grape vines coiled and writhed their way along overhead trellises, succulent bunches of midnight-purple grapes hanging within easy reach. The Count was in a jolly mood, pouring out freshly-pressed lemon juice for them both.

'No doubt you are eager to know more about your birth chart, Signorina McDonagh?' Kitty nodded. 'I believe that my sister gave you a Tarot reading last night?' Kitty nodded again. 'I think you will find that the reading bears out what I learned from your horoscope.'

Kitty's eyes flicked upwards. 'If it says that I am going to be an Empress then it, too, is wrong!'

The Count chuckled. 'Your ascendant – that is, the sign rising on the eastern horizon at the moment of your birth and where the sun is placed at the same moment – is Libra. Libra is ruled by Venus and so, my dear, you have Venus rising.'

'What does that mean?'

'You prefer harmony and peace; you are pleasant and affable, friendly, kind-hearted, and in all things you seek for good balance. Libra is the marriage sign and so you would definitely be happier and more contented in a close, loving partnership with the right man.'

Kitty tut-tutted. 'You and the Contessa should start a marriage agency, I think.'

'That is not a bad idea.' The Count's eyes twinkled. 'Indeed, we might well have inaugurated it when you arrived here. Now, to go on. You are inordinately fond of the voluptuous – in fact, you are something of a voluptuary. Good food, beautiful clothes, jewels, art, music and dancing: all these things intrigue and attract you. Your love of travel and your energy come from having your sun in placement in Gemini, which offsets something of the lethargy attributable to Libra. Now, your House of Marriage.'

'Do not tell me – there is an Emperor in it.' Kitty tapped her nails on the filigree table.

'Oh dear, you do have an aversion to the Emperor, signorina. No, I was merely going to tell you that in your House of Marriage you have the sign Aries, which signifies the type of man who will bring you most happiness.

He will be dashing and bold, assertive, nay, even aggressive at times, energetic, forward thinking, a pioneer in many ways, passionate, single-minded. But then you are passionate also, signorina, so you are well matched.'

'But I am not aggressive nor, I hope, am I arrogant. As you say, I prefer peace above all things.'

'But you have been known to be aggressive in pursuit of peace, I think? For that is the anachronism of Libra the peacelover.'

Kitty shrugged. 'Maybe, but only when I felt justice and right were being threatened.'

'Ah yes, a great one for justice. That, also, is the true Libran. You like Italy?'

'Very much so.'

'That is probably because it is ruled by Gemini. A country which is ruled by one's own sign always appeals to one.'

'So countries have horoscopes, too?'

'Indeed they do. Every country has a national characteristic – or should I say its people do – and these are caused by its sun sign. Every country also has a rising sign, too, and so on, just like human beings.'

'Tell me of my faults please, Count.' Kitty sipped at her fruit juice, a whole universe opening up in her mind.

'A little headstrong, shall we say. Very determined and you can be totally single-minded, if that can be called a fault. Perhaps it is when others have their mind on certain things which you refuse to acknowledge.' The moonstone earring trembled in an invisible breeze, light and dark kaleidoscoping across it.

Kitty's eyes were constantly drawn to the moonstones which the Count wore, for they seemed to churn and flicker with movement all the time out of the corner of her eye, yet when she directed her gaze upon them they seemed bland, creamy, immobile, and the Count apparently unaware of her puzzled scrutiny.

He went on. 'Those born under Gemini the Twins are lively and energetic, quick-witted, easily diverted unless they have a particular passion. The Twins can show themselves in different fashions. For example, you might often find yourself in two minds, have such swift changes of mood that people say you are like two people, be ever seeking a soulmate so that you can make yourself into one of twins. I doubt if you are ever stuck for the right phrase or retort . . .' The Count chuckled, stroking Adam Kadmon who had just insinuated his way onto the astrologer's knee.

'My mother used to say that I would make a brilliant orator one day, but I confess at the time I did not know the meaning of the word.' Conscious of Adam Kadmon's richly topaz eyes upon her, Kitty said: 'I am going to miss Adam when I go back to England. A friend of mine has a young cat called Apollo, but he has nothing like the strong character of Adam or the striking appearance.'

'A cat of one's own is a constant delight. Adam sleeps on my pillow every night, you know. When he decides that it is morning then it is morning, whatever the time of night. Sometimes that is quite valuable to me, because I find that night thoughts are frequently of greater value than those which arise in the hubbub of daylight. The moon rules the imagination, you know, and the deeper recesses of the mind. There is an old saying which you might have heard: Those who wish to revel in the sunrise must first live through the night.'

'Oh, I have done that, all right, the long, long night as yet,' she said wryly.

'Watch the horizon.' The Count's eyes glittered, the moonstone dangling from his ear seeming to give a little leap although his head was still.

Adam Kadmon, as if tiring of the Count's knee, slithered off it, sat for a few moments in majestic pose, inspecting his paws and giving them a cursory wash, and then leaped onto Kitty's knee in one sinuous, tiger-like movement. Once on her knee he turned on his back, paws lolling in the air and began to purr roisterously.

'I have lost a friend,' the Count gave a mock sigh.

'No, you have gained one,' Kitty smiled. 'You've made me feel so much at home here, Count. I did not know what to expect, coming to a foreign country, meeting Italian people for the first time, especially the proud and indomitable Venetians. But never once have I felt ill at ease here, thanks to you and the generosity of your sister.'

'The days of Venice's pride and mastery of the high seas are long over, Signorina McDonagh. It is back to merchanting and magic now, just as we were in the old days before power went to our heads.'

'Did you say magic?'

'Did I say magic?' the Count looked surprised. 'Well, whatever made me say that, whatever did I mean?' He scratched his bushy head, his expression perplexed. 'What could I have meant? Matching, perhaps. We Venetians are excellent at match-making. Yes, I must have meant that.' The Count gazed into the distance, his face bright and innocent.

'Are you – that is, I mean, is it possible that you are a magician?' Kitty asked, a strange sensation sweeping through her as if this scene were a fresco which had suddenly sprung to life in front of her.

The Count seemed not to hear and Kitty felt that it would be impolite to ask the question a second time. Plainly the Count did not want to reply. Adam, who had dozed off, suddenly gave a booming snore, waking himself with a start.

'Oh, Adam, you are adorable,' Kitty said, stroking his soft fluffy fur.

'You told me that you have something else to do while you are in Venice, signorina?'

'Yes, I am visiting Antonio Bartoletti, the fan-maker. He has discovered a marvellous new process for decorating fans. Instead of spending hours hand-painting each leaf of a fan he prints them with a design. That way he can produce large numbers of fans in a much more economical fashion. I want to see exactly how he does this, and collect the fans I have ordered from him. If they go down well in England I shall be a regular customer of his.'

'I hope that you will find time to look round our city. You must not miss the terrazzas and St Mark's, of course – who would visit Venice and not gaze upon its beauty? If you visit the Piazzetta di San Marco you will see the Doge's palace on the waterfront. Look for the winged lion of St Mark that you will see there, for that is the city's patron saint – St Mark, I mean, not the lion.'

The Count's eyes twinkled. 'And there is a figure there of St Theodore, too, if I remember aright. He was the city's patron saint before St Mark. The Doge's Palace is a pinkish colour, most unusual for stonework; you cannot miss it. Walk a little way and you will see the Bacino di San Marco, which means simply the Basin of St Mark. It has been Venice's great harbour for a thousand years. Think of the ships which have plied in and out of that harbour over the centuries and look out across its waters to the Lagoon. Gaze upon the waters which look so smooth, so unruffled, until you look closer and then the light glitters upon them and they seem to be broken into a trillion silvered sequins.

'Little has changed on the Piazzetta since the thirteenth and fourteenth centuries: people still bustle there in the same way, to chatter, to gossip, to sightsee. From the days of the Romans and the Byzantine Empire, we Venetians have been much the same. For all I know, the descendants of the same white swans who bobbed on the waters a thousand years ago are the ones you will see when you look out upon the Bacina and the Lagoon. We love trading, we love gossip, we love colour and excitement. Perhaps that comes of being so cosmopolitan, for we have seen so many other nationalities here – Greeks and Arabs, Persians, Slavs, Egyptians, Byzantinians, Germans, and so on.

'Thousands of pilgrims have passed through Venice on their way from the Holy Land. We can be proud, we can be arrogant even, adventurous and pioneers upon the sea. Sometimes we have over-reached our ambitions, and now is the time for realising that our day is over. We have had too much for too long and we had it too soon. Inestimable treasures have come our way – and many of them should never have reached our hands. Pirate-looted treasures, and so on.'

Kitty wanted to interrupt and say, 'And what of the Pharoah Jewels, Count? Tell me of them and how they came into your possession, for I know somebody who claims that they are his by law.' But she remained silent.

The Count went on. 'In centuries past Venice was the master of Padua and Verona, Ravenna and Treviso, Crete, Cyclades, Corfu, Nauplia, Dalmatia, Monemvasia, Cyprus, Cephalonia. In the late seventeenth century we took the Peloponnese from the Turks, but in 1716 we had to surrender them back to the Turks. Only a proud people such as we can know what it is to surrender.'

'You identify very strongly with your fellow Venetians,

Count. I had to say goodbye to my homeland when I was very young and I doubt that I shall ever see it again.'

'Go back. At some time or other we all have to face our roots. Perhaps we can only go forward when we have gone back? Surely there will be materials, lace, and so on, which you can bring back to England and use in your work?'

'Lace, yes of course. That is a marvellous idea, Count. Yes, I will go back.'

Tears came into Kitty's eyes. Tipperary – the home of her birth, her dead family, the cottage, the scent of peat smoke and potatoes roasted in their jackets on the fire. Nostalgia was like a sick hunger inside her as images flickered through her thoughts.

'Go back,' the Count urged again. 'Do go back.'

'Yes, I think I will.'

Venice was a haunting city, the nebulous ghosts of its past still demanding attention. Now and again as she walked around the city she would see a horse-drawn barge on one of the stretches of water. Enormous and stately, they were caparisoned in rich satins and velvets and the glorious colours of one or other of the Venetian noblemen who lived nearby. Palace after exquisite palace thronged the edges of the Grand Canal. Stone shepherdesses and shepherds adorned their gardens, the statuettes coiled round with columbine and ivy, the lawns neatly cut, shutters closed on the brilliance of the day. On quieter stretches of the Canal, swallows dipped and soared ebulliently.

Kitty knew from what the Count had told her that many of Venice's most noble and important men were now struggling to survive. The count had called them the

Scudati – the fallen – some having reached such a lamentable state that they had to beg. Kitty did see beggars, but whether or not they had once been grand, high-ranking men she could not say. A city built on trade and conquests which had lost much of the former and all of the latter, losing heart, delivering itself to the decay which waited round virtually every corner. For every richly caparisoned horse-drawn barge there were a dozen broken down, creaking, water-logged boats; for every grandly-attired gentleman or lady strolling on the piazzas there were dozens of ragged beggars.

'Poverty is the only thing which has ever invaded our city,' the Count had said. 'In fourteen centuries we have been impregnable and yet it is destitution which has brought us to our knees. The symbolic Marriage with the Sea is still celebrated with as much magnificence as ever at the Church of St Nicolo del Lido. That is, the symbolic union of the ocean and Venice. But the bridegroom is now crippled and toothless and the bride is no longer a virgin.' The Count's eyes twinkled. 'Perhaps Bartoletti can bring a little glory back to our city through you, signorina.'

Kitty marvelled at carved stone bridges over the canals, marble panelled buildings such as the Scuola San Marco, nearly three hundred years old, sculpted angels with wings unfurled, balustrades embroidered with rich carving, but above all she was astonished by the number of cats roaming the city – wild, vulpine, and unfriendly.

The Count had told Kitty how superstitious the Venetians were about the wild cats. It was said that anyone who killed a cat would die within a year and anyone who hurt a cat would meet with a serious accident. Consequently the cats had been allowed to breed as they liked and some of them were pitifully thin, their tiny bones visible, jutting through patchy, mottled fur. Kitty, of course, could not see them and do nothing. She bought fish and meat and bread and every day that she was in Venice she fed them in the same place regularly, so that they grew to expect her appearance and would be sitting waiting for her. She received many stares while she was going about this charitable act, stares of astonishment, or of a patronising tolerance, and occasionally of fury should a beggar pass by. But if one did she would always hand over what food she had with her, for, much as she loved cats, she knew that human beings must come first.

It was Mellyn who noticed that they were being followed as they made their way to the Piazza Angelica where Antonio Bartoletti had his shop.

'Mistress, there is a strange man behind us. He has been following us for some way – indeed, 'tis the same man I saw yesterday when we were in St Mark's Square.'

'A pickpocket, mayhap, Mellyn. The city teems with them – just like London. All cities are the same. We are safe so long as we stay with the crowds.'

'He does not look like a ragamuffin, mistress – he looks like a sailor. He has sea boots on, you know, the baggy kind.'

Glancing back as unobtusively as possible, Kitty saw that the man did indeed look nautical, but his face was not shifty. In fact, he seemed eager to keep his distance. Nonetheless, he had become their shadow.

Mellyn's bright eyes were bulging with curiosity, but Kitty ordered her to look straight ahead as they walked on.

'He will go soon, Mellyn. Anyway, we are nearly at our destination. No doubt Bartoletti will have a servant or two who will deal with the man if he should dare to approach us there.'

Striding on, Kitty did not glance back again. Mellyn did once, but her mistress made such a disapproving noise that she quickly scuttled along, eyes ahead.

The door of Bartoletti's shop closed safely behind them and Kitty introduced herself to the red-checked, plump lady who was overflowing from a chair in one corner. However, the lady, who proved to be Bartoletti's sister, could speak no English whatsoever. At last, after Kitty had said 'Bartoletti' four or five times the woman seemed to understand the message and bustled into the back of the shop. Next came the sound of lilting Italian voices and then, a few moments later, Bartoletti himself appeared, throwing wide his arms and greeting Kitty as if she were a royal princess and his greatest customer. Bartoletti was white-haired and had strangely sloping shoulders, rather like those of a fish. What was more, he suffered from a surfeit of moles: two at the end of his nose, three or four on each cheek, an enormous mountainous one on his forehead, and a company of miniscule excrescences on his chin, and out of each one grew at least one long black hair. Nonetheless, he had a cheerful countenance and a broad smile.

While Bartoletti's sister, Maria, prepared a fruit sherbet for them, Kitty was shown round the workrooms. Normally it took an artist many hours of painstaking, arduous work to complete one fan, and Bartoletti explained how his brother, Guido, had lost his eyesight from years of excruciatingly close work doing just this. It had been this tragedy which had prompted Bartoletti to devise a different method of decorating the fan leaves. If books, broadsheets and newspapers could be printed en masse, why not this most popular of feminine accessories? For some time he had experimented with various methods and it had been a trial and error period with some notable disasters. Meanwhile, the demand for fans had continued to increase.

They served many purposes: they were imperative in hot weather; held in a graceful, dainty hand they served to draw attention to its beauty; they added drama and colour to a lady's outfit; they could be used to express opinions and reactions which a lady could not display otherwise as, for example, when in a moment of anger a lady would click shut her fan with a resounding snap. Then there was the language of the fan, which was of inestimable value to those young ladies, who, heavily chaperoned, wished to transmit their thoughts to a suitor who must keep a respectable distance. In staunchly Catholic European countries where reputable young maidens were never allowed to be alone, and certainly not with a member of the opposite sex, the fan had come into its own. In silence, and in the hands of the adept, it could speak volumes.

'The printing of the fans is simple – I have refined the routine over the years so that my brother can help us. Before we began to print them, of course, he could do nothing but bewail his blindness.'

'I've seen only one of your fans so far. How many designs do you have in all?'

'So far six or seven, signorina, but if demand picks up we can soon produce more. In business it is always a matter of supply and demand, as I am sure you will appreciate.'

Kitty nodded. 'The colours I am concentrating on for my forthcoming collection are peacock blue and green, topaz and oyster – I had the idea of giving away a matching fan with each outfit.'

'To every customer, signorina?' Bartoletti's jaw dropped open.

'No,' Kitty laughed, 'only to my best customers, the ones who return every season to buy outfits from me.'

'Ah, then that is all right, signorina.' Taking out a voluminous crumpled kerchief, Bartoletti wound a corner of it round his fore-finger and dabbed at his forehead tenderly, as if he were ensuring that skin and bones were still in place. Having inspected his extraordinary and brilliant collection of fans, Kitty picked out the ones she required, telling the fan-maker how many she would need and where he should send them.

'Is there any chance of you or one of your printers coming to London to make the fans there so that they are on hand? I can assure you that it would be worth your while.'

'Business is lamentably wretched here, signorina. Venice is no longer what it was – once it was a queen, now it is an ageing and tawdry strumpet.'

'London is as fashionable as ever, Signor Bartoletti, and there is a huge demand for accessories like fans. Fortunes are there to be made by those who have the wit to make them.'

'Fortunes, eh?' Bartoletti dabbed at his brow even more fervently, his eyes glittering acquisitively. He had a slight cast in his left eye, which made it extremely difficult to look him straight in the face, for Kitty was never sure which of his eyes was looking at her.

Later, while sitting in the back of the shop surrounded by fans of every colour, shape, size and design, Kitty sipped her favourite Italian wine and ate two of Signor Bartoletti's sister's delicious lemon cakes, liberally covered in wildflower honey and almonds. Afterwards, Kitty and her maid were escorted back to the Villa Barraccini by Signor Bartoletti's errand boy who was, in fact, extraordinarily tall, muscular and fiercesome in appearance. During the return journey they saw no sign of the sea-booted man who had followed them to the Piazza Angelica.

Kitty had grown to love everything about Venice. It had so many moods and yet they all seemed to blend together successfully. There were the quaint, almost tumbledown, little bridges over the canals, the regal, sumptuous marble bridges carved so exquisitely and showing no signs of their great age. Then there was the terrible Bridge of Sighs, across which condemned prisoners had walked to their deaths.

It seemed strange to see, amongst all the colour, vitality and thronging activity that the gondolas were painted black. When she asked why, she was told that it was so that the Venetians should never forget Martin Faliero, the fourteenth century Doge who had sought to exceed the power and authority that the Council believed he should possess. His sentence had been carried out at the top of the staircase known as the Giant's Staircase in the courtyard of the Doge's Palace, for it was here that he had been beheaded. Those had been the dreaded days of the Council of Ten and the State Inquisition, when the vengeful or malicious could post a letter in one of the openings in the Palace wall accusing their enemies of any crime they cared to concoct.

Once or twice Mellyn would exclaim, saying that she was sure they were being followed as they explored the city, but if the man in sea-boots was still keeping track of them Kitty did not see him.

Frescos and painting were everywhere in Venice. Indeed, Venice itself was like one enormous painting, richly-hued, its moods varying from majestic to poignant. Some of it, like the four magnificent bronze horses stolen from Constantinople and now dominating the entrance to

St Mark's, was breathtaking, startling almost – for who would imagine placing horses in a cathedral?

Inside the Basilica itself were the awesome frescos which had taken no less than seven hundred years to complete, and the Pala d'Oro in front of the High Altar, which had been started by the Byzantinians and completed by their Venetian apprentices. A blaze of rich, dark gold encrusted with jewels – sapphires, rubies, emeralds, pearls, amethysts, yet more jewels added over the centuries by Doges and penitent or grateful nobles. Admiring the Pala d'Oro and captivated by its beauty as she was, Kitty was aware that none of the jewels and the gold blazing before her could compare with the blazing star diamond of the Pharoah Jewels. For a moment a strange, aching longing suffused her: a longing to be holding the Pharoah Jewels, to have them pressed against her body, encasing her throat and forehead, her arms and fingers, so that she became one with the heavenly star, Sa-lu-is, once more.

'All this gold, all these jewels, mistress.' Mellyn's voice brought her back to the present. 'And all those starving cats and children out in the streets, all those beggars, yet here in this Basilica it is afire with wealth for a dead man.'

Kitty looked at her maid with raised brows. Such words from her were virtually anathema, for Mellyn had been raised strictly as a Baptist. Yet what she said was true, and Kitty had thought such things on many occasions before. However, she knew what the Church would say on the subject. Undoubtedly their reply would be something on the lines of 'Blessed are the poor.'

'There's old Sea Boots again, mistress,' Mellyn hissed, and Kitty turned to see a man bobbing out of sight behind one of the massive pillars.

'Ignore him, Mellyn. There is nothing he can do to us

here and we are carrying nothing of value. Besides, he would not dare try to rob us in a church.'

'I do not like it, mistress, I do not like it at all.'

'Stay close to me, there is nothing to worry about,' Kitty said firmly, and with that she continued to stroll around the Basilica, enjoying its tranquil yet mysterious atmosphere.

That night Kitty dined with Count Barraccini and his sister again. They had been warm, hospitable and attentive during her stay, but all the same she felt that she had outstayed her welcome. As they dined on an exotic concoction of pasta, Kitty felt in a poignant mood. When she tried to tell the Count and his sister how grateful she was, they would not let her go on.

'We have enjoyed your visit, Signorina McDonagh. You can have no idea how much you have enlivened our lives,' Estella's rare and youthful smile lit her face. 'My brother and I are old and, some might say, cantankerous. Certainly few people flock to visit us as they once did when we were young. We are pleased to have been able to give you a safe haven while you discovered our beloved Venice for yourself.'

'The Villa Barraccini alone was worth my visit,' Kitty smiled.

'Yes, it is good that you found us in time,' Estella said, but by now Kitty was accustomed to her mysterious pronouncements and she did not ponder overlong on her words. 'There is a time for everything and it was your time to discover us,' Estella went on.

'I cannot remember ever having felt so much at peace before, and it is entirely thanks to you, Conte and Contessa!'

'The peace will go with you wherever you go, even if it is halfway round the world.' Reaching out, the Count touched Kitty's hand lightly and a spring of warmth and serenity began to flow deep inside her.

That night in her room she went to the star-shaped cupboard on the wall just as if she were being guided to it, and, for the first time, the door swung open at her touch. Inside was a painting, a picture of a young and beautiful Egyptian queen with long flowing black hair. She was kneeling down and looking up intensely with love and reverence at a handsome man in majestic robes who was placing around her neck the glittering collar which Kitty recognised as that belonging to Queen Faranefi. Spell-bound by the blazing colours of the picture, Kitty reached out a finger, tracing it over the face of Queen Faranefi, then down to the jewelled collar.

Then as she looked up into the young Pharoah's face, a feeling of disorientation swept through her. He wore a high, oval headdress of gold which concealed his hair, and from the centre of which blazed the star Sa-lu-is. Despite the strange headgear, those arrogant brows and that nobly arched nose and sensual mouth could belong to one person and one person only: Carrick, Lord Cromer.

She looked again at the face of the Queen who was being crowned with the diadem of Sa-lu-is which the man was holding in his strong brown hands. No, the young Queen's face was not hers, most certainly not! Nor was it Carrick Cromer's face. Even to think such a thing was stupidity, nonsense. She, moon over that contemptuous, self-seeking man who thought that she was his biddable slave for him to use as callously as he wished? *Never*! Let him think what he liked of her, it would not alter the truth. She was her own agent, her own mistress. She would do what she wanted, exactly what she wanted, and she intended never to have anything to do with him again, come what may.

CHAPTER SEVENTEEN

'We have a guest for dinner tonight,' the Count told Kitty next morning. 'A merchant, he told me, one who has heard of the Pharaoh Jewels, and wishes to see them. We seem to be becoming a show house here. I wonder how many more will come to view our treasures?'

'An Italian merchant, Count?'

'His letter is from a town some miles distant from here, Roscania, and his name is Aristotle Chieffo, which does rather suggest a man of this country,' the Count chuckled. 'One who has no trouble annotating his accounts himself, I would say. You will not mind a stranger at the table with us?'

'My goodness, no. All friends begin as strangers, anyway. And with your skills as an interpreter, I shall hope to be able to hold some kind of conversation with Master Chieffo,' Kitty smiled.

'Would you like to wear the Jewels for him to see? It is up to you, of course. I would not dream of pressing you to do this. I see by your expression that you hold some doubts. Well, there is no urgency. Wear them, or not, it is up to you.'

'I do not think that I could settle to eating dinner in them,' Kitty pondered. 'Go to a coronation ceremony maybe, but they are hardly meant for the more everyday pursuits, are they?'

'As I have said, it is up to you, my dear. Signor Chieffo will, I am sure, be struck speechless by your beauty whether you wear them or not.'

That night, Kitty was still deliberating over whether or not to wear the jewels. She was dressed in a gown of pallid ivory silk, swathed across the shoulders with gossamer lace of the most fragile kind in the classical mode, but the lace was removable and could be taken off in seconds to reveal a plain scooped neckline which would be ideal to display the Egyptian collar.

Standing before the pier glass in her bedroom, Kitty took off the lace, then fastened it back on again. Mellyn, watching with admiring Celtic-brown eyes, made a tutting noise.

'If 'twere me had the choice, I'd be wearing the jewels to sleep in as well!' she said. 'You could not wait to get here to see them, and now you say no to wearing them for an evening.'

Kitty could not say why she felt this strange ambiguity. Certainly, before, she had rushed to see them, to put them on. She remembered the strange, disorientating effect they had on her when she wore them – was it that which was making her feel so reluctant?

'Take off the lace, mistress, take it off and wear the collar and the earrings – they suit you so. If you don't you'll rue it forever!' Mellyn stood with arms akimbo.

'That is a possibility.' Kitty swept off the lace drapery and turned to smile at her maid, whose face had brightened. 'Yes, you are right, Mellyn. Would you tell the Count that I have decided to wear them?'

Some thirty minutes later, standing before the pier glass in the Pharoah Jewels, Kitty felt the same dizzying sensation as before. There was so much to remember, to look back on, but what she must remember she could not even begin to guess. It was as if she had lost her memory entirely, and must use her senses to find her way about while she wore these beautiful, stunning gems. But she was in safe and happy surroundings. With the Count at dinner, she would feel secure, she knew.

Estella had a megrim and was dining in her chamber. Kitty and the Count had awaited the arrival of Arostotle Chieffo for quite some time before the clanging of the great bell at the front door proclaimed his arrival. A few moments later, a servant announced the approach of Signor Chieffo and then the door swung open, and there he was, the Italian merchant with the imposing name who had dreamed for years of seeing the Pharoah treasures.

Kitty was speechless at the man's appearance. She could not get to her feet, but sat where she was, wearing the jewels, which suddenly felt like boulders weighting her down. Now she knew that her fears had all been justified, that they were in the presence of a villain who would stop at nothing to manipulate people in order to get what he wanted.

For some minutes, she tried to speak, but could not find her voice, and then the Italian merchant was being introduced to her, he was bowing over her hand and his eyes were beacons of admiration, as he greeted her in an accent which was more shattered than broken. What must she do? Expose Carrick now, terrify the Count and ruin his plans for the cosy dinner party? No, she could not do such a thing! Finally she decided to play along with Carrick's impersonation, call him Signor Chieffo and behave as if he were a complete stranger to her. This was what she did, but as the evening progressed and it became obvious that Signor Chieffo had been invited to stay for a few days, she felt that she must speak of her fears to the Count.

Struggling to behave normally was a massive effort. She could hardly swallow and she dared not do more than sip at her wine in case it went to her head. She had to fight an entire siege of conflicting emotions, for, even in the guise of a comparatively humble merchant, Carrick was as dazzlingly attractive as ever to her. If the Pharoah diamonds bewitched and bemused her, then he did the same a hundred times more.

The Count seemed to suspect nothing. He was in fine fettle, jovial, making jests and enjoying himself immensely. Somehow, he seemed to be highly contented at their being together, why, she could not understand. She put it down to his natural conviviality, which he had had little opportunity to indulge.

'Signor Chieffo' was in great good humour, too, displaying a veritable ocean of shattered Italian, so confusing at times that Kitty wondered whether he was speaking English with an Italian accent, or vice versa. As the hours dragged, she coult not wait to reveal her fears to the count, but when he announced that he would retire early, to see if Estella were feeling any better, Kitty was put in a quandary.

'Would you like me to see to the Countess?' she said immediately, but the Count waved his beringed hand.

'That is very kind of you, *cara*, but my sister does not like anyone visiting her when she is ill. Vanity, you know,' the Count's eyes twinkled. 'I am sure that you and Signor Chieffo will find much to discuss. Pleasant sleep to you both. Good night.' And with that the Count was gone. Kitty opened her mouth to call after him, for she was still wearing the Pharoah Jewels and did not know where to put them for safety that night. Then a servant appeared with the casket and in utter relief, aware of Carrick's acquisitive and burning gaze, she removed the gems and placed them in their container.

When the servant had gone, Carrick leaned against the carved plaster fireplace, his eyes appraising her.

'What a pity he took them away – I would have liked you to wear them while I made love to you,' he drawled, his eyes on her breasts.

'You – you *devil*!' Kitty flung herself across the room at him and beat against his chest with fists which were as effective as tissue paper. 'How dare you threaten this dear old man! I know why you are here, you thief! Coming here in disguise, under false pretences, accepting the Count's hospitality when you plan to rob him!'

Carrick trapped her flyings fists as if they were two little butterflies and pressed them to his lips to kiss.

'So now I am a thief and a villain, am I? Is that what you call all the men who bed you, Kitty?'

Cheeks crimson, Kitty opened her mouth to scream out loud, but Carrick instantly put his hard palm across her lips and her scream became a muffled wail. He held her in a manacle-like grip until she became calmer.

'This behaviour is insane, Kitty. The jewels are mine, and I have proof of this. I have only to denounce Count Barraccini and he will be in the kind of trouble which will inconvenience him for some years. Do you want to see him mouldering in some foetid gaol? Venice is infamous for the heartless treatment of its criminals.'

'You would not dare. The Count is no criminal. He is a good, kind, generous man – why should he steal anything? Look at the wealth and riches in this house!'

'The value of the Pharoah Jewels is beyond anything which could be produced today. Their curiosity value alone is boundless. I intend to discover how he got them, and to bring in the law if he does not agree to hand them over to me.'

'You monster!' Tears rolled down Kitty's cheeks. 'You will break his heart. He is an old man, he could not take such callous treatment!'

'Nothing will change my mind. That is why I am in Italy.' Carrick's bronze eyes were burning with a mixture of ardour and what she took to be longing for revenge.

Her hands free at last, Kitty swept away the betraying tears.

'You cannot go on being so cruel and mercenary, Carrick Cromer. You will find out that such behaviour brings its own punishments in the end!'

'What would you think of a few years in an underground gaol, with water pouring down its walls and no light for months on end?' Carrick asked.

'Oh, you plan to have me imprisoned too, do you? Well, please do – I offer myself up in exchange for the Count. Leave him as he is, a happy, healthy old man, and take out your anger on me!'

'How noble, how selfless, *cara*. But then you always were a little nun at heart were you not? At heart, that is, but other parts betray you, do they not? I have only to kiss you and you will let me do anything I wish.' His slumbrous deep gold eyes blazed, and, taking her hand, he placed it between his thighs, pressing it against the steely hardness there so that she could feel every line, every curve of him.

'If that is what will satisfy you, then do what you wish to me, but only leave the Count alone. Promise me that you will not hurt him! Promise me that you will not take the jewels from him! He loves them – they are his life. Please, he has nothing else now!' Kitty begged.

'You ask a great deal – for others. Had you thought of what you could get for yourself if you cared to ask?'

'Then please, promise me that you will do what I ask!' Kitty cried.

'What do I get for a reward?' Carrick's mouth was very close to hers, and he was moving her palm up and down between his thighs.

'Anything – anything you want from me, if you will only promise!'

'Then I agree. The Count will not be hurt, the jewels will stay with him.'

'Oh thank you, thank you!' Kitty felt faint with relief and would have fallen had he not been holding her tightly. The combination of fear for the Count, and the nearness of her lover had temporarily robbed her of strength. Carrick had only to hold her, and all her determination, her vow to have nothing more to do with him, just ebbed away, not even leaving a memory.

'You looked like a queen in the jewels, Kitty. I wish you still had them on . . .' Carrick's sensual voice rippled over her like silvered waters from a magical river. Could its name be Lethe? 'You cannot imagine how I felt when I saw you in them.'

'Perhaps you want them to put on your fiancée?' Kitty's voice was deliberately harsh. 'If it excites you to see a woman wearing a fortune in gems, then you are with the wrong woman. Might I suggest that you visit one of the goldsmiths here in Venice and buy something priceless for Lady Dulcie?'

'Why do you have to bring up her name now?' Carrick's lips were insinuating themselves along her throat, her self-control was taking off on winged feet.

'She is the woman you are to marry. She should be in your thoughts all the time. If I were she . . .'

'What would you do? Admonish me, tell me to stay by your side, and be faithful? Take a whip to me?' Carrick stroked her ears with the tip of his tongue. She imagined that it was rather like being struck by lightning. She felt as if she had been charged with electrical forces, set alight and at the same time reduced to helplessness.

'I can never be in her place, so it is pointless discussing it.'

'You had your chance and you flung it away. You are the most impetuous, wrong-headed female I have ever met.'

'My chance to what? Be your kept whore, your paid mistress in a picturesque little house near the park? That is not for me, I am afraid.' Kitty tried to push him away but knew that she was wasting her energy.

'I see you recall what I said word for word. That suggests it has remained in your thoughts all this time.'

'Of course! It is not every day that a man asks me to be his paid whore.'

'Oh come now, Kitty, all of London knows about your past. It is somewhat colourful, is it not? And that is putting it mildly . . .'

'You still believe all that idle nonsense? I just cannot comprehend how intelligent people can listen to gossip.'

'Ah, praise at last!' Assuming a stunned expression, Carrick put a hand to his heart. 'So you think I am intelligent?'

'Who does not?'

'So it is not your view, then?' He assumed a stricken air.

'The view of hundreds which I merely echo,' Kitty said tartly.

'Oh come now, *cara*, think for yourself. Or has that quality been lost? The girl I remember at Cromer Manor had enough wisdom and judgement to deduce my virtues without being prompted by the commonalty.'

'And to deduce your faults, too. Perhaps it was the observation of those which prevented me from seeing the virtues – if there are any.' Kitty was breathing heavily now, longing to fling herself against him and beg to be taken to bed, but her pride was a splendid armour.

'No man is perfect.'

'Especially not when his name is Carrick Cromer.'

'So I am a fiend, a monster, a rogue and villain – a thief, too, you said? A cutthroat and cutpurse, too, I suppose?' He put his head on one side. 'And a highwayman, a smuggler, footpad and robber, too. Yes?'

'Oh this conversation is inane!' Kitty cried, jumping to her feet in the greatest indignation, to find that Carrick's boot heel was on her hem and that her skirt had ripped from its waistband to reveal much of her underwear and even more of her silk-stockinged, shapely legs with their rosebudded silk garters at the knees.

'Oh, how did that happen!' she cried, looking down in horror.

Carrick had begun to laugh, and he went on laughing as her fury mounted. To her ears, his mirth sounded both raucous and callous, and she wanted to hit him hard, but her skirt had to be held in place. She gave a snort of disgust and headed for the door, but he was behind her instantly, and then as she tried to elbow her way past him to freedom, he scooped her up in one effortless movement and proceeded to carry her across the hall and up the beautiful ornamental stairway.

'Put me down! You cannot do this! We are guests here – we cannot do this, it is unthinkable – dreadful . . . If the Count knew . . .'

'If he knew, he would be seething with envy. Any man would. Who could see you and not want to bed you, *cara*?' Carrick's voice was velvet with sensuality.

'According to you, I never say no, so there cannot be many disappointed lechers around!' Kitty snapped, twining her fingers in Carrick's glossy gold hair and giving a sudden and very violent wrench. He barely winced, but grinned, and continued to carry her onto the upper landing.

'Now where is your chamber?'

'I will never show you, *never*!'

'Then shall I make love to you out here on the landing? That footman down in the hall is looking exceedingly interested in our activities. Shall we ask him to join us?' The slumbrous gold eyes were glittering with amusement.

'Oh you wretch! I shall not listen to such infamy! Put me down!'

'Here? This looks like a soft Turkish carpet – ideal to lie on. Here, let me unhook your gown . . .'

'No, put me down!' Kitty was struggling to express her confusion and embarrassment as mutedly as possible so as not to disturb the household; as a result she was bright pink and extremely flustered. There was also the problem of the torn waistband, which had fallen open when she pulled Carrick's hair and which was now revealing rather more than just a shapely leg.

'Why try to hide your charms, *cara*? I shall have that gown off in two seconds.' Carrick began to unfasten the hooks at the back of her dress, pulling at them roughly in his haste so that more of the fragile material ripped. Then he began to tug off his jacket, and it was then that Kitty leapt away and off into the darkness of the corridors which entwined themselves through the upper part of the villa.

'Come back!' Carrick growled, but she was not going to do that.

She could hear his footfalls behind her, sometimes loud and clacking as they fell on wood and sometimes muffled when they fell on one of the Turkish rugs. It was like being pursued by a hideous, limping monster . . . How dark the house was here – and scary. She very much wanted to turn back, but at this moment darkness was preferable to submission. She was panting now, as much from fear as exhaustion. She seemed to have lost her way – the villa was bleak and ugly up here, no furniture, no rugs, nothing but bare wooden doors, not even a window now and again. The corridor seemed to be growing smaller, suffocatingly close, and her legs were like wooden burdens dragging behind her. Where was she going?

Suddenly, there was nothing ahead. She was at a dead end, She did not want to go back, nor could she go forward. Hands outstretched, she leaned against the oaken panelling, sobbing with fear, her heart thudding, her mind crying to be free of this impasse. As her sobs grew weaker, she heard the sound of his boots behind her, coming closer, and his voice, richly mellifluous, coaxing, billowed over her like a cloak.

Then his arms were round her, his lips on hers, and she was lost.

CHAPTER EIGHTEEN

'You *will* keep your promise? You will not harm the Count?' Kitty whispered as Carrick placed her gently on her bed.

'I will keep my promise.' His face was serious, the perpetual mockery gone from his eyes for a few brief moments, then it was back in force.

'I think we have been enchanted, bewitched, I mean,' Kitty went on as she slid beneath the covers, still in her shift and bodice.

'I certainly have been – but it happened before we met here.'

'Oh, I did not mean like that! Can you not feel a strangeness here – a different atmosphere from that of other houses?'

'It is a romantic Italian villa, what else can one expect?' Carrick was tearing off his clothes at breakneck speed and flinging them across the room.

Mellyn, who had appeared with her face smothered in goosegrease and her hair twisted in curlers like miniature ram's horns, had taken one look at them and fled back to her bed.

'Oh yes, it is that. It was very – well, scary is the word I suppose. In that corridor, I mean.'

'Imagination, I expect. Women are notorious for it, you know.' He grinned, standing for a moment beside the bed as if to let her appreciate the Olympian splendour of his physique before he slipped into the bed with her.

'According to you, women are notorious, full stop!'

'Can we have an end to the sparring now, *cara*? You must keep your promise, too, you know. To give me anything that I want – *anything*, you said.'

At his words, she blushed to the roots of her hair, seeing in her mind's eye what she had left herself open to. Thank the Virgin he was normal – or at least she thought he was, but how did she know? People only allowed others to turn the pages of their books when they chose – he could have kept so much concealed from her. Her heart juddered a little as if it wanted to escape the mesh which was imprisoning it. Beat, beat, tremble, beat, it went, and she could do nothing to stop its betraying sound.

'You will not hurt me?'

'When have I ever done that?' He looked shocked. 'Except of course in the way that you love.' He curved his palm round her breast and it was like a benediction. How right she felt in his arms, as if she were made for him. Perhaps she was, but he was not made for her, and that must not be forgotten. All their togetherness, their intimacy, had been ephemeral. It was her problem that she found it difficult to accept that, not his.

He had said the word she craved to hear, but in the wrong context. Her soul needed his love for food. It was manna which could sustain her through anything. Without it, she must find her own life-support and these interludes, blissful as they were, made it all the more difficult for her to adjust.

She could hear the sibilant slap of waves from the canal beneath her window as a shiny black gondola snaked its way past the villa. The moon was bright and new – a time for new beginnings – and its limpid pearly radiance lit them, so that she could see his gleaming eyes and the lights in his hair, the sensual curves of his mouth which she ached to kiss. Then she was thinking of the stubborn little Queen Faranefi who would not accept her new husband as Pharoah, until she wore the jewels he gave her – after which she was his loving slave. If only there were similar jewels for Carrick to wear – his own Pharaoh's outfit, perhaps. Then, when he put them on, he would love her until destiny decreed otherwise – which would be for all time, of course. If only Sa-lu-is still had its power, she would pray to it, pray that he would fall in love with her.

'Sa-lu-is make him love me!' she whispered, very low.

'What did you say, *cara*? Did you hear that gondola go by? We should be in it, making love with the water beneath us. The bobbing movement would no doubt be a good aid to our own movement . . .' He chuckled, knowing how easy it was to discomfit her when he talked so boldly. 'What better place than a boat for a clandestine meeting?'

'What indeed?' Kitty agreed wryly, thinking of the *Adriatic Pearl* and how shamelessly she had behaved on it. And she was about to do it again! Pulling Carrick's head down to hers, she kissed him soundly, lingeringly, amazing herself as well as him. It was as if she were another person, more boldly daring, sure of herself, with primitive, almost pagan needs and motivations. It must be the spell woven by this house, and the astrologer-magician who lived here; what else could it be? Here was she submitting again, and gladly, when she had vowed she never would again.

Carrick seemed a little taken aback, too, for he looked down at her with brows raised.

'My little passion flower!' he teased, before their mouths ground together as if they could not breathe without each other.

'And you are my sun,' Kitty thought, as they became

twined more closely together, every bone, every fibre and muscle, every square inch of flesh making contact one to the other, so they seemed to be indivisible, inseparable. Now their kisses were sweeter than ever before, scintillating through their bodies, so that there seemed to be silent messages passing between them. How true were they, how much in Kitty's imagination? She heard, *'I love you, oh, I love you!'* but only in her thoughts, for he said nothing. She wanted to hear those words from him more than anything, but only if he meant them. Women who forced men into saying it were asking for trouble.

Strange, she had forgotten why she was in bed with him, that she was here to protect the old Count from disaster. Now, it was as if she had planned this with Carrick, as if they were here together, amicably, sharing a bed with love. She could only put it down to the witchery of this enchanted villa.

In their magic star-chamber, Estella and Count Barraccini smiled broadly at one another before the Count draped their magical crystal with a bright-blue silk cloth gemmed with silvery stars and crescents – a cloth which had once belonged to Lucrezia Borgia, and which was reputed to have miraculous powers.

'We were right, brother,' Estella smiled, thinking of the lovers they had seen entwined in one another's arms, their images strangely silvery and blurred when seen in the magical crystal. 'They are the ones we have sought. All these centuries, waiting, longing, and now they are here with us again.' Tears spangled her lashes and yet she was still smiling. 'Our Emperor and Empress – reborn, really *here* with us again.'

'We must not be overcome by sentiment, sister. We have much to do. Remember the first time they met. It is the same this time – and it is our destiny to bring them together again, so that the jewels will be with their rightful owners once more.'

'You will give them the jewels? What will they think if you do that? Who would part willingly with such treasures?' Estella's hand rested on Lucrezia Borgia's miraculous veil as if she were drawing strength from it – and power.

'I shall find a way. There is always a way. Have we not always been successful in the past? Sa-lu-is has not forsaken us, and we shall not forsake him. When our task is completed, we can rest again. Are you not looking forward to eternal peace?'

'More than anything, brother!' Lifting her hand from the veil, Estella smiled at the gleaming imprint of the crescent moon which glimmered in her palm. The moon and the stars, all satellites of the great Sa-lu-is, their lord and master, all proferring their powers to bring about what Sa-lu-is had ordained. How many centuries he had waited, as had they, his priest and priestess, but now the time was come, the heralding of the new age, when the lovers would rule again . . .

'We can sleep now they are together,' Estella sighed happily. 'How good it will be to sleep again, after all this time. I am looking forward to it. But first I want to know when they will be together for good. Will you tell me, brother?'

The Count beamed, the moonstone in his ear jiggling as if it were greatly amused. On his velvet cushion in the corner of the star-chamber, Adam Kadmon flicked his ears and dreamed of paradise.

Estella sighed, more loudly. 'I can see that I am not to know. Oh, how you do like being mysterious! Still, I should be able to tolerate it after all these years, I suppose. Goodnight, brother.'

'Goodnight, sister.'

When Estella had gone, the Count and Adam Kadmon exchanged a conspiratorial glance. They knew the answers to all things, but they were keeping it a secret – for the moment.

'You did not put anything in my wine, did you?' Kitty asked, as strange shimmering sensations luxuriated through her body. She was lying beneath Carrick, his body gently pressing hers; they had just made love and shared a cataclysmic orgasm.

'Why should I do that? A comatose woman would hardly appeal to me, would she?'

'Knowing you, of course not.' She wanted to ask him what he thought of her in bed, but nothing would allow those words to pass her lips. If she said that, he would know that she cared about his opinion of her. She must treat it all as casually as he did, otherwise, she would be the casualty. She could not bear to see any scorn and contempt in his eyes if he should guess that she loved him. It would give him too much power over her.

'You think I am a rogue, do you not, *cara*? A miscreant of the first water?' Carrick's voice was suddenly soft. 'A rogue who beds his women and then casts them aside in the nearest gutter.'

'Even if I did, it would not mean that I would let you treat me so villainously! There is no way that I am going to end up in the gutter!'

'One ditch is more than enough for you, eh, little colleen?'

'Yes, one ditch is more than enough.'

'I shall never forget how you looked in the Pharaoh Jewels,' he said, changing the subject abruptly. 'They look as if they were made for you. That rich gold and the turquoises goes perfectly with your colouring, and your eyes are lapiz blue. My little Egyptian Queen.'

'I am not *your* Queen!' Kitty leapt to defend herself. 'I am not yours in any way at all.'

'Then I must have made love to someone else just now. I could have sworn it was you – that passion, that response, those searing, heart-stopping kisses, the torrid embrace . . . I could have sworn it was all the great Kitty McDonagh, famous Irish courtesan.'

'You never forget about that, do you, never never, whatever we do, it is always at the back of your mind? I never was a whore, ever, ever, *ever*!'

'What about now, *cara*? What do you consider yourself now after all the times we have bedded together? Respectable lady is hardly the phrase that springs to mind, is it?'

She missed the twinkle in his eyes as she gave a cry of frustration and began to pummel his hard chest with her bunched fists. It was like swatting an iron ship with a butterfly net. Laughing, he crushed her to him, defeating her feeble attempts, pressing her hard against the mattress, grinding her body into the snowy sheets, his mounting desire now very obvious.

'You will not do it again – you have had what you wanted. You promised, you promised!'

'And you promised to give me anything I wanted, remember? Well, I want you again.'

'You – you satyr! You lecher – you . . .'

'Enough, *cara*. Egyptian Queens do not spit curses. They love their husbands devotedly, worship them . . . give them sons . . .'

'Worship you? I would as soon see you burned as a sacrifice. Gods are for worshipping, not mere men . . .'

'Gods, you said gods? I thought you were a Catholic.'

'If you knew that, why did you think me a whore?' she cried.

'Dear me, if Catholicism prevented immorality, most of the world would be beatified. What did you mean by gods, *cara*?'

'Oh how do I know? It just came into my head, that is all. God, gods, what does it matter? *Husband* . . .' The word came out unexpectedly and she touched her hand to her mouth. What had she been about to say? What had he told her about husbands? She could not remember.

'Yes, what about husbands, *cara*?'

'Oh this dialogue is inane. We must sleep now.'

'Sleep? You are jesting. There are seven hours until dawn and we are not going to shut our eyes once.'

He was true to his word. Zeus at his most physical could not have made love with more ardour than Carrick did that night. If she had asked for a sojourn with the Olympian ones, it could not have been more rapturous. One thing puzzled her – the word husband kept spinning through her head, but when she tried to make sense of it, it vanished like a brittle, dried-gold leaf buffeted by autumn winds. She should have learned not to question while she was in this enchanted villa. Just exist, just be, she told herself and all will be well.

To her amazement, an old Irish verse appeared next in her thoughts:

Across the green grass see my colleen a-dancing
With her heart I am joined, and it's marriage we're chancing
There's none other in Ireland I'm wanting to wed
For the rest of our lives 'twill be taties and bed . . .

Oh look at her grace, and her sweet, slender waist
Just to look is to have the most brilliant foretaste
Of the good things in life that're there for the taking
When me and my colleen our thirsts are a-slaking . . .

The words and the tune danced through her head, and she heard her mother's voice singing the words. One of Nora's favourite songs, coming to mind now of all times. How odd. There was no accounting for the tricks the brain played – that had been another of her mother's sayings. Was her brain playing tricks now, bringing back this rush of tender memories? Suddenly she wanted to weep, to give herself into Carrick's arms for his gentle comforting, she had the strangest feeling that if she did, and if she told him why she was weeping, he would want to soothe and cheer her. With all her might, she fought back the tears, because she knew that the relationship she longed for was one she could never have with this gorgeous, tough-hearted, unpossessable man. Weep in his arms? Pour out her troubles to him? What did he care for her problems? She knew what his answer would be. Something on the lines of 'Leave business to men – you have been wilful and stubborn and you deserve all you get,' and she shrank inside at the thought of this reaction, because receiving threats and warnings from him was one thing, but having them thrown at her when she needed sympathy and tenderness was another thing entirely.

'*Cara*, your thoughts are in another world. Am I so lacking in interest? Is there another lover in your mind? Are you missing him?'

Kitty gasped. How could he think that? But it would not do to cry out that he was her only love – for would that not increase his already powerful vanity? A husband might be told that, but not a conceited and arrogant lover.

'Missing another lover?' She paused as if reflecting. 'Well it is true that I did receive a proposal just before I left England . . .' She let her voice trail away.

'Who?' Suddenly, there was a lethal tone in Carrick's voice, and his kisses ceased.

'Who? Oh, one of those interminable, rich young men who languish in London salons and think they deserve to be deified by every girl they set eyes on.'

'Rich? How rich?'

'Of course, you would be interested in that side, wouldn't you? Not as rich as you, Carrick. Who is? Nor does he own an empire, nor is he in business.'

'A wastrel,' Carrick sneered.

'Not quite. He spends his money, he does not fritter it.'

'Tell me his name.' Carrick's bronze eyes were nearly black with passion. She was startled, but hid it well.

'No – it is nothing to do with you.'

'It has everything to do with me. Who is he?'

'What difference will it make if you do know his name? What do you plan to do?'

'Never you mind. Just never you mind!'

'I do not wish to continue this conversation.'

'I shall decide when our conversation ends, not you!'

'What are you going to do – torture me to make me speak? I tell you, I shall never reveal his name, and anyway, I said no. If you had first asked me what my reply was, we need never have had this idiotic argument.' Kitty lay back on the gleaming ivory pillows, looking exotically beautiful with her tumbling, black-silk hair, pale-cream breasts and neck, the faint tea-rose in her cheeks bringing out the blue of her dreamy eyes. She had no notion of the effect she would have had on any man seeing her like that, and if she had, she would have dismissed it airily. Physical love – everyone knew that it meant nothing; that it was, in the words of her childhood, the snare of the devil.

'Hmm, obviously a man of insignificance . . . penniless, no doubt.'

'Quite wealthy, as it happens – and why do you measure everything by money, Carrick? Do you think I am a scheming treasure hunter who makes up to rich men but ignores the poor? If you think that, it cannot do very much for your morale, can it? Do you think I am here just because you are wealthy and for no other reason?'

'Of course I know why you are here – to save your precious, beloved Count from spending the rest of his days in gaol.'

'You think that is it, do you? Nothing else?'

'Would you be here if I had not told you of my intentions to take the Count to law?'

'No – but . . .'

'There you are then,' he interrupted, sounding almost peevish in his pleasure at her agreement. Did it make him so happy to be agreed with even when it went against him? What a strange and unfathomable man he was – but then had she not always known that? Why be surprised when someone behaves as you expect, she thought? Still, she supposed that she had been hoping for some improvement in him, even a little hint of genuine warmth would have brightened her considerably. Just a little sign that he was alive.

'Carr . . .' she began, but he clamped his sensual lips down on hers and the moonlight, billowing down on them so brightly, seemed to have magical powers which could make them commit any folly together. Or that was how Kitty felt. As to the sphinx who at this minute was stroking her white thighs, she could not say.

They did shut their eyes, a little towards dawn, then, when sunlight touched their faces, Kitty woke with a gasp, her hand to her mouth. Looking by her side, she saw an empty space in the bed. It did not even look as if it had been slept in. The sheets were smooth, the pillow plumped up. She had dreamed it all – she must have done. It was the aura of this bewitching, extraordinary house, that was it.

Then the door swung open and Carrick stood there with a gleaming silver tray laden with breakfast for them both. He was grinning widely, his eyes gold in the sunlight, and as he strode across to her, the wine silk dressing-gown he was wearing swung open to reveal his shapely and muscular legs.

'It is time to break your fast, *cara*. What will you have? Pasta with beef? Pasta with mutton? Pasta with vegetables? Or perhaps beef à la pasta? No? Then how about mutton à la pasta? It is always a good idea to get to know the food of the country one is visiting.'

Kitty sat up, and stared at the tray, but all the dishes were covered. Did he really expect her to eat pasta at this time of day? She preferred a light breakfast.

'Well, which will you choose, *cara*?' Carrick's eyes were twinkling vibrantly.

'Could you repeat them again, please – I did not quite catch what you said.' She kept her face straight, as he launched into the descriptions and then came to a sudden halt, as he saw her mouth curving upwards.

'So what *have* you brought me?' she asked.

Placing the tray on her knee, he lifted the silver lids from the chafing dishes. Soufé omelette, *cara*, made with newlaid eggs – Italian, of course, so of a very special and delicate variety – and fresh cream, powdered chestnuts, butter. It was left to rise on a stove until it was enormous, as you can see.' He pointed to the highest fluffy omelette Kitty had ever seen. 'Or would madame prefer quince preserve on brown toast. Italian toast, of course.' Carrick poured out coffee for them both, stirring in thick yellow cream and adding rosemary-scented honey.

'And what is the difference between Italian toast and English toast, My Lord Cromer?' Kitty tried to make her tone severe, but she wanted to laugh out loud. When had she ever seen Carrick like this, so light-hearted, so jocular and full of fun? It was a delight, and she longed to respond in the same way.

Carrick frowned, stroked his chin, pretended to be thinking deeply. 'Could it be that there is no pasta added to English toast?' he finally said, at which she wanted to throw a pillow at him but was afraid she might upset the tray.

'You think you have me where you want me, pinned down by this enormous tray, Carrick Cromer, but you are wrong,' she twinkled.

'If you cannot win their hearts, go after their bellies, I always say.' Carrick lifted his coffee dish to his lips, not meeting her eyes. He must be joking of course.

'You must have a vast collection of the latter then,' she said serenely, helping herself to more honey.

'*Touché*, madame, *touché*!' Carrick grinned, and then they were grinning at one another across the tray in perfect understanding. This blissful state of affairs was to last exactly three minutes and then it was back to the uneasy thrust and parry. Fencing terms for two people who had fallen into the execrable habit of employing their tongues like swords.

'What will the Count think of us not appearing for breakfast?' Kitty was suddenly reminded of her duties as a guest.

'It was his idea that we dine in bed.' Carrick's eyes laughed at her. 'Oh, I do not think he had this in mind –

our breakfasting in the same bed – but nonetheless, he said that he did not expect us downstairs until we were ready.'

'And when did he say this? Have you seen him this morning?'

'You ask altogether too many questions, *cara*. Do you not trust me?'

Kitty narrowed her eyes. Trust him? She would trust an injured warthog or a starving tiger more than she did Carrick Cromer. And she told him so, at which he threw back his head and roared with laughter, his mane of mellow-gold hair bright as a beacon in the morning sunlight. Sun glimmered on his lashes, and she saw that they were a slightly lighter shade of bronze, and shone like pure gold. The sight made her heart quiver. She loved him, ached for him, dreamed of him, yearned for him – but she could never trust him. What was she to do about it?

'My lady has no reply for me?' He touched her cheek with his fingers, gently as mist.

'I am not your lady, Carrick. Your lady is waiting for you in London. Does she know where you are? What would she do if she knew about us?'

'Throw a crystal perfume flask at me? Shower me with talcum powder? Denounce me to all her intimates? Who knows? I have never troubled to consider her reactions.'

'You arrogant, overbearing, presumptuous man.' Kitty cried, reaching for more toast and turning her face away from him as she ate.

'All those, *cara*. You know me well.' He clasped a hand to his heart. 'Perhaps I shall make you my official biographer. I want the complete history of the Cromers put into print, you know.' He paused, tried unsuccessfully to quell the twinkle in his eyes, then leaned towards her, assuming a serious expression. 'You *can* write, I suppose?'

'Oh, you – you poltroon!' Kitty began. Then the tray was being swept to one side, and she was being soundly kissed, despite her mouthful of toast and preserve. She tried to mumble that she would like time to swallow, but he would not listen, and soon she did not care. Breakfast forgotten, they flung aside their robes and melted into one another's arms, naked flesh touching naked flesh, so that invisible sparks seemed to course between them, making them shudder with delight.

Kitty's ebony hair flew out around her like a black velvet cloak borne out by the wind, and the night stars were in her eyes, the enchantment of moonlight in her heart. Whatever witchery was alive in this romantic villa she was no longer fighting it. It now had total control of her, and it was a bliss so beautiful that her mind was assaulted with ecstasy. Let the future bring what it may, she would have this heavenly interlude to remember forever. Divinity on earth, paradise in Venice – this would be what she would recall for the rest of her days.

Afterwards, he whispered against her ear. 'You realise we must both go back to reality soon? I cannot stay here too long – I have other matters urgently needing my attention. I may stay in Italy, but I cannot stay here at the villa another night. Time will not allow.'

She came down to earth with a sickening jolt. It was as good as over already. She wanted to scream and weep and beg him to stay with her – just one more night, just a few more hours, but he was getting out of bed and slipping into his silk dressing gown and the expression on his face was that of all men the world over when they have put love from their thoughts and are now intent upon business.

'You are leaving now?' she said, her voice faint.

'Yes, I must.' He turned to her, and there was a

coldness in his face. Her doting, laughing, teasing lover had vanished. It was all part of the charm he displayed to get what he wanted: her body. When his lust was satisfied, he could not care less for her.

'What about the jewels?' Somehow, she could not see him leaving those behind. They had been the purpose of his visit, after all.

'The jewels?' For a moment, he looked puzzled, as if he did not know what she was talking about. 'Oh, the jewels. We made a bargain, remember? You kept your promise, and I am keeping mine.'

'*You are*?' She could not keep the astonishment from her voice.

'Yes – did you think I would break my word? Yes, I can see from your face that you did.' He came to the bed, took her hands and held them, but he might have been a stranger for all the passion there was in his eyes. 'We made a bargain, and there it is. The jewels will keep the old man warm in his dotage – that is what you wanted, is it not? Your heart would have been broken to see him deprived of his pretty comforts, that is right, is it not?' She nodded, dumbly. 'Well, thank the Lord that you have got what you wanted, then. The Count has his treasures, and you have the satisfaction of knowing that you were responsible.'

'I – I thank you . . .' she stammered. 'Forgive me for – for doubting you.'

He grinned once before leaving. 'Oh if I were you, I would never stop doubting me. It is far safer to continue like that with me. That way, you will never be hurt too much.'

Then he had gone, and she was left alone with the remains of the breakfast and the pieces of her heart which felt just like Aristotle Chieffo's accent of the previous night, shattered.

CHAPTER NINETEEN

They were not to meet again until they were both back in England. It was soon after Kitty had heard the gossip that Lady Dulcie was expecting a child. She heard it from one of her customers as she was pinning darts around her waist. The lady, a vain and ugly woman with a crooked nose and a mind to match, prattled on about Cromer and his Lady Dulcie until Kitty longed to stab the pins into the woman's flesh.

'That is why he has not married her before, you know. Oh, she has the beauty and the fortune, but he wanted to get her with child first, you see. When one possesses such enormous wealth, so many estates and properties and so on, one cannot take the risk of marrying a barren woman, can one?'

Kitty said nothing, affecting an agreeable expression to mask her true feelings.

'Lord, but it has taken him long enough to do the deed! She is three or four months gone, they say. The wedding will be any day now, of course. They cannot wait much longer, it would not be decent. You did her wedding gown, I believe?'

'I did, and her trousseau,' Kitty said, her voice flat.

'He seemed in such a haste to wed her one time and then suddenly it seemed that he had lost interest in her. But that, of course was because he thought she was barren. When so many infants die in the cradle a woman needs to be capable of producing progeny each year. One cannot have enough when so many die young. Lady Bannering had nineteen children, you know, in a matter of twenty-two years, but she has only one living child left, only one who passed the age of five, that is.' The speaker, who was insensitive by nature, suddenly came to her senses, realising that she was talking to an unmarried female who would no doubt one day wish to have children of her own. 'I hope that I am not putting you off producing your own family when the time comes, Mistress McDonagh.' The woman gave a nervous titter.

'My gowns are my children,' Kitty said, somewhat tersely, and after that her client changed the subject.

'There is a lot of talk in the City. They say that Lord Cromer is beside himself with fury.'

'That would be nothing new.' Kitty went on pinning doggedly.

'It is this new trading company – Venice Trading Company, I believe it is called. Lord Cromer says that its founder has an infernal arrogance for encroaching upon his territories.'

'What territories are these?' Kitty asked in all innocence, admitting nothing, for she had told very few people about her new venture. The last thing she wanted to do was attract Cromer's attention. A subtle, gentle encroachment was more in her line, and that was what she had been doing in the months since her return from Venice.

'Oh, there is some old eccentric duke or other. I do not know him personally, but he is a great friend of the King's and he wishes to return to this country to be beside His Majesty in his hour of need.'

'Where does this duke live, Lady Gwendoline?'

'The Sugar Islands – a quite barbaric place. But it is said,' and here Lady Gwendoline lowered her voice, 'that he has a disgraceful predilection for dark-skinned girls, which was why he made his home on his plantation there. Now he wants to return to London with all his property, his art collection, furniture, treasures, etcetera, etcetera. Apparently he has always dealt with the Cromer Trading Company, until now when he has given the shipping of his goods to this newly-established company which I mentioned. That is what has enraged Lord Cromer.'

'I would have thought that such a wealthy and well-established man as Lord Cromer, not to mention his worldwide company, would have thought nothing of losing one shipping consignment. Perhaps it is a matter of masculine pride? And, of course, when one is at the top there is only one way that one can go.'

'It is rumoured that Lord Cromer hopes that the Duke's belongings will go down at sea, thus finishing forever the Venice Trading Company.'

'And what of the poor Duke's possessions? Has anyone asked him what he would think of losing all he has in the world?'

'I do not think Lord Cromer was looking at it like that. I do believe he spoke only in the heat of the moment.'

'That is something he does frequently, I believe. Would you not say that it was his habit to speak out thoughtlessly? Tact and diplomacy are just as important in business as the ability to handle finances and carry out one's commissions on time. Now if I started to tell my customers what they said about one another . . .'

'People speak about me?' Lady Gwendoline gasped. 'They talk to you about me?' Her dark-brown eyes flashed.

'Oh, only to say that they envy your complexion or your

tiny waist, Lady Gwendoline.' Kitty smiled to herself, knowing that the satiation of vanity was like a drug to some women – especially this one.

Mollified, Lady Gwendoline put a tiny jewelled hand to her stomach. 'Well, if they compliment me on the latter it is entirely to your credit, Mistress McDonagh. This new light corset that you designed for me is so much less cumbersome than the old-fashioned variety and it takes quite two inches off my waist.'

'I want some hair ornaments and hats to fit the new flatter wig,' Lady Dulcie Madingley announced. 'And I do not want to be overcharged or I shall take my custom elsewhere. I quite liked the colours that you suggested for me before and I would like them to be put to good use again. I also want my trousseau and wedding dress updated.'

'Updated, my lady?'

'Yes, indeed, that is what I said. Are you still having trouble with your hearing?'

Kitty remained silent but her cheeks went pink.

'Panniers are not so wide as they were a year ago, so I shall want some material taking out of the skirts.'

'Out of the nightrobes too, my Lady?' Kitty said serenely.

'The nightrobes? Why, of course not, you –' remembering that Lord Cromer was also in the room, Lady Dulcie struggled to compose her tongue. 'No, no, of course not. I shall not be wearing panniers in my nightrobes.'

How I wish you were, thought Kitty, the longing to do violence bubbling inside her. By rights you should be wrapped up in a great big cage of metal so that he cannot get at you!

Instead she said, 'Of course, my lady, have the dresses –

brought round and we shall attend to them.'

'And the hats, do not forget the hats for the new lower wig.' She enunciated the word lower as if Kitty were not only deaf but totally ignorant of fashion.

Lord Cromer was growing ever more restive. He had gazed out of the mullioned windows for some time, strolled up and down at the far end of the room, looking at first one then another of the framed sketches of Kitty's most successful designs. He had even at one point sought to catch Kitty's eye, but she had coldly disregarded him. At last, bored with talk of dresses and hats, he had flung himself into the armchair at the corner of the room. The most appalling screeching and yowling was the result, as an enraged and indignant kitten flung its way between his legs, shooting across the room and hiding under the skirts of one of the dress dummies.

Having ascertained that Apollo's son had not been damaged in any way by this, Kitty returned to the discussion with Lady Dulcie.

'What is your kitten's name?' Lady Dulcie asked, for one of her few endearing qualities was that she had a tender spot for animals.

'His name?' Kitty's face assumed an air of sweet innocence. 'Why, his name is Bassanio.'

'What a queer name for a cat! Was he not a character in Shakespeare's Merchant of Venice?'

'I believe so.' Kitty's innocent expression did not desert her for one moment.

And then Bassanio, having summoned all his courage, tore out from the shelter of the model gown to fling himself at Lord Cromer's ankle, where he clung on with every claw fully extended and bit into his leg as hard as he could.

As Lady Dulcie and Lord Cromer left, Kitty stood in

the doorway watching their carriage gather speed. She could have sworn that Carrick's face staring out at her through the carriage window wore an expression of almost anguished entreaty. She consoled herself with the thought that in Lady Dulcie he was getting his just deserts. Perhaps he would consider it all worthwhile when she presented him with his first son and heir, in another four or five months. The wedding would have to take place soon or all the gowns would be coming back yet again to have the waists let out.

Turning on her heel, Kitty went back into the fitting-room of Jade Cottage, which was now her home in the Vale of Health, Hampstead. There were tears in her eyes as she sat down in the chair recently so tumultuously vacated by Bassanio. Within seconds he had clambered onto her knee and was gazing at her with his soulful dark gold eyes, batting her gently on the nose with a furry paw until he had gained her full attention. Cradling him in her arms, Kitty wept a tear or two into the fluffy velvet of his head. The beautiful dream was over, finally and forever. No doubt Carrick had added fickleness to the long list of her crimes, but that could not be helped. Since Venice she had gained the strength to put a vitally needed distance between them. She was no longer his plaything, his little doll, to be picked up, used and flung aside until he lusted after her again. She believed that she had worked through every stage in their relationship and that she was now free of him. Very soon he would be a married man and a father, which should clip his wings, she thought, as Bassanio, having decided that she needed grooming, started to clean her tears away with his rough little tongue.

'Oh, Ba, why couldn't he have been as loving as you?' she said, nursing the soft, warm, pliable little body against her breast.

Lord Huntley was married, his wife with child, and Amalia's infant daughter was flourishing. Everyone around her was either pregnant, newly-delivered of a baby, or trying their hardest to conceive. Work was her palliative, as always, of course, and she was now successfully designing baby clothes. But admiring other people's babies was not like having one of one's own, and Kitty had come from a large family where a new baby had arrived regularly.

Jade Cottage was pretty and in a much sought-after spot in the Vale of Health, overlooking the stretch of water which the locals called the Pond. Bassanio was the best of companions of the four-legged variety and it was true that he slept in bed with her every night, his head on her pillow, purring resoundingly every time she moved. But he was not substitute for the one man she longed for and needed.

One day, as she was walking along the edge of the Heath in a meditative mood, she heard a shout behind her and turned to see Captain Benjamin Hawkley approaching.

'Why, Mistress McDonagh, how are you? You are one of the first people I have encountered since I returned to this country, and how marvellous it is to see you! You do not seem to have changed at all.'

'And you look well, too, Captain Hawkley. How long has it been since we last spoke?'

'Why, it must be all of a year, for that is the time that I have been with my regiment abroad.'

'A year – can it really be that long?'

'Too long, Mistress McDonagh, far too long. I thought of you often and longed to know how you were progressing.'

'You did not write, Captain Hawkley.'

'Ah, but indeed I did, Mistress McDonagh. I wrote on a number of occasions to my aunt, Esmeralda Flanahan.'

'Your aunt is Irish?'

'No, her husband was. He is dead now and, alas, so is she, and that is why she did not reply to my letters, although I did not know it at the time. You see, I had asked her to enquire after your health, to visit you and give you my compliments and to let me know how you were.'

'You could always have written to me direct, Captain Hawkley.' Kitty strode along at a good pace, part of her wanting to be alone but the other part thinking, well, he is a man after all and male company will cheer me.

'I was told that you had moved, you see, and I did not know your new address.'

'I have moved only recently, Captain Hawkley.'

'I was told that you had gone abroad.'

'It is true that I did go to Venice, but that was only for a visit.'

'I see, then I was mistaken.'

'A letter to any of our mutual acquaintances would have found me, I am sure.'

'Yes, you are right.' Hawkley looked chastened.

'How is the young lady you spent so much time with before you went abroad?'

Hawkley swallowed hard. 'Er, do you mean Alice Motleby?'

'Yes.'

'She married Doctor Gage. They are in Holland now, I believe.'

'I had thought that you and she were promised to one another.'

'Indeed not, Mistress McDonagh!' Captain Hawkley sounded shocked. 'Indeed, since I first set eyes on you,

Mistress McDonagh, my thoughts have been totally occupied by your grace and beauty.'

Kitty went on walking, saying nothing for some time. Then she asked Hawkley if he had seen Frederick Argoed since his return.

'I have not, Mistress McDonagh. Have you?'

'Not for some time,' Kitty replied. 'I believe he is now coming to the end of a particularly long poem and he has been shut away for some months composing it. I know the title, that is all.'

'And what is the title, if I may ask?'

'Two Lovers in Venice.'

'Argoed did not go to Venice with you?' Hawkley's voice came out as a squeak.

'Why, Captain Hawkley, what are you suggesting?' Kitty cried.

'Oh, forgive me, Mistress McDonagh, I did not mean that as it sounded. I thought – well, could it be that you and Argoed are affianced?'

'We are not, nor are we likely to be.' Kitty's eyes twinkled. 'I think it could be said that we are both married to our art.'

'My cousin said that you now design regularly for the Queen and her daughters.'

'That is so. They are charming girls and a great support to Her Majesty in these difficult times.'

'Ah yes, the King. His condition worsens, so I hear.'

'Sometimes he is lucid, at others he is quite deranged. All that can be done for His Majesty is being done but, alas, he does not improve.'

'Tragic, tragic. We must all pray for him. You are a Catholic, I believe, Mistress McDonagh?'

'Yes, I am, Captain Hawkley.' Kitty wondered what he was leading up to.

'Would you be willing to change your religion?'

'Change my religion?' Kitty gasped. 'What on earth for?'

'I am a Non-Conformist and my bride would need to be the same.'

'That is between you and your bride.'

'Yes, if my bride meets with the approval of my Uncle Thibault – that is the Earl of Walton – then he will make me his heir. He is a very wealthy man, Mistress McDonagh, but he is a strict Non-Conformist too, you see, and could only accept my marrying a lady of the same beliefs.'

'I do not know why you are telling me all this, Captain Hawkley. It is really none of my business.'

Hawkley, whose eyes had been fixed on Kitty's bosom for some yards, suddenly came to a halt and grasped her hand tightly in his. His palms were revoltingly flabby and damp.

'Mistress McDonagh, as you know, I have been consumed with longing for you since the moment we first met. At that time our union was impossible for a number of reasons. Now you are a lady of some substance and not a little fame, which will please my uncle tremendously, and if you will become a Non-Conformist too, then I would marry you and, in due time, you would be a Countess – the Countess of Walton. I am sure that this would meet with your satisfaction, would it not? Your ambitions . . .'

'My ambitions are my own concern, Captain,' Kitty softened her words with a smile. 'I do not need a man to elevate me, either with his money or his title. You have used the word longing but not, I notice, the word love.'

'That will come in time, Mistress McDonagh.'

'Whose time, Captain Hawkley, yours or mine?'

If he answered 'ours' she might have relented a little

and taken pity on him, but he did not, merely saying that time would tell.

'I do not think that such an important relationship as that between man and wife can be left in the nebuluous hands of time, Captain Hawkley.'

'Oh, you are being unkind to me, Mistress McDonagh! You have no idea how desperate and lonely a man can become when he is abroad with his regiment. I have longed to see your face again, to hear your voice.'

'You have my sympathy, Captain.'

'I need more than your sympathy, Mistress McDonagh. If I could have but a little of your comfort and concern . . .'

'And my heart – what of my heart?'

Hawkley's face flushed. She realised that he appeared to abhor any reference to emotions.

'Your heart,' he croaked. 'I would vow never to break it.'

'Are you good at keeping vows, Captain?'

'I am an honourable man, Mistress McDonagh. My good name means more than life itself to me.'

'So imagine what your uncle's name will mean to you when you inherit it.' Kitty smiled faintly. 'But first you must find a suitable bride to please your Uncle Thibault, a good, decent Non-Conformist girl, of course. And I could hardly be called that, by virtue of religion or otherwise.' Kitty shrugged off Hawkley's hand.

'You would condemn me to a life spent with some boring, witless female?'

'You said a Non-Conformist, Captain.'

'So lacklustre, so mundane, beside you, Mistress McDonagh.'

'Tut, tut, Captain. That hardly sounds like devotional talk.'

'I would be as devoted to you as I am to my God,' Hawkley offered, his face as earnest as he could make it.

'I am a great romantic, you know.'

'If you wish to be courted properly . . .'

'I would hope that any man I decided to marry would know how to court me that way.'

'Then will you allow me to, my dear?'

Kitty wanted to be alone more than anything, the sun in her eyes, the wind in her hair. She had so many thoughts which needed clarifying, but most of all she needed peace from unwanted admirers.

'Will you let me pay court to you?' Hawkley insisted.

'I am sorry, but the answer must be no, Captain Hawkley. Oh, do not think that you do not have my sympathy and my concern, for you do. But you must realise that we have not seen one another for a year and I am now totally involved with my business.'

Hawkley's eyes glittered. 'You are an ambitious young woman. Think how your business will flourish when you are a Countess.'

'You would let me continue with my work after our marriage?'

'Oh, until the first infant arrived of course.' Hawkley's eyes were on her breasts again.

'I see.' Kitty pursed her lips.

'But surely you would not wish to continue when you were with child? What of your health and that of the infant?'

'So really it would be pointless my being a countess for the reason you just mentioned, would it not? Unless, of course, the babies took their time in arriving.'

'I would hope that my heir would be born within a year of our marriage, Mistress McDonagh.'

'I see. You have it all neatly planned. Well, I am glad

for you, Captain, and I hope that you do find the lady of your choice, and very soon, too, for I am told that the longing for an heir can be extraordinarily agonising. Look what it did to Henry the Eighth, after all.' And with that Kitty strode away over the Heath and back to the tranquil haven of her too-quiet cottage.

Hawkley did not give up easily. Gifts arrived at her door daily: flowers and numerous exotic and unusual mementoes of the Captain's sojourn abroad. Calmly Kitty sent back all the gifts, until one day Hawkley arrived on her doorstep, anguished, begging her to keep everything he sent her, saying that he had chosen all the gifts with her in mind and that he wished no one else to have them.

'Captain Hawkley, I cannot possibly accept these gifts, for that would suggest there is a bond between us and I am not prepared to acknowledge that.'

'Believe me, I shall not consider that I have any claim upon you if you accept my gifts.'

'I do not mind the flowers but I cannot possibly accept anything else.'

'Then flowers it shall be.' With a darting gesture, Hawkley grasped her hands, kissing them passionately before turning on his heel and striding away.

Flowers it was: every variety, size, shape and hue. Day after day they arrived until Jade Cottage was bursting at the joints. The scent was delicious, the colours too, but not the purpose for which they were sent. Only Bassanio truly enjoyed them. One day while Kitty was out he demolished the lot, leaving the floor ankle-deep in shredded petals.

After her first startled reaction, Kitty threw back her head and laughed until the tears ran down her cheeks.

Swinging Bassanio up into her arms, she covered him in kisses while imagining Captain Hawkley's face if he ever knew what had happened to his offerings.

The visit from Lord Cromer was like a tornado. Alone, he stormed up to the door of Jade Cottage and hammered furiously on it. By the time Mellyn opened it her legs were trembling.

Moments later Carrick was being shown into Kitty's pretty little drawing-room. Not pausing for civilities, he launched into a tirade.

'This deception has gone quite far enough! I am here to put a stop to it. Stick to your dress designing and keep your nose out of my business!'

Aghast, Kitty stared at him. He was as elegant and beautiful as ever, bathed in honey-gold light from the window so that his bronze hair gleamed like newly-minted sovereigns. He was healthily tanned and the cut of his clothes, although tasteful and expensive, was ruggedly masculine. He did not go in for frills and flounces, black patches and lace ruffles. As she stared at him, wondering what he could mean, she realised that she felt a new strength and conviction. Obviously he had come here thinking that he could order her about as he had done before, thinking that he had absolute power over her. She had been weak, given in to him, been unable to resist his advances. Well, today would be different.

'Do not speak in riddles, Lord Cromer,' she snapped. 'If you have come here with some genuine complaint then let me know what it is.'

Carrick glared, slamming his hand down on the dainty corner table so hard that the crystal vase filled with flowers rattled alarmingly.

'You have stolen my oldest customer and you have done it by fraud and underhand tactics.'

'Ah, you mean the Duke of Warrington. All I did was to offer a lower price than the one you quoted to have his goods shipped back to this country.'

'My price was an excellent one. You had no right to undercut it.'

'Who says that I had no right? If I wish to undercut your prices then who is to say that I shall not? That surely is my own affair.'

'The Duke has been my most esteemed customer for many years. Before he went to the Sugar Islands he was one of Fabian's closest companions. Indeed, they grew up together as boys.'

Turning to the chiffonier, Kitty began to arrange the flowers which stood there in a cloisonnée jug.

'I am sure the Duke would not like to think that you felt he owed you allegiance. Perhaps he is in a fragile financial state and could not afford your rates?'

'When your ship goes down and he loses all his goods he will realise that he could not afford to pay such a low price!' Carrick's jaw clenched.

'That sounds very much like a threat to me, Lord Cromer.' Kitty turned slowly, her face cold.

'A threat it is not, but merely a realistic observation after having viewed one or two of the ships which you hire to do your business.'

'How I conduct my business is no concern of yours, Lord Cromer.' Kitty tapped her nails on the shiny surface of the chiffonier.

'When it interferes with *my* business then it most certainly is.'

'I cannot see that one customer going elsewhere will impoverish you, Lord Cromer. If you lost half your customers you would still be one of the wealthiest men in the country.'

'My fortunes are no concern of yours, Mistress McDonagh.'

'I did not say that they were. But while you are insisting upon concerning yourself with my business I feel it is only right I should do the same with yours.'

'You are a stubborn, hard-headed woman and you think that you can succeed in a man's world, by snatching bread from men's mouths!'

'Am I to take it that you have reduced the wages of your employees because you have lost one person's custom?'

'That is not what I meant and you know it is not. Keep out of the trading business, Mistress McDonagh! It is no place for females. Their brains are not equipped for such endeavours.'

'No doubt your idea of a woman is one who thinks of nothing but new gowns, jewels and producing heirs for you? Might I suggest that you get back to the lady who so aptly fits your requirements and leave *me* in peace, Lord Cromer.'

Carrick's eyes narrowed and in one stride he was across the room. 'You stubborn little vixen! I am going to teach you a lesson once and for all!' he roared, and with that he grasped her round the waist in an iron grip and, flinging himself into the nearest chair, dragged her across his knee and began to wallop her as hard as he could.

'You monster, you *fiend*! How dare you, how *dare* you!' Kitty screamed.

'Just – be – glad – I – am – not – going – to – harm – you – in – a – more – serious – way!' Cromer stormed as he smacked her until her bottom and thighs were red and stinging. She tried to break away from him but she could not for he was extraordinarily strong. 'This will teach you to keep your nose out of men's business, my lady, and if I hear you have been encroaching on my territory again I will come here and do this to you until you come to your senses.'

'You are the most arrogant brute I have ever met – worse, far worse, than your uncle ever was!' Kitty yelled.

'Well, you should know about that,' Carrick rejoindered eyes sparkling, 'for you have bedded us both, you little bawd.'

And with that he flung her off his knee so that she landed in an ungainly heap on the floor in a welter of satin skirts.

'You did not call me that when you made use of my body in Venice!'

'A brief moment's lust – it meant nothing, nothing at all.'

'Any woman would have done, would she not? The lowest strumpet, a street urchin, even a beggar-girl – you do not care who you use when you wish to indulge your animal passions, do you?'

'That is correct, Mistress McDonagh. Anyone would have done, any strumpet would have satisfied me as successfully as did you.' He paused, eyeing her coldly as she struggled for composure, tugging her skirts down over her calves and pulling the tangle of hair from her eyes. 'Yes, anyone would have done. Did you really think you were unforgettable? You will have to do better than that. A few pence can buy me any trollop – they are waiting for customers now across the length and breadth of London.'

'You got me free, *free*!' Kitty screamed after him as he strode to the door.

Turning, his eyes mocking, Cromer said: 'Perhaps that is because you are not worth even a few crusts, Mistress McDonagh. Besides, something that has no price is valueless.'

'Then what of love – *what of love*?' Kitty cried. But he had gone, the door thudding shut behind him. Clenching her fists, she fought back tears. She would die before she took orders from him. No one was going to make her give up her life's work – he had no right to interfere at all. If he came near her again she would get the Beadle to deal with him – a few hours cooling his heels in the stench of the Fleet prison would teach him a lesson, the ungovernable monster! He thought he ruled the world and he thought he could rule her too.

How wrong he was, and Kitty intended to prove it to him.

Part Three:

IN DUBLIN'S FAIR CITY

See how love and murder will out.
William Congreve, 1670-1729

CHAPTER TWENTY

Yes, it must be her imagination, Kitty decided. Unless she were prepared to believe that the man who had shadowed her in Venice was now here in London doing the very same thing. For some time now she had been sure that she was being followed. Yet if it was a footpad or common thief why did he not leap out at her and take what he wanted from her purse? No ordinary thief trailed his victim day after day. Then one night, as she returned from a walk on the Heath in the dusk, she heard a twig crack behind her and, looking round, saw a man creeping up on her stealthily. He was swathed in a cloak and she could not see his face. She took to her heels at once but the man raced after her, following her right up to her own gate. Her servants tore out of the house, giving chase as the man fled. They did not catch him but the cloak was torn from his back and brought to Kitty. Inside its pocket she found a shred of paper bearing the words *Cromer Trading Company* and she raged inwardly. How dare Cromer have her followed and set his spies on her! Who did he think he was that he could control her movements?

After that she ignored the lurking figure – after all, she had nothing to hide – and then one day a footpad jumped out at her as she was walking from a customer's house down a narrow side passage towards her carriage.

It all happened very quickly, so quickly that she did not

have time to collect her wits. Her purse was snatched from her wrist and when she put out her hands to try and stop the man he turned on her, punching her over and over again in the face and throat. The pain was searing. She felt as if she had been stabbed in the eyes. The last punch was particularly cruel, driving deep into the base of her throat. Choking, blind with pain, she fell unconscious in the alleyway.

She lay there unconscious throughout the night, with rain beating down upon her body, saturating her cloak and gown, chilling her through and through. It was nearly noon before she was found, for she had taken a shortcut which few people knew about. Dazed, coughing and weak, she was nursed first of all by Mellyn and then Amalia, who rushed to her side as soon as she heard of her plight.

Had Kitty not been in such pain and so very ill with a burning fever it would have been just like the old days with Amalia. Days passed and Kitty's fever would not leave her. She passed from moments of near normality back into raging delirium while Amalia, desperately anxious, sought to cure her with herbal possets and other well-tested medicaments.

Gifts arrived in plenty: flowers and fruit from Captain Hawkley. A crimson silk shawl from Frederick Argoed, with a copy of his new poem – except that Kitty was too ill to read it, or even to appreciate her gifts. She was slowly but painfully recovering when Lord Cromer arrived, laden with presents for her – more flowers, more fruit, and a pile of interesting books. Kitty would not see him. She told Amalia to send him packing. When he had gone she despatched a note to him saying, '*I see that you think I should eat and be surrounded by flowers, but surely the books contradict your belief that females should remain uneducated lest they take their place in a man's world*?' Having done that she felt very pleased with herself, managing a large smile for Amalia when she brought in some chicken broth and wholewheat bread and honey.

'Why are you smiling, Kitty, my sweet?'

'It is the message I have just sent to that bumptious fiend, Carrick Cromer.' And Kitty repeated what she had written to him.

'I do not see why you are so brutal with him, Kitty, dear. He has been so attentive while you have been ill.'

'Attentive? What do you mean?'

'Why, he has been here once, sometimes twice every day since you were found unconscious.'

'He – he did not see me while I was ill in bed? Surely you did not let him in here, Amalia?'

'Well . . .' Amalia's cheeks coloured a little. 'He seemed so distressed, so very upset and desperate to know the truth about your condition that, well, I did let him in once or twice to look at you. Just to look, of course, nothing else.'

'Amalia! How could you! You let him see me in bed? Oh, how could you?'

'Well, Kitty, my dear, I thought I recalled that he had seen you in bed before, albeit some time ago.' Amalia pursed her lips.

'At least I was conscious then and knew what I was doing – and what he was doing, too. You cannot trust that man!'

'What on earth did you think he would do to you while you were unconscious, Kitty, dear? He came in, looked at you for a few moments, seemed even more distressed – or so I thought – and then tiptoed out, quite white in the face.'

'He did? Are you sure that we are talking about the same man?'

'There is no mistaking the man we are talking about, Kitty,' Amalia said patiently. 'And what I have told you is the truth; he did look white and shocked after seeing you so fevered and delirious in your bed. He told me that he would pay for the best physician in the country if need be, but I told him that we were very happy with the one we had and at that he said he would pay all the expenses of your illness and send you fresh fruit and so on every day until you were recovered.'

'And what did you say to that?' Kitty's voice was faint.

'Why, I thought it extraordinarily generous and kind of him, my dear, and I said that if he wished to do that then, of course, I did not have the authority to prevent him. After all, Kitty, we have not lived together for some time, you and I, and for all I knew he might be your lover again. It isn't something that I could have asked him, you know.'

'So he has been sending fruit and paying my expenses has he? And what happened to the fruit?' Kitty's voice was even fainter.

'Why, you ate it, my dear, of course, what else?'

Kitty thought of the delicious, juicy, nourishing fruit which she had so enjoyed during the weeks of her illness – and all paid for by him, the man she hated most in the whole world. She had taken his gifts without knowing it; she had eaten them! And he was paying her bills! White-hot rebellion surged in her veins. No man was going to pay her bills and most certainly not that one. She would show him that she was truly independent, that she did not need him, that she wanted nothing more to do with him.

She would encourage Captain Hawkley's suit so that he would be more attentive and protect her. It would do Cromer no end of good to be shown the door by a man who had set his heart upon marrying her. A legitimate relationship, that was what she most wanted. In all truth there was no other kind worth having. Sordid, secretive love affairs and such-like were not what she had been made for, nor what she enjoyed. They made her feel debased, humiliated and heartbroken.

Next time that Captain Hawkley called, laden with scarlet, cream and blood-red roses, she was at her most charming. Hawkley, who had entered the room looking very hang-dog, brightened considerably at her warm response and very soon was stroking her hand, his fingers slowly creeping up her arm and lingering in the area of her shoulder, just an inch or two from her breast.

'Kitty, dear Kitty, I have been so desperately worried for you. It is all very well thinking that you are free to behave like a businessman but, when it comes down to it, you are just as vulnerable as any woman.'

Despite her resolve to encourage Hawkley, Kitty felt an immediate antipathy. He seemed to know instinctively how to set her teeth on edge.

'Men, too, are set upon in the streets,' she began, but Hawkley waved his forefinger under her nose.

'Men are hardy, and they cannot come to the same sorry end as fragile females.'

'I do assure you, Captain, I have not as yet come to a sorry end,' Kitty said firmly.

'Think what might have happened to you!' Hawkley put his hand across his eyes and shuddered. 'Out there all alone in the world, with no man to defend you. Kitty, it is my place to protect you and I insist upon it.'

Sighing irritably, Kitty said, 'Captain Hawkley, you cannot have a place in my life unless I wish to give you one, and on that score, my answer is the same as before.'

'*Your head*!'

'My head?' Kitty said, startled, wondering if she were beginning to bleed again.

'Yes, your head – it was damaged during this terrible attack and you do not know what you are saying! When you have recovered your wits . . .'

'My wits, Captain Hawkley, are in fine order, as ever!' Kitty burst out furiously.

'But my dear, how can they be? You were so sweet-natured before and now . . .'

'And now, what?' Kitty's eyes narrowed. To encourage this man was an impossibility. She could not do it. There was only one path open to her: to get away as soon as possible. That trip to Dublin must be brought forward. Amalia would be only too pleased to hear it.

'You are, well, shall we say irascible?' Hawkley affected a tolerant smile.

'*You* may say it as much as you like, but leave me out of it!' Kitty cried. 'Anyone would be irascible being pestered as much as I am!'

'So you call it being pestered.' Hawkley looked truly hurt. 'Is that all you can think of my suit? In truth, Kitty, I wish to marry you.'

'And take upon yourself an irascible, bad-tempered wife with an Irish temper? Tut tut, you would surely rue the day.'

'Never!' Hawkley clasped a hand to his heart.

'I am going away, Captain Hawkley, as soon as I am well enough to travel. It is a trip I have been planning for some time. Let us trust that when I return, I am my old sweet-tempered self again.'

Hawkley gaped, revealing crooked lower teeth crammed together like overlapping almonds.

'Going away? *Where*?'

'That is none of your business. But you will find out

soon enough, no doubt. Now, if you will please leave me, for I am tired.'

Hawkley seemed struck dumb. He walked to the door, his step unsteady, then he turned, his eyes mournful.

'Kitty, please marry me. Let us make your trip a honeymoon. What if you come to some harm while you are away? How could I bear it? The streets are full of brigands and cutpurses!'

Kitty reached out, grasping a china powder bowl on her bedside table. Seeing her intention, Hawkley hurried out, shutting the door just as the dish crashed against it, shattering into a dozen pieces.

Kitty lay back in bed, sighing with relief. Peace at last. She would have Mellyn turn him away if he came again before she left for Dublin. She was settling comfortably into the pillows when she heard the shouts. Someone outside, in the vicinity of her front garden, was very angry indeed. Strange, but the voice sounded like Argoed's. What could he be doing here? He was not due to visit for another two days. Pulling on her peignoir, Kitty went to the window. An extraordinary sight met her gaze.

Argoed and Hawkley were lying on the lawn, legs kicking out at one another furiously. Argoed had a clump of his rival's hair in his grasp and was trying to wrench it out of his head. Hawkley was punching Argoed in a very delicate area indeed, hence the enraged cries. As Kitty stared, amazed at such antics, strands of Hawkley's hair flew into the air, and blood started rolling down his forehead. Sickened, she rang the bell for her maid.

'Mellyn, get the Beadle – somebody, anybody, and stop those two idiots killing one another!'

'Yes, mistress!'

As Kitty turned to the window, she saw a movement on the Heath. A tall, vital figure was striding down towards the cottage, face ablaze. In the next few moments, the two would-be pugilists were being torn apart by powerful hands, one flung to one end of the gardens, the other catapulted into the compost heap beneath the trees. Having sorted them out, Carrick Cromer stood with his legs spread out, hands on hips, a fiercesome expression on his face. Only after the two men had scuttled off, did he let his expression soften. Then, turning towards the window where Kitty stood, he bowed low and extravagantly, like a cavalier of King Charles's time, and he blew her a kiss.

Indignantly, Kitty stepped back, slamming shut the window. Suddenly, she felt faint from all the upset of the past half hour, and she crawled back into bed, her face pale.

Soon afterwards, Mellyn tapped at the door.

'Lord Cromer is here, mistress. He'd like to visit you if he may. He says he has something to tell you.'

'He does, does he? Well, I do not want to hear it!' The shame of having to watch that man separate her suitors with their childish, rowdy behaviour! How could she display them as serious escorts when they grovelled in the wet and mulchy grass like little boys? Cromer would laugh when he saw her with them now. And with good reason. 'Mellyn, send him packing. He is only here because he feels guilty.'

'What do I tell him, mistress?' Mellyn looked perplexed. She knew which of the three men she would like to have courting her.

'To go to hell – no, wait. Tell him to find one of those bawds he spoke of so warmly, and to stop pestering me!'

Dublin was grand and beautiful, a fair city indeed, and the people were friendly, greeting Kitty like a long-lost relative. She warmed to them instantly. They were trusting and childlike, helpful and selfless in a way the tougher, harsher people of London were not. Here, people would pause to pass the time of day and chat warmly. If she asked directions they would be given willingly, without any sign of impatience or coldness. Now that she was back among her own people – her mother and father's people – she felt brighter and more optimistic than she had for many months.

It was ture that Dublin was second only to London for gaiety. Amalia's friends had arranged parties, soirées and balls in her honour, and at these Kitty would appear in impressive and beautiful gowns of her own design. Rumours of Kitty's exotic origins had even reached Dublin, and the fact that during her early weeks there she wore lace veiling to conceal the remains of her bruises was to add to the air of mystery already surrounding her. Amalia, as always, treated the whole thing as an enormous jest.

'If it pleases the people to think that you are a Russian princess then let them do it, Kitty, dear. Have pity on their poor mundane lives – they need exciting rumours to enliven their existence. That veiling that you wear is causing quite a furore, you know. Annabel Barkley asked me if it was to hide your identity – she said she had heard a story that you were an exiled princess who had fled the Russian Court after a terrible scandal involving a love affair. She thinks you are wearing the veiling so that no one will guess who you are.'

Kitty raised her eyes heavenwards. 'Sometimes I wish I could shout something like those famous words of Henry the Second's: "Will nothing rid me of these turbulent rumours?" ' But she grinned, all the same.

'Mystery and intrigue are marvellous for business, Kitty, as well you know. People love to think that they are in possession of an exclusive story or great secret – and it does give you the edge over Carrick Cromer, does it not? He can hardly spread the rumour that he is an exiled Russian prince, now can he? Everyone has known who he is from the moment of his birth. There is no doubt that he grew up in England and no doubt about his parentage. Not that there is any doubt about yours, Kitty, dear, but the people think there is.'

A few days later Alicia, Lady Keneally, asked Kitty to create some designs for her.

'I want some exclusive gowns, Mistress McDonagh, really exclusive. Everyone appears at balls and so on in exactly the same kind of dress and they all think they are exhibiting the very height of fashion when, in fact, they all dress exactly the same. It is so tedious, I find, and I want to look different, very different. You live in London, you know what all the latest modes are there, and I want something which is totally up to date but also quite exclusive to me. Something ingenious, something breath-taking and unforgettable. Cost is no object. Oh, and I shall want to wear it with my rubies and emeralds. There has been much interest in this veiling you wear over your hats and wigs; is this the current fashion in London?'

'No, Lady Keneally, merely something I thought up for myself.'

'I love it!' Lady Keneally cried. 'I absolutely love it! Will you design some hats for me and some head-dresses for evening and all with veiling, please? Pretty, fragile lace. It gives one such an aura of mystery and the male sex do so love a mystery, do they not?'

Not to mention the ladies, thought Kitty wryly, before telling Lady Keneally that she would begin on the designs immediately.

Her days seemed busier than ever though she was here for a holiday, or supposed to be. By day she went out into the countryside to meet the cottagers who had been recommended to her for their craftsmanship. She organised regular supplies of linen and lace, woven materials and worsted to be sent to her in Hampstead. Some would be used for her dress designs, but she also had plans to enter the world of interior decorating. She had seen friends of Amalia's set up home after their marriage and introduce the most garish and offensive colours in their homes. She knew that although society women would spend hours upon their clothes, having fittings and dressing up, many of them affected total boredom when it came to decor. Two friends of Amalia's were marrying within the next six months and both had commissioned Kitty to select colours and materials for their new homes.

It was all very well sending hundreds of miles away to Genoa and Venice, or Paris, but Kitty felt most strongly that one's own countrymen should be supported. There was no sign here in the fashionable section of Dublin of the famines which had recurred regularly during the last century. Amid the splendid Georgian elegance of society's edifices, ribboned by the Liffy, there was only spendour and sumptuousness: a further example of the wealth of the English artistocrats who revelled here. But she knew that when one travelled deeper into the countryside, through County Dublin and into the wilds, there was exactly the same penury and shocking poverty which she had known as a child.

If the potato crops flourished all was well, although it was still a hand-to-mouth existence. Turf, cut from the bogs and then dried, would keep a fire in the hearth, and buttermilk was the main drink, but should the major food harvest fail there was instant hardship. Cottagers would and did die rather than eat the grain and vegetable crops which they grew to sell so that they could pay their rent. Starving was infinitely preferable to being homeless. Kitty wanted to do something for these people – employ their considerable skills, give them regular work, and thereby raise their standard of living. Every man and wife whom she helped in this way would be like her own parents to her and all the children whose lives were made easier as a result would be like her own brothers and sisters.

Sketching designs, arranging contracts with the cottagers and, frequently, if their plight were particularly desperate, paying them a large sum in advance to set them on their way, that was how Kitty passed her days. Her evenings were spent with Amalia in the sumptuous surroundings of the wealthy English who thronged in Dublin. There were magnificent balls at Dublin Castle with its gloriously-coloured rooms. She loved the Wedgwood Room, which was circular and had alcoves carved with a white shell design similar to that on Wedgwood pottery. Dinners were served in splendidly elegant rooms, with glittering chandeliers hanging from the ceiling. Afterwards, there would be dancing in St Patrick's Hall with its glorious frescos on the ceiling, and mirrored walls. Gold pillars lined the walls like sentinels, matching the gold-painted friezes and carved ornamentation. Kitty particularly enjoyed walking along the State Corridor, which had white and gold arches so glitteringly designed that it was like passing under crystal canopies.

At one end of St Patrick's Hall was a gallery for spectators and at the other a gallery for musicians, the hall having been given its name after the institution of the Most Illustrious Order of St Patrick by King George the Third.

'You know what we think of the Order of the Garter in

England, Kitty,' Amalia said, 'well, the Irish feel exactly the same about the Order of St Patrick. If you look up there you can see the Star of St Patrick over the galleries.'

Following Amalia's finger, Kitty saw the eight-starred emblem, one over each gallery, and a strange tingling feeling ran through her veins. It was nowhere near as brilliant or as breathtaking as the star Sa-lu-is in the Pharaoh jewels but it was very similar all the same, and eight-pointed, too.

'The star – doesn't it remind you of the one in the Pharaoh Jewels?' Kitty had to lean towards Amalia so that they could hear one another above the enthusiastic playing of the musicians.

'Yes, it is rather like that now you come to mention it. How strange – I wonder if the two could in any way be connected? But I suppose not, for Egypt is a world away from Ireland. This star is nothing religious, at least I do not think it is. The Knights of St Patrick have their meetings here, you know, although they are actually invested in St Patrick's Cathedral. There are many great names amonst them, Mayo, Granard, Arran, Enniskillen, and so on. We are lucky that the eighteenth century has been so peaceful here in Ireland or we could not have been enjoying ourselves in this beautiful castle.'

'Peaceful for the rich,' Kitty wanted to say, but she knew that would have been too provocative. However much money she amassed – and her fortunes were now considerable – she would always be at heart the penniless Irish girl who had been found half starved in a ditch by Fabian, Lord Cromer.

'Mistress McDonagh.' With dawning dismay, Kitty looked up to see Frederick Argoed bowing before her. Straightening, his glittering and covetous black eyes boring into hers, he said: 'London is devastated without your presence. Ladies do not know what to wear. Gentlemen's hearts are broken. It is reputed that the King himself has taken a turn for the worse since your departure.' Argoed's eyes twinkled, but it was a dangerous twinkle for there was always a look of barely-controlled passion in his gaze, especially when it rested upon Kitty.

He was a strange man – and she always felt happier when she was not alone with him. He had sent her many entreating notes while she was ill and during her recuperation, and he had proposed to her both by letter and in person, but she had always said no, kindly but firmly. She could not forget that last sight of him fighting Hawkley on her lawn. Sometimes his hands would clench and unclench as if he were finding it difficult to restrain his emotions. They were doing that now.

'Mistress McDonagh, would you care to dance with me?' he asked, holding out one narrow and sensitive hand to take hers.

Irish musicians were playing that night and, as always, their efforts were rumbustious, and hearty. Kitty did not know which particular piece of music they were playing at that point but it was refreshingly simple and melodious. She could not help but remember the first time she had danced with Argoed soon after her arrival in Hampstead. Now, he was even more dashing, his wild black hair combining an uncombed disarray with romantic appeal. The bones of his face were strong and spoke of character but his hands were womanish, the nails just a little too long and carefully manicured. He was splendidly dressed in a new suit of dull blue velvet with gold trim on the jacket and breeches.

When they were in the centre of the dance floor Argoed's arm tightened round her like a vise and he pressed himself against her in a most forward fashion. She could feel that he was roused, and she knew what was in his mind, for his cheeks were flushed and he was finding it impossible to keep time with the music.

'Sir,' Kitty began, but Argoed only crushed her to him more tightly, while tremors coursed through his body, and his palms became hot and damp. There was little she could do without causing a furore, so she tried to keep her body as relaxed as possible whilst trying to engineer Argoed to the edge of the floor.

'I am desperate without you, Mistress McDonagh,' Argoed was mumbling in her ear in breathy gasps. 'I sent you my verses but you did not let me know what you thought of them – I could no longer wait for your approval. I had to come here, I had to see you again! Why do you torture me like this? Whatever have I done to hurt you? I want you so much, Mistress McDonagh. My home is yours, my life is yours, and I would lay it down for you this instant if the need arose.'

'I hardly think that will be necessary, Master Argoed, for we are not at war with Ireland at this particular point.'

'Oh, but there are Irish brigands everywhere – thieves, rogues and villains lurking at every corner. Dublin is such a dangerous place for a beautiful young girl and I entreat you to return to London with me.'

He and Hawkley were beginning to sound like one voice!

'So Dublin is too dangerous for me, is it, Master Argoed? Well, I am sorry, but I cannot agree with you there. I find the people here charming, gentle and cooperative.'

'Underneath all that pretentious behaviour they are savages, base savages.' Argoed glared at her. 'The Irish are nothing more than beasts of burden and should be used as such. Their only use is to fill the coffers of English landlords.'

'Are you a landlord here in Ireland?' Kitty said, controlling her anger with increasing difficulty.

'No, but I have friends who are, and it well known that the Irish people are lazy, indolent, dishonest and utterly disloyal.'

Kitty could stand it no longer. Lifting up her foot, she brought it down as hard as she could on Argoed's instep, grinding her heel against his bones. White with pain, he was forced to release his grip. Kitty sprang away, hurrying with as much decorum as possible to Amalia's side.

'That man is insufferable! I vow his wits are mouldered. I have never heard anyone talk such vicious nonsense.'

'What did he say?' Amalia asked, eyes wide.

'Vile, insulting things about the Irish people – how arrogant he is! And it is all possession, possession, possession – wanting to make me his, wanting me to do as he says – he makes Hawkley look a saint.'

'You will have to do something about all these suitors soon, Kitty, you know. You have been dangling them on a string for far too long. I can see fisticuffs ahead. Think of that fight in the garden. Limbs might have been broken had Lord Cromer not come along.'

'It is all a nonsense.' Kitty fanned herself furiously, trying to cool her burning face. 'When a lady says that she is unavailable a gentleman should believe it.'

'But such a statement always incites men to more ardour, Kitty, you should know that. They think that you are holding them at arm's length to make them keener.'

'Then their vanity is extraordinary. I came here for peace and quiet, not to be pursued by sex-crazed men.' She shuddered.

'I have never felt too happy about Argoed, you know,'

Amalia said musingly. 'He is strangely eccentric, a most unaccountable man at times. All that business about that young man he loved – well, it was rather disgraceful to say the least. Then there have been the women.'

'What women? I have heard nothing like that about him.'

'Then I should have told you what I heard,' Amalia said. 'You shut yourself up in your workshop and notice nothing unless I tell you. While you were in Venice he was involved in a rather unsavoury scandal over a young girl – a young maiden, that is, in every sense of the word. She was only fifteen, an heiress and, like most young girls of that age, extremely gullible. He made her pregnant in the hope that her father would agree to their marrying.'

Kitty listened aghast. 'What happened then? Did the father refuse?'

'Not only that, but he took a whip to Argoed, lashing him all the way down the drive from his home. The young girl, poor thing, was so upset that she miscarried, so that was that anyway.'

'The poor child! You should have told me of this before, Amalia.'

'We see so little of one another these days. Besides Argoed does not mean anything to you, does he? Now if I had heard that you were thinking of marrying him I would most certainly have told you this story at once.'

'He has proposed to me repeatedly since I was attacked that night in the alleyway. If I had known how he had treated that young girl I would have said no even more firmly than I did. Why he wants to marry me I cannot think. He can know nothing of my fortunes. As far as he knows, I am a dress designer and nothing else. I have kept my trading concerns secret as much as possible. Cromer found out but then he set his spies on me to do so. Argoed has no spies, nor the money to pay any.'

'Perhaps he believes the rumour that you are the Grand Duchess Tanya who has fled Russia with her priceless jewels to take refuge here in the British Isles?'

Kitty was speechless. 'The Grand Duchess *Tanya*?' she said at last. 'Is that what they are saying now? They have found a name for me, have they? Despite my being in deepest disguise with all those veils!'

Amalia chuckled. 'Ycs, and a character which will hardly meet with your approval. The Grand Duchess is a woman of uncontrollable passions who is reputed to have had one thousand lovers.'

'One thousand . . . I see!' Snapping shut her fan, Kitty rapped it so fiercely on the gilded arm of her chair that a whole sea of curious faces turned in her direction.

CHAPTER TWENTY ONE

Kitty's tranquil interlude in Dublin was over. Somehow Captain Hawkley had found out that Argoed had pursued her to Ireland and now he, too, appeared, pressing his suit with a fervour which made his previous attempts seem anaemic.

'The Earl, my uncle, is in a very fragile state of health, Mistress McDonagh. He is said to have suffered an attack of apoplexy and his physicians hold out little hope of him lasting the year. I am here because of your good heart. I knew that you would wish to help me if you were availed of the truth.'

'I am extremely sorry to hear about your uncle, Captain Hawkley, but I am afraid that my answer remains the same. Please do not waste any more time here with me. Go back to London and set about finding yourself a suitable Non-Conformist wife who will make your uncle's last months happy ones!'

Hawkley's eyes seemed to shrink and darken, his mouth clenching so fiercely that it went white.

'You are heartless. I have come all this way and you are still heartless!' Turning his back on her, he seemed to be trying to control his emotions for his shoulders shook and strange noises came from his chest.

Kitty stepped towards him, her hand outstretched, but at that moment he whirled round and grasped her wrist so savagely that it felt as if it had snapped. Angry, she tried to tug it away, but he refused to let go.

'If you do not release me, I shall cry for help,' Kitty warned, trying to thrust him away with her free hand, at which he proceeded to entrap that one, too.

'I am going to marry you, Kitty, and that is an end to it. In truth, I did not want to shock you – my uncle is near death. He has told me to bring back my bride to England to meet him within thc next few days, or I shall be disinherited. Oh Kitty, you would not do that to me?' His words were pleading, but his eyes glittered with a far more feverish emotion.

'Let me go! Free my hands!' Kitty stamped her foot on his toes, in the way which worked so well with Argoed, but it only served to inflame Hawkley more. Lunging at her, he stamped his mouth onto hers so violently that her teeth juddered, and then he was thrusting against her thighs in a crude simulation of the sexual act.

'We were meant for one another, Kitty. Why are you holding out against me? You know you would like to have me inside you now, you would, I know you would! You would like me *there*, Kitty. I make love well – I would see that you are satisfied, I vow it. How many times, once, twice? Three? I can mange it! I know that you have had many lovers – they say a thousand, but I promise you that none will have filled you like I can.'

'Oh, you swine!' Kitty gasped, then opened her mouth to scream very loudly indeed, but he clamped his hand over her face, almost crushing her nose at the same time.

'It is that curmudgeon Argoed, isn't it? He has had you first and now you think you love him. That is it, is it not? I will have it out with him, the poltroon, the knave! I will settle this once and for all! It is Argoed, isn't it? He has had you, hasn't he? *Answer me*!'

'No, no, no!' Kitty tried to shriek, but Hawkley's hand was clamped as tightly as ever round her mouth.

Suddenly, Hawkley's voice dropped, became an evil sibilant whisper, and that was far more frightening than his shouting.

'Kitty, promise me now that you will marry me and come back to England as my bride, or I will kill Argoed.'

'Kill him? In God's name, but that would settle nothing! A – a murderer cannot inherit.' Kitty's face felt paralysed where Hawkley's brutal palm had been.

'There is a lawful way to murder. Very popular it is, too. There are duelling clubs in plenty in Dublin. High jinks, they think it. I am a crack shot with a pistol and of course my sword arm is much practised as I have been on active service for some years.'

'A duel! Oh, you would *not*!' Kitty gasped. 'Argoed is much smaller – he is no good with weapons. His eyes are bad – he is short-sighted. You would murder him!'

'That is the idea. I see that you love him. Your concern is moving. I promise that I shall not bear you any malice for it when we are man and wife. And I mean that promise, Kitty. I mean it sincerely.'

'I shall never marry you!' Kitty wailed, white-faced.

'Then Argoed will die. He will be shot through the heart within a few short hours. It is as simple as that.'

'Oh, you are a swine!' Kitty cried. 'How could anyone stoop so low?'

'So you will agree to marry me? We shall have a public betrothal here in Dublin, so that you cannot go back on your word? You will agree to a public announcement at the Castle?'

'You cannot mean it about killing Argoed! I shall warn him and he will get away!'

'And I shall follow him, wherever he chooses to go,

until we fight. Inept as he is, his life would be in ruins if he refused to accept my public challenge. He knows that. A man who refuses a challenge is a coward and a blackguard. He would be shunned for the rest of his life.'

'You would kill him if I said no to you?' Kitty repeated Hawkley's words but she sounded dazed.

Her first shock at his threat was being followed by a second, deeper shock as she began to understand what the betrothal would mean. Forced into marriage with a man she did not even like, a man who was showing himself to be a bully and a brute . . . And to save the life of a man she liked even less . . . Hawkley's face was heavy with cruel determination; she knew that he meant every word he said. She also knew that she could not have another death on her conscience. First, her family, then Fabian, then Maddy. She had endured such bitter regret over the way she had failed poor Maddy. If another were to die because she did not care enough . . .'

'Yes, I would kill him. I am an expert at wounding so that death is a lingering agony. He would die with your name on his lips. He would curse you as he took his last breath.'

'You mean – you would tell him why you had shot him?'

'Of course. All Dublin would know by then. How would you feel about *that*?'

'His life – anyone's life – is far more important than my reputation!' Kitty blazed.

'I knew you would feel like that, Kitty.' Hawkley grinned triumphantly, and she knew then that she had placed herself in his power.

The following days passed in a haze. Amalia was struck dumb when she heard of the betrothal, but Kitty would not tell her any of the details. The last thing she wanted to appear was a heroine. Amalia pressed her for information, of course, but Kitty remained obdurate.

'The announcement will be in a day or two, Amalia, at the Castle,' was all she would say.

'Has the man forced you into this with some unpleasantness, Kitty? Lord Frederick would soon deal with him if that were so. Do tell me Kitty, please!'

But Kitty forced a bright smile and said such a supposition was nonsense, while in her mind's eye she saw Argoed lying in a pool of blood, his face twisted in agony. She could not add his phantom to Maddy's, which appeared with unnerving frequency in her dreams.

The Spring Ball at the Castle was the major event of the season. Kitty and her newly-hired Irish seamstresses had worked round the clock to finish the magnificent gowns for Lady Keneally, Amalia, and for Kitty herself. Lady Keneally would be in peacock-green silk studded with jewelled irises in blue and ivory, Amalia in dazzling russet brocade embroidered with silver garlands, and Kitty in sea-blue and sea-green, the Cromer colours, she knew, but still her favourite and which she frequently wore in memory of Fabian.

The panniers were narrower these days, and there were signs that a more classical line would shortly come into vogue. It was entirely due to Kitty's original hatred of the wide and cumbersome contraptions which weighted down the hips like boulders dragging at the waist, and put a stop to light-footed, graceful movement. She had gently indoctrinated her clients, and now was seeing the fruits of her work: the flowing, waterfall skirts with tiny panniers which in no way inconvenienced movement, and the more natural waist, no longer garrotted by the strangling wooden bone corsets.

For Kitty, the ball could have been a momentous occasion. Lady Keneally's delight in her new gown had been transmitted loudly and resonantly all over Dublin, and new clients were already approaching her. It would appear that she would soon be dressing the society leaders of Ireland as well as those of London. What more could she ask? She could provide regular work for all those poor Irish cottagers who had lived at subsistence level for generations, and who were now contracted to provide her with woven materials, linen, lace, and so on. But for Hawkley and the betrothal announcement, she would have been triumphant.

The night of the ball was here and the lights of Dublin Castle blazed like the heavens brought down to earth. Magnificent, brightly-polished carriages swung in through the gates one after the other to disgorge their sumptuously-dressed occupants in the castle forecourt. Lords and ladies of English and Irish ancestry mingled happily together, bowing and smiling, asking after one another's health and offspring. From inside St Patrick's Hall came the riotous cacophony of an Irish jig – the musicians warming up their instruments. Soon, more tasteful and lilting dance music would be heard, with only the occasional discordant note wrongly struck.

Captain Hawkley, resplendent in ceremonial uniform of scarlet trimmed with gold braid, looked remarkably dashing as he accompanied Kitty into the castle, his mouth tilted in a benign smile, his eyes bland. She for her part felt as if she were in a waking nightmare. How had she come to this terrible moment? Hawkley intended to make their betrothal announcement to a packed St Patrick's Hall, at eleven of the clock that night. After that would her life be worth living? She hardly thought so.

Amalia and Lord Frederick did not like Hawkley, or, rather, now that he was about to become affianced to their Kitty, they were prepared to tolerate him, but coolly for the moment. When told of the engagement, Lord Frederick had snorted, 'What, that jumped-up jack-anapes? Kitty deserves a lord not an infantryman!'

'Dear heart, do not forget that Hawkley will be an earl when his uncle dies.'

'Walton's a snide two-faced old badger,' Lord Frederick had snorted again. 'Runs in the family!'

'What does, my dear, a badger?' Amalia had said absently, thinking of her darling Kitty marrying a man she had never trusted, and whom she considered to be an adventurer.

'*Amalia*! Hypocrisy, I meant, hypocrisy! Walton's a Janus. All smiles and affability to your face and rasping acid behind your back.'

'He's quite old now, and very ill, so I hear.'

'As a youth, he spent all his time getting girls with child and abandoning them. The result was he had no legal heirs, which is all to Hawkley's benefit of course.'

'And Kitty's in due course, dearest,' Amalia reminded.

'Yes, maybe. But personalities run in families, d'they not? Look how Carrick Cromer resembles his late uncle.'

'Well, not in every way, husband. Some, maybe. Do you have any proof that Hawkley is a bad match. If you do, you must tell me, or I shall never forgive you!'

'My dear, Kitty will hardly thank us for blackening her fiancé's name, will she?'

'So you *do* know something! Oh, Freddie you must tell me this instant! What is it? What *is* it?' Amalia leaned forward, eyes boring into those of her husband, her hands gripping his.

Amalia recalled that conversation as she and her husband took their seats in the hall. She was filled with misgivings. Had she and Freddie taken the right action? She wished she knew what was for the best. She was dreading the hours to come.

Hawkley plied Kitty with wine to try and elevate her mood, but she felt only despair. Finally, growing impatient with her lacklustre response, he dragged her out onto the dance floor and whirled her round in a breath-snatching polka.

'You are stiff as a sabre – do relax, Kitty!' he hissed at her, but she refused to unbend. Surely he did not expect total submission? If, so, there would be furious battles ahead.

Eventually, growing tired of her chilliness, Hawkley led her to a seat and sat next to her, his eyes never leaving her face for the next two hours. Kitty's only relief was to fan herself furiously. Her ivory ostrich feather fan had a representation of the star Sa-lu-is, printed in the centre panel by none other than Signor Bartoletti to Kitty's specifications. Now and again, Kitty would look at the star, and then up at the balcony nearby where the Star of St Patrick was proudly displayed. How alike they were, and yet surely there could be no connection between them? If only she could leave this noisy, frenetic company and get away from Hawkley's feral gaze. She felt as if she were being stripped of flesh, layer by layer as he gazed at her. How could she have found herself in this appalling quandary? And who could get her out of it? No one, came the sad reply.

It was thirty minutes past ten, and Hawkley's eyes were glinting as he thought of the announcement he was to make soon. And then Amalia came to his side, smiling broadly.

'Captain, would you be so kind as to dance with me? My husband has sore feet after so much capering, and bade me get acquainted with our dear Kitty's fiancé-to-be.' Here, Amalia winked discreetly at Kitty, and then laughingly pulled Hawkley onto the floor.

Kitty was puzzled. She knew how Amalia felt about Hawkley. Loathing was not too strong a word to describe her friend's feelings for the Captain. Yet she had come to dance with him.

And then Kitty knew what was afoot, for a shadow fell across her, blocking out her view of the Star of St Patrick high up on the wall.

'*You*!' she gasped. 'What on earth are you doing here?'

'I am here to save you from yourself, Kitty. I thought you would have guessed as much.' Carrick smiled mockingly.

'Save me from – I need nothing of the sort, my lord! Have you been setting your spies on me again? Did they tell you I was here? You are despicable, Lord Cromer!' Rising, Kitty prepared to speed away.

'Not so fast, my dear.' Carrick's famous steely grip was imprisoning her wrist. 'I am here to tell you something which is vital to your future happiness and security.'

'Oh, you mean you have come as far as Dublin to tell me to give up my company or you will finish it for me, is that it?' Kitty blazed, cheeks crimson as she tried to free her wrist and failed.

'No – it is about this – man – you plan to marry. He is a rogue, a schemer, and a trickster. All he wants you for is your money – he does not love you. He does not know the meaning of love!'

'You are an arrogant, lying monster1' Kitty raged.

By way of reply Carrick dragged her out of the hall and into the nearest alcove in the corridor beyond.

While she continued to try to shout rude names at him he kissed her repeatedly. Within seconds Kitty was too weak with excitement and desire to continue her verbal onslaught. Overpowered by Carrick's kisses and the powerful yet protective way he was holding her so close – tender yet strong, she was overcome by the desperate loneliness and unhappiness which had been gathering inside her for so long now.

'You crazy little vixen,' Carrick murmured. 'Why do we always have to be fighting like this? Why do we rage at one another so? Life is so short . . . Oh, Kitty, Kitty . . .'

A commotion at the entrance to St Patrick's Hall was rapidly growing into a furore.

'What the hell is this?' Hawkley stood before the alcove his face flushed with rage. What the devil do you mean by this, Kitty? I was about to announce our engagement – I looked everywhere for you. But where do I find you? Embracing this man like some cheap strumpet. Cromer, it is time you got your just deserts and I intend to see that you get them!'

Taking his silk-embroidered gauntlets from his belt, Hawkley stepped towards Cromer, slapping the gauntlets across his cheeks, first one then the other. 'I challenge you to a duel. Pistols at dawn in Phoenix Park!'

'I accept,' Carrick growled.

'Oh no, no, not again!' Kitty cried, and then she fainted.

When Kitty came round she was in one of the private staterooms of the castle with Amalia bending over her solicitously.

'Oh Kitty, poor Kitty, what you have been through! Where will it all end?' Amalia was saying as Kitty opened her eyes.

'Where is he – they?' Kitty whispered.

'They both stormed off for an early night, I should imagine, in readiness for the duel.'

'Oh,' Kitty moaned, seeing Carrick riddled with holes, blood gushing from his wounds, as he collapsed dead on the ground. 'Amalia, find me a messenger. Get Hawkley back. Tell him I will marry him now, this minute, if he will call off the duel.'

'Their honour is at stake, Kitty, my pet. You know what men are like. He challenged him publicly and Carrick accepted publicly.'

'But it is all about me, Amalia! Hawkley is in dire financial straits, he needs as much money as he can get, and he must have his uncle's fortune. Huge gambling debts. Carrick told me all about it.'

'Gambling debts, eh?' Amalia removed the vinegar-soaked cloth from Kitty's forehead, re-dipped it, squeezed it out and replaced it on her brow.

'We have no time to waste, Amalia. You must send a messenger after Hawkley – tell him to come here *now*, tell him to bring a priest! I will marry him tonight if need be.'

Hawkley was sweating profusely. Challenging a short-sighted inexperienced duellist like Argoed was one thing, but challenging a skilled swordsman like Carrick Cromer was another. Biting on his nails, pacing up and down his room, swilling glass after glass of wine, Hawkley felt as if he were being stretched upon the rack. He had just received Kitty's message that she would marry him immediately if he would call off the duel. She had also told him that she would not marry him if the duel went ahead. So at least he knew where he stood. If he ran off, his name would be tarnished; he would be finished in society and Kitty would certainly not marry him. The alternative was to stay to fight Carrick at dawn, before selected seconds and, no doubt, a crowd of curious bystanders.

It was true that Hawkley had been abroad with his Regiment, but this had been interspersed with periods of leave when he had indulged his favourite vice of reckless gambling. During his service abroad, he had learned many things. He had learned how to kill; how to garrot; how to creep up on an enemy as silently as a panther and then knife him in the back. His pistols lay side by side on the table; beside them was his stiletto sheath knife, a long, thin, fine, shiny blade which carried murder at its tip.

Hawkley picked up the dagger, holding the icy cold steel to his cheek. It had been his faithful companion on many a lonely night in enemy territory. It would be so again tonight, for Carrick Cromer was just as much an enemy as any foreigner on battle-strewn soil. Putting on his most concealing cloak, the dagger tucked in his belt, Hawkley crept out of his lodgings and headed for Lord Cromer's rooms.

Carrick was asleep in bed when his bedroom door opened slowly and Hawkley tip-toed into the room, nothing heralding him but the tiny creak of a floorboard. He was a cool and accomplished killer, nothing gave him away, not even a wildly pounding heart. At the side of Cromer's bed he stopped, looking down at the sleeping man, and then he raised the murderous, needle-like knife over Carrick's heart.

CHAPTER TWENTY TWO

As Hawkley lunged down with the blade, Carrick's arm swept up to intercept it. The blade scored deep into Carrick's arm, slicing through a vein, so that a jet of blood drenched Hawkley's face and chest. In the fierce fight which ensued, and despite the serious loss of blood, Carrick managed to hold off his assassin, leaping out of the bed and crashing with his full weight against Hawkley. Chairs and a table were overturned and smashed into splinters, but Hawkley had everything to lose and was determined that before he left this room Cromer would be dead.

He could not last much longer having lost so much blood.

At that moment, Carrick's door burst open. The innkeeper and his two sons rushed in and behind them the innkeeper's wife and their three daughters, their hair in rag curlers, their faces shiny with goose grease, and their eyes agog.

'Stay back!' Cromer shouted, determined that this was one fight he would carry out to the bitter end with no man's help but his own.

Shocked and alarmed to see that the fight was now being witnessed, Hawkley lost much of his courage – in fact, his major instinct as soon as the door opened was to flee as fast as he could, and take the first ship to safety, whatever its destination. In fact he tried to evade Cromer's grip, tried to make for the door, but was pulled back and landed with a crash on the floorboards, the impact taking his breath away.

'Why are you here? Tell me why you are here!' Cromer roared, taking Hawkley by the collar and shaking him furiously. The dagger had fallen from Hawkley's grasp and was lying a few feet away from them, its blade glinting evilly in the moonlight streaming through the window.

'Get off me, you swine,' Hawkley choked, tears of rage welling down his cheeks. Then, in one swift movement he brought his boot up between Carrick's legs with brutal force. While Carrick was twisting away Hawkley got his fingers round the dagger and turned it in his opponent's direction, ready to plunge it into Cromer's heart.

Women's screams rang through the room. The innkeeper reached for the nearest chair to bring it down over Hawkley's head, but there was no need. Hawkley's hand, slippery with Cromer's blood, failed to point the dagger in the right direction and as Carrick flung himself across his assailant to evade his boot, the dagger, so sharp, so thin, sank into Hawkley's side, fatally slicing through his liver.

'You – bloody – cur . . .' Hawkley gasped as he died, struggling to remain conscious long enough to voice the words which he was sure would wreck Cromer's life. 'Your – bitch – Dulcie – ask – her – who – made – her – pregnant! Look – in – my – box!'

And with that Hawkley died.

Ashen-faced, Carrick slumped against the wall. He could see blood everywhere – on the bed, on the floor, on his nightshirt – and he knew that most of it was his. He heard the horrified clamour of the innkeeper's wife and daughters as they all hurried towards him in a bunch, and then he lost consciousness.

'Well, it looks as if the legend of the Habsburg emerald is true,' Amalia said. Kitty, who was still desperately shocked after hearing of the events of the night before in Carrick's room, stared up at Amalia dully. 'Do you not remember?' Amalia went on. 'I told you ages ago. The emerald was given to the Empress Isabella by her adoring husband Charles the Fifth. Theirs was one of the great royal love matches of history. Ever since – and I believe that there are facts to prove this – whenever someone who was not truly in love has worn the Habsburg Emerald it has brought them nothing but disaster.'

'Carrick has been wounded, not Lady Dulcie,' Kitty said, her voice low.

'So you do not agree that to lose Carrick Cromer as her husband is a disaster?' Amalia's eyes twinkled.

'Yes, it is a disaster,' Kitty said soulfully. 'The most awful disaster imaginable.'

'Are you going to visit him – he was quite badly wounded, you know. He lost a great deal of blood and is very weak. But I believe that he is being well cared for by the innkeeper's wife and daughters. I believe that they vie with one another to wait on him hand and foot.'

'I can believe it,' Kitty said. 'Yes, of course I am going to visit him. The only thing that prevented me from rushing over there the moment I heard was the thought of seeing him so badly wounded. Oh, Amalia, you do not think that he will die?'

'I do not think that there is any likelihood of that – he is immensely strong, very hardy. But, just in case, I would get over there as soon as I could if I were you.' And with that she went to the wardrobe and took out Kitty's cloak.

Tears filled Kitty's eyes when she saw Carrick lying in bed heavily bandaged, his face as deathly white as the swathing linen.

'Kitty, I must apologise to you,' he said huskily, his eyes glazed with weakness. 'I have lost you a husband. But it was through no fault of mine, you must believe that.'

'He is no loss!' Kitty cried. 'He was everything that you say he was and more. This morning I received a letter from his sister-in-law – a widow. He got her pregnant, poor woman, and then when he found out that she had no money he ditched her. The baby is two years old now, poor mite.'

'We have made an unconscionable mess of our lives, Kitty.' Carrick's voice grew even more husky as he took her hand. 'But it is not too late, you know.'

Hating herself for having to mention her name, Kitty said: 'But what of Lady Dulcie?'

'There were letters in Hawkley's box in his lodgings. They were brought round to me this morning. You may read them if you wish, but the gist of them is that he was having an affaire with Dulcie, and the child she is carrying is his. She is an immensely wealthy woman, you know. It seems that he has been trying to get as many women as possible with child in the belief that one of them must eventually marry him. Gambling on it, you might say. With you, he probably considered it Russian roulette . . .' Despite his pallor, Carrick's eyes twinkled.

'Oh Carrick, are you heartbroken over Lady Dulcie?' Kitty could think of nothing else but her beloved's feelings. At the very least he must be suffering from injured pride.

'Kitty, my darling, that woman has hung round my neck like a millstone from the moment our marriage was arranged as children. You cannot know how marvellous it is to be free of her! It was she who told Hawkley that you were an heiress – because she wanted to get you married and safely out of the way.'

'She knew that I – that we . . .?'

'Yes. She found out, do not ask me how, but people talk you know. So she got Hawkley to have you followed – with a view to finding out what you were up to. She knew that he needed to marry soon, and they planned to marry well: Dulcie to me, and Hawkley to you, then carry on their secret liaison.'

'Why did Dulcie not consider marrying him?'

'For the simple reason that he was penniless and unreliable. As a lover, while she had my name, fortune and protection, he was a little excitement to relieve her boredom. As a spouse, he would have been a very bad companion and supporter. Even if he had inherited his uncle's estates, he would have needed all the money to pay off his debts. He owed many thousands of pounds. Possibly Dulcie became involved with him before she knew the truth about his character.'

Kitty rested her head on Carrick's shoulder, shuddering at the thought of such wretched morals.

'Then there was the other matter which Hawkley found out quite by accident.'

'To do with Dulcie?'

'No, to do with you. Do you have any memory of being followed in Venice? Yes, I thought you might have seen someone, for your eyes are sharp. It was Hawkley's man, sent to find out what you were doing there. The man, I do not know his name, found out all about the Count and the Pharaoh Jewels and of course after that Hawkley was insensible with longing to have you as his bride.'

'Why should my acquaintance with the Count make any difference?' Kitty looked puzzled.

'You made a huge impact on the Count, Kitty. He was always an eccentric old man – very strange, as you may have found out. Oh, I had my spies on the look-out too! A few weeks ago, his sister Estella died, and he made a new will.'

'Estella is dead? Oh, I must write to him at once! Poor man, he will be so lonely without her.'

'Prepare yourself for a shock, Kitty.' Carrick held her hands gently so that his warmth flowed into her body. 'Hawkley found out about the new will, and who was now the Count's beneficiary, and he then pursued that person hot-foot.'

'Who is it, then?'

'You. It is all yours, the villa, the art treasures, the paintings and of course the Pharaoh Jewels. Of course, you know that an ancestor of mine was the original owner, but that doesn't matter. They are yours now.'

'Mine? But the Count? Surely, while he is still alive . . .?'

'Sadly, the Count's body was lifted out of one of the canals only a few days ago. He had been – well, I will spare you the details, but suffice it to say that he did not die by natural means. As far as I am concerned, if Hawkley did not do it himself, then he paid one of his minions to do so.'

Kitty burst into tears. 'That darling old man, who was such a pet, so kind to me, so gentle and generous! Oh, how could anyone do that?'

'The culprit is dead now, Kitty. And the Pharaoh Jewels are back in the Cromer family.'

'Back in the Cromer family? What do you mean?' Kitty looked at him through a curtain of tears.

'We are never going to be parted again, Kitty. It would have come to that even if Dulcie had been a paragon of virtue. There was no way I could continue trying to struggle along without you. It was madness of the most foolish kind. Will you marry me? Here in Dublin if you like, I do not care where so long as it is soon.'

Kitty stayed silent for long moments. So much had happened in the last few hours. That poor old Count . . . She could not as yet realise what it would mean being his heir, being the owner of the priceless Pharaoh Jewels. Yet somehow, strangely, she felt as if she had always owned them. Somewhere, in the dim, shadowy recesses of her memory, she knew that she had worn those brilliant starry gems, a royal regalia, and that this man lying beside her, this man whom she adored with a passion which shook her, was the man who had given her those jewels in those long-ago distant days. And with that thought came the knowledge she had fought so violently to deny: of that moment when she had opened the star-shaped cupboard in the Count's home and seen the painting of herself being crowned by a man in Emperor's robes. She had refused to admit that the man had been Carrick's double, but he had. Now, she no longer wanted or needed to deny it. Whether the painting had been real or an hallucination did not matter. It had existed for long enough to revive her memory of the time when she and her royal husband had together worshipped the star, Sa-lu-is, and loved one another in a former life . . .'

Kitty adored Carrick; he was her only reason for existing. She knew that she could not live without him, but she had been stubborn before, all those centuries ago, refusing to admit that they were made for one another. Then the little widowed Queen had fallen in love with her Emperor, and they had married and from that moment had known the meaning of divine joy in one another . . .

Despite all that, Kitty had learned many other things during her more recent encounters with Carrick, and she was mindful of these when at last she spoke, her voice sweet:

'And what would our marriage entail?' She hid her face

from him so that he could not see the rapture in her eyes. First, she must clarify her position.

'You will close down your trading company, of course.' Carrick's voice was firm.

'Just as I thought!' Leaping up from the bed, Kitty reached for her cloak. 'Is there nothing that you would not stop at to get rid of your competitors?'

Grinning, Carrick went on. 'But it will become affiliated to the Cromer Trading Company. How do you like the sound of the Cromer and McDonagh Trading Company, my darling? You will of course continue to have full control over your own business interests as before. Why not? In many cases you have succeeded better than I ever did. The way you have won customers . . . I do not know how you do it.'

Kitty thought that she could tell him. It was something to do with having Venus in the ascendant, she was sure, but he would think her mad if she said that now. The fire faded from her eyes, the cloak fell from her fingers, her heart filled with gladness. Gently she sat down beside Carrick, a broad smile on her face.

'That sounds like a merger after my own heart, Carrick my love.' And she leaned forward to kiss him tenderly on his cheek, very much aware of his tanned muscular body beneath the shirt and the voluminous bandages. She had never loved him more than at that moment. But even so she had all her wits about her. Was it total capitulation on his part? Looking up, she saw a suspicious twinkle in his eyes. Would he keep his promise? Did he really mean what he said? She believed she knew how to test him.

'Our merger, my darling,' she said, smiling sweetly, 'the Cromer and McDonagh Trading Company, you said?'

'Yes. I mean it, Kitty – if you are agreeable, of course.'

'I rather like the sound of the *McDonagh* and Cromer Trading Company,' Kitty said artfully.

'McDonagh and Cromer!' Carrick cried, all the old fire returning to his eyes. '*McDonagh* and Cromer!'

'Yes, that is what I said, my darling. McDonagh and Cromer. It is such a little thing to ask, isn't it? A little gift for your bride. After all, ladies are supposed to come first, are they not?'

'*McDonagh* and Cromer . . .' Carrick said again, but his face was alight and he burst out laughing.

'You see, I do not want to lose my identity.' Kitty explained, laughing too.

'I do not think that there is any danger of that, my beloved. You are a woman and a half and I am not the only person who will swear to that.'

'So what is it to be?' Kitty put on her most winning smile.

'Is this a major condition of our marriage?'

'It is.' Kitty knew that if she did not hold out for what she wanted now, showing her mettle right from the start, Carrick's forceful personality would gradually overpower hers, for however much he loved her, he would always be a Cromer.

'You want an answer now?'

'I do.' Adoringly, Kitty caressed his cheek. 'If we do not decide it now we will still be arguing at the altar.'

That thought amused them so much that they both burst out laughing again.

'Then McDonagh and Cromer it shall be, Kitty. My God, I hope I've learned something over the past years. A man has more to lose by stubborn intractability than he ever has by capitulation.'

'My darling, how right you are.' Reverently, Kitty sank into his arms for a blissful celebration kiss.

She knew that there would probably be more storms ahead, for they were both powerful personalities and no doubt their fight for mastery would involve them in many colourful and sometimes riotous moments. But she knew that she was more capable of handling Carrick now – had she not had a thorough apprenticeship at it? He was very much the dominant male and getting his own way was a lifetime's habit to him. But one habit could just as easily be replaced by another, she would see to that. Whatever happened, she knew that in his arms, with his love, she would be fulfilled. It really did not matter which of their names came first, for, ideally they would be equals and she would work towards that end.

It was over now, the torture and the torment, the loneliness and the desperate fight for survival. Here, in Dublin, the Emperor had been reunited with his Empress. Count Barraccini had said that she would have to go back before she could go forward. How right he had been and she would never forget him.

The feuding and the fighting were over forever. Now it was time for the loving.